Boccaccio in the Berkshires

Boccaccio in the Berkshires

a novel

Alan Govenar

DEEP VELLUM PUBLISHING
DALLAS, TEXAS

Deep Vellum Publishing
3000 Commerce St., Dallas, Texas 75226
deepvellum.org · @deepvellum

Deep Vellum is a 501c3 nonprofit literary arts organization
founded in 2013 with the mission to bring
the world into conversation through literature.

First edition, 2021

Scripture quotations are from the King James and American Standard Versions of the Bible.

Support for this publication has been provided in part by grants from the National Endowment for the Arts, the Texas Commission on the Arts, the City of Dallas Office of Arts and Culture's ArtsActivate program, and the Moody Fund for the Arts:

ISBNs: 978-1-64605-160-1 (hardcover) | 978-1-64605-161-8 (ebook)

LIBRARY OF CONGRESS CONTROL NUMBER: 2021940875

Front cover design by Justin Childress | justinchildress.co

Interior Layout and Typesetting by KGT

Printed in the United States of America

Prologue

IN THE MIDDLE OF THE ROAD, I felt safe. Immune. Even if I wasn't. I was willing to trade one danger for another. Never too close to people on the sidewalk. But in harm's way if a car turned the corner too quickly or sped down the side streets I walked every morning to clear my head.

I'm average weight. Average height. Average. But not exactly ordinary. The kind of guy who likes to watch and listen. Growing up, I wasn't the smartest kid, but I was smart enough to stay away from bullies and jocks, nerds and ne'er-do-wells. When I was in grade school, my teachers often complained that I didn't participate enough in class discussion. I was an *A over F student*—meaning that I got an *A* for being creative and an *F* because I didn't follow instructions. I did my assignments, but they were rarely what the teacher was looking for. If they said write a story in the first person, I didn't stop there. I'd take an observer's point of view and fancied myself omniscient. I loved that word *omniscient*—all-knowing. I felt like it gave me a power I didn't have in real life. I could insert thoughts and ideas into my characters based on what I imagined they were feeling. Needless to say, I broke the rules. And wasn't unduly rewarded for my efforts.

In high school I was a B/C student and managed to get into Navarro College, a small liberal arts school in Corsicana, Texas, but

I never graduated. I got a job as a bagger in a grocery store and did odd jobs on the side and met a curly-headed girl about my age at a gasoline pump outside a convenience store. We both tried to insert our credit cards into the slot at the same time. And when our hands bumped, we started laughing and talking, and before long, we were dating. After a couple of months, we wanted to get married.

But she got sick.

She went to visit her mother in California, and when she came back to Texas, her symptoms developed quickly—sore throat, a dry, hacking cough, fever, shortness of breath. And on the day that she was rushed to the hospital, I tested positive for the virus and was ordered to quarantine for fourteen days, even though I didn't have any symptoms.

I was a total wreck. Every second of every day was excruciating. I couldn't sleep, and I hated being awake.

The last time I saw my girlfriend was on FaceTime. She'd been intubated and was connected to a noisy ventilator. She couldn't talk. She struggled to raise her arms and hold her hands in the shape of a heart. All of a sudden, her body convulsed. And her face seized up in pain.

There was no funeral, only a memorial service that was streamed online.

I shut down. I went through the motions of doing what I had to do to get by. It was as if wherever I went, I wasn't really there. Part of me was absent, trapped in an avalanche of mourning, and the harder I tried to dig myself out, the deeper I sank into the abyss. Even saying my girlfriend's name aloud hurt. Burying her in an unmarked grave in my heart helped.

I began to search the internet for asymptomatic people like me. After a couple of days, I joined an online chat room. We were all in our twenties. We were all hurting—grieving from something terrible that had happened to us, something that we could barely talk about.

Even though all of us had tested negative after our quarantines, we still wondered if we might get sick.

We all figured it was a good time to leave home and hibernate someplace else, while we still could. We didn't talk much about our day jobs, other than to assure each other that we had enough cash on hand that we could afford to take some time off. But none of us knew where to go. "A cabin in the wilderness," Eleanor said. "Not just an ordinary cabin," I chimed in, "a big one with ten bedrooms, where we could all live together for at least two weeks, or until it felt safe to come back to civilization."

I joked about doing something similar to *The Decameron,* a collection of novellas written in the fourteenth century by the Italian author Giovanni Boccaccio about a group of friends who sheltered themselves in a villa outside of Florence to escape the Black Plague. Initially, everyone thought my idea was nuts, but they came around. "After all," I said, "Ten of them. Ten of us. Seven women. Three men."

Maggie, who was the first to jump on board, even found a place where we could all stay. It wasn't exactly a cabin. It was a "Berkshire cottage" near Tanglewood, on the outskirts of Stockbridge, Massachusetts, that was owned by a friend of her father's who had inherited the place but didn't want to live there. He'd been trying to liquidate it for a few years, and with the economy crashing around him, he dropped the price from $14 million to $8.5 million. But still there were no buyers.

Maggie said she was speechless when her father told her that the property owner wasn't going to charge us any rent, as long as we chipped in for a cleaning service after we left and paid a pro rata share of the utilities for the time we were there. There was an additional benefit: the cottage was furnished, staged for best effect for potential buyers.

One by one we signed on. Getting there would be easy for Maggie in Manhattan, Barb in Brooklyn, and Cynthia in Boston, but travel for some of us was more complicated. I was in Texas. Max was in Seattle, Eleanor in San Francisco, Richard in St. Louis, Josette in New Orleans, Sandra in Atwood, Kansas, and Hannah in the Amana Colonies, south of Cedar Rapids, Iowa. But the distances didn't seem to matter. With the virus becoming more prevalent, we were all more than ready to be someplace other than where we were.

After a few days, we were chatting online every night, around 10:00 p.m. Central Time, even though it was, at first, tough to coordinate our schedules and time zones. But once we got into the same headspace, we couldn't get enough of each other. Zeroing in on a date when we'd meet in the Berkshires became easy. The last hurdle was deciding whether we should see what each other looked like before making a final commitment.

Max thought it was a must. Richard, Barb, Josette, Maggie, and Sandra were on the fence. Hannah, who was raised in something called the Community of True Inspiration and was totally against the idea, suggested a conference call, saying, "That way we can at least hear each other's voices. It's not about what we look like. Trust God. That's who brought us all together in the first place."

The mention of God was a turnoff for Richard, who explained that he was agnostic. And once he said that, we knew we each had to say something about our religion, or lack of it.

Josette was the first to speak up. "I'm a woman of faith. But I don't really practice an organized religion. I guess you could say I'm nondenominational, meaning I'm into the Bible, but I'm also a believer in Voodoo."

"Voodoo? You're not in a cult, are you?" Hannah asked.

"No way! I have Haitian roots. In my family, Voodoo means believing that humans are spirits who inhabit the visible world."

"Not sure what that means," Barb said.

"It's deep . . . and beautiful," Josette added.

I wasn't sure what to say. So I said nothing.

Then Cynthia blurted out, "I'm a closet Buddhist. I keep it to myself, because I'm still figuring it out."

Sandra maintained, "Religion is completely personal."

Max said, "I second that!"

And that was it. Just a conference call. No Skype. No Zoom. No FaceTime.

Maggie sounded relieved and quickly refocused the conversation to logistics. "Once we're together, we have to practice good hygiene, masking, and social distancing."

We all had to agree to share the household expenses and responsibilities. Each of us had to pay for their own travel.

Eleanor took a deep breath and said, "Let's not *overrun* ourselves with details. If something doesn't feel fair, we'll talk it out."

Richard chimed in, "First and foremost, it needs to be fun. Sheltering together isn't a jail sentence."

We were, in one sense, freeing ourselves from rules that might get in the way, even though we all knew we had to be vigilant about each other's well-being. In such a huge house, we all felt there would be plenty of space for that to happen. But the question that kept coming up was what we were going to do when we were together.

We agreed that we wouldn't watch TV—it was too noisy and too intrusive, and we'd spend too much time trying to decide what to watch. If we wanted to listen to music or keep up with the news, we had to keep it to ourselves. The goal was to bond as a group, supporting each other as best we could given all that we were going through.

Richard said he was a wine connoisseur and was willing to bring a case of some of his best stash—that is, if everyone was a wine drinker. One by one, everyone said, "Of course."

Sandra told us that she loved to play Scrabble, but only four of us could play at once. She had a big collection of other games. But no one seemed to like that idea.

Barb countered that social distancing was impossible with board games. And Maggie droned, "It's not like we're contagious."

"At least not that we know," I said, having barely survived those awful days when I was losing my girlfriend.

Hannah commiserated with me, admitting that the tragedy she had experienced was unspeakable. But then she quickly changed the subject to *The Decameron,* which she had ordered the day after I mentioned it, and which sparked an *a-ha* moment once she started reading. To pass time we could tell each other stories, like they did in *The Decameron.* Our stories could be made-up, real, whatever.

"But we need to give the stories a new twist," Maggie said, "to heighten the drama of the moment. Maybe we should try to mimic the exaggerated way the stories were told in *The Decameron.*"

"Sort of like charades?" Hannah asked.

Maggie giggled, "Not exactly. More like a one-person show in an off-off-Broadway theater."

Richard was upset. "I haven't read *The Decameron* and I'm not sure I want to."

"The point is, we just tell each other stories," I said. "They can be from *The Decameron,* or wherever."

"It all sounds crazy to me." Sandra complained.

Barb mumbled "Uh" a few times and finally said, "I like the idea."

"What happens if it's boring?" Josette asked.

Richard balked, "Or if it gets out of hand, we need an exit strategy."

"No censorship," Max insisted.

Eleanor said, "Participating in the storytelling sessions should be voluntary. If you want out, you can be out."

That was exactly what I was thinking. And that's what we decided. Not long after, we headed to Massachusetts.

Looking back, what happened during those fourteen days in the Berkshires hardly feels real. My memories are blurred around the edges by the intensity of what we all experienced. When I think about the ways we bonded, and how some of those same bonds were fractured, I'm left with an emotional aftertaste that's at once painful, ludicrous, and oddly liberating.

Somehow, I survived and found something I didn't even know I was looking for.

Day 1

THE HIGHWAY STRETCHED OUT IN FRONT of me, winding into the horizon and swirling back. Part of me was pumped up on adrenaline; the rest was Silly Putty. I had been driving for two and a half days, stopping only when I had to. For gas, to pee, for coffee and junk food. Pulling off into rest areas to sleep for a couple of hours here and there, slumped over the steering wheel or leaning back in my seat.

I knew I was getting closer and studied the license plates of the cars in front of me, wondering about the people inside. Who were they and where did they come from? I started imagining that I knew them and that they knew me. Just feeling that we might somehow be connected muted my feelings of isolation. I wasn't completely alone. And as the miles passed, the distance between the billboards strung along the roadside seemed less.

The ground fog on the Massachusetts Turnpike glowed orange in the pink morning light as the Berkshires came into view, the dew rising through the groves of white pine and hemlock, striped maple and moosewood. Turning onto Ice Glen Road, I was stunned. What Maggie had called a *cottage* was actually a mansion, one of the last remaining Mediterranean Renaissance Revival estates in the Berkshires, commissioned in 1915 by the wealthy New York paper merchant William H. Jones and built on 68.8 acres surrounded by mountainous terrain and lush rolling hills. A replica of a villa in the Italian Sabine Hills, the house came to be known as *Villa Carolina,* named for Jones's daughter, although the name was changed to *Villa Delicia* after the property was sold to the industrialist Elijah Smithberry.

A woman with dusty blond hair stood at the front door, but, as I approached her, she stepped back and waved me forward, careful to keep her distance.

"Are you Maggie?" I asked. And she nodded, "Yeah, that's me. And you're . . . Richard?"

"Nope. Just Andy."

We were both a little startled to see each other, not knowing what to expect. Maggie was statuesque, with blue eyes and a pearly complexion. I was self-conscious and brushed back my hair. Maggie raised her eyebrows ever so slightly, as if she were surprised that I was prematurely gray.

I thought I was the first to arrive, but then I saw a yellow Hummer parked on the far side of the large driveway. Walking toward me was a man wearing a red sweater and khaki pants. He looked as if he'd just stepped out of a Ralph Lauren ad. "I'm Max," he shouted, and then started rambling on, "I cheated. I took a plane to Boston and then hired a private driver. Life in Seattle was terrifying. We had the first confirmed virus case in Washington State. And within weeks, Seattle confirmed its first death."

Maggie thrust her hands to her hips and said, "Make yourself comfortable. I wish I could join you, but I'm in charge of hospitality—at least until everyone gets here."

The house had thirteen bedrooms and twelve bathrooms, in addition to ten other rooms, including a huge kitchen, a full basement, a den, a living room with a fireplace and a hand-painted ceiling. The hallway from the pantry and mudroom led to a glassed-in veranda that opened out to the manicured lawn of the estate.

Max carried his suitcase inside, and Maggie motioned for me follow her to the back of the cottage.

"The garden," she grinned, "is in bloom year-round, with perennials and seasonal plants, from exotic flowers to vegetables."

"I've never seen anything like it," I said, amazed by its grandeur.

"I've heard," Maggie continued, "that a *mano fico* was found by a gardener when he was turning the soil sometime in the 1920s."

"A what?"

"A *mano fico* is an Italian amulet of ancient origin that is molded or carved in the shape of a fist in which the thumb is thrust between the curled index and middle fingers."

"I don't get it."

"Andy, it's erotic."

My eyes met hers and she smiled, "But we can never know for sure what it really looked like, because soon after it was discovered, it disappeared. The gardener, who people say must have been close to eighty, died of a heart attack, and he didn't have any known heirs. He lived as a hermit, and, like a lot of people around here, was an amateur antiquarian who collected all kinds of stuff, from old newspapers and scraps of paper to bottle caps and letter openers. When they cleaned out his belongings, no one knew what happened to the *mano fico*. Apparently, it was lost or stolen, but the fact that it was missing only added to the mystique of the garden.

"Rumors spread that the garden was so fertile that lovers from around the world wanted to be married there. And in the 1970s, after years of rebuffing wedding planners, the Smithberry family began to offer the garden for rental. It was soon after Delicia Smithberry, who had wed Darren Wilcox Jr. there, gave birth to twins, surprising her doctors, who were certain that it was impossible for her to get pregnant after her fallopian tubes ruptured when she was a teenager.

"These days, townie kids like to hang out in the garden, doing whatever it is they think they can get away with. You know, it's a place to make out and make love. And I suppose there are even pregnancy-challenged couples who come to the garden with the hope of renewed fertility, even if they couldn't afford to get married there in the first place. I don't how much they charge, but I've heard it's a fortune."

I was impressed, but a little put off by Maggie's tone. It was clear that she was a woman of means.

"Andy, relax. You look so tensed up."

"I'm fine. It's just a lot to take in."

The cottage and its grounds were incredible. It was hard to believe that whoever owned it was letting us stay there for free. There had to be a catch. But I couldn't figure it out. It just felt too good to be true.

It was obvious that Maggie had been busy cleaning. There were ladders and rags and vacuum cleaners scattered through the rooms. Some of the furniture had been covered with drop cloths, and Maggie said it was kind of creepy, taking them off and folding them up, expecting to find something underneath, some vestige of the people who had once lived there, even if it was mostly staging.

Everything looked barely touched. There wasn't much period furniture, and a lot of what there was, like the twenty-five-foot wraparound sofa in the living room, had a contemporary, custom-built vibe. When I sat down on the comforter on my bed, it smelled brand-new. The feather pillows on the bed were perfect. Nothing was musty.

I unpacked slowly, not wanting to rush out of my room. I wanted to savor the canopy bed and the lace curtains and the plush towels in the bathroom. I was losing myself in the details, the satin texture of the wallpaper, the lace doilies on the dresser, which had so many drawers that I didn't know where to start. I placed my underwear in one, my socks, T-shirts, a couple of shirts and sweaters in another. But I opened each and every one of the drawers to see if there was something inside. They were all empty.

I stretched my arms over my head and flopped backward onto my bed, kicking off my sneakers and loosening the belt on my jeans.

I struggled to keep my eyes open. I was exhausted, recalling everything I had endured to get here. The middle of the night was the eeriest. Only a few cars. Mostly eighteen-wheelers barreling along, passing me when I should have been passing them. And as I neared Stockbridge, the roads became narrower and darker. Every time I saw a deer crossing sign, I eased my foot onto the brake and flashed my high beams, worried that a huge buck was going to dart in front of me and crash into my car.

There was a knock on the door. It was Max. "You ought to come downstairs. Cynthia's just arrived with a trunk-load of goodies—two coolers packed with lobsters and clams, and a case of Chablis and White Burgundy."

I pulled my cell phone out of the front pocket of my jeans and checked the time. It was past noon. I had slept longer than I thought.

When I got downstairs, Maggie and Cynthia were in the kitchen, joking around with lobsters in both hands, ready to drop them into a huge pot of boiling water.

Max was at the kitchen sink, pulling the corks from a couple of bottles of wine, gloating that we were going to have a feast.

I looked outside and saw someone unpacking a Jeep Cherokee.

"That must be Richard," Max said, "He looks like the outdoors type. Down vest and hiking boots."

Maggie giggled and asked Max if he had ever been horseback riding.

He shook his head *no.* And Maggie started talking to Cynthia, who said, "I'm from an old Yankee family. My mother likes to brag that my ancestral grandparents came over on the Mayflower, but she doesn't have any proof. As a kid, I believed her, though now I wish I could find some kind of DNA evidence."

A horn was honking. We trickled outside. Three cars followed each other into the circular driveway in front of the cottage. But only one of them parked. The others were Ubers, the drivers popping their trunks at almost the same time, while the other car pulled off to the side. In the Ubers were Barb from Brooklyn and Eleanor from San Francisco, and in the other car was Josette from New Orleans.

Barb had taken Amtrak from Penn Station in New York City, and Eleanor had flown in from Oakland, where she had been staying with her brother and his family. Her apartment in San Francisco was being remodeled.

Josette had driven her red Mustang from New Orleans and boasted, "I hit the open road and floored it most of the way. In record time."

Hannah, who had split her trip into two days, stepped forward and extended her elbow in my direction. "I'm so excited to finally meet in person."

I felt the same. But I expected her to look different. She was about five feet tall with frizzy braided hair. And her wire-rimmed glasses slipped down her nose as she talked, drawing attention to the pointiness of her chin.

Sandra was talking with Cynthia and Richard, but when she saw Hannah approach me, she did the same. Sandra was broad-shouldered and overweight. She was wearing blue warm-up pants and a pink hoodie.

I helped Hannah carry in her two suitcases, then offered a hand to Barb, "Thanks, but not needed," she said, pointing to her knapsack, "Only brought a few changes of clothes, a computer, and toiletries."

For her, the cottage seemed overwhelming. She lived in an efficiency apartment in a brownstone in Brooklyn and said that she'd probably need a map to find her way around the cottage and the grounds. Barb was a native New Yorker who bragged that she could navigate the subway blindfolded but couldn't find the exit in a shopping mall. She worked at a shoe boutique in lower Manhattan.

Josette drawled that she was *jet-lagged* from all the driving.

Cynthia was more proactive and insisted that it was time to eat.

She scooped out the steamer clams and lobsters and plonked them into the sink, twisting off the heads with her gloved hands and cracking the shells before placing the tails and claws neatly onto three serving trays.

Sandra gasped, "That's a lot of food, and I hope you all enjoy it. But I guess I forgot to tell you that I'm a vegan with a very particular diet. I came prepared, though. In the trunk of my car, I have a case of almond milk, four jars of cashew butter, dried apricots and cranberries, and a huge Tupperware filled with a couple dozen homemade granola bars, crackers, cookies, and a bunch of other stuff for sharing."

"That's wonderful," Maggie said.

Josette rifled through the drawers' cracking tools, picks, and forks, while Max melted five sticks of butter in a small saucepan, watching as the fats separated and sank to the bottom and a foam rose to the top. Then he skimmed off the foam and poured the clarified butter into the dipping bowls that Barb had lined up on the kitchen counter.

Cynthia stacked plates and napkins and directed us to form a line to serve ourselves, each of us separated by about six feet. Then, with a wine bottle in each hand, she led us to the twenty-four-foot mahogany dining table, set with linen place mats and goblets, surrounded by ten armchairs, upholstered, Maggie said, "with dark brown leather cushions and damask fabrics that looked like they might have been made in Florence."

Once we were all seated, Cynthia raised her wine glass in a toast: *L'chaim*—to life. And Max cheered, *Salute*—to health, and Hannah bowed her head in prayer: "Our Father, who art in heaven, hallowed be thy Name."

Richard glared at Hannah, sipping his wine. "I don't want to be rude. But please, remember, I'm agnostic."

Josette said, "Good for you. If we want to pray, we can."

"Is that so?" Max asked.

"Okay, too much, too soon," Josette replied. "No offense. We have plenty of time to get to know each other better."

The table fell silent. We all looked at our plates, and after a few bites, the conversation switched to small talk.

Richard seated himself next to Eleanor and asked, "Is 'Eleanor' a family name? I'm into genealogy. I know 'Richard' sounds humdrum, but, in my family, it has a long history."

Eleanor smiled, "I was named for Eleanor Roosevelt, who my mother thought was one of the most amazing women in the twentieth century—in politics, diplomacy, human rights. I could go on and on. And believe it or not, there's now an Eleanor Roosevelt Barbie doll."

Max rolled his eyes, and Barb said, "Personally, I hate Barbie dolls."

"So do I," Josette nodded.

Eleanor glowered, "Enough said."

Max cleared his throat and started rattling off the latest virus statistics.

Richard scoffed, "Personally, I think everything might be overstated. I'm trying not to panic."

Eleanor asserted, "We've got to listen to the doctors."

Cynthia agreed. "That's right. Trust the scientists."

"Can we change the subject?" Josette pleaded, "I thought the purpose of our getting together was to do something different. I need a break from all this virus stuff."

I zoned out and focused on peeling back the membranes of each of my steamer clams, swishing them around in a steamy cup of broth from the cook pot, dipping them into the clarified butter, sliding them ever so slowly across my tongue into my mouth, and savoring every bite.

Richard cooed, "The French Chablis is perfectly dry with flavors of citrus and pear, a wonderful counterpoint to the saltiness of the soft-bellied clams and the sweetness of the Maine lobster."

I didn't really know what to say, other than *thank you* to Maggie and to Cynthia for the great food and wine.

They both smiled. And the mood in the room transformed.

Josette's face brightened.

Max sighed.

It was time to plan what remained of the day. Maggie took the lead with the cleanup, doling out assignments. Cynthia picked up the place mats and carried them onto the deck outside the kitchen to shake them out. And I wiped the table with a soft cloth.

We all went into the living room and spread out on the sofa and side chairs, upholstered with an elegant mix of brocade, houndstooth, and striped prints with muted terra cotta tones. It felt like a Hollywood set for a film in which we all had parts but hadn't yet learned our lines, because the script was still being written.

Cynthia wanted to open another bottle of wine, but when she asked if there were any takers, no one piped up. "Okay, then. I'm off to explore. So much to see."

"Where you going to start?" I asked.

Cynthia smiled. "Not sure. As much as I like nature, I like people-made things more."

"I like them both," I said, "I love living on the Gulf Coast. Sailing is great. But messing around with broken-down sailboats is better, not that I've had much luck fixing them. But I keep trying. One of these days I'm going to get it right."

Cynthia nodded, "I want to know how things are put together and how they're used. Like the structural beams in the basement. The shelving in the den. That old shed in the back of the cottage, and how it connects to what's around it. The stable. The path through the garden. I want to go poking around."

Maggie entered the room in a flourish, whirling around, carrying a shopping bag with small plastic bottles of water that she tossed to each of us.

Richard whispered an apology to Josette, who still seemed upset by the way he had jumped on her after Hannah's prayer. He sounded sincere, but I could tell he wanted us all to hear what he was saying.

Maggie spoke up, "Before we go off on our own, I'd like to talk a bit about the ground rules that I think we should follow. In keeping with the spirit of *The Decameron,* I think each of us should take turns being queen or king for a day, not to order anyone around, but to keep us together as a group."

"Without question," Cynthia concurred.

"But what about the storytelling?" Eleanor asked.

"Well, for one thing," Max said, "the stories can't be too long."

"Or weird," Richard grinned.

"Actually, weird is okay," Maggie laughed. "Let's try to connect to *The Decameron*. Not necessarily in content, but in the way we express ourselves."

I wasn't sure I got what Maggie was talking about. And neither did Josette, who muttered, "What do you mean by that?"

"It's like I said in our last chat, a little bit of theater can't hurt," Maggie replied.

Hannah asked, "Do we have to make up stories? Or can they be true?"

"True?" Sandra wondered.

"Personal," Hannah said, "You know, about us, and what we're trying to make sense of in our own lives."

"It doesn't matter, as long as the stories are entertaining," Maggie beamed, and Richard added, "If you need therapy, this is probably the wrong place for you."

Cynthia yawned, "Let's continue this conversation after we've all had time to decompress."

We all applauded Maggie's plan and went off in different directions. The dreaminess of the afternoon carried me to the lily pond. I sat down on a boulder, propping my elbows on my knees so that I could cradle my chin in my hands. The water was calm, but the lily pads were bare.

I heard rustling in the leaves. And as the sounds got closer, I recognized Josette's high-pitched chattering. Eleanor was with her. I got up quickly and moved on, hoping that they hadn't seen me. I needed time to myself, time to put the day in perspective. I rarely drank wine in the middle of the afternoon, and the fogginess in my head made it hard for me to think clearly. Since my girlfriend died, I didn't really like talking to people much, because the conversations seemed to always land on death. I was working on refocusing my life and thought getting away from Texas would help. I walked back to the cottage and went up to my room. I undressed quickly and slid under the comforter, wiggling my way to the center of the bed, sinking my face into my pillows, wishing I were a caterpillar spinning a silky cocoon.

Day 2

I WENT TO THE BATHROOM AROUND 6:30 a.m. and couldn't fall back asleep. My body ached for more rest, but my mind was awake, thinking about how I'd been avoiding social media. Facebook, Instagram, and Twitter pissed me off, especially since my girlfriend died. Most of the messages I received had to do with her. I knew all my friends and family meant well, but every word was a reminder of what I was struggling to forget.

I leaned back against the headboard of my bed and stared into the darkness. The morning light seeped around the edges of the curtains and into the room, bringing the shapes and colors of the furnishings to life. I felt like I had won the lottery. First prize. A luxury vacation I couldn't otherwise afford.

I squirmed back under my sheets and dozed off, dreaming that I was on a raft drifting down a stream in a forest I didn't recognize. The current was running fast, and I started thrashing around, only to wake up just as the whitewater rapids up ahead came into view.

I lifted myself out of bed, one leg at a time, and trudged into the bathroom to wash my face. My hair was a mess. And instead of looking for my hairbrush, I put on a Boston Red Sox cap I found on the shelf above a terry cloth robe in the closet.

I hadn't brought any slippers and was about to put on my sneakers when I saw a pair of rubber flip-flops in a basket next to the shower.

Downstairs, everyone was up—Richard, Max, Maggie, Eleanor, Cynthia, Josette, Barb, Sandra, and Hannah.

Maggie handed me a cup of fresh brewed coffee, and I joined the others, milling about the room.

Maggie announced, "I picked up some bagels and lox as I was leaving Manhattan. And there's more than enough for us all to share. A kind of welcome breakfast. But we also have eggs, milk, orange juice, and some stuff that qualifies as vegan in the refrigerator."

Max clanged the side of his coffee cup with his spoon, expressing his appreciation with a loud *mwah*.

Cynthia and Eleanor cringed. Richard backed up, as did Barb.

Sandra stammered, "I have to admit. I'm a germophobe, and just the sound of kissing, these days, terrifies me."

"We're easily six feet apart from one another," I said, "Everything's okay."

"Except that Max's mask is hiked up over his lips and nose," Sandra sneered. "I think it's time for each of us to sanitize."

Richard grimaced.

Maggie acknowledged Max with a sincere *thank you* as she left the solarium to prepare a tray with bagels and lox.

Sandra followed her, asking if she'd donned rubber gloves before handling the food.

Maggie nodded yes, but Sandra didn't let up. "How many pairs of gloves and what kind of face masks are available for the group?"

Maggie was stumped. "I'm not sure. But there's plenty."

"Well, it's not that I'm paranoid. I'm just careful, extra careful, for good reason."

Max was defensive. "But we're all asymptomatic. Isn't that enough?"

"Maybe," Sandra snarled. "We could be carriers."

I sighed, "Whatever that means."

The room tensed up.

Eleanor and Cynthia each said she'd brought a couple of boxes of gloves and N-95 masks, to be used and shared as needed, but, at this point, they hoped social distancing and handwashing were enough. There were pump-bottles of hand sanitizer in every room of the cottage.

Max glared at Sandra, "Why on earth did you agree to come? Especially given all your concerns."

Sandra shrugged her shoulders, "I needed to get away."

Barb added, "If we aren't careful, our sheltering together is never going to work."

"That's right," Richard said. "We have to remember. We're not required to be here. It's a choice that we all made."

I zoned out, gazing at the floral patterns on the porcelain vases and lamps on the tables around me. Sunlight streamed through the windows of the solarium, illuminating the white cushioned wicker sofas and swivel chairs with an ethereal glow.

The platter that Maggie carried in must have been four feet long and was filled with bagels, lox, cream cheese, sliced tomatoes, capers, chopped onions, and half-sour pickles. Cynthia refilled our coffee cups and offered glasses of water or seltzer.

We served ourselves, one by one, and while we were munching away, Maggie reminded us that the agenda for the day was simple. "Please, take more time to enjoy the cottage and the grounds. Go a little deeper into the spirit of place than you did yesterday. Walk, hike, stroll, nap, whatever feels right. Let's reconvene at three on the veranda, where there are five twelve-foot couches arranged in the shape of a pentagon around a six-foot square firepit. It's the perfect place for storytelling and afternoon tea."

When we split apart, I hurried to catch up with Maggie, and, when she sensed I was at her side, she slowed down. For a minute, I didn't know what to say. From a distance, I hadn't fully realized how much I was attracted to her. She was about my height and had the face of a model. But her manner of speaking was completely disarming.

"I'm so glad to finally meet you, Andy. Thanks for buddying up. Is everything okay?"

"Well, to be honest, I'm not sure I can stay at the cottage. I mean, it's wonderful, but I worry that I'm going to bring everyone else down. Just listening to Sandra and watching how everyone else responded to her makes it difficult for me to speak up. I'm just not ready. And I'm not sure if I ever will be."

Maggie looked at me with compassion. "Andy, I understand. You've got to do what you've got to do. You're free to leave whenever you wish. There won't be any hard feelings. But I do hope you decide to stay, because I have a feeling that your presence, regardless of what you talk about, could really give the group an energy that it otherwise wouldn't have."

Energy wasn't exactly what I felt at that moment, but I appreciated her confidence in my ability to do something I didn't think possible.

She invited me to go horseback riding with her, though she could tell from my body language that I didn't know how. Maggie smiled, "Maybe next time." And we went our separate ways.

• • •

When we gathered for afternoon tea on the veranda, everyone seemed more laid-back. It was chilly outside, but the firepit kept us warm. Maggie rolled a cart from the kitchen with ten cups, three steaming teapots, and an assortment of Kusmi Teas. Barb passed around white paper napkins, and Eleanor carried a tray with biscotti.

I overheard Cynthia telling Eleanor about the shed near the stable and that there was something about it that didn't fit in. "It's such an anomaly," she said, "kind of an afterthought, or maybe the shed predated the cottage. Architecturally, it doesn't make sense." I wanted to ask her what she meant, but there wasn't time.

Once everyone was seated, Cynthia nominated Maggie to be the first queen. No one objected. Cynthia reached into her purse and pulled out a small plastic tiara and placed it on Maggie's head. We all cheered. It made perfect sense.

Maggie said, "I'm truly honored that you have picked me to be queen for the day. All I want is for everyone to try to be happy."

Max straightened up, and Richard did the same, announcing almost in unison that they were doing the cooking and cleanup tomorrow. Cynthia led the applause. Eleanor hooted, and Maggie squealed.

Eleanor and Hannah said their hands were cold, and Maggie pulled out a couple of cashmere throws that were neatly folded in drawers built into the frame of the couch.

Eleanor was surprised: "Cashmere? I thought everything at the villa was a fake. You know, for staging."

Maggie laughed, "Well, these are on loan from my mother, who insisted, once she found out what we were doing, on loading me down with something special. They're from our family cabin in Maine."

"Family cabin?" Cynthia asked, "Does it have ten bedrooms?"

"No, no. Only five. But I don't want to talk about that. I don't want you to get the wrong impression."

"We get the picture," Barb said matter-of-factly, and Max smirked, "And it has a gilded frame."

Maggie shook her head and pulled out more cashmere blankets. We each got a different color: forest green, strawberry red, ochre, sienna, and different shades of blue, brown, and tan.

Hannah wrapped herself in her throw and leaned forward, telling everyone she hoped she could tell the first story.

We were all pleased. A volunteer.

Hannah prefaced her story by telling us that before her family moved to the Amana Colonies, they had lived in Rome, New

York, until she was in second grade. Her father was stationed at the U.S. Air Force Research Laboratory: "I never knew exactly what he did, but it was top secret and it had something to do with information science and technology for fighter planes. My mother taught kindergarten in a little school near the Oneida Nation, and many of the kids in her class were from Indian families who were proud of their heritage, even though it always seemed to me that some of the parents and grandparents who came to the holiday parties at the school had chips on their shoulders. I didn't understand at the time the extent to which Indians, well, Native Americans, had been mistreated.

"When I was in kindergarten, it was hard for me, being the teacher's daughter. All the kids thought I got special treatment, but that wasn't the case. If anything, my mother was harder on me than anyone else. One time, she even sent me to the discipline corner for just talking out of turn. I was so mad and hurt.

"I didn't want to go to the annual Christmas party, because I thought everyone was going to make fun of me. I often heard the kids talking behind my back. But there wasn't much I could do. So I made a point of sitting by myself, away from the cookies and punch, on a folding chair near the window. It was snowing, and watching the snow blanket the ground outside comforted me in ways that I didn't really comprehend at the time.

"Thank goodness, my mother left me alone. I was lost in my thoughts, struggling to find my way out, when an old Oneida woman sat down next to me without saying a word. And after I don't know how long, she said that watching the snow was one of the biggest joys of her life. Then, she whispered, 'The snowflakes speak to me.'

"Her voice was gentle, but her face was wizened, and her hair was scraggly, and one of her eyes tilted up and the other drooped down. If I didn't know any better, I might have thought she was an old witch. At her side was an oversized straw bag, embroidered with what

I assumed were Oneida designs. I wanted to ask what they meant, but inside my heart was jumping up and down. I slid backward in my chair, and just as I was getting up, she said she had something for me and reached into her straw bag and handed me a corn husk doll.

"'She will always be your friend,' the old woman assured me.

"I took the doll into my hands and laid her on my lap. Her red and white gingham dress was tied with a sash. She was so pretty, but she didn't have a face.

"'And for good reason,' the woman said. 'Long ago, the Great Spirit of the Haudenosaunee people told the Corn Spirit that she could make a doll from her husk, and the Corn Spirit gave the doll a beautiful face. And the doll went from village to village to play with the children, but she was uppity and boasted how beautiful she was. So the Great Spirit called to her. And the corn husk doll went to the Great Spirit's lodge, and, while she was there, she looked into a pool of water and admired the reflection of herself. And the Great Spirit warned her that if she kept thinking she was better than anyone else, she would be punished. But the corn husk doll didn't listen and went to other villages to show herself off. And the Great Spirit called to her again, and when the doll went back to the Great Spirit's Lodge, she gazed into the pool of water and once again admired herself. And the Great Spirit told her, "I have given you one warning; now a great punishment will come upon you." But she wouldn't say what was going to happen. So, the corn husk doll left the lodge and went on her way. And when she saw another pool of water, she rushed to see herself again, but, when she looked into the pool, she didn't have a face. And since that time, the Haudenosaunee people do not put a face on their corn husk dolls. This is to remind people to never think that they are better than anyone else, or a great punishment will fall upon them.'

"The end," Hannah said. "Or maybe, to be continued."

We all clapped. Hannah blushed and stood up. She scanned our faces without saying anything more. Then, she reached to her side and opened a felt zipper pouch that was attached to her purse. Inside was her corn husk doll, but she didn't lift it out, explaining that it was too fragile. The husks were dry and brittle, and the doll's gingham dress was tattered. Hannah handed me the felt pouch and asked me to pass it to the others. We each had a special moment with the doll, except for Sandra, who waved her hands in front of her face and said abruptly, "We should all be wearing gloves!"

Hannah acted hurt, as if Sandra's rejecting her doll were a personal affront.

Sandra recoiled. "I just looked at my phone. I know I shouldn't have. I know I'm breaking the rules, but . . . uh . . . twice as many people have died from the virus today. And a chill shot up my spine. Look, my hands are shaking. I'm okay. Enough!"

Before anyone of us could respond, Sandra cleared her throat and muttered, "Forgive me. Please. I'm sorry. I really am. I need to tell my story."

Max and I nodded *okay.* Richard cringed. Josette closed her eyes. Maggie glanced at Cynthia and Barb, who looked like they wanted to say something but were holding back. Eleanor excused herself to use the restroom. And just about when Sandra was going to start, Hannah said, "I'll pray for you."

Sandra acted as if Hannah's prayers meant little to her. But there was some hesitation in her voice, as if she were having second thoughts.

After Eleanor took her seat, Sandra began: "Once upon a time, there was a scarecrow who had no friends. She worked day and night in a wheat field. The work was not difficult, but it was very lonely, especially when it stormed. She endured freezing rain and drizzle, drenching rain, and blizzards that roared across the fields without remorse.

"On sunny days, the scarecrow loved to watch the birds. And

sometimes she even waved to them. But the birds never answered or even acknowledged her, because they were afraid of her. At night, the scarecrow was so unhappy that she often cried herself to sleep. And when she awoke in the morning, she could hardly lift her head up.

"One spring day, the scarecrow did something she wasn't supposed to do: she threw some seeds high into the air, but the birds ignored her and acted as if tempting them was really just a trap. The birds cackled and cawed, and the scarecrow felt even worse than she had before she tried to help them. No matter what the scarecrow did, the birds avoided her. No one wanted to be her friend.

"One day, out of nowhere, a blind crow fell at the scarecrow's feet. The crow was shivering and starved. And the scarecrow knew that if she didn't help him, the crow would die. Each day, the scarecrow fed the blind crow seed, and the crow got stronger in a couple of weeks and was finally able to fly. But before the crow took off, the scarecrow asked him why the birds never wanted to be her friend. And the crow cawed, 'Because your job is to scare us. You treat us like we are evil, and we're not. We only want to survive, like you.' And the scarecrow swallowed hard. 'It's not true. I'm not evil.' But the crow didn't believe her and flew away.

"The scarecrow was crushed, and, later that night, she said to herself that she'd had enough. She needed to leave the wheat field forever. And as she dragged her feet across the wet field, she started moaning, and she moaned so loud that she woke up the farmer, who had been sound asleep with his family in his house next to the wheat field. The farmer was frightened and angry and woke everyone up. They ran outside, and the farmer screamed that the scarecrow was possessed by the devil and that if he didn't set fire to the fields where the scarecrow walked, his wheat crop would be forever doomed. When he lit the fire, it spread quickly, and before dawn the wheat field and scarecrow had burned to the ground.

"When the crows overhead saw the smoke rising, the blind crow was very sad, and he told the other crows in his flock about how the scarecrow had saved his life. And the flock of crows could hardly believe what they were hearing. They had misjudged the scarecrow, who was only doing her job to protect the wheat. She wasn't evil.

"Ashes swirled around in the wind. And the blind crow could feel the presence of the scarecrow flying side by side with the flock. The scarecrow had finally made peace with the birds who had not understood her. And out of respect to the scarecrow, all of the crows decided that they must dress in mourning. And this is why, to this day, all crows are black, in memory of the scarecrow who wanted to be their friend."

Sandra welled up when she finished her story.

None of us seemed to know what to say.

Max scratched his head with the index finger of his right hand. Maggie looked confused, and the faces of Josette, Richard, Barb, Eleanor, and Cynthia went blank.

Hannah turned toward Sandra, wanting to be compassionate, whispering, "I will pray for you, and . . ." But she didn't finish her sentence. Sandra was recoiling again.

I could tell that Sandra identified with the scarecrow. She was an outsider, a self-described misfit who was desperate to make friends. For her, joining the chat room appeared to have had a significance that was somewhat different from its meaning for the rest us.

Sandra started coughing, covering her mouth as she got up.

"Are you okay?" Maggie asked.

"I just choked on my spit. I'm all right."

"Would you like some water?"

"No, no. I'm fine. I'm just tired. I'm ready for bed. I know it's early."

"Nothing like vacation," Barb said, "Having a little time off. Wow! I work every day from 11:00 am. to 7:00 p.m."

Sandra shook her head, "I wish. I'm a waitress in a breakfast joint in the middle of nowhere, Kansas. I wake up at 4:30 a.m. and I'm at work an hour later. We open at six, and sometimes the truckers are waiting in line."

"Sounds awful," I said.

"You don't know what awful is. Well, maybe you do. But I will tell you, the biting cold before dawn only makes it worse."

Day 3

I GOT UP EARLY. BURSTS OF sunlight splintered into my room, waking me. I dressed quickly without showering. My khaki pants and chambray shirt were wrinkled, but it didn't matter. I pulled on a cable-knit sweater and laced up my hiking boots with a silly grin on my face. It was already shorts weather in Texas.

I hurried downstairs and through a back door into the garden. On the veranda, I saw Hannah and Josette, keeping their distance from one another but engaged in what sounded like an intense conversation. It was obvious that they weren't on the same page. Josette's face was animated, and she was jabbing her right index finger in Hannah's direction, extolling the virtues of Voodoo and how her faith had transformed her life.

I could barely understand what she was saying, her words muffled by the heavy cotton mask covering her mouth. I stayed back but moved in a little closer when Hannah started speaking, countering Josette's exclamations in a soft voice.

"Please, understand, Josette, I only want to share with you a verse from a sacred book often read by those of us who are part of the Community of True Inspiration: 'Oh, Holy Trinity, lead me entirely away from earthly things, direct my whole physical and spiritual being toward the course of eternity. Unite me with Thee and let me be here one with Thee that I may also be with Thee in eternal glory.'"

When Josette and Hannah saw me, they became more circumspect and seemed a little embarrassed.

Josette was frowning, ruffling her hands through the woolen shawl draping her blue and red Haitian dress, and Hannah straightened her black Amana Colonies sweatshirt.

I nodded *Good morning*, and they did the same. But I sensed what they were talking about, and I just picked up where I thought they might have left off and asked Hannah, "Why do you whisper when you talk about God?"

Hannah looked surprised. "Andy, I only speak loud enough so that those who are truly listening can hear."

"That's heavy," I answered, not wanting to sound disrespectful.

And Josette asked me, "Why are you always in such a rush?"

I tried to explain what I was going through. "I'm not really rushing. It's just that ever since my girlfriend died, I've needed to walk more, even if it's only in my apartment. If I do five thousand steps in the morning and then again in the afternoon, I feel more together. The self-discipline keeps me focused on the here and now, not on what happened six weeks ago."

Hannah nodded, and Josette shook her head. It didn't seem to be the answer she was expecting. And I moved on.

In the crags and crannies of the trail there were still ice and patches of snow. I pulled the compass from my fanny pack and navigated my way into the Beartown hills toward the gorge called Ice Glen, which I had read about when I was at Navarro College. Nathaniel Hawthorne had described the gorge as "the most curious fissure in all Berkshire" and he was right. Thousands of years ago, all of the streams around Ice Glen flowed south to north, while it was aligned east to west. But all that remained was the evidence that the water flow had carved the deep ravine and boulders from the gorge walls. There were no streams today.

The terrain was tough uphill. But the views were spectacular—the towering ash, white pine, and hemlock trees, some more than one hundred feet high and 150 years old, standing tall, in stark contrast to the hobblebush, the striped maple, and the delicate fronds of the maidenhair ferns. Approaching the V-shaped mouth of the glen, I stopped, nearly out of breath. I had been trekking as fast as I could, racing to escape my thoughts of the past, but now I was slowing down, immersing myself deeper into the transcendental beauty around me. *Transcendental.* I knew what the word meant, but to experience it firsthand was much different.

I closed my eyes, inhaling the woods, tasting them, sweet and sharp on my tongue. A new path spread out in front of me, marked with yellow rectangles, crossing a bridge and railroad tracks before turning back into the forest.

By the time I got back to the cottage grounds, I didn't want to know how much time had passed. The clouds were thickening, and I was perspiring.

Sandra was standing in the garden waving, but not at me.

Josette and Hannah were walking in my direction, and behind them were Maggie and Max. Maggie was carrying a plastic bag, and, when we were all together, she handed us N-95 masks and gloves, saying, "I know these are probably more than you need right now. But just in case . . ."

Sandra was pleased that Maggie had brought masks and gloves. "I'm sorry if I scared you last night when I started coughing. I just took my temperature, I'm normal."

Sandra passed us her thermometer. None of us had a fever.

Sandra stammered, "We need to be more vigilant. It isn't just me that's at risk. We all are." And then she offered to leave the cottage for good, if that was what everyone wanted.

By then, Richard, Barb, Cynthia, and Eleanór had joined us. We looked at each other with a jumbled mix of emotions—frustration, compassion, and just plain bewilderment.

Hannah said, "It's okay, Sandra. We're all just getting to know each other."

Cynthia added, "Sandra, if you get back on the road now, it could be a death sentence. You're already so exhausted and stressed out."

Richard, Max, and I were neutral and had nothing to say.

Josette mumbled something about wanting to build a Voodoo shrine in the garden. Maggie rolled her eyes, "No way."

"Why not?"

"First of all, we're only guests of the owner of the property and he has asked us to not mess things up. The cottage is still on the market. And if a prospective buyer were to show up, it might be a turnoff."

"I only want to build a temporary shrine. A place that can bring us closer together."

Maggie's face went blank.

"A place where we can pray to God to protect us."

"With Voodoo?"

"Yes. Something terrible could happen. Voodoo is powerful. It came to New Orleans in the early 1700s, Africans brought it from the Slave Coast of West Africa. And once it got to New Orleans, Voodoo was infused with the city's dominant religion, Catholicism, and became a kind of Voodoo-Catholicism hybrid. Just because I don't look Black, it doesn't mean I'm not. My ancestors were Creole, of mixed racial origin. Some were enslaved, and others were free people of color."

Sandra cheered up. "I love the idea of a Voodoo shrine."

Josette was surprised, "Really? You said you were from Atwood, Kansas."

"Well, that's where my family ended up. My grandmother was from New Orleans, and when I was about five or six, she came to live with us. She had breast cancer, and my mother wanted to take care of her. And I used to do what I could to help, you know, bringing her slippers, cleaning her glasses, simple things. And she had all kinds of trinkets, little beads and things, and every time I did something for her, she'd give me something, telling me they were passed on to her from an old Voodoo queen who had magical powers. Well, one day, when my mother saw and heard what she was doing, she snatched from my hand everything my grandmother had given me and threw it all away. I cried for days. And as I got older, I never really got over it. When I was a horny teenaged girl, I had fantasies that one day I'd meet my own Voodoo queen."

"That's wild," Josette said, "I want to know more, but now's not the right time. I just want to get started. Building a shrine is good for the soul."

"Well," Sandra smiled, "Maybe, just maybe, it can help restore the sense of belonging that we all seemed to feel in our chat room."

Eleanor and Richard voiced their concerns that instead of bringing us together, the shrine might push us further apart.

Josette was upset. "What do you mean?"

Maggie replied softly, "Josette, I don't want to do anything that's going to divide us."

"What's going to divide us, Maggie, is trying to censor what we really need to do to give us some peace of mind, some relief from everything that's bubbling up among us and out in the world."

I didn't want to listen to any more arguing. I separated myself from the group and headed toward the cottage. Max, Hannah, and Cynthia did the same.

The sky darkened. Thunder and lightning cracked above the tree line, and it started to rain as we ran toward the house. Maggie, Eleanor, and Richard chased after us, but Sandra and Josette stayed behind.

Once I was back on the veranda, I watched Maggie, Eleanor, and Richard rushing toward me, and, in the distance, I saw Sandra and Josette jumping up and down, as if they were celebrating the rain in a way none of us could, connecting in a way that seemed to bring them closer together but at the same time isolated them from the rest of us.

Maggie was dripping wet, but she waited for us all to be in earshot before drying off. "Remember, the next storytelling session begins at 3:00 p.m." I wasn't sure I wanted to participate.

I was starved. I hadn't eaten breakfast, and it was past noon. Cynthia followed me into the kitchen, and we rummaged through the refrigerator. I wanted scrambled eggs and offered to make some for Cynthia, who looked at me like I was from Mars. I didn't understand what was wrong, but then I saw the water pooling at my feet. My hiking boots had tracked mud across the kitchen floor.

Cynthia reached for a mop and some rags in the broom closet and handed them to me. This was the last thing I wanted to do, but I had to clean up my mess. First, though, I had to pull off my socks and boots. I leaned against the counter and struggled to balance myself on one foot and then the other. Cynthia was amused, teasing me that I was the biggest klutz she had ever seen.

I blushed, and she said, "To be honest, Andy, I can't find the words to describe how I'm feeling."

"Well," I said, "Sometimes less is more."

I rinsed the mop in the kitchen sink and propped it on the counter. Cynthia chided me, "That's not a very good place to leave the mop." I was embarrassed. And before I could grab the mop, she lifted it and placed it in a bucket in the broom closet. Then she threw another couple of rags at me. "Now you need to sanitize the sink and the counter."

"Okay, okay." I did what she said, and she laughed, "That a boy, Andy."

I forced a little grin. "So, do you still want scrambled eggs?"

Cynthia nodded, and while I melted the butter in the omelet pan, she put two slices of bread in the toaster and set the table with forks and condiments—salt, pepper, marmalade, and fig jam. Then, she divided up the coffee left in the pot on the counter and heated two cups in the microwave.

When the eggs and toast were ready, we sat at opposite ends of the kitchen table and shared a late breakfast that neither of us had planned. We found ourselves gazing into each other's eyes off and on, connecting in a way so different from anything I had ever experienced that I had to look away. My girlfriend had a Texas twang, Cynthia, a Boston accent, brown eyes, and thick chestnut braids. I was really attracted to Cynthia and part of me felt guilty. It was as if the spirit of my girlfriend were hovering over me, watching me drift into a subliminal place with someone else.

"Those were some of the best scrambled eggs I'd ever had, Andy."

"Huh? Actually, they were pretty ordinary."

She giggled. "Well, sometimes, ordinary is best."

"It must have been the farm-fresh eggs."

I got up to wash the dishes and the omelet pan and excused myself. Cynthia leaned forward and said, "Not so fast. Don't go just yet. I want you to tell me more about you. Yes, Andy, your eggs were that good."

But then, Maggie, Max, and Hannah came into the room, talking loudly about the latest virus news. Forty-one people who worked in a chain grocery store had died, and thousands more had tested positive. I rinsed my plate in the sink, hoping the running water would drown out the grim realities of the virus. I glanced at Cynthia and tried to say how much I had enjoyed my time with her, but the words got stuck in my throat.

Cynthia stayed in her seat, and the others joined her around the table.

I blurted out, "I need to shower and nap."

Maggie bobbed her head , holding her nose, and waved me away. Cynthia smiled. And I grabbed my socks and boots up from the floor and exited the kitchen quickly, wondering if I was leaving too soon.

• • •

When I came back downstairs, no one was on the veranda. I was early for our storytelling session and was hoping that I'd get a chance to talk more to Cynthia before we met as a group, but she wasn't around. I sat down close to the firepit and leaned back and relaxed, grateful to have a few minutes of quiet before everyone else arrived.

Soon enough Hannah walked in with coffee and tea. Eleanor followed with two bags of lemon cookies she had brought from San Francisco, and everyone started to filter in and take their seats. Richard and Max teamed up and saved a place for Maggie, who was stepping down from her throne and passing her crown on to someone new.

Josette was telling Sandra about the dos and don'ts of making a Voodoo figurine. Maggie tapped her spoon on the side of her teacup and announced that, after long and mindful consideration, she had picked Max as her successor.

We all clapped, and Maggie asked Max to kneel as she tried to fit her plastic tiara onto his head, but then pulled it back and placed it in his hands instead, laughing, "If I'm not careful the sacred crown might snap in half."

Rain pattered on the glass roof.

Josette asked if she could light some candles she had in her suitcase. She always traveled with votives.

I said, "Perfect," and Cynthia glanced at me as if she were amused.

Josette scurried off to her room, and while she was gone, Max chattered on about his day job. "I never thought I'd become a chiropractor, but I didn't get into medical school, for reasons I'd rather not discuss."

"I think you can do more to help people as a chiropractor," Richard said, "You have wonderful hands."

"Yes, I believe that. Helping people is a blessing, and being hands-on makes me happy."

"Me, too," Richard laughed, "In fact, I need a little spinal manipulation. My body these days is so tense." And Max smiled.

When Josette returned, she tiptoed into the room and spread ten candles around the veranda, five on the floor and five on tables. Then she tossed matchbooks to each of us so that we could light them at once.

We did what she asked, and the effect was enchanting and soothing.

Hannah confided, "The flickering candles are transforming the veranda into a sacred space that makes me want to pray." Then, she bowed her head, clasped her hands, and recited the first lines of Psalm 23: "The Lord is my shepherd; I shall not want."

Cynthia repeated the words after her. And I remembered hearing them for the first time when I was in third grade.

Josette's eyes teared up.

Richard sat sternly in his chair, and Maggie surveyed the room, seemingly focused more on the rain and the waning afternoon than on what was being said.

Max raised the plastic tiara into the air and proclaimed. "Time for the storytelling to begin."

Richard stood up, as if he and Max had already planned the order of events, and began his story: "Long ago, just days before the opening of the Great Exposition of 1889, an Englishwoman and her daughter traveled from Jaipur, India, to Paris, France. They arrived at Gare de Lyon around 9:00 p.m., where they were met by the driver of a closed carriage, who loaded their two pieces of luggage under his feet because he feared, if they were visible on the top of the coach, thieves would descend upon them and steal their belongings. When they arrived at the hotel, they requested separate but adjoining rooms. But unfortunately, this was not possible. The manager apologized profusely and said that the best he could do was to put the mother in a room on the third floor and her daughter on the fourth floor directly above it. Both the mother and daughter were very tired, and each went to her room to rest.

The daughter promised that she'd come to her mother's room in two or three hours to be sure that she was comfortable. But the daughter was more exhausted than she thought, and she fell asleep without removing her clothes. So it wasn't until about three hours after midnight that she went to her mother's room. But she didn't want to knock on the door, because, if her mother was asleep, she didn't want to wake her. So she went to the hotel desk, and the night clerk followed her to her mother's room. But when he opened the door, they saw that the room was empty. The daughter was confused, thinking she had made a mistake, and called the chambermaid, who rushed to meet her but knew nothing of her mother's room. In fact, the chambermaid remembered that the daughter had arrived at the hotel alone. Needless to say, the daughter was very upset, and she returned to the hotel desk and asked the clerk to show her the guest book that both she and her mother had signed when they checked into the hotel. The clerk was, of course, very courteous, and opened the guest book, telling her as politely as possible that there was only her name in the register and that no one saw another woman at the time when she arrived. The daughter shouted that she was going to call the police, and the clerk pleaded with her to calm down, advising her to do what she must do. Well, when the police arrived, they spoke to the clerk and summoned the carriage driver, who had, the daughter insisted, taken her and her mother from Gare de Lyon to the hotel. But once again, much to the daughter's dismay, the driver recalled ferrying her alone from the station. The daughter was completely distraught, and, in the morning, the police picked her up and had her admitted for evaluation at Sainte-Anne Hospital Center in the Fourteenth Arrondissement that had been opened as a psychiatric center by Napoleon III in 1863. There, she received experimental electroshock therapy that at first seemed to help her but ultimately worsened her condition.

"By the time she was discharged, she was heavily sedated and was allowed to travel back to her home in England, with the condition that she must be accompanied by a nurse. After more than a year, the daughter's physicians convinced her that her mother had vanished, not supernaturally, but willfully, to escape criminal charges that had been leveled against her. Reportedly, she had been involved, unknown to her daughter, in a surreptitious plot to extort funds from an Indian bank, which she claimed had embezzled her deposits.

"But then, out of the blue, the daughter received a letter from her mother's chambermaid, who confessed that she could no longer bear the burden of the treachery and deceit to which she had been forced to acquiesce. In fact, the mother had died, while the daughter was sleeping, of the bubonic plague, which she had mysteriously contracted in Constantinople from a snake charmer whom she had tipped in the street.

"The daughter was stunned. The snake charmer. And the daughter recalled that this poor man had looked so ill that she had stayed away, but, apparently, her mother had gotten too close. However, the daughter didn't understand how it was possible that her mother had not transmitted the disease to her. And the chambermaid said it was obviously the will of God that she should survive.

"The chambermaid admitted that covering up the disappearance of the daughter's mother was deviously planned and executed, because if it had become public that a woman had died from the plague, the Paris Exposition would never have opened, and millions of dollars would have been lost.

"In France, investigations were launched to track down and punish the perpetrators of this heinous deed, including a cadre of investors in the Paris Exposition, the hotel clerk and carriage driver they paid to lie, and even one of the doctors at Sainte-Anne's. Ultimately, they were all arrested, but the court deemed the chambermaid's evidence inadmissible because she, too, had accepted a bribe. So, all were set free. However, months later, rumors circulated in Paris that each of the perpetrators had been tracked down and tortured by the ghost of the vanished woman, who, some say, threw acid in their eyes, blinding them, before slitting the jugular vein.

"Upon hearing this news, the daughter collapsed, and when she regained consciousness, it was unfortunately evident that she had gone insane, and she was deemed a danger not only to herself but to others who tried to help her, especially older women who reminded her of her mother. The court ordered her committed to a psychiatric hospital in London, but the people in her village stood up in her defense, and the judge, without precedent, granted them custody of her, provided that a trust be established to provide for her perpetual care. In the village, stories about the daughter were passed on from one generation to the next. And for the next fifty years, men, women, and children did as their forebears had promised. It was considered an honor to serve as the daughter's caretaker. Each year, a lottery was held, and the one who drew the lucky number was bestowed with the responsibility to help the daughter with her daily life and was provided with a residence and a healthy sum to cover household expenses. Much to everyone's amazement the daughter aged more gracefully than her peers. And as her body became more fragile, her face never wrinkled and she retained the countenance of the beautiful young woman who had traveled to Paris with her mother, hoping to attend the Great Paris Exposition, which many, to this day, believe was the dawning of the modern age.

"So, my friends, the legend of the vanishing woman lives on, a lesson to us at this terrible time: the deceived will be vindicated, and the truth will one day be told."

Richard sighed and sat down, acting a little troubled by the lack of immediate response.

He pointed an index finger at Max, who was quick to say, "Well done. I was impressed by how Richard was able to allude to the virus without actually mentioning it. Clearly, the deception to which the daughter was subjected mirrored the way our president has downplayed the pandemic and then scrambled to cover up his mistakes."

Hannah said, "I appreciated the moral of story."

Barb squirmed in her seat, "I'm not sure whether or not there was a moral."

Hannah responded, "Ultimately, good triumphed over evil."

"But the perpetrators were never convicted," Barb countered, "and the poor daughter ended up insane. Justice never prevailed."

"Except," Hannah maintained, "she was vindicated in the lessons that were passed on to the next generation."

"To be honest," Barb said, "the story was kind of boring, but Richard made it more interesting than it actually was by playing around with the tone of his voice."

Maggie interjected, "I agree, the performance made it work, carrying me unexpectedly through the silliness like a hot air balloon on a windy day. I liked the exaggerated diction, and the way it sounded archaic reminded me of *The Decameron*."

Richard perked up. "Thank you; that means a lot. I like playing with voices. In fact, that's why I picked that story. I work in the hospitality business."

Cynthia laughed, "No wonder you know so much about wine."

Richard continued, "I own a bed and breakfast, a mini-boutique hotel in a historic neighborhood in St. Louis. And as much as it might seem hard to believe, I enjoy working the front desk. I like pretending, so sometimes I take on different personalities for my guests, who, quite frankly, don't know the difference. But I had to temporarily close the hotel because of the pandemic."

Max wanted to know more, but Richard shook his head, "Later. I don't want to monopolize the conversation."

Eleanor asked, "Does anyone want more tea?" and I offered to help.

In the kitchen, Eleanor and I talked softly, wondering whether exchanging stories was really doing us any good. She was skeptical, and so was I.

When we brought the teapot and another bag of cookies back onto the veranda, Josette and Sandra, who had not commented on Richard's story, asked to be excused so that they could work on their Voodoo shrine.

Maggie exhaled loudly.

Josette brushed back her hair and said, "I loved your story, Richard. And we'd stick around a little longer to talk about it, but Maggie's starting to act up."

"Act up?" Maggie asked in a sarcastic tone. "You know the way I feel about your Voodoo shrine."

"Yes, I do," Josette replied, trying to sound respectful, "Rest assured. I'll take down it all down at the appropriate time."

Richard shuddered, and Max winked, "No need to worry, Maggie. It's okay."

Maggie glared at Sandra, then at Josette, who finally acknowledged Maggie's disapproval and reluctantly conceded, "Okay, we'll pause our work on the shrine until we can work out the details."

Maggie pursed her lips and did her best to let go of her frustration by asking, "Will someone please tell us another story?"

Max interrupted her, "Lest we forget, I am the king. And, dear friends, it's up to me to decide what we are going to do next."

Josette and Sandra sat down without saying anything more.

Max quickly swiped his hand through the air and announced, "I'd like everyone to direct their attention to Eleanor, who has agreed to lead us in some yoga exercises. I do believe now is the perfect time. Please, Eleanor, help us to recenter and affirm our commitment to each other."

Before anyone could object, Eleanor moved to the center of room. "I urge all of you to participate. Chair yoga melts away stress. Believe me, the techniques and exercises that I practice are tried and true.

"Let's begin with Ujjayi breathing," Eleanor instructed. "Sit up tall at the edge of your seat. Place your hands on your waist. Take a deep breath in through your nose, expanding your inner self through your sides and abdomen. Now, exhale slowly."

Eleanor demonstrated and told us to repeat the exercise for ten breaths. And one by one we did what she said.

"Now turn right and gaze into the eyes of the person sitting next to you. Then turn left and do the same thing with the person on the other side of you. Again. Again."

To my right, Barb's opalescent eyes opened wide, and when we connected, it was as if we were meeting for the first time. There was something about her that felt both familiar and strange. Her makeup was heavier than I had realized, covering a thin scar that ran from below her left ear to her chin. I wondered what had happened to her, but I didn't want to ask.

I turned toward Max, to my left, and he frowned. I could tell that he thought I was staring at him, but I wasn't. I focused on the roundness of his face and his pale blue eyes protruding ever so slightly through their narrow sockets above his cheeks. Clearly, I was making him uneasy. So I looked back at Eleanor, hoping she could give me some guidance on what to do next.

Eleanor rubbed her palms together. "The next exercise is *Cat-Cow*. Inhale and arch your back and look up at the ceiling. Exhale through your spine, pulling your abdominals in and rounding your back. Repeat this movement five times."

Sandra complained, "I have some kind of kink in my glutes, and arching my back makes me hurt more."

Eleanor tried to reassure her. "Yoga can help." But Sandra acted like she didn't believe her.

I wished I'd seated myself across from Cynthia. I liked looking at her. There was something about her eyes that turned me on in ways I didn't really understand.

Eleanor swiveled around in her seat. "Now, let's try *Sun Salutation Arms.* Sit tall, inhale slowly, and raise your arms up, pressing your palms overhead. Now exhale. Float your arms back down to your sides. Repeat five times. This lengthens the spine and releases the tension in your shoulders and neck."

With each exercise, the oxygen levels on the veranda seemed to rise. Breathing was easier. My body loosened up.

"Now," Eleanor continued, "let's do *Eagle Eyes.* Stretch your arms out to each side. And then bring one arm under the other in front of you at shoulder height. While bending your arms at the elbows, twist your arms so your palms meet each other. Hold for five breaths, then unwind and repeat with the opposite arm on top."

When Eleanor finished, she brought her palms together and bowed her head: "Namaste."

Maggie did the same. "Namaste *Khush Raho*. Be happy."

Barb sprang up out of her seat and playfully bowed to Eleanor, and then to King Max, who acknowledged her with a regal gesture, placing both arms behind his back and thrusting his chest forward in a show of confidence and pride, his head held high and his chin jutting out.

Barb giggled, but then her face crumpled. Fighting back tears, she apologized. "I know it's getting late, but I have to tell a story that's . . . uh . . . like a cancer inside me."

Max gulped the tea from his cup and surveyed the room to see how all of us felt about staying longer to hear Barb's story. We nodded in unison.

Barb blurted out, "I don't mean to be a downer, but, being from New York, I'm just torn up inside. I know we've been able to escape the wrath of this terrible disease, for now. But to be honest, I am tormented by survivor guilt. I feel like I'm being crushed, and, sadly, no yoga exercise can take the pressure off. That said, I loved everything we just did with Eleanor, but instead of relieving my stress, I feel worse.

"I know I shouldn't have brought my cell phone with me to the veranda, but I did. And while Andy and Eleanor were getting the pot of tea, I heard it ding, and I saw a text message from my sister about her husband and the virus. It said: 'Hysterical!!!! Sam is dead!!!'

"I know I need to call my sister, but I don't know what to say. Should I leave here and go back to Brooklyn? But what good would that do? My sister has little kids, and I probably couldn't see her or them, anyway.

"I remembered the last time I saw Sam. I was stuck in my apartment. In quarantine. Ten days after I tested positive. I was asymptomatic. Sam left a Tupperware container outside my door with veal marsala, porcini mushrooms, and grilled vegetables that my sister had made for me, knowing it was one of my favorite meals. And I opened the door to thank him.

"Could I have possibly infected him without knowing it? Was I standing too close to him?

"When I got my first test, it had nothing to do with Sam, or my sister. It was because someone in the store where I work was friends with someone who had the virus—someone I didn't know.

"At that point, no one told me I had to go the doctor. But I did anyway. And when they said I didn't meet the testing criteria, I went to a private clinic and paid for it. I had to wait a week to get the results, and when I did . . . well, I don't know why I'm rambling on about me. All of us have gone through the same thing. It doesn't make me any more special to talk about it. If anything, all of you are probably thinking I should just shut up."

Max raised his teacup above his head, as if it were some kind of royal chalice, and asked that we observe a moment of silence to mourn the death of Barb's brother-in-law and others who had died from the virus.

Barb was sobbing. Cynthia broke the social distancing rules and brought her a box of Kleenex.

I wanted to hug Barb, and Cynthia. I was shaking inside and could barely contain my craving for physical contact.

Max asked Barb, "Is there anything we can do?"

Barb wiped the tears from her cheeks and shook her head *no* as she stood up and hurried away.

Josette and Sandra started talking again about the Voodoo shrine, and Hannah prayed, "'Lead us not into temptation, but deliver us from evil: For thine is the kingdom, and the power, and the glory forever.' Matthew 6:13."

Max leaned forward in his chair and said, "I think it's time to adjourn. But before we do, I hereby name Cynthia the next queen."

We all clapped, relieved that our session was over.

Josette and Sandra pulled back their chairs, as if they were getting ready to leave, but they didn't. Josette cleared her throat, and Sandra coughed softly.

Max exited the veranda, with Richard and Cynthia following behind him.

My stomach ached. Too much caffeine. Cynthia could tell I wasn't feeling well and passed me a plate of cookies. "These might take the edge off, but then again, they could make it worse."

I grinned and thanked her, then went upstairs to get my coat. I needed some fresh air. But when I stepped outside, it was blustery and cold. I wasn't sure if I was doing the right thing. Staying inside with Cynthia might have been a better idea.

I could hear my girlfriend saying my name, beckoning me into the night, massaging me with the warmth of her voice, her touch, her hands easing their way around my waist. I didn't know where I was going. And as the darkness embraced me, I couldn't let go.

But the farther I walked away from the house, the lonelier I felt. An owl hooted from a tree somewhere in front of me. I tried to echo the sounds I heard. And my girlfriend disappeared, without a word.

Day 4

I DREADED GOING DOWNSTAIRS. I HAD a sour taste in my mouth. Sleep had been tough. But when I saw Cynthia at breakfast, my mood changed. "Queen for a day," she giggled, showing off her red shawl and twirling around.

The sky was clearing, the tree limbs that outlined the perimeter of the cottage were dusted with frost, and the grassy lawn was covered with an icy glaze of frozen dew.

When Hannah came into the kitchen, she was beaming. "What a glorious morning!"

Cynthia brought the pot of coffee she had just brewed to the kitchen table, and we swapped small talk about the weather, the landscape, the cottage. I told her that being in the Berkshires was helping me to come to terms with everything I'd left behind. But I knew it all sounded so vague. Cynthia seemed to understand what I was going through, but she didn't want to share much about her life, either. Instead, she focused on what she was doing now. "I really want to find out more about the shed," she said, "There something about it that seems so strange, out of place, but at the same time, important. The shed, Andy, really turns the scientist in me on. I know all of this must sound weird."

"Not exactly."

"That's good. I need to be careful to not say too much too soon. It's not that I don't trust you."

I looked into her eyes, wondering whether my feelings for her were truly real.

Richard appeared and said, "I'm really worried about Barb. I heard her crying all night. And when I knocked on her door on my way downstairs, she didn't answer."

None of us knew exactly what to say. I asked if I should try to talk to her, since she had kind of opened up to me the day before. Richard shrugged, and Hannah said, "Barb probably called her sister. No telling what happened."

"Sometimes," Richard added, "reality takes its own time to settle in, and, when it does, it can punch you in the gut so hard that you can hardly breathe."

I could tell that he was worried about Barb, but from the way his voice was cracking, I figured it also had to do with something terrible that had happened in his own life. We were all damaged, wounded by the unspeakable, and just thinking about Barb brought me down. The problem was that I didn't know how to talk about it. Maybe none of us did. It was as if we were all looking for distractions, things that helped us to pretend that nothing was really wrong.

Sandra and Josette entered the room laughing. Each had a small incense burner in her hands, and they placed them side by side on the kitchen counter, rambling on about sandalwood and the benefits of essential oils.

Richard told them about Barb, and they quieted down, wafting the incense smoke into the air with the backs of their hands.

Maggie was right behind them and was about to snatch up one of the incense burners when Eleanor, Max, and Barb trudged into the kitchen.

Barb's eyes were puffy from crying. She reached for a napkin and patted her cheeks.

While we all chattered away, Barb sat down by herself at the kitchen table and tilted her head backward.

Max exclaimed, "I want to make pancakes!"

Cynthia, Richard, Hannah, and I nodded our approval, but Barb, Eleanor, and Maggie said they didn't have much of an appetite.

Max clumsily mixed the batter and poured dollops onto a heated griddle, flipping them onto a big platter and covering them as quickly as he could. But by the time he served us one at a time, the pancakes were cold. I looked at Cynthia, and she whispered that we'd better eat them anyway, and we did, without talking to each other or anyone else.

When we finished eating, Cynthia told us she wanted to push the storytelling later in the day, perhaps into the early evening, but didn't want to do so without the consent of the group. She wanted her reign as queen, brief as it was, to be as democratic as possible. So, we all voted, and it was unanimous. Storytelling would begin at seven thirty.

With the time settled, Cynthia urged us to spend the day by ourselves: "Reflect on yourself and the others in our group. Are we becoming friends? Or adversaries? Clearly the tensions we internalize might be starting to get the best of us. It doesn't matter what you do. But, please, today, try do it on your own—reading, napping, hiking, horseback riding, whatever. Be good to yourself, so you can be a better person when we're together."

Eleanor was disappointed. "I didn't come all the way from San Francisco to be alone."

Cynthia was adamant. "It's not about being alone. It's about getting in touch with our inner selves." Eleanor left the kitchen in a huff.

As much as I agreed in principle with Cynthia, I hoped for more social contact, too, especially with her, even though I sensed that wasn't going to happen, not anytime soon.

Maggie seemed okay with Cynthia but said, "Frankly, I feel

thwarted by Sandra and Josette. No matter what I say or do, they seem determined to build a Voodoo shrine."

Cynthia griped, "Look, you told us on day one that we could do whatever we pleased. Their shrine isn't going to do any harm. If anything, it will be good for them, and who knows, maybe for us."

Maggie stormed out of the kitchen, with Richard and Max following close behind.

After everyone had left, I stayed behind, offering to help Cynthia clean up. She was on a mission, scrubbing the sink, wiping the tables and chairs with sanitizer, pulling pots and pans out of the cupboards, stacking dishes on the counter. A total overhaul.

Cynthia grimaced, "Cleaning is a kind of therapy for me. It's not couples counseling."

I stepped back, stunned by her terseness, but didn't respond. I just wished her well and slipped away to the veranda.

Richard and Max were on the couch, and they weren't six feet apart. They were wearing masks and latex gloves and their fingertips were touching. But when they saw me, they pulled their hands apart.

Max had a silly grin, and Richard said, "I couldn't believe Cynthia asked if we were making friends or adversaries. That's ridiculous. For me, coming to the cottage is one of the most amazing things I've ever done. I never expected I'd meet someone in person who actually reminds me of someone I lost, who meant so much to me. It's like he's come back to me."

I nodded. "Yeah . . . Sounds a little weird."

"Oh, but it's not," Richard said, "I've told Max all about him. In fact, Max has the same color eyes."

"I see. I mean . . ."

"It's okay," Richard continued. "I know you know how hard it is. You're living it. We all are. When my partner, Jack, got sick with the virus, I panicked and he moved into one of the guest rooms in my B&B so that we could do what we were supposed to—masking, social distancing. And when I got tested and found out that I was asymptomatic, it became clear he must have gotten the virus from me, because when I was working the front desk, I was interacting with people every day, and who knows what they had or where they came from. So I shut the B&B down and hired a nurse to take care of him. But the nurse got the virus, too. And they both were admitted to the hospital. Well, the nurse survived, and Jack died of a heart attack just when it seemed like he had turned the corner. His fever was down, and his doctor thought he was getting better."

I was fidgety, and, when I looked at Max, I could tell that he was, too, but he didn't say anything while Richard was talking. But when he was done, he changed the subject. "Who started the chat room in the first place? Andy, were you one of the last to join?"

"Yeah, I guess. And when I did, I think I heard someone say Maggie started it. Which makes sense, since she seems to have the greatest expectations."

Richard laughed, "Well, if that is in fact true, she should lighten up."

I leaned back in my chair, stretched my feet in front of me, and dozed off, half listening as they talked about how ridiculous it was that Maggie was so bent out of shape over the building of a Voodoo shrine.

When I opened my eyes, Max and Richard were gone. Sitting across from me was Barb, who said, "I liked watching you sleep. Did you know that you're a nose twitcher?"

I was still groggy, and she giggled that I was doing it again.

I straightened up in my chair and told her I was glad she was feeling better.

"Not really," she mumbled, "My sister laid a big guilt trip on me. And I can't shake it off."

"I know, it's tough. The moment I think about the death of my girlfriend, I stew about it. I sink into a strange abyss and struggle to claw my way out."

Barb sobbed, "It's my fault. My brother-in-law is dead because of me."

I gritted my teeth. "It's not your fault. How were you supposed to know that you were an asymptomatic carrier? There's so much about the virus that we, and even the doctors, don't know."

Barb got up and apologized. "I shouldn't have said that."

I struggled to find the right words and finally blurted out, "There's no need for an apology. You haven't done anything wrong."

Barb stammered, "I have to accept responsibility for his death. I'm alive and he's not! And my sister's kids have lost their father."

Cynthia hurried onto the veranda and asked what was wrong. Barb cried out, "Everything!" and charged outside into the garden, where she bumped into Hannah, who was kneeling on a rubber pad with a trowel in her hand, pulling weeds and preparing the soil for planting.

I grabbed my jacket and scarf from the mudroom coatrack and headed outside. As I got closer, I overheard Hannah praying and slowed down so that I could listen to what she was saying: "God of love and mercy, embrace dear Barb whose heart today is burdened with grief. Grant Barb space to shed her tears. Hold her close through the coming days."

Barb was weeping, and, as I passed by, Hannah glanced at me with an expression that I couldn't exactly figure out. Was she attracted to me? Or was it the other way around?

Outside the stable, I heard the horses neighing and then saw Maggie, who was brushing the mane of Harry, the gelding. She was surprised to see me and asked if I wanted to join her for a ride. She was wearing riding boots, blue jeans, and a tight leather jacket. Her cheeks were ruddy, and her hair was tied into two long braids that draped over her shoulders.

I had to admit that I'd never been horseback riding and that, while it sounded like fun, I was kind of scared.

Maggie joked, "Then Daisy is the perfect horse for you. She likes city slickers."

"Look, I'm not exactly a city slicker. I'm from Texas, after all."

Maggie tied Harry's reins to a fence post and led me into the stable, pulling a bag of sliced apples from her fanny pack and handing them to me, instructing me to give the old mare a snack.

I started to push my hand between the slats in the gate to Daisy's stall, but Maggie motioned for me to take a step backward, reassuring me that Daisy would come to me and appreciate the snack all the more. Daisy neighed and poked her nose forward, eating the apple quickly out of my hand and then licking my palm.

Maggie opened the gate, and Daisy nuzzled up close to me. Maggie pulled the bridle off the rack in the stable and undid the halter so she could slide a band down over Daisy's nose and slip the crown back over her ears. Then she put the bridle on and slipped the reins up over Daisy's neck. And when all was secure, Maggie handed me the reins while she placed the saddle on Daisy's back and cinched the straps.

Then she pushed a step stool alongside Daisy to make it easier for me, helping me to place my foot in the stirrup and pull myself onto the saddle.

I was nervous, but it was easier than I had expected. Sitting in the saddle, I felt like I had really accomplished something. Daisy was calm, and, in my mind, glad to have me on board. Maggie explained, "Now, remember, Daisy was basically trained to perform three different gaits: walk, trot, and canter. And since we're going onto narrow trails in the woods, we're mostly going to walk, and maybe trot when the ravine opens up."

High cumulus clouds hovered above the landscape. As we moved forward, the tree line resonated with the sounds of squirrels and birds that seemed to sense our trek into the woods.

Daisy was everything that Maggie had described—gentle and

smart. She knew I was inexperienced but somehow made me think I was in control. Seeing the world from horseback gave me a perspective I had never experienced. The forest came alive. And while I was awestruck by the expansive views, I knew I had to be more vigilant, watching for low-hanging branches and ducking my head, acutely aware that if I didn't, I was going to get knocked to the ground.

Maggie was ecstatic, keeping pace with me and, sometimes, teasing me that I looked like a young Don Quixote who had lost his way.

After about half a mile, the trail sloped upward through a grove of hemlock trees and forked in front of us. Maggie slowed to a stop and dismounted, tying off her reins around the trunk of a sturdy white pine, and then helped me to do the same.

"Up ahead," she said, "that's Laura's Tower, named for the grief-stricken daughter-in-law of David Dudley Field, a former minister in Stockbridge, who came here to find solace in this wonderland of birch trees and mountain laurel after the untimely death of her husband and children."

Maggie scurried up the cast iron stairs of the tower, and I chased after her. It was a game, and she was winning. When I got to the top, I could barely catch my breath, and she tittered, "You're in terrible shape. Do you ever work out?"

"As much as I can. I walk a lot. I used to do more, lifting weights, sit-ups, planks. But after my girlfriend got sick, I didn't do much, and, since she died, I've done less."

Maggie pouted. "Just days before joining our chat room, I lost one of my oldest friends, an emergency room nurse at New York Presbyterian Hospital. He was only twenty-seven years old, and we'd known each since we were kids. We'd never dated, but in hindsight, I think we might have been on the verge of taking the next step. But when he got sick, he didn't take it seriously enough. It was before anyone knew how deadly the virus was, and by the time he told me, he was already too far gone. He was in the emergency room and coughing so loud he could barely talk. And the last thing he said was that his lungs felt as if they were filling with pus."

Listening to Maggie talk about her friend cast a shroud over the panorama of the Berkshires swirling around us. The sky was silky blue, but the clouds floating over the rolling hills were thickening. Mount Greylock, the highest point in Massachusetts, loomed in a strange haze that Maggie said obscured our views of the Catskills of New York, to the west, and the Green Mountains of Vermont, to the north.

Maggie admitted, "If my friend hadn't died and the virus wasn't raging, I doubt the property owner would have given permission for us to use the cottage. But I'm starting to worry that coming here might have been a bad idea."

I struggled to reassure her that she had done the right thing. "Gathering ten strangers together was bold and incredibly generous, even if it doesn't seem to be working out exactly as you imagined."

"Really? I'm not so sure. I may have made a huge mistake."

Maggie was antsy, stroking her braids as if she didn't know what else to say or do.

I followed her back to the horses, where she rewarded them for their patience with more sliced apples, then helped me to get back in the saddle.

Maggie turned Harry in the direction of the Ice Glen Ravine, but then decided it was time to head back to the cottage.

The smell of hemlock intensified as we plodded our way back down the trail. Harry lunged forward into a trot and canter, and I did my best to keep up. If Daisy hadn't known the way back to the stable, I might not have gotten there.

Maggie was glad to get back. I thanked her for taking me along, and she asked, "Would you like to join me for a cup of tea?"

I shook my head *no, thanks,* feeling like I was letting her down. But I just needed more time to get myself together. I didn't want to talk any more about death.

An uneasy silence settled around us. We walked toward the cottage side by side without speaking, but as we got closer to the garden, we drifted apart.

• • •

When we convened in the living room for storytelling, Cynthia welcomed each of us, but she made a special point of extending her hand or elbow without touching as we took our seats.

Max was giddy, goofing around with Richard as he picked up the bellows from a stand next to the fireplace and squeezed out some musty air that smelled toxic.

Sandra scowled. But Josette seemed oblivious, lifting a small cloth figurine out of her purse and waving it in the air as if deeply immersed in some kind of incantation.

Hannah raised her hands and whispered, "'But the Lord is faithful, who shall stablish you, and keep you from evil.' 2 Thessalonians 3:3."

Josette took a deep breath and glared at Hannah.

Eleanor folded her arms across her chest and bowed her head.

The blood drained out of Barb's cheeks, leaving her skin pale and her body shivering. She rubbed her palms together, as if trying to get warm.

Max tensed up. And Richard muttered, "Talking about religion in mixed company is dangerous."

Maggie was circumspect, but when I looked in her direction, her eyes brightened up, inviting me to sit closer to her. But as I moved toward her, Barb asked me if I could bring her one of the cashmere blankets from the veranda. And while I was handing it to her, Cynthia recited a traditional Buddhist prayer:

Just as the soft rains fill the streams,
pour into the rivers, and join together in the oceans,

so may the power of every moment of your goodness
flow forth to awaken and heal all beings,
those here now, those gone before, those yet to come.

Barb welled up as the color was beginning to return to her face.

Cynthia was glowing.

I was restless. And for a reason unknown to me, I couldn't stop thinking about food. I was still kind of hungry. I had made myself a roast beef sandwich, which I ate by myself before coming to the living room. I had no idea what the others had eaten for dinner, but the kitchen was spotless, and, apparently, Cynthia's cleaning therapy had the effect she had hoped for.

I expected Cynthia to ask us about our day, but she didn't. Instead, she was proactive and asked Barb to please start the storytelling. I was surprised, especially since Barb had been so dejected. But Barb's eyes brightened, as if Cynthia had flipped a switch inside her, and once she began, she had a poise and grace that belied her grief.

"There was a homeless man who lived in an abandoned tool shack in an alley a couple of blocks from my apartment. I wasn't sure what he had inside his little shack, but there was a cord that poked through the ramshackle roof that appeared to be connected to an electrical pole nearby.

"On my way to the subway, I'd seen this guy sitting on the curb near the alley where he lived. It was like he was guarding the shack, but somehow thought it was smarter to stay away from it during the day, because he didn't want to alarm the tenants in the buildings nearby. I'm sure they knew he was there, but I guess the guy thought that if he only slept in the shack, they'd leave him alone. Which they did.

"Most of the time when I saw the guy, rain or shine, he pretended he didn't see me. He wasn't a panhandler. If anything, he appeared self-sufficient, and even had enough food that he could feed the pigeons, who flocked around him as he scattered his table scraps on the sidewalk. But he looked like a bum with a stinky peacoat, grimy jeans, and ratty old sneakers with holes in the toes.

"Well, one day, I saw him talking to the pigeons, telling them to get in line before he fed them, and that was exactly what they did. I'd never seen anything like it. This guy was actually able to train them to come to him when he called, and to fly off with a whoosh of the back of his hand.

"So, I decided to go up to the guy and talk to him. Once again, he acted as if I wasn't there, but I wouldn't leave. And finally, he stood up and barked at me that I was invading his space.

"Half of me was scared, but the other part was determined. I wasn't going to give up. And I guess he sensed that, and he marched away, laughing as if, if I wanted to play hide-and-seek, he was going to win. I told him it wasn't a game. But before I could finish, he ran off.

"So I headed off to the subway, and, as I walked downstairs to the tracks, he jumped out in front of me, taunting, 'I told you so. I told you so.'

"What had I done? I mean, I wanted to be his friend, and now I was becoming his enemy. He scoffed that I was privileged, and he was not.

"But I didn't respond. I stared at his face, and he at mine. His skin was pitted, and his beard was splotchy. And his hair was frizzy, and one of his eyes looked like it was made of glass, and the other didn't seem to focus right, because he bobbed his head back and forth in front of me, as if he couldn't really see me.

"I didn't know what to do. I asked him to leave me alone, but he wouldn't budge. So I pushed through the turnstile, bumping into him. Then he stepped aside and whispered that I had his permission to pass. And then he jumped over the turnstile and climbed down onto the tracks and disappeared into the subway tunnel.

"I worried that once the train came and started up, it was going to speed into the tunnel and kill him. I started screaming for help, and a policeman came running toward me. And I babbled on and on about what had happened, and the policeman took a few notes, but when he asked me if I had seen the guy before, I said no. The policeman could tell that I was lying, but he didn't challenge me. He just handed me a card with a telephone number to call if I had more information and turned around, leaving me alone on the platform.

"So I waited for the next train and got on, went to work, and headed home later than usual. I met a friend for drinks and sushi and was kind of tipsy when I left the subway for my apartment.

"As I walked by the alley where the homeless guy lived, I saw a light on in the tool shack and was surprised he actually had electricity. So I tiptoed down the alley to get a closer look. And when I was outside the shack, I heard the guy talking on what I assumed was a cell phone.

"But then I heard the flutter of the pigeons, and, one by one, I watched them enter the shack. It didn't make any sense. But then I saw the guy come out of the shack carrying two oversized birdcages, each with five or six pigeons inside. It was so strange. I had no idea what was going on. But then, in a glint of light, I saw a pigeon leg dangling out of one of the cages, and attached to it was a small cylindrical band.

"I couldn't believe it. They were carrier pigeons, but I didn't have any idea what they were doing and where they were going. I wanted to follow the guy, but I was exhausted. And when I made it back to my apartment, I conked out for a few hours but then tossed and turned the rest of the night. In the morning, I could barely eat and had to hurry to the subway because I was going to be late for work. And as I passed the alley, I saw the guy sitting on his curb, pretending that he didn't see me, as if nothing had happened.

"That night, I got off work early. I had a plan. I was going to follow the guy and see where he went with those birdcages, even if it took all night. I grabbed a bite to eat on my way home, stopping at my favorite halal stand for a lamb gyro at the corner of Prince and Broadway, and then went to Joe's Coffee for a double espresso and a slice of almond cake. I was stuffed, but I wasn't weighted down. I was energized.

"When I climbed the stairs out of the subway in Brooklyn, I took a different exit and walked on the opposite side of the street, taking a slightly different route to the backside of the shack to be sure the homeless guy didn't see me.

"I sat on the stoop of an old brownstone, acting as if I was waiting for someone to come home, and no one bothered me. The sunset was amazing—kind of like orange and yellow saltwater taffy stretched out across the horizon. It made me think of Coney Island and the great times I had when I played hooky from school with my friends.

"As the sky darkened, the guy came out of the shack, beckoned his pigeons inside, and emerged with his two cages. I stayed about ten feet behind him, stopping every once in a while just in case he turned around.

"When he got to the subway, he raced downstairs. He was on a mission, swiping his MetroCard and hurrying to the end of the platform. I did the same, and when I saw his silhouette in the shadows, I positioned myself about six yards away from him. But when the train stopped, I moved closer and scrambled onto the same subway car as he did. And when he sat down, I didn't. And when he turned in my direction, I looked away.

"Finally, at Columbus Circle, he got up and exited the train. I followed him, staggered between people.

"He moved quickly into Central Park, scanning the benches for homeless people—sitting by themselves, men and women of all ages, each with some kind of physical disability, crutches at their side, amputations, bandaged arms or ankles, each leaning back and flashing a peace sign as he passed by, as if it was a signal that had been planned in advance. And when the guy stopped, he set his birdcages on the ground and put a latex glove on his right hand and passed another glove to the person on the bench. Then he opened the gate to one of the cages to let a single pigeon out, carefully placing it in his hand, carrying it in a gentle embrace, his fingers wrapped tenderly around its torso and wings, handing it to the person on the bench, who said *thank you.* And the guy nodded, picked up his birdcages, and moved on.

"Over the next couple of hours, the guy delivered nine pigeons to nine different people, and then headed back to the subway, back to Brooklyn, back to the shack.

"The darkness shielded me from view, and once the guy was back inside his shack the pigeons he had delivered circled overhead, and one by one, they landed at the door to the shack and filed in, where, I assumed, they were fed and rewarded for coming home.

"Waiting was hard, but somehow, I managed to do it, leaning, sitting, doing jumping jacks, pacing up and down the alley, until all the pigeons were back and he flipped the light on inside. I tiptoed up to the shack and listened. He was talking on his cell phone, reading messages aloud that were carried from Central Park to the shack by each of the pigeons. And while I couldn't hear every word, I could tell that the guy was telling the people he called that so-and-so was safe and still very much loved his family. In a couple of instances, the person who sent the message via carrier pigeon was apologizing for something they had done wrong. Each of the calls lasted about five or six minutes, and when the guy was done, he flipped out the light and apparently went to bed.

"I was flabbergasted. Who was this guy? And how was he able to train the pigeons and fulfill his mission to help others who were more disadvantaged and at risk than he was? Was he really homeless?"

Barb stopped talking. And she sat down without saying another word. We all clapped.

Richard oohed, "In a strange way, the guy in the shack reminds me of my great-grandfather Henry Wilcox Evans, otherwise known as the 'Millionaire Tramp,' who devoted his adult life to trying to help homeless and migrant workers. Evans was an heir to a wealthy St. Louis family; he told a reporter from *The New York Times* in 1905, when asked about the fortune he had inherited, that 'I have not worked for it, it is only mine to give to others.' As a young man, Henry studied theology and tried to establish a monastic order that he called the Brotherhood of Forgotten Men but failed. He later moved to Zurich, Switzerland, where he joined the Worldwide Welfare Association and became a vegetarian. In 1930, he moved back to St. Louis and founded the Union of Itinerant Workers and published a biweekly broadside called *The Homeless News* that called for social reforms and published poetry by homeless writers."

Eleanor shouted, "Cool, cool!"

Maggie seemed amused, but also troubled by the story. "I'm concerned that Barb's story, and Richard's addendum, romanticize homelessness in a way that's detached from reality. In my neighborhood in Manhattan the conditions for the homeless are dire and the lack of services available to them is an abomination."

Max stood up and said, "So what are you going to do about it?"

Eleanor was irritated by the way Max cut off Maggie. "You're acting out. You're too macho. Let her speak her mind."

Max was defensive. "I'm everything but macho. If anything, I worry I might be too gay. I've endured enough ridicule to last a lifetime."

Cynthia looked surprised. "I didn't even know you were gay."

Eleanor wasn't fazed and reiterated, "Max, please. Stop being so rude to Maggie."

Barb muttered, "I've heard enough. You're missing the point."

Eleanor said, "Indeed."

And Cynthia added, "Thank you, Barb. Your story touched a chord in me that I didn't know was there."

Hannah prayed, "'He that hath pity upon the poor lendeth

unto the Lord; and that which he hath given will he pay him again.' Proverbs 19:17."

There was an awkward silence. None of us had anything more to say. Eleanor stood up and walked out of the room, followed by Richard, Max, and Barb. Josette and Sandra said that they were going outside.

Maggie, Cynthia, and I stayed behind, not knowing exactly what to do next. For me, it was very strange. I liked them both, but in different ways: right brain, left brain.

Cynthia offered to open a bottle of white wine, and I chimed in that I was starving. Cynthia laughed, "You're always thinking about food," and we all moved into the kitchen, where we sat around the table, sipping wine and snacking on grapes and Camembert cheese that Maggie served with sliced apples, joking, "It's a good thing Daisy, the old mare, isn't around."

Day 5

WHEN I STOOD UP AND POKED around for my flip-flops in the darkness of the morning, I felt a strange vibration under my feet. At first, I thought something was wrong with me. But when I sat down on the edge of my bed and picked the rug off the floor, I saw a note that Cynthia had written: *While you were horseback riding, I made you a surprise. A thank-you for offering to help with my cleaning project. I hope I wasn't too harsh. Wired into the rag rug is a foot massager. Hannah wove the rag rug on a handloom she brought from the Amana Colonies and placed it in your room as a gift from her. Yours is extra special. Cynthia.*

I couldn't believe I hadn't noticed it sooner. I was certain I had walked across that rug when I'd gotten into bed and when I got up in the middle of the night to pee. But, apparently, I hadn't stepped on it right. Now I ran my fingers along the warp and weft of the rug and followed the wires to a pressure pad.

I lay back in my bed. Too much to think about. Too soon. But I was too awake to fall back asleep. I rolled over onto my pillow, eyes wide open. And then I saw that a wire from the rug was stretched taut along the bedpost and was connected to some kind of transformer that was taped on the back of the light fixture attached to the headboard. Ingenious.

By then, the light in the room had brightened. Early morning sun streamed between the curtains I had forgotten to close all the way.

It was time to get dressed. And when I opened the door to my bedroom, Cynthia and Hannah were in the hallway talking to Max and Barb. We hadn't voted for the next queen or king the night before, and they were bantering back and forth about what we should do.

I thanked Cynthia and Hannah for their gifts. And Cynthia said, "I'm so glad the foot massager worked, especially since the only parts I could find I scavenged from the shed near the stable."

Barb joked, "Don't forget. There's a secret language hidden in some rag rugs. The color patterns can be symbolic of ancient mythologies about fertility, protection, and the afterlife."

Hannah giggled, "Well, my rag rugs have a significance that's not that complicated. I'm carrying on a tradition that I learned from my great-grandmother, who started making rag rugs when she was eight years old in the Amana Colonies. The carpets and rugs that she made were functional. They met an important need, bringing comfort to her friends and family in the Community of True Inspiration. Granny used a loom that was so big, her parents built their house around it."

Barb laughed, and Hannah said, "It was the most amazing house I'd ever seen—that is, until, of course, I came here, to this cottage. Nothing compares to this."

Cynthia hurried downstairs, worried that the egg-and-bacon soufflé she had made for our breakfast might burn if she didn't take it out of the oven soon.

I followed behind her, asking if there was anything I could do, and she said, "Please, do me a favor. Check on Sandra. She might need some help with her vegan hash brown casserole. Josette was working with her, but she pooped out."

In the kitchen, Sandra was busy chopping vegan chipotle sausage and pointed me toward garlic cloves to mince and onions to dice. And while she seemed grateful for my help, she acted suspicious of my motives.

Sandra was wearing a purple tank top, showing off her biceps, but accentuating her pudgy tummy that was pierced with an oversized belly button ring.

I kept to myself, focusing on the garlic and onions, and, when I was done, she handed me a bunch of carrots and a cup of white mushrooms to slice, acknowledging me with a twisted grin that made me hope that maybe, just maybe, we weren't that different after all.

Sandra finished assembling her casserole, blending together the spices and veggies and topping it with vegan cheese and a drizzle of creole hot sauce that Josette had brought from New Orleans. She slid the baking dish into the oven and excused herself, saying she wanted to check on Josette.

Cynthia was preoccupied with her soufflé, which looked absolutely perfect, and invited me to have a taste. She poked a spoon into the light, puffy crust, and it deflated as she scooped out a tablespoon-sized serving for me that was delicious.

Cynthia was methodical. And that was increasingly more evident in everything she did, from how she filed her fingernails to the way she organized pots and pans in the cupboard.

When I asked her about her day job, she said, "Well, I'm a mechanical engineer by training, but, at heart, I'm a tinkerer, a scientist who loves to make Rube Goldberg machines."

I laughed, "What's a Rube Goldberg machine?"

"Well," Cynthia explained, "they're named after the cartoonist Rube Goldberg, who invented them, contraptions designed to do simple tasks in an overly complicated way."

"I see. Mostly, I do odd jobs—from digging fence post holes to working as a sous chef in seafood restaurants near where I live. I live in Palacios, a small town on Matagorda Bay in Southeast Texas. I do whatever I need to get by, and that's enough. My rent's cheap, and the climate is great, except when the mosquitoes take over the place. I'm used to it, but usually I try to leave town from early June to Labor Day. I have a college friend who owns a big old house and pizza joint in Durango, Colorado, where I'm able to live and work pretty much whenever I want, except the pandemic has changed all that. But when I leave here, he says I can still use the extra room that he mostly keeps vacant, calling it 'Andy's Place,' in my honor. Sometimes other guests stay there, in which case I go camp in the national forest nearby until it's okay to return. But I'm not sure I'm up for going to Colorado this year."

Cynthia started mimicking the way I talked with my hands but stopped when Maggie came into the kitchen. She was carrying a tray of croissants that she had picked up at a bakery in Stockbridge. Eleanor and Richard were at her side, and each had other goodies, creamery butter and an assortment of cheeses, marmalades, and homemade jams.

Eleanor was excited. "I went for an early morning drive, and it was marvelous. And on my way back, I pulled into a rest stop to watch the sun rise over a steep cliff when I heard what sounded like two cars crashing into each other. I was so shocked I couldn't move, and out of the fog came six Jersey cows, and, as they got closer, I saw the silhouette of an old man in bib overalls limping after them. I got out my car and the man shouted for me to stay out of the way. His trailer had jackknifed into an oncoming vehicle and flipped onto its side, and his Jersey cows got out. Within minutes, two younger farmers arrived to help load the cows back into another trailer. It was surreal.

"Well, the old man approached me and thanked me, even though I didn't do anything but watch. He was wearing a surgical mask and rubber gloves and said that someone had told him that humans sick with the virus might be contagious to cows.

"I didn't know how to respond, so I just listened, and he told me that he was on his way to transfer his cows to another pasture when the accident happened. Fortunately, no one was hurt. But by the time he finished telling me about his family farm, he was complaining that he might be forced to dump hundreds of gallons of milk because he couldn't take them to market. So I told him about us, and he said that he wanted to give us some milk because I was so kind to help. And I followed him back to his farmhouse in the fog, and he loaded me up with ten jugs of fresh raw milk.

"He was so proud of his milk that I couldn't say no. But I had to tell him the truth, that there was no way we'd be able to drink all of that milk, and he said he already knew that. I was confused, but then he opened up. He had an idea that I could help him with distribution to those in need. All of the kids in Stockbridge were out of school, and the schools were the biggest consumers of his milk. He said the kids and their parents knew that the milk from Jersey cows was the most nutritious, containing more protein, calcium, and vitamins overall—especially more Vitamins A and B1 per gallon—than Holstein milk.

"I was convinced. And when I asked what exactly he'd like me to do, he said that he was going to make calls to some of his family and friends in town to tell them I would be leaving a gallon of milk on the front porch of their homes, starting today.

"I wasn't ready for this, but I agreed, on the condition that I'd only make nine stops, so that there would be one gallon left for the cottage. 'Fair enough,' he said and instructed me to take a seat on the oak tree stump in front of his barn, and he'd get me a list. Then he turned around and went back inside, and, after about ten minutes, he reappeared and folded his list into the shape of a paper plane and threw it to me, so that he wouldn't have to get too close.

"So, I drove into Stockbridge to make my deliveries. It was fun."

Eleanor looked tired.

I asked her if she was really going to do it again. And she nodded. "In fact, I'm headed back there after breakfast to pick up another load." And I offered to help.

Eleanor perked up, and Cynthia called us to the table for the soufflé. Sandra took her vegan casserole out of the oven and placed it on a tray. It was piping hot, and we all served ourselves.

Once we were all seated, Hannah said grace: "Lord, for the meal we are about to eat, for those that made it possible, and for those with whom we are about to share it, we are thankful."

Richard rolled his eyes but said, "Amen," along with everyone else.

While we ate, Barb started talking about the deep disparities in the way the health care system was able to respond to the growing number of virus patients. "The wealthy private hospitals in Manhattan," she complained, "are able to increase patient capacity quickly, ramp up testing, and acquire protective gear, while public hospitals in Brooklyn are scrambling to fix roof leaks and maintain intensive care units separated by plastic tarps and duct tape."

Maggie was defensive. "Well, some of what you're saying may be true, but believe me, nurses and doctors everywhere in New York City—in all five boroughs—are struggling with the same grim reality."

"But the reality is," Barb said with an air of disgust, "most of the people dying from the virus are Blacks and Latinos."

Cynthia didn't want to take sides and said, "Look, when it comes down to it. You're both right. You're really talking about two pieces in the same impossible puzzle." But neither Maggie nor Barb was satisfied. The news about the virus was getting worse every day. And while living in the cottage was a luxurious escape, Barb grumbled, "It's like all of us are in denial. Let's face it. White privilege has seized control and won't let go."

Josette took a deep breath. "As you know, I'm not white, and I'm certainly not privileged. My family lost everything but their lives in the aftermath of Hurricane Katrina. And the house where I grew up in the Ninth Ward was razed and is still an empty lot littered with trash and overgrown with weeds sixteen years later."

"Point taken," Sandra stammered, and Max said, "I second that."

"Me, too," Cynthia continued. "But now, in the interest of time, not to make light of anything that has been said or what will be discussed further, I want to announce that I have selected Sandra to be the next queen."

Sandra stood up and joked, "If no one tries my vegan casserole, each and every one of you is going to be banished to the garden in the next few days to plow and till the soil in preparation for my spring planting."

I looked at her in disbelief. I'd already sampled her casserole and liked it, as had most of us. But none of us wanted to hurt her feelings. So one by one we passed her our plates and she divided up the remainder of the casserole, smirking, "If you don't taste or smell the spices, you might be suffering from anosmia, and that could be an early sign of infection, even if you are otherwise asymptomatic."

No one responded. We all nibbled on her casserole and thanked her as best we could for all her hard work.

Max and Richard volunteered to help in the garden, as did Hannah, Cynthia, Josette, and Maggie. Barb said she needed time to herself. And I wanted to go with Eleanor to see the dairy farmer and pick up more milk to deliver.

As we were getting ready to leave, Sandra asked us when we should reconvene for our storytelling session. Max blurted, "Early teatime—3:00 p.m.," and no one objected.

Richard said, "I heard about a pastry shop in Stockbridge that I want to try." And Max joined in, "If it's safe, I'm going into town with you. I've always wanted to host a high tea with all the accoutrements."

Both Cynthia and Maggie acted surprised that I opted to go with Eleanor instead of hanging out with them, looking at me like I was playing hard to get.

Eleanor was different. She had red hair and freckles and wasn't exactly my type. There was something androgynous about the way she carried herself that made me feel safe.

Eleanor asked if I would drive, since she had borrowed Richard's Jeep Cherokee for her early morning outing.

"No problem," I said, "But first I have to unload my camping gear to make room for you and the milk."

"You're actually a camper? You don't look like one."

I snickered, "I love the woods."

"Well, mostly, I'm a city girl," Eleanor responded, "who hardly ever leaves the Bay Area. But I've gone hiking a few times in Muir Woods and was blown away by the redwoods."

I was envious. I'd only been to San Francisco once, and it rained the whole time I was there.

Eleanor said, "I'm a freelance feminist, meaning I work as a consultant for different organizations focusing on expanding and protecting the rights of women and girls. These days, the incidence of domestic violence against women is out of control and the number of child abuse cases is spiking."

"That's horrible!"

"It's a struggle. But I'm in the trenches, fighting."

"I'm impressed."

"Don't be. There's so much more to do."

"That's the truth. I just wish I knew where to start. There's not much I can really do to change the world in Palacios, Texas."

"You've got to start somewhere," Eleanor said and looked at me as if I were from another planet. I got a sinking feeling in my gut.

"What makes you happy, Andy?"

"Not sure. 'Happy' isn't a word I use much these days."

"Do I make you happy?"

"Huh?"

"I don't mean to put you on the spot."

"That's good."

"I just speak my mind. For better, or worse."

"I . . . admire that."

"So, tell me, what are you thinking?" Eleanor asked, "It's like you've finally just noticed that I never wear bras and don't shave my legs."

I didn't know what to say. I couldn't tell if she was coming on to me or trying to turn me off. She was so blunt that I couldn't believe she was the same person who appeared to be so reticent.

"I'm sorry, Andy. I don't know what's gotten into me today."

I nodded, and she turned on the radio and channel surfed until she found a hip-hop and contemporary R&B station.

By the time we got to the dairy farm, I started to relax. And when she introduced me to the dairy farmer in the bib overalls, he said he was flabbergasted that she had brought a friend to help deliver more milk in town.

My car wasn't as roomy as Richard's Jeep Cherokee, but the old man managed to squeeze in ten more gallons of milk—loading them into the trunk, on the floorboard, and stacking what he could onto the back seat. It didn't take him long to put together another list and say, "Now that I have a cell phone, I can speed-dial my calls. It kind of makes me feel like Santa Claus, bringing goodies to the kiddos in town."

Eleanor and I laughed. And before we left, she asked the dairy farmer, "Should we come back in the morning?"

The old man scratched his head, "You must be really bored over at the cottage."

"Just want to help," I chimed in, and he shrugged. "I appreciate that. Truly. But I don't want you to wear yourselves out too fast, too soon."

Eleanor grinned, and I said, "See you tomorrow."

When we got into town, Eleanor and I took turns dropping off the milk jugs.

"I'm so much faster than you," Eleanor gloated. And I didn't challenge her. I was tired, and my back hurt.

As we headed back to the cottage, Eleanor started talking about her grandmother in San Francisco.

"She was a hippie who somehow managed to buy a place in a

rundown building back in the day in the Haight. You know, Haight-Ashbury. But she never talked much about the sixties, because, I think, she worried it would make me want to drop acid or something stupid like that. But she was a die-hard flower child who wore long dangly earrings and beaded peasant tops up until she got sick. For me, she was invincible, and, when she was diagnosed with the virus, I didn't believe it. She kept telling me she was okay, that her temperature was normal, even though I knew it wasn't. Every day she woke up with a big smile, as if whatever was wrong with her had disappeared. But her hacking cough wouldn't go away, and, when I told her I needed to take her to the hospital, she refused, insisting that hippies didn't need doctors. They needed good karma. I knew better but for her sake wanted to believe her, but I knew I had to get tested, and, when I did, I tested positive. Asymptomatic. I was a basket case. And while I was in quarantine, my grandmother died. When her home health aide found her in her bed, her body was all shriveled up, but she had a little grin on her face and a lollipop in her mouth."

"That's awful."

"To say the least. I felt so guilty. And when I hooked up with our chat room one sleepless night, it was just what I needed, talking to a bunch of people who seemed to understand what I was going through without having to say too much about it."

Back at the cottage, everyone was still working in the garden. Even Barb had joined the others. Eleanor said she wanted to pitch in, but I needed a nap. Every other breath I was burping up survivor guilt. I kind of wanted to open up about it but worried that, if I did, I was going to bring everyone else down. I could listen and try to be sympathetic. But talking about what had happened to me just made more self-conscious.

• • •

When I got up from my nap, the light in my room was flickering. I looked outside and the reflection of the sun off an aluminum panel in Cynthia's hands was blinding. The adjustable mount had slipped, and she was trying to fix it. I hurried downstairs, and, as I inched my way toward her, I had spots in my eyes but could tell that she had a wrench in one hand and a screwdriver in the other. She was on her knees, and, as she stretched forward, the back of her jeans slid below her waist, revealing parts of her bottom that I wasn't supposed to see.

I called out to her, wanting her to know I was approaching so that she could straighten up before I got too close. But it didn't seem to matter. She was in her zone, and nothing was going to yank her back to reality.

"I'm headed to the shed," she said, "I want to install this jerry-rigged solar panel on the roof, so I can warm it up inside. As it is now, it's freezing."

"Do you think it's really going to work?"

"Maybe . . . but the most I can probably do is focus the sunlight more intensely," Cynthia said with a straight face, but then laughed, "If there was a space heater lying around that I could use, it would be a lot easier and, no doubt, more effective."

Maggie hurried toward us. "What do you think you're doing?"

Cynthia glanced up. "Playing."

"Did I hear you saying something about bringing that thing to the shed?"

"I just want to try it out," Cynthia said.

"Just be careful. The shed might not look like much, but, from what my father's told me, it means a lot to the property owner. Some kind of sentimental attachment, I suppose to his past."

I was distracted. Richard and Max were teasing each other in the distance. Max had his arm around Richard's waist, and when they saw me looking at them, he pulled it away. I was amazed that they were openly coupling up.

Were they getting it on when no one else was around? What difference did it make? Why should I even care? In my daydreams, I was making love to Cynthia and Maggie, separately and together, in the woods, rolling around in the hayloft at the stable, sinking deep into the fertile loam of the garden. Barb and Eleanor, and Hannah, were there, too, standing in different corners of my bedroom. Waiting to see what I was going to do next. And in the ether of my afternoon nap, the face of my girlfriend appeared, just for an instant. I could hear her laughing, pleased that I was finally having fantasies about women other than her.

Cynthia wiped her brow with a red bandana she pulled from her back pocket, then brushed the dirt from her jeans.

I wanted to reach for Cynthia's hand and take it into mine, but I knew it wasn't possible. Or was it?

Cynthia asked, "Is something wrong?"

"I'm . . . okay. Just tired."

And I sauntered away, asking myself why I couldn't just open up to her. I went through the veranda into the kitchen to get a glass of water. Maggie was putting away groceries that she said Richard and Max had bought in town.

Maggie smiled, "I'm going for a horseback ride before the tea. Would you join me?"

"I'd like to, but I'm pooped. I need more rest, even though I just got up about an hour ago."

Maggie frowned, exaggerating her dismay by rolling back her lower lip. Her eyes met mine, and I felt myself melting inside. But instead of sticking around, I decided it might make me feel better to explore more of the cottage. I heard Josette and Sandra chatting in the hallway. So I took a route that avoided them and led me through the dining room and living room down a few stairs and up a small incline into the den, where I found Hannah curled up in a tufted leather chair. Hannah was glad to see me. I sat down in a chair across from her, and she rocked forward and back in her seat, as if she wasn't sure what to say. We were both a little uneasy, having never been alone together in the same room.

Hannah thumbed through the pages of the book in her lap. It was thick and unwieldy, and she smiled as she told me that it was called *Amana: The Community of True Inspiration,* written by Bertha M. H. Shambaugh and published in 1908 by the State Historical Society of Iowa about the history of the Amana Colonies and the importance of the *Psalter-Spiel,* a 1,285-page volume of hymns. The *Psalter-Spiel,* Hannah giggled, was a "best-seller in the Community of True Inspiration, probably because of its subtitle: *Psalms after the Manner of David, for the Children of Zion, or a Collection of Old and Newly Selected Spiritual Songs, Brought Together with Zeal for the Blessed Use of All Souls Desirous of Salvation, and Sucklings of Wisdom; but Particularly for the Congregation of the Lord.*"

I didn't know how to respond and stumbled around with my words. "It's not that I'm not . . . well . . . frankly, I don't know what it all means. And I hope I don't sound critical."

"Don't be ridiculous. You're being honest with me. May I read a passage I was studying when you walked into the den?"

I nodded *okay.* And without hesitation, she began: "'The last 111 pages of the *Psalter-Spiel* are music. The hymns themselves are printed as prose, two columns to a page, the verses being numbered consecutively. To add to their effectiveness certain hymns are written in the form of acrostics, the initial letters of each verse spelling out such admonitions as: *Strive with fear and trembling that ye may be saved.*'"

Hannah paused and was about to continue when I pointed to two birds that had lit on the sill of the window across from us. Hannah perked up, "Wow! They're warblers. Listen closely, the male is singing a slow, soft, sweetly whistled trill. The pitch is mostly even but rises and falls as he speeds up. Look, he's ready to fly off, with the female close behind."

I was impressed by Hannah's knowledge of birds and Scripture, both of which I knew so little about. And I asked, "Why did you join the chat room? You're . . . not like everyone else."

Her eyes welled up, and she said, "Well, I'm not that different. My parents contracted the virus and were hospitalized late."

Hannah had been working in a meat processing plant but was asymptomatic, and, when several of her fellow assembly-line workers got sick, she quit and got herself tested. Her results came back negative a week and a half later, two days before she joined the chat room and decided she needed a change of scenery.

"I've never been much of anywhere, Andy, and I worry that wherever I go, I'm not going to fit in. For me, being here at the cottage is wonderful, but it's tough being thrust into a world that I don't seem a part of. And . . . I don't want to pass judgment. But sometimes I feel that everyone but you is weighing down the cross I must bear."

"Actually, I'm pretty much like everyone else. Hurt. Looking for something, but I'm not sure what it is."

"But you're willing to listen."

I leaned back in my chair. And as the light dimmed in the room, the morning became afternoon. I had trouble keeping my eyes open. Hannah suggested that I take a little snooze. And she picked up her book and continued reading to herself.

I wondered if Hannah had ever had a boyfriend. And while she was prim and proper, I could tell, when she rattled off trivia about the warblers, that she also had a playful side, more like a girl than a woman.

My body loosened up. Just being in the same room with Hannah, without speaking, comforted me in unexpected ways. It was as if the rag rug she had made for me was a raft floating out to sea on the gentle waves of a summer day.

Around three o'clock Sandra came into the den ringing a little bell. It was time to meet in the living room for high tea and storytelling.

Hannah and I followed her out of the den. I hadn't really slept, but I was rested and whispered to Hannah how much I had enjoyed our time together, and she blushed. Sandra heard me and rolled her eyes. In the living room, everyone was already seated. Richard was serving tea, and Max was passing serving tongs and a tray filled with tiny brioche sandwiches, pecan crumpets, lemon cranberry cupcakes, and vegan scones with clotted coconut tofu cream.

Once we all had our tea and goodies, Sandra announced that the Voodoo shrine that she and Josette were constructing was almost completed. Maggie swallowed hard but apparently had given up on her efforts to stop them. Hannah looked disturbed. And Barb and Eleanor seemed excited.

Sandra rang her little bell, and the living room quieted down. Max crouched forward, then pulled himself out of his chair with a hyperbolic gesture of pomp and aplomb and began his story.

"A few years ago, in an undisclosed location, a convent was raided by federal law enforcement officials. There had been reports that the convent had been the site of illicit activities for more than three decades. But the Church has denied any misconduct.

"The story broke when a groundskeeper, on the condition of anonymity, came forward after a member of his garden crew was literally caught with his pants down in the room of one of the nuns in the convent.

"Now, this particular convent did not require that its nuns be virgins, a fact that made this remarkable order of special interest to women seeking refuge from the perils of the heterosexual world. That is, of course, not to say that all the nuns were heterosexual.

"In a sworn deposition, the groundskeeper revealed the lurid and systematic attempts of the gardener to not only seduce nuns in the convent, but to also blackmail them to preserve the secrecy of their indiscretions.

"The gardener, in his testimony, contradicted the groundskeeper and produced evidence, in the form of audio recordings and cell phone videos, that the groundskeeper was complicit in the crimes committed and, at times, functioned as a pimp for prospective gardeners, who sought coveted positions in work crews at the convent.

"It should be noted, for the record, that, while the lasciviousness of the gardeners was despicable, there were unexpected outcomes for the convent and the nuns, who were able to not only satisfy themselves with men of great sexual prowess but to also earn a livelihood that exceeded that of their peers. The gardens at the convent were meticulously cared for and were known worldwide for producing different prize-winning varieties of roses. Horticulturalists from around the globe frequented the convent and were willing and eager to pay huge sums of money for the stem cuttings to propagate their own plants.

"Clearly, those of you who have read *The Decameron* will no doubt note the striking similarity of this tale to the Third Day, First Story, of that incredible book, which recounts the adventures of a young man named Masetto who pretended to be deaf and mute to curry favor with the nuns. In this case, the gardener suffered from macular degeneration and had only limited peripheral vision, meaning he was only able to identify the nuns that he serviced through his unparalleled sense of touch.

"The relations between the nuns and the gardener evolved slowly. He had actually started working in the garden when he was a boy, the son of a poor village widow, and over the years he was mentored by the groundskeeper, who taught him the names of all the plants in the garden. And as his eyesight began to fail, he learned to identify the plants by touch. Macular degeneration set in slowly, and while his center vision waned, he cultivated an uncanny ability to use his peripheral vision to navigate his way and care for the plants he so loved. And in turn, he was loved by the nuns, who gravitated to him, because they believed God had imbued him with a special gift.

"The nuns came voluntarily to the gardener with empathy in their hearts, understanding all too well that being legally blind was a huge obstacle in his day-to-day activities. Working side by side with the gardener as he tended his flowers and vegetables gave the nuns a rare opportunity to interact in close proximity to him, sometimes touching his hand or helping to guide his hoe or rake as they combed through the soil.

"Ironically, following a tradition that began centuries ago, the nuns at this particular convent chose the names of colors to identify themselves in what they called the Grand Palette of Our Lord. With this in mind, it was relatively easy for the gardener to learn the names of each of the nuns, who he always addressed in the most formal manner.

"The first nun the gardener lured into his lair was Sister Red, whose voluptuous body was described in a police deposition as having the distinct character of a Titian model. Records show that when she followed the gardener into his tool shed, she was giggling for no apparent reason, although Sister Blue later remarked that it was her impression that the breasts of Sister Red had brushed against the chest of the gardener before they had departed.

"In the tool shed, police discovered under a large plywood plank a trapdoor that led to an underground compartment containing a luxurious mattress, presumably stolen from one of the unoccupied guest rooms in the convent, that was fitted with the finest silk sheets and an assortment of goose down pillows, encased in hand-crafted fabrics and embroidered with delicate lace patterns, which some believed had been imported from Belgium.

"The police were told that each of the lovemaking liaisons began with a ritual that included the burning of incense and the lighting of votive candles surrounding the bed.

"Under intense questioning, Sister Green revealed that during her session with the gardener, she had heard him pray *Dear Lord, forgive me for what I am about to do* as he lowered himself onto her naked body with passion and lust. Other nuns also remembered what they thought were prayers before, during, and after each sexual encounter, though the words coming out of the gardener's mouth were often incomprehensible.

"To be admitted into the tool shed, each of the nuns was sworn to secrecy about whatever transpired. And reportedly, the interactions between the gardener and the nuns were not always consummated. In other words, the gardener was not always able to perform in the manner that had been promised.

"At the trial, the gardener, in a plea agreement granting him immunity, confessed to the moral crimes he had committed, insisting that his sex with the nuns was consensual and that he was only doing what he was ordered to do by the groundskeeper, who disguised himself with a mask embroidered with exotic flowers and accepted all payments that were made. In his defense, the groundskeeper denied that the services provided by the gardener were ever sold but, instead, were only performed in exchange for a voluntary contribution that was designated for the purpose of helping the gardener have the surgeries and treatments necessary to restore his eyesight.

"Sister Purple, however, when she saw the gardener, recognized him as a male prostitute she had once been introduced to when she herself was working the streets of an unspecified city in the mid-Atlantic states. When confronted, the gardener, records show, recoiled and, in a fit of rage, tried to suffocate the nun in his bed. Screams from the tool shed were heard by the abbess of the convent, who was working nearby in the garden.

"The abbess charged into the tool shed, leapt through the trapdoor, and pounced on the gardener, who, in his struggle to free himself, fell backward, hitting his head on the bed frame with such force that it caused swelling in his brain and left him partially paralyzed from the waist down. Sadly, the nun, who survived this vicious attack, died from an undetected blood clot that surged into her heart while she was being treated by the paramedics who arrived on the scene.

"In the weeks that followed, the abbess pleaded to the court to show mercy to the nuns, who had been deceived and had kept silent because they feared retribution from the groundskeeper. Investigations were launched on the local, state, and federal levels. And unfortunately, nothing other than circumstantial evidence was ever produced until a yellowed semen stain was found on a white habit belonging to Sister Orange. And after DNA analysis, it was discovered that it had a chromosomal match with the pimp groundskeeper, who was arrested and convicted, with a sentence of life in prison without parole.

"Court records show that each of the nuns lured into this tangled web left the convent to repent for her sins and to form a nonprofit organization, funded in part by an anonymous trust, to support the much-needed counseling and treatment for women who, like them, had been victimized and abused.

"The gardener was permanently disabled and confined to a wheelchair, with degenerative cognitive problems resulting from his head injuries. But instead of turning him away to fend for himself, the abbess allowed him to continue to live at the convent in solitary confinement until the end of his days. All of the tools were removed from the shed, and the mattress from the secret compartment was moved aboveground, and an accessible outhouse was built to meet the daily needs of the gardener. I have been told that the nuns currently in residence at the convent brought the gardener three meals a day and were known to pray with him, reading aloud the Bible, from beginning to end, over the course of each year, from January 1 to December 31, and then starting over again.

"The story here, my friends, has, once again, an important moral, a lesson about the power of lust and forgiveness, which I leave to you for your own assessment and judgment in these uncertain times in which we are now forced to live. The end."

Max's face went blank. It was as if all emotion had drained out of him. I realized that he had improvised much of his story, and while he intended to tell a modern-day version of Boccaccio's tale of Masetto, new details emerged as he spoke.

We all looked at each other, but no one said anything. Finally, Sandra rang her little bell and encouraged us to have another cup of tea.

Richard clapped and Maggie, Cynthia, Eleanor, Barb, and Josette joined in.

Hannah seemed uncomfortable, shaking her head, as if she wanted to say how much the story turned her off, but she didn't. She closed her eyes and stretched her neck backward until her head touched the top cushion of her seat, and then she suddenly popped forward, saying she needed some fresh air.

Sandra looked disappointed. "Hannah, please stay a little longer, or at least until I can properly adjourn."

Hannah reluctantly agreed but glanced at me, like she was hoping I would come to her defense, which I did, saying, "Participation in the storytelling sessions is completely voluntary, and if we choose, for whatever reason, to leave, there should be no repercussions."

Sandra tensed up and barked, "If we don't respect the wishes of the queen, then why go to the trouble of having one?"

Maggie was irritated, "For me, Max's story was perfectly appropriate and very entertaining."

"Maybe, if you're a pervert," Barb scoffed.

Maggie was defensive. "Please, that's not fair. It's obvious that we're all beginning to show symptoms of cabin fever. We all need to lighten up."

Hannah whispered, "'And when he was at the place, he said unto them, pray that ye enter not into temptation.' Luke 22:40."

In unison, Maggie, Cynthia, and Barb said, "Amen."

As much as I wanted to be supportive, I detached. I liked the idea of getting some fresh air.

Richard sighed, "I'm ready for a glass of wine," and Max nodded, "Me, too."

Josette asked Sandra if they could resume work on the Voodoo shrine.

Maggie stood up and left the living room in a huff.

Sandra, despite her misgivings, quickly adjourned our meeting.

I asked Hannah if she wanted some company when she went outside, and she shook her head *no*.

But from across the room, Barb said, "I'm down for a walk."

I could tell that Cynthia wanted to come, too, but she said instead that she was going to tinker around in the tool shed and asked Eleanor if she was interested in seeing her newest Rube Goldberg invention, leaving me in the awkward position of having to do something with Barb that I really wasn't in the mood for.

Barb had been so depressed that no one wanted to do much of anything with her. And as we walked into the garden, I kept my distance, hoping that she might decide to leave me alone. But then I had second thoughts and was kind of ashamed of myself for trying to avoid her.

I heard Barb humming. And as we walked side by side across the garden, she said, "I like being with you, Andy, because I can identify with your grieving."

I didn't know how to respond. I tried to not show my sadness, but to her it was obvious.

Barb donned latex gloves she pulled from her pocket and offered a pair to me, telling me that she wished she could hold my hand, if only for a few minutes.

Barb and I stretched our arms across the space between us and held hands without saying anything to each other. But as we passed the tool shed and stable, I saw that Cynthia and Maggie were watching us.

Everything was becoming too complicated.

I heard Josette and Sandra chitchatting behind us, and Barb and I let go of each other's hand. Barb ran off into the woods by herself, and as much as I felt compelled to follow her, I knew I had to try to explain what we were doing before Josette, Sandra, Maggie, and Cynthia came to their own conclusions.

So, I just blurted out the truth. "It isn't romantic. We were simply sharing a moment of mutual support. We're grieving."

I felt a little stupid, but it all made sense to Cynthia, who stepped forward and said, "I understand, Andy. You should go look for Barb and see what you can do to comfort her. We all know that it's tough for her right now."

"It's tough for me, too," I said under my breath, and hurried off to find Barb. And when I finally found her, she was sitting on a tree stump crying. I tried to console her, but she grimaced, "There's nothing you can do. Nothing anyone can do."

I reached for her hand and she stood up. Side by side, we wandered through the woods toward Ice Glen Ravine. I didn't know what more to say, and neither did she. Somehow, just being together was enough. I kept thinking about Barb's brother-in-law. But I knew talking about him was only going to make both of us feel worse.

As we neared the ravine, I slowed down. Barb pulled me forward, wanting to go deeper into the forest. I stuttered, "It's getting dark, and, to be honest, I'm a little worried we're going to get lost." And she joked, "Look, I have a crackerjack sense of direction. In the subway, that is." The sun eased its way into the horizon, and the sky glowed orange and violet as we made our way back to the cottage.

Day 6

ELEANOR WAS PERTURBED. SANDRA HAD SLIPPED a note under her bedroom door, informing her that she was her choice for the next queen.

"I'm only going to do it," Eleanor grumbled, "if someone can come up with a gender-neutral title. Something other than 'queen.' 'President,' maybe, or even something as simple as 'leader.'"

"It's just a game," I said. "It's your turn to be in charge. The title has no true symbolic meaning."

Eleanor was miffed, and when she saw Sandra, Josette, Richard, and Max chatting together, she ranted on about the core values imbedded in our use of language and the need for social change: "Even Boccaccio understood these fundamental principles. He lived in a world where women had lower social standing than men. But he chose to cast the women in *The Decameron* as having the upper hand in most male-female relationships. If anything, he favored women as the stronger sex in terms of both good and evil. Women not only wielded more power but were more lustful and cunning. And in those instances where men appeared to triumph or surpass women, they usually did so through scheming and deceitful means."

Josette cringed. "I suppose. But for me, *The Decameron* is mostly about white hetero privilege during a time when most of the world was impoverished and suffering. There are no direct references, at least that I remember, to people of color or to same-sex love."

"But same-sex love is implied," Max said, "In Dioneo's story on the fifth day, he focuses on Pietro di Vinciolo, a rich man who appears more interested in men than in women. Which is kind of amazing, considering that in the Middle Ages, acts of homosexuality were harshly punished by the courts, often by castration or hanging."

I'd heard enough and went downstairs. What they were saying made sense, but their bantering grated on me.

In the kitchen, I opened the refrigerator and saw that someone had bought a gallon of fresh-squeezed orange juice. My favorite. I poured myself a glass and joined Cynthia and Hannah, who were on the veranda nibbling on croissants and sipping tea.

Cynthia was talking about her newest Rube Goldberg invention in the shed and invited Hannah and me to see it in progress. Hannah said she wanted to do some reading, but I liked the idea of just being with Cynthia.

I was ready to go, but Cynthia said that I'd better eat something first and suggested that I grab a croissant. And while I munched away, she bagged up a couple of apples and slices of cheese to take with us.

As I walked with her across the garden, the lawn glistened with morning dew. The sun streamed through Cynthia's hair, making her more attractive to me than ever before. There was something about her that enticed me to come closer but also pushed me away. She was independent and headstrong, and I had the feeling that she was open to love but not going out of her way to find it.

I followed Cynthia into the shed and was amazed. All of the garden tools were neatly arranged against one wall, and opposite them were the pulleys, electrical wires, and mismatched parts and pieces of scrap wood and metal that she was using to make her inventions. In the middle of the space was an old wooden table with spindly legs, covered with an old sheet and stacked with a plastic organizer with sixteen little drawers, each filled with screws and nuts, nails and fasteners of different shapes and sizes.

Cynthia explained that she was making a device that could grind, weigh, and dispense spices through a series of metal tubes into mixing bowls that rotated on a motorized plastic lazy Susan that she had discovered under a stack of newspapers in the corner.

I was wowed by all of the detail that went into Cynthia's thinking and planning, especially since the thrill for her came from using the junk she found in the shed.

Cynthia seemed proud of herself, and rightly so.

There were two folding chairs leaning against the back wall of the shed, and Cynthia asked me to sit down. I opened one of the chairs and Cynthia said, "I have a surprise. Now, close your eyes." And I heard her slide the table to the side. Then with a flashlight in her hand, she raised her voice, "Look at this!"

It was a trapdoor, and, as she opened it, she shined her flashlight into what appeared to be some kind of underground compartment, joking that maybe it had belonged to the gardener in *The Decameron.*

I shook my head in disbelief, telling her in a sarcastic tone that I didn't think it was more than five hundred years old. And we both laughed.

Cynthia said, "I haven't started to explore the compartment yet, because it's going to be a very messy job."

I wanted to help explore but remembered how defensive she was when she was in the middle of her kitchen cleaning project. The shed was her turf. But I reached for a broom leaning on the wall behind me, anyway, to see how she'd respond. And she said, "It's going to take more than a broom to do what's necessary to excavate this site."

Cynthia picked up a shovel, handed it to me, and grabbed a spade for herself, pointing to the mound of dirt that was piled up around the rungs of the ladder that led into the compartment. Then she poked around with her spade, worried that it might cave in, and, when it seemed safe to proceed, she told me step-by-step what I needed to do.

The mound of dirt was denser than she had thought. Apparently, it had gotten wet and dried into a block. "Heavy limestone content," Cynthia said, "kind of like a natural cement."

While we worked, Cynthia talked about growing up in a brownstone in the Back Bay area of Boston, within walking distance of the Charles River. "My father was a reptilian biologist, and my mother was a biochemist who worked most of her life analyzing enzymes and other molecules to research the effects of drugs and food on biological processes. I was an only child, and, by the time I was ten years old, I had unlimited access to an electron microscope in my mother's lab. By the age of fifteen, I was doing computer modeling and discovering the morphology of the earthworms I pulled out of the rose garden in front of our house. I applied to MIT after my sophomore year in high school and got in, though I ended up dropping out in the middle of my freshman year, because I just wasn't ready socially. I could handle the coursework, but my classmates resented me."

I didn't have much to say, other than that I was a general studies major at Navarro College and that when I stopped going to classes, I didn't have any real sense of direction.

Cynthia smiled. "Andy, you are a breath of fresh air. No pretense. No hidden agenda, at least that I can discern. But I still don't know you very well."

I assured her that the only agenda I had at this point was to stay healthy and not let the realities of the virus drag me too far down, though I did spend a lot of time wondering what would have happened if I had married my girlfriend, who was much more career-driven than I was. Somehow, I imagined that I would have made a good househusband.

Cynthia glanced at me like she was only half paying attention, but I sensed that I had touched something deep within her by the way she pressed her lips together. But she didn't seem ready to talk about it. Instead, she focused on our excavation project. We weren't making a lot of progress, not because of any lack of work or motivation. It was just the pace at which Cynthia chose to proceed. I could tell that she took great pleasure in analyzing every step.

After a couple of hours, Cynthia said, "I think the underground compartment might predate the cottage and that the shed was erected on top of it. But what puzzles me the most is why someone would have gone to the trouble of building a shed when they had apparently not explored what was underground."

I asked her how she knew this, and she was beaming: "Because each of the layers of dirt exhibited different degrees of compression, meaning that their creation may have been separated by months or years, maybe even a decade or more."

Cynthia wished she had brought the micrometer she had in the tool kit in the trunk of her car to measure the thickness of the fragments of the layers we had removed.

I asked her how long she expected our excavation might take, and she joked, "As long as we want. We're just having fun."

Cynthia straightened up, brushing dirt from her jeans, and I did the same.

We both knew it was time to get back to the cottage. I couldn't believe that we'd actually spent most of the day in the shed. Everyone was probably wondering where we were. Neither of us had any idea what Eleanor, now that she was in charge, planned for our storytelling session.

As we neared the cottage, we could see that everyone had gathered around the firepit. I watched the sun slide behind the clouds to the west and looked at Cynthia, the shadows softening the profile of her face in the cold air of early spring.

When we got to the firepit, no one seemed very concerned that we had been off by ourselves for so long. Maggie had just gotten back from what she described as a spectacular horseback ride.

Eleanor was talking calmly with Barb, and Hannah was sitting with Max and Richard, explaining what she had been reading in the *Psalter-Spiel.* Max didn't seem particularly interested, but Richard did and said, "I don't really practice a religion, but the name *Psalter-Spiel* has a certain ring to it."

When Cynthia and I sat down, Eleanor got out of her seat and identified herself as the Supreme Leader, a title that she said Sandra had conferred upon her, after a lengthy and at times heated discussion, to indicate, in a gender-free manner, both the importance and the silliness of her role.

Cynthia and I wondered where Sandra and Josette were.

Maggie said, "I saw Josette and Sandra hiking around in the woods gathering feathers for their shrine, and both of them promised that they'd be back for the storytelling session at three."

"Great," I replied, shocked that everyone was acting so well-behaved.

Richard, forever the optimist, announced that he was mixing martinis, provided that we all wanted one. "I know it might seem like a Manhattan thing," Richard gushed, "But I love martinis." We all raised our hands. All voted yes, including Hannah, who admitted that even though she was a teetotaler, she'd likė a little taste.

Max motioned for us all to follow him into the living room, where Richard opened the bar cabinet in the credenza. Maggie went to the kitchen for a bucket of ice. Eleanor joined her, taking the hors d'oeuvres that Max had prepared earlier out of the refrigerator and arranging them on a silver tray with garish-colored toothpicks so that we could serve ourselves slices of cheese, dates, pimentos, and spicy boiled shrimp. Then she filled a small bowl with sealed packets of salty mixed nuts and crackers.

Richard's martinis were strong, and, after just a few sips, I felt kind of tipsy, as did Hannah, who started slurring her words. Eleanor offered her a glass of water, which she accepted gratefully, setting her martini glass on the end table beside where she was standing, telling us without words that she had had enough.

Cynthia, Eleanor, and Maggie were all giddy but very much in control, and, when Josette and Sandra entered the living room, the three of them clapped. Maggie joked, "Well, now that I'm under the influence of Richard's martinis, I'm ready for the Voodoo shrine, even though I don't know what I'm expected to do."

Josette snarled, "My Voodoo shrine is not a game or a toy. It is a sacred place of holy dedication, a place to praise God and other divine beings." Maggie stood up and glared at Josette, and Sandra stepped between them. Maggie took a deep breath and then sat back down, griping that she was only trying to be conciliatory. Josette turned away, and, once again, Sandra intervened, telling Maggie and the rest of us that she and Josette had decided to move the shrine into the woods, so as to not offend anyone who might object.

Josette gazed at our faces and drawled, "I'm not looking for acceptance, but at the very least, I'd appreciate some kind of acknowledgment of my right to worship in accordance with my personal beliefs."

Maggie said, "I never intended to hurt anyone's feelings."

Eleanor sighed, and I perked up.

Richard asked if anyone wanted another martini, and only Max raised his hand.

Cynthia sampled the spicy shrimp, and Hannah nibbled on a slice of sharp cheddar.

Eleanor moved into the center of the room and called the storytelling session to order, urging us to return to the agenda at hand, closing her eyes and spinning around, as if she didn't know who was going to be next. But when she stopped and pointed the index finger of her right hand at Cynthia, I—and probably everyone else—knew that her choice had already been planned.

Cynthia asked for a few minutes to collect herself, laughing that she was still feeling the effects of a single martini. "I'm still in a liminal space, somewhere between one point in time and another." We all waited patiently for her to continue. And after a few minutes, she said, "Silence is always soothing. I'm ready to begin."

She stretched her neck backward and then lowered her chin.

"My story is based on a dream that a friend of mine named Rebecca had before I left town. It was so vivid in her mind that she felt compelled to call me in the middle of the night. And when I fell back asleep, I wasn't sure which details were part of Rebecca's dream and which were actually mine.

"In any event, the exact nature of the two dreams that merged in my consciousness will never be fully known. I could go on and on. But, as a scientist, I am obsessed with specifics, even when I don't know what they are. I have long wanted to participate in sleep studies and polygraph testing to discover the intricacies of how we differentiate between truth and fiction when we are asleep.

"I know all, or some, of this might be boring to you as listeners, trying to follow this somewhat plotless account of a dream I only remember because, I must confess, it has left me with feelings of desire that I am still grappling with. So what I am about to tell you is more personal than perhaps it should be and is entirely out of character for me, given that many people I know think I am analytical to such an extent that I am essentially devoid of emotion.

"Well, on the night in question, sleep came easy. I submarined into my pillow and didn't come up for air until Rebecca's telephone call jarred me back to consciousness. Her voice was panicked. And she described in excruciating detail the trouble she had getting comfortable in her bed. She had cramps in her glutes, subdermal itching in her shins, and uncontrollable twitching in her toes. She took a Flexeril, but it took hours for her to relax enough to doze off. And when she did, she felt like she was being lifted up and carried outside by someone she couldn't see, who lowered her with a mechanical crane onto a soft mattress in the bed of a pickup truck circling a place called Quantum Lake, which was populated by mating ducks and geese somewhere in the middle of nowhere. Rebecca didn't know who was driving, but it didn't seem to matter, because she felt secure.

"But then Rebecca heard a voice telling her that she needed to change vehicles. The pickup truck slowed to a stop. And the crane lifted her out of the truck and placed her in the driver's seat of a Mercedes convertible that was waiting for her in an empty parking lot. The keys were on the dashboard, and, after Rebecca buckled her seat belt, the roof of the car rose behind her and locked into place. The car was on autopilot, driving on roads she couldn't identify. And before long, she was in line at a car wash. There must have been twenty people ahead of her. And while she waited, the MP3 player in the car began playing Beethoven's Ninth Symphony. But as she moved forward, the instruments in the orchestra began to drop off—oboe, bassoon, contrabassoon, another oboe, two clarinets, timpani, a bass drum, three trombones, one trumpet, a triangle, another trumpet, a piccolo, and the chorus. By the time she reached the middle of the car wash, all that remained were the cymbals, crashing through the mechanical devices that foam, rinse, and dry.

"Now, it was at this point in Rebecca's dream that she snapped awake and called me. But I was groggy and had trouble listening, though I stayed on the phone long enough for her to settle down.

"And when I drifted back asleep, I was, without being aware of it, plunged into Rebecca's dream, which I began to believe was my own.

"My vision was blurry. My mind was mush.

"I was powerless.

"Lights were flashing on and off.

"And as the car was pulled on the conveyor into the car wash, I realized that Rebecca had disappeared, and, somehow, I had taken her place in the driver's seat.

"The tire dressers in the car wash kicked in and locked onto the wheel rims, and the car jolted to a halt.

"I was trapped.

"An oxygen mask dropped from the ceiling of the car, and, when it was even with my mouth, it automatically strapped itself around my face. The oxygen was pure and intense, and everything around me became crystal clear.

"I saw a strange man sitting next to me in the passenger seat. And he was ecstatic to be with me, even though I couldn't recognize who he was. And he shouted that I was nuts for believing anything that Rebecca said.

"And as I tossed and turned in my bed, I wondered who this man could be. Was he a predator? A rapist?

"I was horrified.

"The windows to the car burst open and water rushed inside. I was screaming, but no one heard me. But the man comforted me, massaging my arms and legs, caressing me, enveloping my body in his. The car rocked back and forth. And a series of rapid, rhythmic contractions surged through me, as the Boston Symphony Orchestra exploded into the orgasmic crescendo of Beethoven's *Ode to Joy* in my brain.

"And I woke up, hot and sweaty. And the man vanished. Except that in Rebecca's dream, which she recounted to me the next morning, the man transformed into the body of her husband, who rolled over, his arms flopping up and down, as if he were in the throes of a terrible nightmare. Then it dawned on me: the man in my dream was Rebecca's husband, who had tried to convince me to not leave Boston for the Berkshires. In my dream, he was in my bed. In reality, he was not. Somehow, I had occupied Rebecca's dream, without either of us knowing it at the time. I had been half asleep when she called, and, through the mysteries of dreaming, her experience was transferred to me. I became someone I am not in my dream, and somehow, now that I am aware it, I am forever different. I have never lusted for Rebecca's husband, but, to be honest, feeling her desire awakened something in me, and, hopefully, my dear friends, in you."

Cynthia paused, and when she said, "The end," she looked only at me, gazing into my eyes as if transfixed by something even I didn't know was there.

My hands were tingling. Was Cynthia talking about me? And her?

Hannah grimaced.

Josette winced.

Barb patted her thighs.

Richard chuckled, and Max stroked the bridge of his nose with his fingertip.

Maggie poured herself another martini, took one sip, and dumped the rest into the bar sink, drawing attention to herself in such a way that a wave of discomfort rippled through the room.

Cynthia sat down next to me.

Maggie was annoyed. "The whole story was just so . . . vulgar."

Barb was irked by Maggie's response. "Have you really read any of *The Decameron*? It's filled with everything from the erotic to the tragic, from steamy sex innuendos to fetishized foreplay. It's hard to believe that it first appeared in print in 1353 but wasn't published in a full English translation until 1886."

Maggie groused, "I'm just fed up! If I have to hear one more story like that, maybe we should start thinking more seriously about how and when we are going to disband."

Max and Richard looked at each other as if they were bummed out by Maggie's tirade.

I wanted private time with Cynthia, but, when I asked her if she'd like to go for a walk and maybe get back to our excavation project, she told me bluntly that she wasn't in the mood. I said that I understood, and she nodded but then seemed to have second thoughts about my leaving her alone. Our eyes connected, but I stepped back and told her that I needed to do laundry and probably talk to Maggie, who had apparently misunderstood the moral of the story.

"Moral of the story? There was no moral."

"Well, maybe you're right. But . . . it seemed . . . uh . . . some good came out of it all. I mean, the narrator, er, you learned something about yourself that you didn't know."

"Andy, you're missing the point. I'm done talking about it," Cynthia said and then backed away.

As I walked out of the room, Hannah asked, "Would you like to meet me in the library in about an hour? I'd love to read you another passage in the *Psalter-Spiel*."

"Uh, okay. I'll try," I replied. And Hannah blushed, realizing that Cynthia and Barb had overheard her invitation to me.

I tried to catch up with Cynthia, who sensed that I was behind her and turned around and said, "Have you ever heard of a biographical fallacy? It's when you conflate the identity of the storyteller with the story being told."

I looked at her in disbelief, and she rushed off.

Sandra asked Richard and Max if they wanted to accompany her and Josette for a preview of the Voodoo shrine, and they said they'd be honored but that they were going to have another martini first.

Josette cleared her throat and motioned for Sandra to follow her, apparently dismayed by Sandra's overture to Max and Richard, who were already sloshy and, in her estimation, not in the right mindset to experience her shrine. Sandra quickly exited the room with Josette at her side.

I headed for the horse stable and found Maggie in the hayloft. The horses were neighing, and Maggie was thrilled that I had come looking for her. She shouted for me to climb up to join her, and, as

I grabbed hold of the ladder, she laughed, "Tighten your mask. This is one of the smallest lofts I've ever seen."

"I'm in good shape," I replied, and she extended her hand and pulled me into the loft next to her.

It was weird. Here we were, about three feet apart, Maggie in a lotus position and me struggling to cross my legs.

Maggie could tell that I was starting to feel self-conscious and said, "What I like most about you, Andy, is that you're funny."

I stretched my legs out in front of me and leaned back against a bale of hay.

"I mean, what makes you funny is that you're so lovable, kind of like a teddy bear with a silly grin."

"Is that so?"

Maggie scooted herself closer to me and laid her head on my thigh, giggling, "I just want to cuddle up."

I brushed her hair lightly with the palm of my hand.

"Sometimes, I do stupid things, just to see what kind of response I might get, like mouthing off too much after Cynthia finished her story or getting into another verbal duel with Barb, Max, or Sandra or Josette. It's the actress in me."

Maggie acted so self-deprecating that I relaxed. And she rolled over onto her side and massaged the inside of my leg with the palm of her hand, reassuring me, "Don't worry. I'm not trying to seduce you. I only need a little physical contact to feel human again."

I took a deep breath, "Me, too."

Maggie shimmied closer but then inched back so that we were no longer touching.

"Being a stage actress in New York City is hard enough, but, with the virus, it's been impossible."

"So . . . uh . . . what's been your favorite role? You know, as an actress."

"Oh, Andy, don't go all starry-eyed on me. I don't want to tell you about anything I've done in the past. I want to feel new again. For me, reminiscing about the past is fatal."

There was nothing more to say. She was right. What we did with our lives in the present was all that really mattered.

Maggie sat up. And I tried to stand but bumped my head on one of the rafters, and Maggie whinnied like a horse, joking that it was time to get our feet on firmer ground and go riding. And I followed her down the ladder.

Mounting Daisy was easier than last time, though Maggie still needed to help me get positioned right. But once I was in the saddle, I felt like Daisy remembered me. She could probably tell by how unsteady I was that she needed to be extra vigilant. The last thing she wanted me to do was fall off.

Maggie set the pace with Harry with what she called a two-beat trot, a faster gait than I had tried before. Daisy followed Harry with precision, never veering from the trail through the woods into an open field where early spring wildflowers were starting to pop out in the winter-worn grass. Maggie slowed Harry to a walk, and Daisy eased up. As we moved along side by side through the landscape, Maggie talked about the dainty rue anemones. "Check out their slender stalks and delicate blossoms, each with five or ten white petals, whose subtlety might be lost in a garden, but seeing them sprouting through the dried birch and hemlock leaves has a beauty that leaves me speechless. And that's saying a lot, because I love words."

In the distance, I could see a herd of cows grazing. Their fawn coats glistening in the late afternoon light made me think of the dairy farmer whose milk Eleanor was delivering in Stockbridge. I wanted to help her but wasn't sure I wanted to wake up every morning at dawn to join her.

The air was moist, and Maggie said, "I can smell the rain that's moving our way." When I didn't respond, she sensed that I was preoccupied, which I was. It was like my girlfriend was calling to me, but

I couldn't find her. Maggie trotted out in front of me to turn around. The sun was dropping fast, and the muted tones of dusk settled on the horizon as we rode back to the stable.

Day 7

IN THE MORNING, THE THUNDER WAS rumbling so loud that we all got up early, each of us stationing ourselves at different windows to watch the lightning crack through the darkening clouds. The wind picked up, and the rain whipped across the grass, shattering some of the clay pots on the perimeter of the garden and pummeling the cottage with sleet and pea-sized hail.

Maggie shouted, "Step back from the windows! I know how devastating these storms can be."

The lights in the cottage flickered and went out.

Barb screamed. Water was surging under the door to the veranda, soaking the carpet. Eleanor ran to get bathroom towels to plug the leak, but nothing seemed to work. Cynthia pulled a mop from the broom closet and started wiping up the mess. Richard and Max pushed the couch against the back wall, and Eleanor and I carried the end tables and lamps into the living room. Maggie scoured the cupboards for the emergency weather radio she thought she had seen when she was stacking dishes.

Josette and Sandra donned their hooded rain jackets and bolted outside to retrieve the tools that they had left when they were working on their Voodoo shrine the day before.

Maggie stomped on the floor. Nothing was where she thought it was, and the power drill and miter saw that Sandra had been using were no doubt ruined.

Barb yelled, "We have to stay calm!"

Maggie barked, "The last time I got caught in one of these storms, lightning fried the power grid, and there was no electricity for days."

Hannah was so agitated that she could barely speak. She'd found a box of candles in the basement, but, as she was rummaging around, water began seeping onto the floor. She struggled to move the boxes that were stacked in the corners, but the water level was rising. It was only a matter of time before the basement would be flooded.

Maggie hurried toward the basement door and rushed down the stairs, hollering that we needed to get everything out immediately. Max, Richard, Cynthia, and I formed a kind of relay line, taking the boxes and crates that Maggie handed to us and stacking them in the kitchen.

After about an hour, we were able to relocate everything that seemed most at risk.

We were exhausted, and it was only 9:30 a.m. The rain was letting up, and Maggie said she needed to go to the stable to check on the horses. I wanted to go with her but figured it would be better to stay at the cottage, just in case the storm got worse, which, according to Maggie, was likely.

Eleanor called 911, and the dispatcher who answered confirmed that the power grid was, indeed, out and then informed her that the Stockbridge Police and Fire Departments remained committed to the needs of the community as they dealt with the pandemic. Eleanor switched the call to speakerphone so I could listen in, and we couldn't believe the formality of the dispatcher's response. "Given the limitations of staff and resources, our officers are only able to respond to the most critical calls. And should assistance be needed, it is essential that officers be notified of any symptoms of fever, cough, muscle aches, and sneezing. Notification of any flu-like symptoms helps our officers to be prepared to assist while protecting themselves from unnecessary exposure. Having this information will not delay a response but simply allows them to maintain their professional protocol."

Eleanor was shaking when she got off the phone. She was disappointed in herself for not telling the dispatcher that we were all asymptomatic. But even though we had tested negative after fourteen-day quarantines, I started to worry that we might still be contagious, or that one of us might have gotten reinfected.

Someone had to take control, and Eleanor looked at me with a twisted smile and said, "Andy, it's your turn to be king or supreme leader, or whoever or whatever you want to call yourself."

I wasn't ready and suggested that Maggie should probably be in charge, since she knew more about the house and more about Stockbridge and the surrounding area.

Maggie snickered, "I'm glad to be chief of staff. But I know all of you are sick of me telling you what to do."

Barb seconded that and complained, "I guess, we're just too set in our ways, and we're all not even thirty years old."

Sandra and Josette barged into the kitchen. Josette was crying. Her shrine was a total loss. Everything was scattered in bits and pieces. It was a wreck. Sandra promised to help with the cleanup once the weather cleared. But when Eleanor told her that the power grid had been hit by lightning, she gritted her teeth as if she were going to explode, but didn't.

Cynthia tried to be consoling. "I'm so sorry. I know how much the shrine means to you."

"To me, to all of us," Josette sobbed.

"And once we get through this," Cynthia said, "maybe I can help."

"Thanks, but . . . I know what to do."

Hannah was disappointed. "Perhaps it shouldn't be rebuilt. I worry that its destruction might have been divine retribution." Josette recoiled, and Hannah apologized, saying that she didn't mean to be judgmental. "'Judge not,'" she said softly, "'and ye shall not be judged: condemn not, and ye shall not be condemned: forgive, and ye shall be forgiven.' Luke 6:37."

Josette nodded, "Amen." And in that moment, Josette and Hannah connected, if only by a thread.

I agreed to be king for the day, hoping that the storm was over. But as the day wore on, everything was in question. I could tell that Richard was thinking about leaving, but when I overheard Max arguing with him about being a "traitor to the cause," I knew he wasn't departing anytime soon.

We all managed to scavenge enough food to satisfy ourselves, but we were each on our own. Cynthia had heard about my horseback ride with Maggie and didn't want to talk to me, apparently because she felt some kind of betrayal. I guess after my being away for hours, she was suspicious. I couldn't really process all the emotional baggage that I had, she had, and Maggie had. We were all coming from such different places. And it was like the boy-girl thing that was budding was more of a fantasy than a reality, even if Maggie had massaged the inside of my thigh. I wasn't really ready for a relationship, and Maggie and Cynthia, I think, were aware of that.

Without electricity, the interior of the cottage was eerie and mysterious, and as I wandered around, I felt more alone, more separated from the others, my memories of my girlfriend deepening my sense of loss and abandonment.

I saw Hannah walking toward the den and followed her, startling her, because I got too close, not intentionally, but somehow blanking out, for an instant, on the need for social distancing. I told her I was sorry that I never showed up yesterday, and that, if she was still up for it, I'd like it if she read to me.

She asked me to sit across from her. She had a copy of the *Psalter-Spiel* in her satchel but also had a Bible, which she opened in her lap, asking me if I was familiar with 1 Corinthians 13. I wasn't, and she started reading aloud: "'If I speak with the tongues of men and of angels, but have not love, I am become sounding brass, or a clanging cymbal. And if I have the gift of prophecy, and know all mysteries and all knowledge; and if I have all faith, so as to remove mountains, but have not love, I am nothing. . . .'"

Hannah was beaming and asked me if I could feel God in the words.

I nodded *yes*, as if I were seeing Hannah for the first time. She had taken off her wire-rimmed glasses to read, and her face appeared more beautiful than I had noticed. Her braids were looser, and I could see that the color of her hair was nuanced with shades of blond and chestnut.

Hannah positioned herself to read more to me, sensing that I wanted to talk, but I didn't. Being with her was enough, and in the quiet that grew between us, I felt at peace.

Hannah explained, "Paul wrote his letter to the Corinthians in about 53 AD, when he was in Ephesus, a city on the west coast of today's Turkey, about 180 miles by sea from Corinth, and while he was there received troubling news about the community in Corinth regarding jealousies, rivalry, and immoral behavior."

The way Hannah talked about the Bible amazed me, even though I had trouble believing everything she was saying. Religion had not been a very important part of my life, and, if anything, I resented how it had been weaponized by politicians and evangelicals alike.

Hannah was surprised by my candor and said, "I wish politicians would leave religion alone. For me, the meaning of religion is deeply personal. It's what we carry in us every day. It's what keeps me going, ever since I was a child."

I leaned forward and asked, "What attracted you to Christianity?" And she moved closer to me, her lips quivering.

"Suffering," she whispered, "Suffering."

Once again, I was speechless. And Hannah opened up that it was a long story, and said if I didn't have time to listen, she understood. Completely.

I joked that there wasn't much else to do. It was nasty outside. And we were stuck inside without electricity.

Hannah forced a little smile and said, "It's painful to tell." And then she paused, tearing up.

"I was seven years old and was as happy as I could be. I had just started second grade, and I loved my teacher, Mrs. Drummond. She was about the same age as my mother and had a very similar disposition. She was kind and thoughtful, always helpful, without ever raising her voice. If someone didn't do their homework, she wanted to know why, and if there was a legitimate excuse, like being sick or not understanding the assignment, there was no punishment, only encouragement.

"My father at that time was working on an assembly line in a meatpacking plant in Cedar Rapids that was the largest plant in Iowa and the fourth-largest in the world. My mother was a clerk in the East Amana country store, which catered to some locals but mostly to tourists, who came through wanting to learn about the Colonies and to buy the handicrafts that were made there, everything from jams to toys and rag rugs.

"I was an only child, but I knew my parents were trying to have another. My father wanted a son, not that he didn't love me as his daughter. He adored me, and we played games in the backyard after he came home from work, and we watched TV together on weekends. Pancakes and Saturday morning cartoons were two of his favorite things to do. And he'd cuddle me up at his side or bounce me on his knee. He made me a dollhouse and built me a fantastic activity board to teach me about tools and gadgets, with pulleys and zippers and anything else he could think of.

"But one day I came home from school and saw my father's car in the driveway much earlier than usual, and there was a white van parked next to it that I didn't recognize. And when I knocked on the front door, my father rushed me inside. My mother was on the couch, and she was having trouble breathing, and the man standing at her side was Dr. Johnson, who I went to see for my annual checkups, but I never knew he made house calls.

"In a few minutes, the EMTs arrived and took my mother to the hospital, and my father and I followed the ambulance in his car. On the way, he told me that my mother had had a miscarriage and that she needed to have a hysterectomy, which meant, he said with a frog in his throat, that she could never have another baby.

"My mother was in the hospital for about a week, and when she came home, she was so weak that she needed me to help her with little things, like pulling up her jeans and tying her sneakers. My father took some of his vacation time, and, before he went back to work, he called me into the living room, where he said we were going to have a family meeting. And we all sat together and prayed. We had never gone to church much, but I recognized some of what they were saying. And when they were done, my father said that they had decided to take in a foster child, who, if everything worked out, they might adopt. My mother explained that foster children were often orphans who either didn't have any parents, or whose parents were not able to take care of them for any number of sad reasons.

"I was excited. I was going to have an older brother. It was like a dream come true for my father and mother. And a couple of weeks later a boy named Johnny came to live with us. He was about twelve years old, and he was very shy.

"My parents gave Johnny the bedroom next to mine, which had mainly been used for storage. My father bought posters of some of the stars on the Chicago Bulls and the Chicago White Sox that he thought Johnny would like, and together, they put them up on the walls. And my mother knitted Johnny a sweater that was midnight blue with red piping around the neck. Johnny loved everything and seemed so grateful to be part of our family. And he especially loved me. He said he'd always wanted a little sister and he couldn't have wished for anything more.

"After school, Johnny and I played all kinds of games. Scrabble and Monopoly were our favorites. Johnny was competitive but not aggressive. He was always so gentle, and, at night, he liked to read to me at bedtime. But one night, he told me it was hard to read because his eyes were hurting, and he wondered if we could touch each other in a different kind of game, to see if, with our eyes closed, we could identify our different body parts. It all sounded so easy, but once we got started, it was more complicated than I thought. When I reached for his hand, he wiggled his fingers around, and I couldn't tell the difference between his index finger and his middle finger. And we laughed and laughed, and then he asked me if I could find his *pee-pee,* and I wasn't sure what he meant. So, he lifted my hand and placed it on his tummy and said that I should just walk my fingers down from there between his legs. And that's what I did, and when I got to his *pee-pee,* it was soft and teeny, and he said that if I massaged it, it would grow in the palm of my hand. I couldn't believe it. And when it got bigger, I pulled back. And he said that was okay, so long as I didn't open my eyes. And I did exactly as he told me, and then he said he was so proud of me. I was happy, and so was he. And he went to his room, and I fell asleep.

"The next night, we played Monopoly, and this time Johnny placed the game board in the middle of my bed instead of on the little table we usually used. And when we were done, Johnny congratulated me for winning and asked if we could play the touching game again. And we did, and Johnny said it was so much fun he could hardly find the words to express how he was feeling. And that made me so glad.

"Every night, Johnny and I played board games, followed by the touching game, which seemed to last longer each time we played. And one time, some sticky liquid spurted out of Johnny's *pee-pee* and he giggled *oops* and he ran out of the room to the bathroom to get a tissue to clean it up.

"But in the hallway, my father stopped him and asked him what he was doing. And I could hear them talking. So, I cracked opened my bedroom door and saw that my father was very upset. Johnny's *pee-pee* was poking through his underwear and was oozing more of that sticky liquid.

"Well, the next day, when I came home from school, Johnny wasn't there. And my mother told me that something had happened and he had to move out. The boy's home where he had been living needed him back. I was so sad, I cried and cried for days. I missed Johnny so much, and my parents did what they could to console me. But they never explained to me what Johnny had actually done to me.

"It wasn't until years later that I realized that I had been molested. I started having strange feelings about boys, and, around the time I got my first period and started to learn about sex, I began to understand what had happened to me. I wanted to talk to my parents about it, but I never did, because I knew how much it hurt them to know what Johnny had done to me.

"But I suffered. As a teenager, I was afraid of boys, and if anyone ever tried to kiss me or touch me, I pushed them away. And to be honest, Andy, I have never told anyone this story, and now that I'm telling it, I'm not sure if I've made a mistake. But you're such a good listener that, I guess, I felt I could . . ."

Hannah was weeping. I wanted to take her in my arms and comfort her, but I knew I couldn't. I felt so bad about what had happened to her and reassured her that I would never tell anyone her story.

And she said, "Well, the truth of the matter, Andy, is that when my mother was diagnosed with the virus, she called me on my cell phone and told me that she needed to talk to me about something that happened when I was a little girl. I was horrified. I couldn't believe it. I felt trapped in between the lines of a terrible tabloid cliché. Both she and my father had to check themselves into the hospital while they were physically still able to do so. They both had high fevers, dry coughs, and severe difficulties breathing. And I needed to self-quarantine for fourteen days. So that's what I did, and, after eleven days, my mother died. And before my father passed away three hours later, he was gasping for air but somehow mustered the strength to tell me that he and my mother had been racked with guilt every second since that fateful night when they found out what Johnny had done to me, without ever asking me to go into any of the details. And we cried together on the phone. He was wheezing but still seemed coherent. And then he asked me for forgiveness.

"I was in tears, and he continued, his voice cracking, remembering the words to a passage from the beginning of James 1 that he hoped would nurture me in times of sorrow: 'Count it all joy, my brethren, when ye fall into manifold temptations; knowing that the proving of your faith worketh patience. And let patience have its perfect work, that ye may be perfect and entire, lacking in nothing.'"

Hannah sighed and thanked me for listening.

"Thank you, Hannah, for opening up to me and sharing . . . your pain. I'm so sorry to hear how you've suffered all these years."

Hannah stood up and, as she was saying that she needed some time to herself, Maggie charged into the den, screaming, "Two of the windows in the living room are cracked! We need to board them up before the glass shatters!"

Hannah and I followed Maggie into the living room. Max and Richard were struggling to nail two large sheets of plywood they had found in the basement onto the window frames, and I ran outside to see what I could do to help.

The rain pelted my back. I was freezing. The temperature had dropped. I planted my feet in the muddy flowerbed beneath the windows and leaned my shoulder into the plywood. But it kept pulling back in the gusts of wind.

Sandra bolted out the front door, grabbed the hammer out of Max's unsteady hands, and quickly pounded a row of nails into the plywood, securing it to the window frame. She moved over to Richard, who was more adept than Max but was still wrestling with the other piece of plywood. Cynthia and Josette were at his side, and together they were able to position the plywood. But while they were working, the glass shattered into the palm of Josette's right hand. She was bleeding, shrieking, "I need a Band-Aid! A Band-Aid!" But it was obvious she needed a bandage, and maybe stitches. Josette was in shock. Hannah, who saw what had just happened, hurried to her side and wrapped her hand in a bathroom towel.

I tried 911 on my cell phone, but there was no service. I shouted to Maggie and she scrambled back into the cottage to get a first aid kit. Eleanor was already inside looking and hadn't located much other than a bottle of hydrogen peroxide and a box of Band-Aids. Barb found only a tube of Neosporin and a couple of Ace bandages in the cabinet above her bathroom sink.

In the den, Maggie grabbed a sewing kit from a drawer under one of the bookshelves and handed it to me. Then she remembered seeing a first aid kit in the stable and darted out of the cottage, but, when she got to the stable, Harry and Daisy were wild, kicking on the doors to their stalls. They were spooked, and there wasn't much Maggie could do. The first aid kit was her priority, and by the time she got back, Cynthia and Sandra had carried Josette into the cottage. Hannah had spread out a blanket on the marble entry room floor, and we propped Josette onto two cushions that Eleanor had taken from the couch on the veranda. Josette was losing blood fast. I needed to do something to help. I looked at the sewing kit and pulled out a needle and a spool of thread. Impulsively, I threaded the needle and sterilized it with some rubbing alcohol that Maggie had retrieved from the stable.

I squeezed the gash in Josette's hand and positioned it between my legs, so that I could stitch the wound together with the sewing needle to stop the bleeding. Sandra shouted, "Stop! Stop!" Josette flinched in pain, and Eleanor and Hannah restrained her. I didn't really know what I was doing, but it was all I could do. And somehow it worked. But Josette was woozy, and Sandra sat by her side, trying to comfort her. Hannah ran to get her car to take Josette to the emergency room at the Stockbridge hospital. And together, Eleanor, Sandra, Cynthia, and I helped Josette to her feet and buckled her into the back seat of Hannah's car. And with Josette's head cradled in Sandra's lap, Hannah sped off.

The living room was a wreck. We had saved much of the carpet, but some of the furnishings were no doubt damaged from the mud we had tracked in and the debris that had blown inside when the window shattered. Maggie said she needed to get in touch with her father in New York City so that he could contact the owner of the property and inform him what had happened.

After about an hour, the wind died down and the rain slowly let up. Everything seemed under control, at least to the extent that we had done our best to mitigate the most immediate problems. We were all exhausted. One by one, the rest of us went upstairs to shower and change clothes, except for Maggie, who said she had to return to the stable to take care of Daisy and Harry. I offered to go with her, but she saw that I was shivering and insisted that I stay in the cottage.

We agreed to meet in the den at four thirty for our storytelling session, though I wasn't sure if anyone would show up.

• • •

I had trouble walking downstairs to the den. My right knee was swollen, and I had bruises on my shoulder from my desperate attempts to keep the plywood in place over the window frame. I had somehow lost touch with what I was feeling until I was able to catch my breath, and then, in the loneliness of my bedroom, my body seemed to shut down, and, when it restarted after a very short nap, I was sore. My muscles ached, and my fingertips were raw.

I heard Cynthia in the kitchen. She was speaking to Sandra, who was sobbing. What they were saying was inaudible, but the tone of the conversation was clear. Sandra was worried, and Cynthia was sympathetic. But when I stepped into the kitchen, they both stopped talking, as if the conversation had something to do with me.

I didn't want to seem paranoid, so I just went with the flow, though I knew that I probably looked jittery. Cynthia was glad to see me, but Sandra refused to talk to me and left. I asked Cynthia what was wrong, and she was blunt. "In your attempt to stitch up Josette's wound, you punctured a nerve in her hand."

I was stunned. "I did what?"

"And sadly, Andy, the damage might be permanent."

I thought I was going to faint. I steadied myself against the kitchen counter, and Cynthia said, "Luckily, the doctor on call was able to perform emergency surgery. But the outcome is still unknown."

Josette was going to be hospitalized for at least a couple of days, and her hand would be immobilized for about a month. And once they removed the bandages, she could start the long and arduous process of occupational and physical therapy.

Unfortunately, because of the virus, Josette was allowed no visitors. The hospital in Stockbridge was small and understaffed.

I swallowed hard. I felt so bad. But then Cynthia said, "If you hadn't tried, Josette might have bled to death. The glass severed part of the radial artery, one of the two major arteries in the body that bring oxygenated blood to the forearm and the hand to maintain proper metabolic activity."

"If Josette loses the use of her right hand, I'm not sure I can ever forgive myself for being so impulsive, so stupid. I should have tried to wrap her hand in some kind of tourniquet first before picking up that sewing needle."

I appreciated Cynthia's empathy for Josette, and for me. But I suspected that she still felt I'd made a mistake.

Cynthia inched her way closer to me, and our eyes met. And we both let go of any inhibitions we had and hugged each other tightly, pecking each other's lips with a delicate kiss, masks and all. It was wonderful but strange. I closed my eyes, losing track of time, and when I opened them, I saw Barb glaring at us. Sandra was at her side, and I pulled away from Cynthia.

I stepped backward, and Max, Richard, Eleanor, and Hannah joined us. Max said, "I'll tell you what. I'm going to make hot chocolate for the storytelling session. Good thing we have a gas stove," and Richard chimed in, "I'm certain that would be what Josette would want us to do."

Sandra scoffed, "You don't have a clue. You have no idea what Josette's thinking. She's not even reachable by phone, and, if anything, she's still in recovery from her surgery."

Richard defended Max adamantly, "Please! Max is only trying to alleviate some of the pressure by doing something fun."

Sandra stormed out of the kitchen and accidentally bumped into Barb, who pleaded with her to not run away from this very difficult situation, reminding her that we came to the cottage to help each other and that meant sticking together when it got tough.

Sandra calmed down but refused Max's hot chocolate, which he was making with the Jersey cow milk that had been given to Eleanor by the dairy farmer. And Max said, "Well, I'm even going to make a special hot chocolate for you with almond milk." Sandra was surprised, and, as we all moved into the den, she bit her lower lip, "Thank you, Max," but she wouldn't look at me.

When everyone was seated, I asked everyone to bow their heads in a moment of prayer for Josette. Hannah whispered *Amen,* and Richard did the same, as did Max and Barb. Cynthia and Sandra were silent.

Maggie was standing in the doorway, wiping her brow with a hand towel. Her hair was disheveled, and she said, "As much as I want to just crash, I know I need to be with all of you."

I could barely talk but somehow managed to apologize to everyone for what I had done.

Cynthia was upset and spoke up, "It wasn't Andy's fault, and, from my point of view, he probably saved her life."

Everyone was quiet.

Maggie sat on a folding chair she pulled from the closet. And I announced that I had decided that Eleanor should tell the next story.

Richard and Max paraded around placing candles wherever they could. No one knew when the electricity might come back on, and the candlelight was comforting, even if it wasn't yet dark.

Eleanor was pleased, saying that she had expected that she was going to be next, since everyone but her, Josette, and me had shared stories.

"Mine," she began, "is about a trip that I took to India when I was a teenager. I had a friend named Amaira who lived with my family for a month while she was an exchange student at my high school in San Francisco. And her family was so appreciative of our hospitality that they invited me to visit them in Mumbai and travel with them across Rajasthan to Jaipur, Jodphur, and then to the Taj Mahal in Agra before flying home from Delhi.

"I arrived in Mumbai on a mild January day. The pilot said the temperature was in the mid-seventies, and I couldn't wait to get outside, but, when I got out of my seat, I was a groggy mess. My mother had given me an Ambien to help me sleep on the plane, and I couldn't shake it off. I had zonked out somewhere over the Pacific Ocean, and, by the time we landed, all I could think about were the elephants and snake charmers I had imagined in my sleep.

"Amaira was so happy to see me, and, as we exited the arrival terminal of Chhatrapati Shivaji International Airport, she gushed on and on about its spectacular design with a long-span roof covering seventy thousand square meters without an expansion joint, one of the largest of its kind in the world. I was overwhelmed. But at the same time, I felt like I was stuck in the middle of a giant mushroom. Amaira laughed and said that I was very perceptive, explaining that the design motif of the mushrooming molded coffered panels throughout the airport derived from the teardrop-shaped eye of the peacock, India's national bird.

"Once we settled in the back seat of the taxi taking us to Amaira's house, I strained to see the Mumbai skyline in the distance, but my window was smudged, and the landscape was hazy.

"Amaira said the pollution in Mumbai could be terrible, but, for her, it was still the City of Dreams. I started to doze off, and Amaira elbowed me playfully in my side, giggling that the plans for my stay had changed. She was now engaged to be married to a man named Nikhil. The wedding had been arranged years ago but had not been announced until December 26, a public holiday in the Indian state of Haryana called Shaheed Udham Singh Jayanti, in honor of the birth anniversary of the legendary Udham Singh. Singh was a revolutionary freedom fighter who assassinated the British administrator Michael O'Dwyer in 1940 to avenge the 1919 Jallianwala Bagh massacre of more than four hundred men, women, and children that he had witnessed when he was twenty years old.

"Amaira didn't really understand why her parents had picked Shaheed Udham Singh Jayanti, of all days, to announce her engagement, other than the fact that her father was from the state of Haryana. In any event, Amaira had mixed feelings about marrying Nikhil. For her, arranged marriages were old-fashioned and out of sync with today's world. She was sorry for not telling me what was going on in advance of my trip, but, in all honesty, she said that she hoped I might be able to help.

"I was shocked that Amaira wanted me to go with her for their first in-person meeting. I was terribly jet-lagged, but Amaira assured me that if I kept moving, I'd be fine. And when I got to her house, her mother welcomed me, preparing chai and a tray of delicious Indian goodies—kaju kothimbir vadi, a popular Maharashtrian dish made with a chickpea flour batter, cashews, and spices; kalmi vada, a golden fried delicacy from Rajasthan made with dals and fresh hari chutney; and pinaca, a sweet snack from Goa made with a mixture of jaggery and coconut rolled in rice flour.

"After tea, Amaira showed me to my bedroom and said that I should unpack quickly because we were to meet Nikhil in the lobby of the grand Taj Mahal Hotel in just two hours, and the traffic was going to be awful. I asked Amaira what I should wear, and she said anything was okay but then invited me to pick a sari from her closet, since we were about the same size.

"I followed Amaira into her room and was awed by the possibilities. Amaira offered to dress me, and I let her do as she wished. And she picked an embroidered saffron-colored blouse and a green sari for me and a red chiffon sari and gold blouse for her, symbolizing, she said, passion and sensuality.

"When I looked in the mirror, I didn't recognize myself. If anything, I felt kind of ridiculous, with my red hair and freckles, dressed in a sari. Amaira said I looked beautiful, and that was enough for me.

"In the taxi, I conked out. The traffic was excruciating, and my eyelids weighed me down.

"At the Taj Mahal Hotel, we were met by a bearded doorman, a five-foot-eleven Sikh in a cream-colored tunic and pants with an embroidered cummerbund, who welcomed us with folded hands and a traditional Namaste greeting. And as we walked into the lobby, Amaira told me that in 2008, when her father was on his way to work nearby, gunfire broke out and Pakistani terrorists stormed the hotel and set it afire, killing thirty-one people during a three-day siege. 'Thank God,' Amaira said, 'he wasn't hurt. He hid in an alley and was spared. And when the hotel reopened twenty-one months later, it once again became one of the favorite tourist destinations in Mumbai.'

"Amaira thought it was weird that Nikhil wanted to meet at the

Taj, but she was glad that I was with her. To me, it was so strange that they had never even seen each other, other than in photographs that had been exchanged by their parents.

"Nikhil recognized Amaira immediately, but, when she introduced me to him as her American friend, he acted disappointed. This had not been discussed in advance, and my being with Amaira made him uneasy. Nikhil was dressed in a Western-style business suit, and as he led us to the Sea Lounge, he focused his attention on me without saying a word, apparently trying to make me uncomfortable. Amaira ignored him and explained to me that the Sea Lounge was known worldwide for its colonial charm with its art deco furnishings and unparalleled views of the Arabian Sea. The maître d' escorted us to our table, and I was totally wowed. Nikhil made sure that Amaira's and my seats faced the sea and that his was directly across from Amaira.

"Amaira was shy and didn't say much, but, when he asked how she felt about their upcoming marriage, she flinched but quickly regained her composure and told Nikhil bluntly she wasn't sure if she could love somebody who had been picked for her by his parents.

"Nikhil was concerned. Apparently, in his mind, all of the details and logistics had been settled. He opened his briefcase and pulled out a brochure for a new apartment complex in the center of Mumbai, where he thought they would live because of its proximity to the office tower where he worked.

"Amaira laughed and replied that just the thought of moving into the confines of a luxury apartment in the middle of the city was unappealing. Nikhil continued, as if he hadn't heard a word that she said, pointing out that the apartment, for which he had already paid a deposit, had two bedrooms—perfect for a new family—since he anticipated that their first child would be born during the second year of their marriage.

"Amaira frowned, and Nikhil tried to reassure her that he would provide for her, hiring a maid and a nanny to help care for the child. Of course, he said, the apartment would have quarters for these domestic servants that would be more than adequate.

"Amaira was angry. Not only was Nikhil dismissive, he was rude. When the waiter came to take our order, Nikhil chided him for interrupting his conversation and insisted that he return once he had decided what would be best for his guests. I couldn't believe how chauvinistic Nikhil was. The last thing I wanted him to do was order for me.

"Nikhil became sarcastic, informing us in a formal tone that it was his duty to provide for us. Amaira sank deeper into her seat. Once again, she tried to interject her feelings, but, every time she uttered a word or two, Nikhil shut her down.

"My sympathies were with Amaira, who shifted around in her seat, disgusted by Nikhil's behavior.

"Nikhil, sensing how agitated Amaira was, instructed the waiter to bring three glasses of the lounge's finest champagne, smiling that champagne was perfect any time in the afternoon.

And when the waiter returned and placed the champagne flutes on the table, Nikhil proposed a toast to his future bride.

"Amaira burst out of her chair, standing up, champagne glass in hand, took a tiny sip, and then surprised Nikhil by splashing the rest on the tablecloth in front of her. Nikhil was stunned. Amaira was terrified at what Nikhil might do, but he did nothing. And she politely excused herself by saying that it was an accident, when I, and surely Nikhil, knew very well that it was a courageous act of defiance.

"Amaira gestured to me, and, together, we marched out of the Sea Lounge toward the entrance of the hotel, where the Sikh doorman called us a cab. And we headed back to Amaira's house, rejoicing that we had triumphed, and Amaira was finally at peace.

"But as we neared Amaira's house, she began to worry, not so much because she had rejected Nikhil and the arranged marriage, but about what her parents were going to do to her and what repercussions she, and they, were going to be subjected to. Amaira asked that I not talk about what had just happened. She needed time to figure out what to do before her parents found out. I assured her that I'd say nothing. But I worried that I was somehow going to get caught in the middle.

"That night I was so jet-lagged that I slept soundly until about four o'clock in the morning, but then I couldn't fall back asleep. I was so turned off by Nikhil's chauvinism. I tossed and turned and struggled to get comfortable, but my bed and pillow were hard. And in the darkness, I heard someone chanting in another room. I wasn't sure if it was Amaira or perhaps her mother, but I knew I couldn't ask whoever it was to stop. And I decided to get up and call American Airlines to see if I could somehow change my return to San Francisco. I'd had enough. I needed to get out of India as soon as possible.

"Little did I know that the walls were so thin in Amaira's house that my talking on the phone woke her up. And when I was done, she knocked on my door. And I told her that I had changed my ticket.

"Amaira was dismayed at first, but she completely understood, explaining that it might be best if I did leave, because her parents were going to be furious. I didn't want to abandon Amaira, but I knew that, if I stuck around, it was only going to get worse. Amaira was relieved and said she appreciated my compassion for her. And then in an excited voice she told me that never in her life had she been able to experience in one day all of the Navarasa—the nine emotions: Love (Shringara), Laughter (Hasya), Sorrow (Karuena), Anger (Raudra), Courage (Veera), Terror (Bhayanaka), Disgust (Bibhatsya), Surprise (Adbutha), and Peace (Shantha).

"In the morning, Amaira arranged for a taxi to take me to the airport. And I thanked her parents and left. I couldn't believe I had only been in India for a day and had spent two days getting there and had another two days ahead of me to get home. It was as if my time in Mumbai was a dream or, perhaps, like a folktale I remembered that I heard when I was a little girl but somehow never mentioned to Amaira, when in fact Amaira was so much like the heroine of the story. Maybe Amaira was the incarnation of Princess Rukmini, whose brother Prince Rukmi had arranged her marriage to Shishupala, the crown prince of Chedi, when she had her heart set on marrying Krishna, whose valor she had admired since she was a child. In desperation, Rukmini sent her trusted aide with a note she had written to Krishna confiding in him that he was the only husband for her and that, if he would not have her, she would give up her life. Rukmini pleaded with Krishna to kidnap her on the day of her wedding. And Krishna, having heard of Rukmini's beauty, agreed, even though he wasn't sure if he should approach her family because of her brother Rukmi's allegiance to his sworn enemy, Jarasandha, who was also favored by Shishupala. But Krishna was not deterred and went bravely to the temple where Rukmini said she would meet him. And on her wedding day, when Rukmini was leaving the temple, she looked in the crowds for Krishna, but she didn't see him. And just as she was about to leave, she felt someone hold her from behind. It was Krishna. He lifted her into his chariot and sped away with her brother Rukmi in pursuit. And after Rukmi was defeated, Rukmini begged Krishna to spare her brother's life, which he did, cutting off half the hair on his head and half the moustache on his face, humiliating him before letting him go. Then, Krishna returned to his home in Dwarka with Rukmini and married her.

"On my flight back to San Francisco, I wondered if Amaira would ever find her Krishna, and I promised myself that I would never lose touch with her. And we stayed pen pals for years, and, finally, about three years ago, we were able to get together again in person. She had graduated from medical school and had accepted a residency in the emergency room of a hospital in San Francisco. She had never mentioned her parents in any of her letters, and I didn't dare ask what happened after I left. I knew it was complicated, and, if she had anything that she wanted to share with me, she'd do it. But when we met, one of the first things she told me was that her parents ultimately accepted her decision to reject Nikhil, but at the same time, they considered her ineligible for marriage. Amaira knew she could never live in India again. She was ready for a new life in the Bay Area. She loved her job, and we met up often for lunch or tea or just sitting on a bench in a park somewhere, giggling about stupid things that had happened to us in the course of our day. And after a while, she started dating an attending physician with whom she worked, and it wasn't long after that that they were married by a justice of the peace without telling anyone. And after that we didn't get together as often, and, sadly, she contracted the virus and died three weeks later. And when her husband called and said that she had passed, I didn't believe him. Had it really been three weeks since I had last talked to her? I had so many questions, but her husband didn't want to talk. I didn't know him very well, and when I asked if there was anything I could do, he simply said no. Amaira had been cremated and her ashes had already been sent back to her parents in India. I wished Amaira's husband well and he said thank you and ended the call. My eyes welled up, but tears never came. I finally understood what Amaira had once told me—I experienced, like her, all of the Navarasa, the nine emotions, in one day: Love, Laughter, Sorrow, Anger, Courage, Terror, Disgust, Surprise, and Peace. Namaste."

Namaste echoed through the den.

Max said, "I'm ready for yoga," and Richard rolled his eyes.

I arched my back to look up at the ceiling, exhaling through my spine, pulling my abdominals in, and rounding my back.

Cynthia straightened up in her seat and stretched her neck backward.

Memories of Amaira's death seemed to wash over Eleanor,

leaving her face with an empty feeling that I sensed was overpowering. She patted her eyes with her fingertips, keeping the tears that were welling up from running down her cheeks.

I told her that I was moved by her story, sympathizing with her loss and complaining that not enough was being done to protect the nurses and doctors who worked every day to save the lives of the sickest people.

Barb started ranting, "Our world is doomed! Our world is doomed!" Maggie raised her hands, pleading with her to stop. Barb snarled and stomped out of the room.

Sandra stood up abruptly and said, "I'm going to the hospital in Stockbridge to check on Josette," and I asked if I could join her. Hannah and Cynthia wanted to come along, too, muttering that they needed a break from the cottage.

Sandra exhaled loudly, as if she had been holding her breath, not wanting to lash out at me. But the expression on her face said it all. She knitted her brow and flared her nostrils, reminding us in a stern voice that visitors, other than family, were not allowed. "If we all go, we'll all get sent home. But if I go alone, I might have a chance."

Reluctantly, I gave in. And Hannah and Cynthia backed off.

I pleaded, "I really need to talk to Josette."

"Now is not a good time, Andy," Sandra scoffed. "You're a huge part of the problem. Not the solution. And if you truly want to help Josette, then leave her alone."

Cynthia snapped, "Sandra, I don't understand why you are being so mean. The gash in Josette's hand was an accident."

Maggie shouted, "Enough!" And Sandra left the den in a huff.

Hannah was visibly shaken and excused herself.

Maggie said in a sarcastic voice, "I need a shower, but the truth is I'm more hungry than dirty."

No one thought that was especially funny, but the words

coming out of her mouth were at least a departure from the tension in the den, and everyone seemed to relax.

Eleanor liked the idea of eating. "I've been craving tuna fish for the last couple of days. I hope we have some. I forgot to bring any. And just thinking about it makes me want it all the more."

Maggie motioned to Eleanor to follow her into the kitchen.

Cynthia looked at me like she was hoping that we could go off somewhere together, tilting her head from side to side and beckoning me with the index finger of her right hand.

Maggie saw what Cynthia was doing and turned away, and the inseparable Max and Richard accompanied her and Eleanor into the kitchen.

I stumbled toward Cynthia with an awkward gait that I exaggerated the closer I got to her. And she giggled, "You're too silly," and then asked, "Would you like to sit and talk for a while? Even though I'm not sure where we should go. The downstairs of the cottage is a wreck, but upstairs, in the bedrooms, there's still some semblance of order. Of course, I don't want to make you more uncomfortable, but my room is tidy, and there are two high-backed chairs where we can sit catty-corner to each other."

But as we exited the den, Cynthia changed her mind, telling me that she needed to go outside. The sky had cleared, and the late afternoon sun flushed red on the black and white marble tiles of the vestibule floor in front of us. Cynthia sneezed, and I stepped back, and she sneezed again, explaining, "This is the time of year when my allergies act up. I'm not allergic to much, but grass pollen is the worst. Don't worry. I'm not getting sick. I just need a decongestant."

She reached for a little plastic pouch in her fanny pack. As I watched her fumbling around, I tried to imagine what it might be like if we coupled up. But just thinking about it made me wince inside. It was too soon. I liked being with her. But I also liked Maggie, Eleanor, Hannah, and even Barb, all in different ways. It was amazing, not because I imagined that any or all of them were emotionally available. It was as if I were a kid in a candy store, fantasizing about what I probably couldn't have anyway.

Cynthia finally found the decongestant, and I trudged behind her as she rushed into the kitchen for a glass of water. Maggie stared at her, and Barb said she was concerned. Eleanor insisted on taking her temperature, and Cynthia agreed. Eleanor pulled a digital thermometer from her purse, and, once she saw that Cynthia's temperature was normal, everyone calmed down.

Cynthia nodded, acknowledging their vigilance but not uttering a word. And when we got into the hallway, she said, "I'm going to the shed. You want to come? But, please, don't feel obligated."

"Of course," I said, "that's exactly what I want to do."

The grounds of the cottage were still sopping wet. Just as we were about to step onto the grass, Cynthia remembered that she had seen a few pairs of rubber boots in the mud room. To get them, though, Cynthia said, we had to walk around the cottage and enter from the rear. She didn't want to go through the kitchen. She needed a break from Maggie and Eleanor.

Cynthia was determined, and we managed to get around the cottage without our sneakers getting too wet. And as we pulled on our rain boots, Cynthia joked that wearing them always made her feel like a duck, teasing me with silly quacking sounds, urging me to move quickly so that we could get to the shed before dark.

We saw Eleanor and Maggie watching us from the kitchen, but we were not deterred. And when we got to the shed Cynthia was surprised to see that storm damage wasn't as bad as she had expected. There were no windows in the shed, and the wooden walls had apparently been treated with some kind of water-resistant material that had held back the pelting rain. Even the dirt under the trapdoor was relatively dry. Cynthia and I picked up where we had left off and continued to excavate, but this time Cynthia had brought her micrometer. And as much I was ready to start shoveling, she asked me to wait while she began charting measurements of the stratification in the layers of dirt.

I was impressed. It didn't take her long, and together we dug deeper into the underground pit, coordinating our efforts, Cynthia with a spade, me with a shovel. Systematically, we cleared off the wooden ladder.

When it seemed safe to go down the ladder, Cynthia picked up a rope she found in a corner of the shed and tied it around her waist, asking me to hold the loose end tight as she grasped the ladder. She worried that what she called the "compartment" might actually be the remnants of an old well, and with the water table so elevated, she didn't want to drown.

I laughed, but she said, "I'm dead serious. The walls around me could collapse."

Cynthia carefully lowered herself into the compartment, and when she reached the ground, she unfastened her safety rope and disappeared from view. I shouted to her, worried something was wrong. But then she called up to me, "It's incredible down here. It's so much larger than I thought. Before going any farther, I need more supplies."

Slowly, she climbed back to the surface, telling me that she wasn't prepared to stray too far from the ladder. The flooring was solid but creaked as she inched forward. "The ceiling seems to be about six or seven feet tall, and, in the shadows, I see the outline of what appears to be a desk, and maybe a bed frame." Cynthia was inspired and tried to figure out how she could gather the supplies she needed to explore the compartment further.

But then she said, "The bigger issue for me is that I don't want to talk about what we've discovered with the others, particularly since I don't know exactly what we're going to find when we go down deeper. For now, let's keep it a secret between us."

I gazed into her eyes and nodded *okay*.

Day 8

SANDRA GOT BACK TO THE COTTAGE around three o'clock in the morning. But all the doors were locked. I heard her pounding on the front door, shouting for someone to let her in. I pulled myself out of bed, not knowing what to expect. Downstairs, Hannah and Barb had candles in their hands and were already talking with her, trying to calm her down. But when Sandra saw me, she went ballistic and charged at me. "When you had that sewing needle, I pleaded with you to stop, but you wouldn't listen. I tried to protect Josette. But you sewed up her hand anyway!"

I was horrified and backed away as quickly as I could. Sandra stopped short, about three feet away from me, and fell to her knees, sobbing.

Hannah shrieked so loud that before long, everyone showed up. Maggie demanded that Sandra apologize for making such a ruckus, but she cried out, "Never!"

I turned around and hurried back upstairs to my bed. I was shivering. The shrillness of Sandra's voice sent chills up and down my spine. I wrapped myself in my blanket, and when I finally warmed up, I didn't want to get up. I stayed in bed until about nine.

At breakfast, Sandra was still frantic, rambling on that Josette's hand was infected and she was delirious. The nurses had blocked her from Josette's room and threatened to call a security guard.

But somehow, she muscled her way through. And finally, after a fifteen-minute stand-off of shouting and insults, the floor supervisor intervened and made an exception.

Sandra passed the virus clearance test. She didn't have a fever or any exposure to anyone with the virus in the last fourteen days. But she was only granted a half-hour visit with Josette, who barely had any idea who she was talking to. Josette was slurring her words, and, when Sandra came closer to her bed, she screamed that evil spirits were descending upon her. She was hallucinating and had to be sedated.

Sandra said she left Josette's hospital room in a state of shock. The nurses led her to the waiting room, and, when she quieted down, advised her to go home, which she did, even though she didn't want to leave.

Cynthia and Hannah tried to comfort her and led her to the veranda.

The cottage was humming with a sound I hadn't heard before, and the electricity was back on. In the hallway, I overheard Maggie telling Max that her father had called the owner about the power outage and that he'd pay for a generator, so long as we stayed at the cottage until all was up and running. Parked outside, there was an eighteen-wheeler with a giant generator on its trailer.

Eleanor asked me if I wanted to help her with her morning milk deliveries, and I told her that I was ready whenever she was.

Max was making tea for Richard, who was still in bed. Barb was eating a bowl of cereal, and I sat down next to her. No one had been giving her much attention. But she seemed better and grinned, "Thanks for joining me. Everyone else seems to be avoiding me." As she munched away, I said, "Guess what? You're my choice for the next queen." Barb flinched, and I did my best to let her know that I truly felt she could help us come back together as a group. "After all you've been through, I mean, clearly, we all have problems, but yours have only gotten worse in real time. I just think you can help us get back on track. Your story about the homeless guy was maybe the best one yet."

Barb listened intently and promised, "I'll try, but I'm not very optimistic because I feel like no one, other than you, really gets where I'm coming from."

Eleanor signaled to me that she was ready to leave. She was unable to reach the dairy farmer by phone and was worried that something had happened to him. We'd heard on the radio that a couple of small tornadoes had touched down near Pittsfield, about ten miles away.

"So, what is it about the dairy farmer that makes you want to check up on him?" I asked, "I mean, I don't want to sound insensitive."

Eleanor shook her head, "I guess, I'm a do-gooder. When anyone is in need, I just want to try to help. And to be honest, Andy, I think you're the same way. I mean, the way you jumped in and stitched up Josette's hand."

"Well, I'm not so sure I did the right thing.

"But you made the effort. That's what matters."

Eleanor eased into the passenger seat of my car with a mask and a box of sanitizing wipes, concerned that the gallons of milk we were going to load into the trunk might have passed through more sets of hands than we knew about. I had thought the dairy farm was relatively small and employed only a few workers, who I assumed were family members. But Eleanor said that she had read online that it was actually a much bigger operation, with most of the milk being sold to cheese companies in Vermont.

Driving into the countryside cleared my head. But the landscape was more torn up than I had expected. The storm had ravaged the fields, uprooting small trees and scattering brush and leaves onto the road. The sky was mottled with clouds, and the air was gritty. And when we got to the dairy farm the front gate was chained shut.

Eleanor phoned the dairy farmer again, but there was no

answer. So she got out of the car and tried the call box mounted on a metal fence post. After a few minutes, a man with a booming voice answered. "Old Charlie had a heart attack and had to be rushed to the hospital in the middle of the storm. Fortunately, he's alive and underwent triple bypass surgery early this morning."

"Oh, no!" Eleanor exclaimed.

"Don't worry about Charlie. He's a tough old bird."

"What about the milk that needs to be delivered in Stockbridge?"

"It's already been dumped. Two of the Jersey cows were sick, and the milk might have been contaminated."

Eleanor was bummed out, and I tried to console her, but didn't really know what to say. "I'm . . . uh . . . sorry, but with all that's going on these days, part of me is just numb. I'm hurting in so many ways, I'm not sure what's worst. I suppose I have no one to blame but myself."

Eleanor looked at me with sympathetic eyes. "I've been there, done that, felt guilty for things that were out of my control, like Amaira dying of the virus when I didn't even know she was sick." As much as I appreciated what she was saying, I was stuck in a different place. I was sinking in the quicksand of my own guilt because I was the root of the problem. I was the one who'd been out of control, thinking I could stitch up Josette when I didn't really know what I was doing.

I asked Eleanor if she minded if we took a detour back to the cottage. I wanted to stop at the hospital in Stockbridge to see how Josette was doing. Eleanor nodded *okay* and turned on the radio and surfed around until she found a station blaring hip-hop and contemporary R&B. And after a few minutes, she zoned out and didn't say anything more until we got to the hospital. But when I parked the car, Eleanor reminded me that it wasn't my fault. I really wanted to believe that, but I didn't. I had to accept responsibility for my own actions, and it was eating me up inside.

At the hospital, a nurse wearing a mask appeared, and, keeping her social distance, said, "I'm not really supposed to give out patient information. But I can tell you Josette seems to be improving. She's responding well to the antibiotic treatment, but she isn't out of the woods yet."

Eleanor gently placed her hand on the sleeve of my jacket, telling me without words not to jump to any conclusions.

The ride back was quiet.

As we neared the cottage, Eleanor said, "It's so tough to get a handle on everything that's going on. But I'm glad we were together today."

"Me, too."

Eleanor smiled, "Thanks for coming with me to Charlie's place," and then went upstairs to her room.

Cynthia was in the kitchen, wiping the counters with sanitizer. She looked up and asked, "How'd it go?"

"It's a long story," I sighed, "with a bad ending."

"It sounds like my morning," Cynthia said, "Sandra was difficult, to say the least."

I shook my head, not wanting to talk about Sandra, and Cynthia held back the details about what had happened while Eleanor and I were away. I gave Cynthia the update on Josette, and, when I told her that the nurse had said Josette wasn't out of the woods yet, she grimaced.

"Do you think I should move out?"

"Of course not, Andy. In my mind, if anyone should leave, it's Sandra."

I was completely drained and couldn't decide if I should go back to bed or stick around.

I was hungry and opened the refrigerator door to see if there was some yogurt or juice, and Cynthia offered to make some eggs and toast.

I was grateful and sat down and watched Cynthia do her thing at the stove.

The eggs were perfect—soft-scrambled with melted cheddar—and the rye toast with plum jam was wonderful.

Cynthia rambled on about the shed and how she'd found a helmet with a rechargeable head lamp in the basement of the cottage. She was ready to resume work on the excavation project and asked if I'd like to join her. And as pooped as I was, I couldn't refuse. Anything that would take my mind off the Josette situation, I was game to do.

Maggie slogged into the kitchen, her arms dangling at her sides, saying she felt like a rag doll. There was so much to do, and not enough hours in the day to get it done. Cynthia and I asked what we could do to help, and Maggie furrowed her brow, grumbling that she wished that was possible. Mostly, she had to make phone calls. Water remediation was the first priority. Carpet and upholstery cleaners. Finding a glazier to replace the windowpanes in the living room. Painters. Getting estimates. Meeting the repairmen. Reporting back to her father. Approvals by the owner. The tasks were endless.

I had second thoughts about going to the shed, but Maggie insisted that we go, though I sensed that she wanted me to stay back. I was on the fence. Maggie or Cynthia?

Cynthia said she needed to gather up a few things she had left upstairs, and while she was gone, Maggie complained, "The energy of our chat group is fizzling out."

I felt pretty much the same way. "Staying together in the same house is a lot harder than being in a chat room."

"Point taken."

"What's bothering you the most?"

"It's like no matter what I do, I can't connect. I really want everyone to come together as a family. Okay, maybe 'family' is the wrong word."

Cynthia appeared, and Maggie shut down.

"Are you okay?" Cynthia asked.

"I'm fine," Maggie answered. "I'm fine."

Cynthia had packed a box lunch and a satchel with her helmet and tools, and, as she reached down to pick them up, Maggie was curious. "So, what are you really doing in the shed?"

"Oh, not much," Cynthia said, "Just straightening up the tools and digging around." Maggie rolled her eyes, "Sounds like a science project."

Cynthia laughed, "Well, I guess that's what it is."

I followed Cynthia out of the kitchen through the veranda to the garden, where Sandra was working to rebuild the Voodoo shrine she had started in the woods with Josette. Maggie didn't really approve but didn't make any effort to stop her, especially since Josette had been so badly injured. And when Sandra saw me, she planted her feet in the soil, her hands on her hips, and snarled, "I've talked to a lawyer about what recourse Josette might have for what you did to her, especially if she loses the use of her hand."

I was dumbfounded.

Sandra leaned forward and poked an index finger in my direction, barking, "You know, you could be criminally charged and sued for civil damages if it's determined by a court of law that your *attempt* to help Josette actually made the situation worse or injured her further."

I didn't want to listen and continued walking. Cynthia rushed beside me and tried to assure me that Sandra's accusations were ridiculous. But I wasn't so sure.

When we got to the shed, we saw that the door was ajar. Cynthia worried that someone might be inside, and, when she stepped into the interior, she screamed, "What are we going to do?"

I wasn't especially concerned. From my point of view, there was nothing of value to steal. But for Cynthia it was a problem. This was her project, and any tampering with the site could mess up her analysis of the data she was collecting.

Cynthia pulled on the chain connected to the single light bulb in the middle of the ceiling, and it snapped off in her hand. But she was prepared and asked me to get the needle-nose pliers in her satchel so that she could grab hold of the few links of chain that were left on the edge of the bulb socket. She turned the light on with a flick of her wrist.

Cynthia pushed the table against the back wall, laid out the tools she had brought with her, and detailed her plan of action. This time, the first thing she wanted to do was to check the stability of the ladder leading into the interior compartment. She lifted the spade and jabbed each of the rungs to see if they were secure. Once she was confident that neither of us would be injured, Cynthia buckled a tool belt around her waist and positioned the helmet and lamp on her head. Slowly, she descended into the compartment and directed me—flashlight in hand—to follow her.

Illuminated, the interior compartment was more expansive than either of us had thought. There was not only a desk and bedframe, but an old wooden file cabinet stuffed with documents and drawings. As we pulled them out, we discovered that most were handwritten on a parchment-like paper. Cynthia gave them a closer look and determined that the writing was in German and Italian.

The drawings, which looked to have been made by an architect, contained a schematic of the interior design of the room. The drawings also seemed to confirm what Cynthia had suspected: there was another level beneath or connected to where we were standing. But as we looked around, we couldn't locate an entry point. We didn't see a trapdoor or a ladder.

The walls were more solid than the shed above us and were layered with dust, grime, and cobwebs that Cynthia surmised might have been there for decades, if not centuries. As she ran her gloved hands across the walls, she marveled at their construction from rectangular, quarried blocks of stone. She pulled a screwdriver from her tool belt and scraped between the stones, noting that there was a lime mortar, like what was used during the Middle Ages. As she worked her hands along the surface, two of the stones gave way. When we looked into the hole behind the stones, we saw what appeared to be the opening of a tunnel.

Cynthia pushed against the stones in front of her and was able to loosen more of them. Each seemed to be mounted on a steel rod, with some kind of gear system that made it possible for them to turn on an axis point. But some of the stones wouldn't budge, no matter how hard we tried. After an hour or more underground, we decided to stop digging.

Cynthia glanced at her watch and said, "It's already two o'clock. I want to get a closer look at some of the documents and drawings. I'm fluent in both German and Italian, and, while the language seems archaic, I think I can make sense of what's there."

We climbed back up the ladder. I knew Cynthia wanted to continue working, but she could tell that I was exhausted. So, she handed me a bottle of water and a smoked turkey sandwich that she'd packed, and together we sat at the table, scooting back the pile of documents and drawings that we had somehow managed to ferry up the ladder.

When we were done eating, Cynthia said, "I suppose we should head back to the cottage. I heard someone say that the storytelling session starts at five thirty. And we need a little time to rest up."

"That's the truth. Otherwise, I might doze off. And cause more damage."

"Damage?"

"You know what I mean."

Before leaving, Cynthia installed an old padlock she'd found in the mudroom of the cottage on the door of the shed. She was certain that we were really onto something, something big, and didn't want anyone snooping around.

I dreaded going back to the cottage. "So, what should I do if Sandra attacks me again?"

"Ignore her. Turn the other cheek. If Sandra becomes aggressive, be passive."

I knew Cynthia was right. I had to move on. But it was tough. I couldn't let Sandra bait me into saying or doing something I might one day regret.

• • •

It was quiet when Cynthia and I got back to the cottage. I was dragging, but Cynthia was energized and immediately grabbed her laptop.

She couldn't wait to research the techniques used to dismantle the walls without destroying the core stonework.

I ambled off by myself, hoping I could stretch out on the couch in the den. But I was hungry and headed for the kitchen, where I saw Barb at the stove.

She was surprised to see me and said in a cheery voice, "I'm making Italian *confetti* treats, like the kind they made in *The Decameron,* for our storytelling session."

She was chopping dried apricots and dates and sprinkling them with cinnamon and ground cloves before mixing it all together with honey and shaping little balls that she placed on a cookie sheet in front of her. She slid the first batch into the oven and made another, this time with chopped almonds and pumpkin seeds.

Barb gushed, "I'm actually a connoisseur of *confetti.* I've loved them ever since I was a kid, when I used to buy little bags of them at a penny candy store in Little Italy that was about two blocks from where I lived in New York City. Each morsel was homemade by an old lady who ran the place and called herself 'Granny.' Little did I know at the time, they were almost identical to those described in *The Decameron. Confetti* shows up in Story Three of Day Seven in a rant about monks who preach abstinence but treat themselves with imported wines and boxes of candy."

Barb was chattier than ever. I listened as best I could, but I was wiped out. I didn't want to seem rude, but I knew that if I didn't nap, I was going to be miserable later. The last thing I wanted to do was doze off in the middle of our storytelling session.

I grabbed a few slices of cheddar from the refrigerator and thanked Barb for all the trivia and, most of all, for making the *confetti* that I could hardly wait to taste.

When I got to the den, Hannah was in her reading chair. She glanced up from her Bible, and I said, "I need some rest. And if you don't mind, I'd like to sack out on the couch."

Hannah seemed confused, "The den isn't private."

"That's what makes it just right. I like being in the same room with you."

Hannah blushed.

I stuttered, "I'm also trying to avoid Sandra."

"I understand."

"I'm torn up inside."

"God was with you, Andy, when you stitched up Josette's hand, and God is still with you."

"Have you heard any more news about Josette?"

"Well, not exactly. Sandra called from the hospital. Josette's infection is under control."

I plopped down on the couch to take off my sneakers.

"Sandra's waiting to speak to her doctor about what happens next."

I was relieved and raised my feet onto the cushions. I laid my head back against the pillows and drifted off to sleep with Hannah's lovely face in mind.

But when I woke up, Hannah was poking me in the side. "C'mon. We gotta go. Barb's about to start."

I jerked up, stepped into my sneakers, and quickly tied the laces.

By the time we got to the veranda, Maggie was passing around a tray with pieces of Barb's homemade *confetti*, and Richard was bragging that the Chardonnay he had picked was the perfect pairing with the sweets.

Cynthia pointed to the glasses on the credenza, and I picked one up, my head still a little fuzzy.

Barb tapped her wine glass with a teaspoon and called the storytelling session to order.

Maggie stood up and began without hesitation: "In my story, I have chosen to adopt an exaggerated tone, echoing the syntax of Boccaccio or perhaps, more accurately, what I imagine the dour Middle Ages to have sounded like. However, I must confess that the narrative I am about tell is based on the Seventh Day, Eighth Story, as it appears in *The Decameron*. To dismiss any accusations of plagiarism, names and situations have been changed arbitrarily. In other words, believe what you wish and disregard the rest. It's all a little crazy.

"In 1914, a young woman named Tabitha, the daughter of the fifteenth-wealthiest man in the world, married William H. Jones III, the son of a rich investment banker, who lived in a lavish residence on Park Avenue, within walking distance of the Armory. The Armory had been completed just a year earlier.

"While the marriage had not been arranged per se, it had been expected ever since Tabitha and William were born within two days of each other. Their parents had known each other for years, beginning in the early 1890s, when they met as members of The Four Hundred, a listing of the notables in New York society during the Gilded Age that was compiled by the legendary Mrs. Astor, the grande dame and arbiter of elegant taste.

"Tabitha and William attended different but equally prestigious private schools, though Tabitha, of course, was in many ways deprived of the benefits afforded to William, because of the simple fact that she was a girl who was being groomed to become the dutiful wife of a fine, upstanding man and was never given the opportunity pursue a career of her own making. But she cared less about a career than about the financial benefits that an arranged marriage would bring to her. From her perspective, as an overly protected virgin with a pittance of monetary allowance, once she had wealth and luxury, everything else—from sex to children and, of course, happiness—would inevitably fall into place. The prenuptial agreement that both William and Tabitha signed gave them unrestricted access to an irrevocable trust of many millions of dollars that their respective parents established to support them together and separately for the rest of their lives, provided, of course, they never divorced.

"The wedding of Tabitha and William was the social event of the spring season. Tabitha loved to dance, and, according to one account, she refused to leave the reception, to the dismay of William, who stormed out with his closest friends, only to return drunk to the couple's new apartment on Park Avenue.

"On their first night together, William, in his inebriated state, announced that he was bisexual and that Tabitha and he were to have different bedrooms, connected by a common door that could be locked or opened at will, depending on his sexual needs on any given night. Needless to say, Tabitha was distraught, and her fantasies of conjugal bliss were all but obliterated.

"That night, Tabitha cried herself to sleep, startling Robert, William's valet, who happened to be walking by her bedroom door after bringing yet another Scotch to William. By then, William had already blacked out, and it was pointless for Robert to leave the drink, which would no doubt be discarded in the morning. Robert tapped lightly on Tabitha's door, his serving tray in one hand, and, when Tabitha opened the door, she was startled to see this man, whom she did not recognize, carrying a drink she had not ordered.

But instead of turning Robert away, she invited him into her room, and, while the details of what happened next are unknown, gossip spread quickly the next day among the maids that Tabitha had indeed unexpectedly found the bliss she had been hoping for.

"Well, Robert and Tabitha continued to see each other surreptitiously on nights when William was consorting with harlots or too drunk to notice what was going on in the bedroom that adjoined his. The plan that Tabitha devised was for her to tie a string to the big toe of her left foot and to dangle the string out of the window, and, when Robert was ready to come to her room, he tugged on the string to let her know that the *magic time* had arrived. If all was clear, Tabitha released the string, and the maid led Robert to her bedroom.

"Over the course of the subsequent months, Robert and Tabitha were able to enjoy their passionate liaisons, usually on Mondays but sometimes on Tuesdays or Wednesdays. But one night, Tabitha's maid was ill, and her substitute had trouble navigating through the darkness of the bedrooms and mistakenly tied the string to William's toe instead of Tabitha's. And when Robert tugged on the string and William unknowingly turned over in his drunken stupor, the substitute maid led Robert to William's room. Without thinking, Robert undressed quickly and slipped under the covers. And quite to his chagrin, as he pulled himself closer to the body he thought belonged to Tabitha, he realized, upon touching William's hairy back, that he was in the wrong bed. William was horrified, and, in a rage, kicked poor Robert and pummeled his face, blackening both his eyes before coming to his senses and realizing that the man in his boudoir was not a perverted intruder but instead was his hapless valet.

"The next morning William confronted Tabitha, who denied any romantic involvement with Robert. William, of course, knew differently, but rather than divorcing Tabitha, he deemed her act of infidelity a license for him to more actively pursue his own improprieties and decided that it was in his best interest not to fire Robert. But he needed to assert his authority over Tabitha and punish her accordingly. To do so, William confided in her eldest brother, Eugene, about her misdeeds. Eugene, who had bullied Tabitha when she was a child, told William that he would discipline her by charging into her room on that very night, disguising himself with a black hood, and spanking her butt with a pussy willow. But unknown to William and Eugene, their conversation was overhead by Tabitha's maid, who, by then, was back at work, and who dutifully informed Tabitha of their intent.

"Tabitha, in turn, told Robert, and Robert decided that he would take Tabitha's place in her bed, while she hid in his valet quarters. And as planned, Eugene barged into Tabitha's room in the middle of night, and, when he raised his pussy willow, Robert sprang from the bed and ripped Eugene's hood from his face, cursing him at the top of his lungs, waking William, who charged through the door connecting his room to Tabitha's. But Robert held his ground and demanded that William be banished from Tabitha's room forever. William was furious, but he was ultimately rendered powerless when Robert informed him that he had secured signed affidavits from three of his harlots and that he was prepared not only to turn them over to the police but also to release them to the press if William did not leave Tabitha alone.

"In the morning, nothing was said of this encounter. That night, when Robert visited Tabitha, they professed their undying love for each other. And from that day on, they lived as happily ever after as was possible, given the circumstances of their lives. Their romance, of course, remained a 'secret,' as Tabitha and William never formally divorced in accordance with their prenuptial agreement, thereby affording themselves the pleasures of the annual dividends from the irrevocable trust their parents had established on their behalf. Photographs in a recently discovered album attest to the beauty that Tabitha retained, despite the realities that she no doubt endured but somehow managed to overcome. Records show that Tabitha, against all odds, pursued a college degree in forensic social work and spent her last decades as a volunteer, counseling runaway teenage girls and advising them on the legal remedies available to them to counter the abusive treatment of parents and spouses alike.

"According to legend, as no public announcement was ever made, Tabitha died from a massive heart attack on July 4, 1957, after having what was rumored to be the best sex of her life. Robert passed away exactly one year later.

"William, it was gossiped, contracted syphilis at the age of fifty from one of his harlots. And when he had one of his legs amputated due to a diabetic infection, he was confined to an undisclosed facility on the Upper East Side, where he went blind and lived, defying all expectations, until his death at age eighty-three."

Richard sighed, "What a horrible story."

Max, however, applauded and proclaimed, "Well, well. All I want to do right now is open another bottle of Chardonnay and drink myself into oblivion while we talk about the cruelty and vigilante justice in Maggie's unseemly tale."

Maggie stood up. "My story has little to do with vigilante justice. For me, the lesson of the story is straightforward: one bad deed deserves another."

Cynthia weighed in, "It's difficult to determine who the real protagonist was, given that both Tabitha and William were villains in their own ways. Poor Robert was a victim, much like a prostitute who does what must be done to survive."

Barb countered, "C'mon, Robert was in love with Tabitha, because, surely, by the time of their deaths, their sex lives were more of a fantasy than a reality."

Max disagreed, "Well, I'm not so sure about that. I deeply believe that his libido lived on, even after his passing, and transferred to the person he loved the most during his lifetime."

Eleanor scoffed, "That's ridiculous!"

I was amused.

I expected Hannah to be disgusted. But instead, she said, "I was impressed by how well the story evoked the spirit of *The Decameron*. For me, the moral is plain and simple. It makes me think of Ephesians 4:22–24: 'Put away . . . your former manner of life . . . corrupt after the lusts of deceit . . . that ye be renewed in the spirit of your mind, and put on the new man, that after God hath been created in righteousness and holiness of truth.'"

Maggie was excited, "Yes, exactly. The story of Tabitha, William, and Robert is a warning about what not to do, but it's also a story of true love—illicit as it was."

I wondered why Maggie had picked this story. What was she really trying to say? Did it have anything to do with me? Or was she revealing something about her own life that she couldn't talk about?

Maggie thanked Hannah for sharing the Scripture.

Hannah was thrilled and added: "'. . . present your bodies a living sacrifice, holy, acceptable unto God . . .' Romans 12:1."

Max cringed, "I'm sorry to say, Hannah, but sometimes you make me remember parts of me I'd rather forget. I was forced to go to Vacation Bible School the summer of my thirteenth birthday. And as much as I resented it, I came home enlightened and confessed to my parents that another boy and I had fondled each other in the pool and ended up sleeping together in the same bed."

Hannah recoiled and, in a shaky voice, replied, "I have one more Scripture I'd like to share before heading outside for a walk. 'Your iniquities have separated between you and your God, and your sins have hid his face from you, that he will not hear.' Isaiah 59:2."

Max frowned, "You have no right to judge me."

Hannah turned toward Max and said sternly, "'Judge not, that ye be not judged. For with what judgment ye judge, ye shall be judged: and with what measure ye mete, it shall be measured unto you.' Matthew 7:1–2."

Max shrugged, "Whatever."

Richard poured wine for Eleanor, Maggie, Max, Cynthia, and me. Hannah left the room, smiling, saying that she was at peace and hoped we were, too.

After Hannah left, I was ready to leave, too, but I sensed that Eleanor and Cynthia wanted me to stick around. Max and Richard were tipsy and becoming obnoxious. But when Sandra marched into the room, I almost choked. There was something about her demeanor that reminded me of an SS officer in a World War II movie.

Sandra's tone was gravely serious. "First, the good news. Josette is going to be discharged later tonight, earlier than expected. She doesn't have a fever, and there's some worry among her doctors that, given the surge in virus patients, it's critical that she be sent home as soon as possible. Second, I had a long talk with the police concerning the report that needed to be filed about the incident, and that discussion led to a more detailed dialogue about Good Samaritan laws, which might come into play once the police and the insurance companies get involved."

My heart sank. I stared at Sandra, and her face went blank. I had nothing to say, and neither did she.

I savored my last sip of wine and exited the room. I felt everyone staring at me, but I didn't look back.

Day 9

THE REPAIRMEN ARRIVED EARLY AT THE cottage, waking me from a deep sleep. My stomach was knotted up and my right hand was numb from the way my head was positioned on the pillow crumpled on top of my forearm. I wrapped myself in my terrycloth robe and cracked open the door to get a better sense of what was going on. Then I headed downstairs.

I could hear Maggie coordinating the work crews, which all seemed to be demanding her attention at the same time. The glaziers were busy replacing the window glass, and the carpenters and painters were assessing what needed to be done next to fix cracks and damage in the trim and framing. The carpet cleaners hauled in their hoses and vacuums to sanitize the living room, veranda, and other areas of the cottage where the rain had seeped in. Cynthia was spot-cleaning the seat cushions of the chairs and couch, and Eleanor was wiping down the credenza, end tables, and any furnishings that might have been contaminated.

It was overwhelming, and I rushed back upstairs. I wasn't ready for this.

Just then, I heard a big thud followed by moaning, and, when I looked down the hallway, it was Josette. She'd slipped on the hardwood floor outside her bedroom and broken her fall with her good hand but bumped her bandaged hand against the doorjamb. I hurried toward her and reached down to help her up, but she motioned me away. "Please! I've been advised not to talk to you until the facts and causes of my injury are established and documented."

Stung, I said, "I'm so sorry. I was only trying to help." Josette turned away and managed to stand up by herself, lifting her bandaged hand back into its sling as she limped off.

I was a mess and retreated to my bedroom to shower, shave, and brush my teeth. But every step forward seemed like two steps back. When I pulled on my jeans, the zipper got stuck, and the more I yanked on it, the more its teeth got entangled in the denim. Finally, I gave up and put on another pair of jeans and threw on a flannel shirt. While I was lacing up my hiking boots, there was a knock on my door.

It was Hannah. Her face was glowing as she looked into my eyes, "I was thinking about you all night. I have another Scripture to share with you, if you want to listen." I nodded, and she whispered, "'. . . by faith into this grace wherein we stand . . . we rejoice in hope of the glory of God. And not only so, but we also rejoice in our tribulations: knowing that tribulation worketh steadfastness; and steadfastness, approvedness; and approvedness, hope: and hope putteth not to shame; because the love of God hath been shed abroad in our hearts through the Holy Spirit which was given unto us.' Romans 5:2–5."

I lowered my chin to my chest and closed my eyes, meditating on what Hannah had just said, but, when I looked up and opened my eyes, she was gone. I worried that I had somehow hurt her feelings. But when I went downstairs for breakfast, she was talking with Eleanor and Barb as if nothing had transpired between us.

Sandra and Josette were in the back corner of the kitchen, rattling on about their Voodoo shrine. They glanced in my direction but didn't acknowledge that I was there.

No one wanted to talk about the ramifications of what Sandra had said about Good Samaritan laws, and neither did I.

After breakfast, Barb announced, "Josette is my pick to be the new queen for the day," and then asked her to post the time for our next storytelling session on the refrigerator. Josette seemed ambivalent, glad to be named queen, but, at the same time, she acted a little miffed that she hadn't been chosen sooner. "There is no need to post a time. I've already decided. Storytelling is going to be at 6:00 p.m. in the garden. You'll all need to wear a jacket because it's going to be chilly, if not downright cold."

Max said, "I'll make hot toddies," and Josette laughed and mentioned that, as much as she appreciated his offer, no alcohol would be served. Sandra applauded, and she and Josette left the room.

Max was hungover, and Richard escorted him upstairs, saying, "I'm really behind on my email. I've got to check in on my B&B. The girl I hired to watch the place texted me that a pipe burst."

"Details, details. I have a headache," Max said. "I'm so out of touch. But then again, I planned it that way. After all, I do have a private practice. And I canceled my appointments, not that I had many, before I left town."

Cynthia asked me if I wanted to go with her to the shed. Hannah, Eleanor, and Barb planned to stay behind to help Maggie. The repairmen were going to be working at the cottage all day.

Cynthia grabbed a heavy wool sweater and a small toolbox, and I got my down jacket.

Outside the air was raw and damp. But Cynthia was happy: "I love dreary weather. I do!"

Josette and Sandra were in the garden, and Sandra was showing Josette where she wanted to reconstruct the framing of their shrine. There was a sawhorse, a couple of sheets of plywood, and six two-by-fours stacked beside them. As we walked by, Sandra pulled a few tools from the box—a saw, a hammer, a screwdriver, and a plastic box with nails and screws.

Josette was complaining, "My right hand is useless. Useless!"

Sandra tried to console her, "I'm ready to do whatever you want me to do. Just tell me."

Josette perked up, chanting, "I can feel the spirits rising from the soil and hovering over the shrine. 'For, behold, the day cometh, that shall burn as an oven; and all the proud, yea, and all that do wickedly, shall be stubble: and the day that cometh shall burn them up, saith the Lord of hosts, that it shall leave them neither root nor branch. But unto you that fear my name shall the Sun of righteousness arise with healing in his wings; and ye shall go forth, and grow up as calves of the stall. And ye shall tread down the wicked; for they shall be ashes under the soles of your feet in the day that I shall do this, saith the Lord of hosts.'"

Cynthia stopped and offered to let them use the electric drill that she had in her satchel, but Sandra was skeptical, acting as if borrowing it might in some way obligate her to Cynthia and even to me. When Cynthia told her that she was only trying to be helpful, Sandra sneered, "No need to go out of your way for us."

Cynthia marched off in front of me, shaking her head, disappointed. But by the time I caught up with her, her mood had changed. The shed was her solace, and, when she stepped inside, she sighed.

I was still reeling from the awkwardness of our interaction with Sandra and Josette, but Cynthia did what she could to make me feel better. She pulled a baggie filled with pieces of Barb's *confetti* from her satchel and said, "Just looking at them gives me a sugar rush."

I was so glad to be with Cynthia in the shed. But it was still kind of strange. It was like the shed was our escape from the cottage, which was intended to be an escape from the reality of our day-to-day lives. But now the escape from the escape was weighing me down.

Cynthia didn't want to focus on my convoluted obsessing and did her best to encourage me. "Andy, you need to let go of everything that's bothering you and make the most of what we are doing right now." She handed me a flashlight and shovel, then donned her helmet and pried open the trapdoor with the spade.

Cynthia lowered herself into the compartment, and I followed close behind. The ladder seemed more unstable than before, but I figured this was more a reflection of my state of mind than a structural flaw. But when Cynthia looked around, she screamed, "Someone's tampered with our excavation site. Again!"

What didn't make sense was that she had padlocked the door to the shed and no one had a key but her, which meant that the intruder must have found the key in her belongings.

I asked Cynthia if she thought someone was watching us with a surveillance camera that was imbedded somewhere in the ceiling or in the mortar of one of the walls. She laughed, "Possible but unlikely, but, then again, if there is a camera, maybe it's installed outside the shed, perhaps on one of the eaves of the stable."

Cynthia climbed quickly up the ladder, and I told her I was going to check the ceiling and walls, just to be sure. But I didn't find anything, and neither did Cynthia, who concluded, "Someone must have been watching firsthand what we were doing. And from my point of view, the only person it could be is Maggie, who not only knows more about the cottage and its environs than anyone in our group but is probably at the stable right now while we're working. And Maggie is the only one who had access to my room, especially when we were all downstairs."

Cynthia wasn't deterred. But she was concerned that if Maggie found out what we were really doing, she might try to stop us. What Cynthia had discovered needed to stay our secret until she at the very least figured out how to loosen the stones in the back wall.

Cynthia scraped at the limestone mortar between the stones, and, while most of it was difficult to scratch off, there was one section that crumbled into her hands, leaving a gap wide enough for her fingers. And once she had brushed away the fragments of mortar, she felt a small lever, which she was able to jar forward with her screwdriver, activating the gear system on which the stones seemed to pivot. The wall opened before us! Cynthia and I were stunned. And once the stones separated, we saw a cavernous corridor that was tiled in mosaic patterns that reminded Cynthia of what she had seen years ago in the Medina of Fez, Morocco.

Before entering the corridor, Cynthia wanted to be sure she would be able to seal it off again when we left. She pulled the lever back toward her, and the wall closed. She was pleased that the gear system was operational.

Cynthia tightened her fanny pack and tool belt. "I think it might be best if you didn't come with me at first. The flooring could be unstable, and if, for whatever reason, it caved in, you could go for help."

I nodded *okay* and she said, "Well, I started reviewing the handwritten documents in German and Italian, but I'm still confused. While the drawings indicate there's another level beneath the compartment, the documents only discuss the corridor in front of me that's supposed to narrow into a tunnel that extends for nearly two hundred meters and leads to a subterranean hot spring, surrounded by different species of ferns and algae, some of which the writer believed were edible."

Cynthia stepped into the corridor but had gone only ten feet when she had to stoop because the ceiling sloped down and stalactites of different sizes obstructed her view. She removed a small pick from her tool belt and scraped samples of what appeared to be calcium salts into a vial she pulled from her fanny pack.

I shouted to her to be sure she was okay, and she stepped backward, away from the stalactites, and turned around, assuring me that she was fine. But when she got back to the compartment, she started coughing, apparently from the calcium dust she had inhaled. I handed her a plastic bottle of water and she took a big gulp, but the coughing persisted.

Cynthia sat on the floor of the compartment, propping her back against the stone wall, then leaned forward, gasping for air. I massaged her back, and her breathing finally evened out.

It was time to return to the cottage, but Cynthia pleaded with me to stay a little longer. She wanted me to see the corridor and the tunnel up close, and she needed to examine the calcium samples she had collected. She had brought some kind of chemical test kit in her satchel, and she organized a rack with a few test tubes that she placed between her legs. But before she got started, she handed me an N-95 mask, gloves, and a pair of goggles, and I inched my way into the corridor, sliding my hand across the mosaic tiles, trying to avoid the stalactites, but it was an obstacle course. A few of the stalactites broke off from the ceiling and shattered onto the ground.

I could hear Cynthia telling me to be more vigilant, but I had a hard time talking to her through the mask. The ground was uneven, and I didn't want to trip. And as I proceeded deeper into the tunnel, I heard a strange gurgling sound, which I assumed had something to do with the hot spring that Cynthia had seen referenced in the Italian and German documents. But I couldn't see very well. My goggles were fogging up.

The walls on both sides of me bore a slick film that was thin and watery, but, as I went deeper into the tunnel, it seemed to have a greasier texture. Then I felt something crawling on my hiking boot. My flashlight revealed a small lizard tracking past my ankle and slithering up my leg into my underwear. I squirmed around and grabbed my crotch, trying to loosen its sticky feet from my groin. I quickly unzipped my jeans and the reptile popped out on the ground and scurried away. I swiveled the flashlight around but got just a glimpse of its tail as it burrowed into a hole in the ground.

I was lightheaded and had to steady myself against the tunnel wall as I worked my way back through the corridor into the compartment. And when Cynthia saw me, she said, with a laugh, "You look like you've seen a ghost. Your skin is pasty white, and your zipper is down."

When she asked me if I had peed my pants, I was mortified. I knew she was only joking, but the way she was acting made it all the more difficult for me to tell her what had happened. When I did, though, she said I was *too cute,* questioning whether the creature was actually a lizard, explaining, "One of the only lizards to be found in New England is the five-lined skink. But it's largely extinct in this region of the country, though they have been documented around the Housatonic River in Litchfield and New Haven Counties."

I asked how she knew so much about the five-lined skink, and she reminded me that her father was a reptilian biologist whose idea of a family vacation was traipsing his kids through the woods to see who could find the most species of lizards and salamanders.

There was so much about Cynthia that wowed me. She loved what she did, whether it was making things or exploring some place where she had never been before. But she was a moving target, and sometimes her thoughts seemed to sprint out in front of her, and I could barely catch up.

She asked me what the five-lined skink, if it was one, looked like, and I said I wasn't sure. Once it popped out of my pants, it was gone so fast that it was impossible for me to remember what I had seen for only a few seconds.

Cynthia tossed me a bottle of water and motioned for me to sit down beside her, which I gratefully did. I needed a break. And she giggled, "Let me tell you what you missed. Five-lined skinks are sleek and slick. They are usually about five to eight and a half inches long, including the tail, and have rows of tiny scales that wrap around the middle of their body. On their backs are white or yellowish stripes, but as they age, their coloration varies; the stripes darken, and the tail often turns gray. Males are much more territorial than females, especially when they're breeding. The color of their heads and jaws often becomes an orangish-red as a display of aggression. Male skinks have been known to bite their attackers, but generally speaking, never chomp into humans."

I was relieved. But I couldn't wait to get back to the cottage to shower.

Cynthia took my hand and then pulled away from me, giggling, "I don't think five-lined skinks are carriers of the virus, but you can never be too cautious."

Cynthia jerked down on the wall lever and the stones slipped into place, closing off the corridor from view. Then we climbed the ladder out of the compartment, padlocked the shed, and walked as quickly as we could to the cottage. Cynthia swung her arms back and forth as if she were in a race. I took giant steps to overtake her, but, in the end, I knew she was going to get to the garden before I did.

The air was brisk and the light was stark, and, as we neared the cottage, we could see the silhouette of the shrine that Sandra and Josette were erecting. It was carefully placed on the perimeter of the garden on the east side of the veranda and was constructed with mounds of dirt outlined with a series of irregularly shaped rocks, flower vases, and incense burners. Josette appeared to be meditating, her palms pressed together in silent prayer.

Cynthia approached Josette with a gentle plea to allow us to be with her in this very special place. Josette turned toward me, and, as she revealed the prayer beads between her hands, she asked me to join her in praying the first two verses of Psalm 51. She looked deep into my eyes and waited patiently for me to steady myself. And once she began, I repeated the words after her: "Have mercy upon me, O God, according to thy lovingkindness: according unto the multitude of thy tender mercies blot out my transgressions. Wash me thoroughly from mine iniquity, and cleanse me from my sin. For I acknowledge my transgressions: and my sin is ever before me."

Josette placed her gloved hand on my forehead: "I am breaking the rules of social distancing for a divine purpose, and, because of that fact, we will not be at risk."

Cynthia stepped back, shaking her head in disapproval.

Josette waved her prayer beads in the air, and Sandra lit the candles surrounding the shrine. Incense wafted in the air.

I looked at Josette and nodded.

Maggie, Hannah, and Richard filtered out of the cottage and gathered around us.

Maggie frowned.

Richard was beaming.

Josette prayed, "Create in me a clean heart, O God; and renew a right spirit within me. Cast me not away from thy presence; and take not thy holy spirit from me. Restore unto me the joy of thy salvation; and uphold me with thy free spirit. Then will I teach transgressors thy ways; and sinners shall be converted unto thee. Deliver me from blood guiltiness, O God, thou God of my salvation: and my tongue shall sing aloud of thy righteousness. O Lord, open thou my lips; and my mouth shall shew forth thy praise. For thou desirest not sacrifice; else would I give it: thou delightest not in burnt offering. The sacrifices of God are a broken spirit: a broken and a contrite heart, O God, thou wilt not despise."

My face flushed red.

Cynthia was shocked.

Everyone began chattering among themselves. Josette reached for my right hand with her left and droned an incantation in a language I didn't recognize as she lifted my arm, touching my fingertips to the sling that held her right hand, saying loudly, "Only through your confession of sin can you be healed."

Cynthia pronounced Josette's proselytizing unacceptable. Maggie agreed and insisted that, unless Josette relented, the storytelling session should be adjourned.

The group was silent until, finally, Josette said, "So be it."

Sandra echoed, "So be it."

"Richard," Josette drawled, "please tell us your story."

The wind picked up; the temperature was dropping fast. Maggie,

Cynthia, and Hannah excused themselves to get blankets, and, as they handed them to each of us, we all seemed to feel better, conceding that somehow in spite of all the acrimony and Josette's incantations, we were still bound together, whether we liked it or not.

Richard cleared his throat and began, the candles flickering around him. And as he spoke, his words flowed in a tone that was more solemn than I had expected. "Dear friends . . . oh, to say the word friends, what does this mean? Especially at a time when our relations with one another are so strained. For me, true friends are not people who make your problems disappear. They are the people who care.

"Before we came to the cottage, we knew little about what was actually going on in each of our lives, other than the fact that we were all asymptomatic, and the sickness and death we had witnessed was weighing us down, motivating us to seek each other out in a chat room we found online, and then to leave our homes to shelter in place with people we didn't really know.

"So here we are. I had prepared one story," Richard said, "and now I feel compelled to tell another, inspired by Boccaccio's Eighth Day, Seventh Story, about a man named Antonio, who concealed his background from everyone he met. Even his closest friends had no idea where he was from or what he did to support himself. But that said, he was completely gregarious. Every night, he frequented different bars in New York City, though his identity was different in each of the venues where he was known as a regular customer.

"Most of those whom he spent the most time with thought that he suffered from some type of multiple personality syndrome, because he was a chameleon of sorts, and the styles of clothing that he wore varied from night to night, but it was completely clear that he favored Italian designers, principally the cruise wear of Cucinelli and Zegna, the garish patterns of Etro and Gucci, and the staid elegance of Isaia.

"Antonio was a hunk who worked out three times a week at a gym in Midtown, and it was there that he met a woman named Rina who was so beautiful that he pursued her with a zeal that defied any good reason, because she had dutifully, on the day of their very first meeting, informed him that she was deeply in love with someone else.

"One afternoon, when by coincidence their workouts ended at the same time, they exited the gym together, and he invited her to join him for a drink at the bar at Eight, located at 8½ West 57th Street, a place where he would not be recognized, because he had never been there, but had heard was an *in* place to go.

"Much to his surprise, she agreed, but after one drink she said she had to leave, because she was meeting her lover for dinner at a restaurant nearby. But before they parted ways, he asked her for her address, to which he said he would like to deliver a special gift.

"A few days later, he brought her a potted Dendrobium orchid; these are more enduring than many other varieties and are often recommended for people, like her, who might otherwise be afraid to grow orchids. But unfortunately, she wasn't at home. However, her lover was in her apartment and unknowingly buzzed Antonio in. Needless to say, it was an awkward moment that left Rina's lover wondering if she had been unfaithful to him.

"Antonio, sensing his jealousy, decided to return the next day. But this time, Rina was ready for him and hatched her own plan to mitigate the suspicions of her lover.

"When Antonio arrived at her apartment, Rina instructed her maid to greet him and to take him to an interior courtyard of the building reserved for residents and their guests. Antonio was delighted and followed the maid with great anticipation for the liaison he hoped to have with Rina. But after an hour of waiting, neither Rina nor the maid appeared, and when Antonio tried to leave the courtyard, he discovered that the metal gate was locked. And as dusk descended and darkness filled the courtyard with an eerie glow, the air grew colder and colder, much like it has done today in the Berkshires.

"Antonio was freezing, and, as the hours passed, he grew weak but managed to insulate himself by wrapping his body in trash bags that he scavenged from a dumpster outside the gate, reaching between the metal bars that had imprisoned him. Little did Antonio know that Rina had been watching him with her lover at her side, mocking Antonio's foolishness to convince her lover of her devotion to him. And that night, the passion between Rina and her lover soared to new heights.

"In the morning, after her lover left for work, Rina went to the courtyard to revive Antonio, who by then was beginning to lose consciousness. Rina apologized, explaining that she had been so preoccupied with a crisis that involved her brother and mother that she had completely forgotten about him after her maid had left for the day.

"But Antonio didn't believe a word that she said. The fingertips on his left hand were frostbitten, necessitating emergency treatment. And Antonio scrambled to get away from Rina as quickly as he could and vowed revenge.

"Weeks passed, and Antonio recovered, slowly regaining most of the use of his fingers, and, once the bandages were removed, he resumed his bon vivant lifestyle with a vengeance. He trusted no one.

"When he finally returned to the gym to work out, he saw Rina and did his best to avoid her, until she approached him to once again apologize for her negligence. And while Antonio's first impulse was to ignore her, he realized his opportunity for revenge. Rina was weeping and confessed to him that, in fact, she had wanted to be with him instead of the man who was at the time her lover, who had seduced her with lavish dinners and a pearl necklace that she later determined was a fake. Not only was her lover a liar and a jealous madman, but he was also cheating on her and was even caught in her bed with her maid in the middle of one afternoon when he was certain that Rina was still at work.

"Antonio feigned sympathy and invited her to accompany him to a friend's country house about fifty miles outside of New York City. Rina was excited, but, when she opened her arms to hug him, he pulled back, saying that his fingertips were still tender and he needed to be careful not to reinjure himself.

"The drive north on Route 9 along the Hudson River was dreamy, and Rina was so smitten by Antonio that she was willing to do anything to please him. When they got to the country house, the first thing Antonio wanted to do was to take Rina up the water tower to see the breathtaking views of the rolling hills of Duchess County. But the ladder was narrow, and Antonio urged Rina to climb ahead of him, so that if she were to lose her footing, he would be able to steady her.

"But when they reached the platform on top of the water tower, Antonio backed away, saying that he had marveled at this view many times by himself, and that it was his wish that Rina have the same experience. But Rina was nervous and said she was afraid of heights. Antonio told her that the only way to overcome her fear was to confront it alone.

"Antonio promised that he would return in about half an hour, but as he climbed down the ladder, he decided to implement the strategy he had devised to teach Rina a lesson that she would never forget. And when his feet touched the ground, he unlatched the ladder from the pulley system that supported it, thereby stranding Rina on the platform, without her knowing it until she grew impatient and called for Antonio to help her climb down.

"Antonio, relishing her discomfort, failed to respond for more than two hours. The sun rose high in the sky, beating down on Rina's face, melting her mascara and makeup and burning her delicate skin to a ruddy hue. By the time Antonio hoisted the ladder back in place,

Rina was dehydrated, and her fluffy summer dress was drenched in perspiration and other bodily fluids I will not even attempt to describe.

"Antonio apologized, mocking Rina's lie when she abandoned him, by telling her that he had been preoccupied by a crisis involving his mother and brother. But unlike Rina, who did little when he was suffering from frostbite, Antonio rushed Rina to the emergency room of a local hospital, where she received treatment for the unsightly and painful blisters that had formed on her cheeks and forehead and caused her face to swell.

"Rina refused to speak with Antonio for months, but, as she healed, she was overwrought with a gnawing sense of guilt that she was the cause of her own undoing. And in time, she realized that she was doomed to bear the scars on her face for the rest of her life.

"Antonio, haunted by his own evil deed, also suffered complications. And while he was told that his fingertips would one day regain their sense of touch, they never did. The end."

Sandra glared at Richard and clamored, "To be honest, Richard, your tone of voice was insulting, and the abject depravity of your story was a total turnoff."

Josette raised her left hand and stammered, "Ye have heard that it hath been said, an eye for an eye, and a tooth for a tooth: But I say unto you, That ye resist not evil: but whosoever shall smite thee on thy right cheek, turn to him the other also."

Hannah chimed in, "Yes, indeed. 'But I say unto you, love your enemies, bless them that curse you, do good to them that hate you, and pray for them which despitefully use you, and persecute you.' Matthew 5:44."

Maggie scoffed, "I've heard enough."

Barb rolled her eyes, and Eleanor snickered, "That story sounded so much like *The Decameron* that it makes me want to go reread the reference."

Richard stretched his neck and head backward. Max donned a fresh pair of gloves and took Richard's hand in his. Sandra reprimanded him, "It's as if you're wearing gloves as a style statement."

Max flipped her the bird and exited the garden as quickly as he could.

Everything had gone from bad to worse. Cynthia whispered, "Andy, I'd like to spend more time with you. In private." I nodded and neatly folded my blanket, offering to take hers and mine back to the veranda.

Maggie stood up. "Not so fast! No one leaves the garden until I say so. We need to discuss what we, as a group, are going to do next. Everything is becoming so . . . dysfunctional."

Eleanor objected, "I need more time to think about it," and Barb clapped her hands. Sandra, Josette, Hannah, Richard, and Max left en masse.

Maggie was fuming, but she bit her lip, holding back her outrage and refocusing her attention on Cynthia and me. "No one, obviously, is listening to me, and both of you are just as bad. But at least I feel I can communicate with you. Please, may I join you for whatever? I know I'm imposing."

Cynthia was dismayed. But I could tell Maggie was in need and said, "Yeah, I get it. Sure. We don't really have any plans, and you're welcome to hang out with us, somewhere out of harm's way, wherever that might be."

Cynthia acted like I was right and warmed up to Maggie, who suggested that we go into the basement, where there was an old sofa and a couple of overstuffed chairs. It sounded great to me, and Cynthia agreed.

I followed Maggie and Cynthia into the kitchen to the basement door, expecting that downstairs would be musty and damp. But when Maggie flipped on the lights, it was totally different. The ceiling and walls were paneled with end-matched tongue-and-groove knotty pine planks. And there was a small fireplace, with a cord of logs stacked neatly in a wrought iron rack.

The sofa and chairs had fatigued leather cushions, and on the floor was a kilim rug with an elaborate rust- and bone-colored tribal design. Cynthia and I sat on opposite ends of the sofa, while Maggie opened the flue and damper above the fireplace and gathered a few logs to start a small fire.

"I just wish we could all get along better," Maggie said, and Cynthia asked, "Isn't it unrealistic to think we can all become friends in such a short time?"

"Everyone just seems to pull back when someone starts to speak up," I added. "You know, say what they're really feeling, afraid, maybe that they're going to hurt someone else's feelings."

Maggie laughed, "If anyone's guilty of holding back, it's you, Andy, especially as it relates to Josette's accident. Sandra and Josette are jumping all over you. You act complacent. Resigned."

I knew Maggie was right, and the anxiety that had been eating away at me surged up. "What am I going to do if Josette presses charges against me? What if she really makes good on Sandra's threats to get a lawyer?"

Cynthia sighed, "I wish you'd stop asking such ridiculous questions. Sandra and Josette are needling you because they have nothing better to do. Ignore them and they'll leave you alone."

Maggie disagreed. After all, Josette might be disabled for life, and, from what she had overheard, Sandra was vetting litigators in Western Massachusetts. "Josette," Maggie said, "I sense isn't completely on board with Sandra, but the more Sandra hammers on her, the more likely she'll be willing to go along with whatever Sandra's cooking up."

I asked Maggie if she knew anyone who might represent me, and she said, "I can ask my father who he thinks might be best. I'm glad that you're starting to see the merits of getting legal counsel before the crap hits the fan, because, once it does, there's no turning back the clock."

Cynthia concurred, "As much as I don't want to believe it, Maggie is giving you sound advice. If you don't get in front of what is inevitably headed your way, it's going to run you over before you even have a chance to defend yourself."

What I had hoped was going be some downtime was everything but. Maggie said I looked pale.

Cynthia got up and told me to lie down, but Maggie joked, "Andy, I think you should lower your head between your knees first because you look like you're going to puke all over me, the sofa, and the rug. And I don't want to clean it up."

I forced a little grin and Cynthia knelt down and unlaced one of my hiking boots, and Maggie decided to unlace the other. I laid my head back on the cushions, and they lifted my legs onto the sofa and giggled as they pulled off my socks.

Cynthia smiled, "Andy, your feet are so cute." And Maggie said, "'Cute' isn't exactly the word I would use. But on the plus side, they aren't stinky."

Cynthia pulled a small tube from her purse and squirted hand cream onto the instep of my right foot, then handed the tube to Maggie, who did the same to my left foot, though some of it oozed between my toes. When I jerked my foot away, Maggie said, "Just because you're ticklish doesn't mean you can kick me in the face." We all laughed, and Cynthia and Maggie massaged my feet, almost in unison.

I closed my eyes and drifted away into the ozone of my imagination, fantasizing that I had time-traveled to a faraway place where I was completely at peace. When they finished, my eyelids sprang open, but I didn't want to get up. It was the first human physical contact I'd experienced in months.

Cynthia and Maggie seemed delighted, and they looked at

each other as if they knew I was totally turned on and so were they. Cynthia and Maggie stepped back to put on the masks they had in their purses, then moved closer to me. I fumbled around and managed to pull my mask from my back pocket and lowered it over my nose and mouth as quickly as I could, just as Cynthia and Maggie descended on me, loosening my belt and easing my jeans off my waist and positioning them below my knees.

Maggie massaged my thighs, and Cynthia inched her fingers onto my balls, and then they switched off and playfully teased me until I was fully aroused. My head sank deeper into the cushions, and my glutes tensed up as my pelvis rocked up and down in their hands.

I was hot, and they were steaming, each of us hypnotized by a music that we all seemed to hear, soaring to a crescendo in an indescribable ode to joy. Our bodies separated ever so slowly, and I dozed off. When I awoke, Cynthia and Maggie were sitting across from me, their eyes flickering, as if we were sharing the same dream.

Upstairs, Hannah and Josette were arguing, and the sound of their voices was getting louder and louder.

I dressed quickly, and Cynthia and Maggie perked up. Maggie brushed her hair, and Cynthia straightened her sweater, which was bunched up under her breasts.

We hurried into the kitchen, thinking that maybe we could help, but it seemed futile. Hannah was more upset than I had ever seen her, and Josette was just as smug and arrogant as ever.

Hannah snapped, "Just because you quote from the New Testament, it doesn't make you a Christian."

And Josette countered, "No matter how hard you try, you do not *own* the Bible, because, in the end, it belongs to anyone who cares enough to read it."

Hannah backed off.

Cynthia, Maggie, and I refused to get sucked into their fight and walked past them without making eye contact with either of them.

Then we saw Sandra in the back corner of the kitchen, scowling at us with her arms folded in front of her, curious to find out what we were doing in the basement. But we ignored her, and each of us went up to bed, looking back at each other as we opened our doors, marveling at what had happened and wondering if it could ever happen again.

Day 10

LIGHT AND SHADOW DANCED TOGETHER THROUGH the gap between the curtains in my room. *Ring around the Rosie, Ring around the Rosie* echoed in my head before I fell down, slipping on the rag rug that Hannah had made for me. I was half asleep and still dreaming. Cynthia and Maggie were taunting me to either join the game or stay out. I tried to do both.

When I went downstairs for breakfast, Cynthia and Maggie looked like they were waiting for me. I nonchalantly opened the refrigerator door and offered to get them juice and yogurt, and they said they'd already eaten.

Cynthia joked, "I can tell something's bothering you by the way your upper lip is quivering."

"Oooh!" Maggie added, "She's right. Did we do something we shouldn't have done?"

"It was innocent," I said, measuring my words, trying to sound reassuring.

"It was a little weird," Maggie cooed, and Cynthia giggled.

I was still groggy. "Sometimes what we don't understand we appreciate all the more."

Cynthia shook her head, "Yes, that's true."

Maggie smiled, "Enough said," and seemed to relax but then asked in a more serious voice, "I know you two have been up to something in the shed. And I'd like to know more."

Cynthia acted as if she'd been expecting Maggie's question and began, "Well, first of all, Maggie, I want you to know I was drawn to the shed because I'm a tool person. As an engineer, I'm always on a quest to understand what makes things work, and how they're designed and built."

Maggie was amused. "I know that, and I do admire your commitment, but I wonder whether or not whatever it is you're doing is truly worth the trouble."

Cynthia took a deep breath. "Look, every day I go to the shed I learn something new, but, at this point, I can't provide details."

"Well," Maggie said, "from what I've seen, there isn't much there."

I tried to intervene, but neither of them seemed interested in hearing what I had to say. Cynthia was acting paranoid and overly aggressive, and Maggie was pissed off.

Finally, Cynthia admitted that she had padlocked the door because there was evidence of an intruder. "I just didn't want to see any of the property owner's belongings disappear."

Maggie looked at her in disbelief and said, "Oh, really? Just remember. Digging under the shed is forbidden."

I excused myself and said that I needed to get something from my room.

Maggie called out for me to come back, reminding me that it was Day Ten at the cottage and that we needed to schedule a group meeting to determine how and when we were going our own ways.

I reluctantly turned around, and, just as Cynthia was about to talk, Sandra and Josette walked into the kitchen, accompanied by a stranger, who handed me two envelopes and said, "You have been served."

The man exited quickly, but Sandra and Josette stayed behind, watching me as my jaw dropped in disbelief.

Inside the first envelope was a subpoena for me to give a deposition in the civil suit that Josette had filed against me and in the second was a letter from a Stockbridge police lieutenant advising me that I was a person of interest in a criminal investigation of Josette's injury.

Maggie shouted for Sandra and Josette to back off, but they didn't budge. Max, Richard, Eleanor, Barb, and Hannah trickled into the kitchen. Cynthia pleaded, "Please, we need to stay calm."

"The charade of playing king and queen is over," Maggie announced. "From now on, I'm in charge. Everyone is required to attend our group meeting at five o'clock this afternoon."

No one objected. And for a few minutes, everyone quieted down.

Attempting to add some levity, Richard broke the silence and said, "Sounds important. I wish I'd brought a suit and tie."

Maggie yelled, "Enough!" and left the room. Cynthia and I followed close behind her. In the foyer, Cynthia apologized to Maggie, who said she needed to apologize, too, not only to Cynthia, but to me as well. It was stupid to argue about the shed, considering my impending legal problems and everything else going on. Maggie said, "I've called my father on your behalf, Andy. He'll know what you need to do."

I looked at her apprehensively but thanked her nonetheless. I was so out of my element.

But then Cynthia shifted gears and appealed to Maggie for more time in the shed, saying that she wanted to take me with her to get my mind off all of the BS that was raining down on me. Maggie gave in, reminding us, "Whoever's snooping around the shed might be dangerous."

Cynthia didn't appear especially concerned, but, then again, she hadn't really told Maggie the truth. And I was starting to worry that we were going to find something we'd wish we hadn't gone looking for. When we got to the shed, the door was wide open. The padlock was on the ground, but it wasn't broken. Someone had removed the wood planks to which it was attached. Cynthia stepped cautiously inside, taking the spade that was propped against the wall and handing it to me, and then grabbed the shovel for herself—just in case we needed to defend ourselves.

Cynthia slid back the table covering the trapdoor, and, when she looked inside with her flashlight, everything appeared to be the way she had left it the day before. Then she asked if I wanted to go first, handing me the flashlight as she donned her miner's helmet.

I grabbed the spade with one hand and lowered myself into the underground compartment slowly. When my feet touched the ground, I was relieved but still a little shaky inside. Cynthia passed me the shovel, then eased her way down with her satchel in one hand and a knapsack with a couple of bottles of water in the other.

Cynthia wanted to do a more thorough inventory of the papers in the file drawers and asked me to dust off the chair next to the table, as well as part of the bed frame, so we could both sit down. I put on a pair of latex gloves that Cynthia gave me and wiped the chair seat first, but the dust was thick and a little gooey, as if something had dripped onto the surface. Cynthia passed me some disinfectant from her satchel. The spray was effective, loosening the grime and making us feel a little safer and more comfortable.

Cynthia pored over the documents that she emptied from the file drawers, arranging them by subject and then by date, if any. It was becoming clear to her that someone had used this area not only for storage but as an office, or maybe a fallout shelter. But there was no evidence of food or other supplies.

I was impatient and wanted to explore deeper into the tunnel, and Cynthia said, "I'm okay with that," and laughed. "But there might be spiders or snakes, or lizards that aren't as friendly as the first one you encountered." Cynthia pulled the wall lever, and the entrance opened before us. But when we stepped into the corridor, we noticed footprints that we hadn't seen before.

Cynthia was alarmed, but I told her I wasn't. I was happy to have something to distract me from everything that was going on.

In a serious voice, Cynthia noted that the patterning of the footprints revealed that whoever went into the corridor apparently left in a hurry. The tracks were smeared and seemed to indicate that the person had slipped and fallen. On one of the mosaic tiles, there was a trace of blood.

Cynthia couldn't figure out exactly how the person had injured him- or herself. The tiles were smooth, but she speculated, "Perhaps the person was carrying some kind of pointed object or tool, and, when he or she tripped, they were cut or stabbed, or maybe an existing wound that was bandaged had opened and oozed a little blood."

I began to think that it might have been Sandra and Josette and asked, "Why would they go to the shed and mess around with what we were already doing?" Cynthia replied, "Maybe they want to exact revenge on you, Andy, and figured one way to do that would be to booby-trap our excavation site. But apparently something prevented them from doing that, and they changed their minds. And they decided to get a lawyer and go to the police instead."

Cynthia and I joked about the goofy Sandra-and-Josette scenario we were imagining, but we did know for certain that there had been at least one intruder and that we needed to proceed with caution. Cynthia maintained that since we'd found a trace of blood, the corridor should be treated as a possible crime scene. We needed to gather whatever evidence we found, because it could be useful later. Cynthia took a DNA test kit from her satchel and collected a blood sample from the tile and sealed it in a tube.

"Where'd you get that?" I asked, amazed that she actually had a DNA test kit.

"It was in the tool kit in the trunk of my car. Believe it or not, it was a Christmas present from my parents."

Cynthia decided to abandon the documents that she was sorting, thinking out loud that it would be best if we coordinated our efforts in exploring the corridor and the tunnel. We squeezed between the stalactites and Cynthia wondered, "What if the stalactites were actually calthemites, secondary deposits formed from concrete, lime, mortar, or other calcareous materials outside a cave environment?"

The deeper we went into the tunnel, the more I expected to see lizards or some other sign of life. The ground was slick with some kind of watery residue that Cynthia was concerned might be seepage from drainage pipes overhead. The support system for the tunnel was a strange mix of two-by-fours and boulders that were propped in an irregular configuration that Cynthia observed was more ordered than it had first appeared.

After about ten yards, the tunnel widened into another underground room with a ten- or twelve-foot cathedral-like ceiling. The ground was sandy, and there was evidence of a firepit that had left a blackened circular shape in the middle of the room. Cynthia poked around in the ashes, and when I turned my flashlight in her direction, I saw a glint of light reflected in the sand. I knelt and smoothed my hand on the surface and saw what seemed to be some kind of pendant. And when I brushed off the sand, I recognized it as a *corno*, or *cornicello*, meaning "little horn," an Italian amulet or talisman that was worn to protect against the evil eye.

Cynthia was surprised that I was able to identify it, and I explained that my girlfriend was Italian and always wore a gold *corno* that had belonged to her grandmother on a thin chain around her neck. But finding this *corno* in the sand was a sad reminder of what I was trying to forget.

Cynthia could tell that my talking about my girlfriend was a downer, but she was quick to say that she saw it differently. "I think it's divine intervention. It's perfectly aligned with the documents I've been reading, which were written by an Italian who was presumably involved in the construction of not only the underground compartment but the corridor and tunnel as well. But what happened in this room is still a mystery.

"I'm not an archaeologist," Cynthia said, "but the engineer in me is certain the walls are not man-made. We're standing in a cave that was likely prehistoric but had obviously been adapted for other purposes over the course of decades, if not centuries." Cynthia leaned against the wall directly in front of me and knelt, combing through the sand as she systematically moved toward me, wishing she had a sifter because she could feel tiny pottery shards and chips of glaze, which she scooped up into a plastic bag she had in her fanny pack.

I followed Cynthia's lead, and, about a foot behind me, I saw another shiny object that turned out to be a *mano fico*.

Cynthia knew what it was, and I told her about Maggie's story of the gardener at the cottage finding one years ago.

"Really?" Cynthia asked. "Incredible! The gardener must have known that he was onto something, but he didn't know enough."

"But where did he get the documents and drawings?"

"No telling. For all we know, they might not have even been his. Someone else could have put them in the file drawers for safekeeping. But this is where he must have kept the *mano fico,* or maybe he just dropped it when he was poking around."

"Somehow, I expected it to be more elaborate."

"Andy, it's beautifully crafted and contains the most essential elements. The *mano fico* represents a woman's genitals, and the hand gesture signifies intercourse. But like the *corno,* the *mano fico* is also used for magical protection against the evil eye."

Cynthia motioned for me to sit on the floor of the cave with her. She inched her hand across the sand, and, as I eased in next to her, she massaged my thigh with her fingertips. I was turned on. She giggled, "I love being with you . . . because you're so gullible."

I balked at the word gullible, and Cynthia said she didn't mean it in a negative way. "It's just that you're such a newbie when it comes to science. But you're trusting and passionate without really trying."

I didn't feel particularly passionate, but Cynthia smiled, "Oh,

Andy, you're working so hard to hold back your sex drive that it makes you sexier."

I closed my eyes and laid my head on her thigh, and she stretched out her legs. I rolled over, and, in the quiet of the cave, we connected in ways I had never thought possible without ever taking off our clothes.

By the time we stood up, we were both a little unsteady, holding onto each other to regain our equilibrium. We weren't ready to leave. Cynthia wondered if the tunnel extended beyond the cave in the direction of the cottage, but she couldn't find the entry point. The walls seemed solid, but, as we moved around the cave, she saw a section of what appeared to be quarried stones that had been covered in plaster and rubbed with dirt to make them blend in with the wall. Cynthia chipped away the plaster with a wire brush. Then she asked me to help push against the stones and discovered that they weren't stones at all. They were wooden frame boxes, layered with painted papier-mâché that broke apart to reveal an opening in the wall that was too narrow to crawl through.

Following the light on her helmet, Cynthia reached inside with her hands but then jerked back. "Wow! I can't believe it!"

I craned my neck over her shoulder. "What is it?"

"It looks like the fingertips of a skeletal hand that's encrusted in some kind of calcified sludge."

The bones were brittle and began to crumble. Cynthia picked up as many fragments as she could with tweezers from her tool belt and placed them into a stoppered test tube.

Then she pulled a small pointed probe from her fanny pack and poked around, and the encrustation around the hand cracked open, exposing the long, bony fingers of a skeleton that was bejeweled with gold rings mounted with gemstones and diamonds. Cynthia was awestruck, and I rushed over to see for myself.

We looked at each other in disbelief.

We didn't know what to say. And all of a sudden, I started worrying about the intruder, and how he or she might be lurking in the shadows behind us. But before I could say anything to Cynthia, she darted away, working her way back through the tunnel and the corridor into the compartment, shouting, "I need to be sure there's no one else in here."

When I climbed the ladder out of the underground compartment, I was nearly out of breath. Cynthia was sitting on a folding chair, musing that it was likely that the intruder was not Maggie, Sandra, or Josette, but instead was someone who knew more than we did. But the gnawing questions were *why* and *how*.

I wondered, "Maybe we're just being used. Maybe we were only given use of the cottage because whoever owned it, or had knowledge of the skeletal remains with the gemstones and diamonds, needed a couple of twenty-somethings like us to do the exploring for them. And the reason the cottage was on the market for so long was that they didn't really want the property to be sold, at least not until the hidden relics were found and removed."

Cynthia hypothesized, "Yes. In fact, the bejeweled skeleton or, perhaps, skeletons that have yet to be uncovered, might actually be more valuable than the cottage and its grounds. I've read a lot about relics of this kind after seeing a couple on display in small churches on a school trip to Germany when I was in junior high school.

"Around 1578," Cynthia explained, "workers in an in Italian vineyard accidentally discovered that a hollow along Rome's Via Salaria led to a catacomb. And after painstaking excavation, researchers proved that the catacomb was full of more than five hundred thousand skeletal remains, presumably dating back to the first three centuries following Christianity's emergence, when thousands were persecuted for their religious practice. When the Catholic Church learned of this discovery, priests and parishioners alike believed they were a godsend, since many of the skeletons must have belonged to early Christian martyrs. In Northern Europe, especially Germany, where anti-Catholic Protestants had vandalized churches and plundered their sacred relics, these holy skeletons became sought-after treasures. And when churches received the skeletons, parishioners often adorned them with golden clothing and sometimes even filled their eye sockets and imbedded their teeth with rubies, emeralds, and other precious gems. But during the Enlightenment, these bejeweled skeletons were deemed excessive, and many were hidden away or disappeared."

Cynthia stood up and signaled for us to go back underground, but, before we did, she reattached the broken wood planks and moved the padlock to the inside of the shed door; that way, no one could enter without our knowing it.

As we made our way slowly back into the tunnel, I began to have second thoughts and asked Cynthia who we could tell about our discovery. "At this point," she said, "we need to be really cautious. Because, as much as I believe Maggie, I'm starting to have doubts about her father, who's friends with the property owner. I need time to send off the blood sample and bone fragments I've collected for DNA testing and then try to consult with forensic specialists to help analyze the data."

Inside the cave, Cynthia measured the dimensions of the hollowed-out cavity that contained the bejeweled hand, trying to determine whether it was connected to a full body or was in proximity to other skeletons that had been placed inside. And at the same time, she tried to figure out how to seal off the wall so that what we had done to excavate it was not so obvious.

Cynthia said, "We need some of kind of plaster to patch up the wall, but there's no access to water. So I'm not sure I'll be able to prepare the right mix of dirt and calcium deposits to make it look untouched."

I offered to go back to the cottage and get a bucket of water, but

Cynthia was concerned that if I went by myself, I might get cornered by Maggie or Sandra or Josette or someone else demanding to know what we were doing in the shed.

Instead, Cynthia thought that possibly we could involve someone else in our escapade, someone who wouldn't freak out and go blabbing to everyone else. I suggested Hannah or, perhaps, Eleanor, or even Barb. Hannah, Cynthia worried, was too moralistic and would likely feel like she was lying. Eleanor and Barb were better options, though Eleanor seemed preoccupied with the dairy farmer and keeping up with her advocacy work in San Francisco. So we settled on Barb, who was principled but also was an out-of-the-box kind of person. After all, she was willing to track a homeless guy and his carrier pigeons.

While Cynthia went back up the ladder to call Barb, she asked me to gather up the broken pieces of plaster that she had removed and to grind them with a rock into finer sediment in preparation for making a paste to smear on the wall once we were able to get some water.

I was glad to help, even though I didn't really understand why Cynthia wanted to go to so much trouble to cover up what we were doing. She said she had a plan, and I believed her.

But when she returned, she said she had decided against calling Barb. I remembered seeing running water and buckets in the stable, which was so close to the shed that no one, other than Maggie, could possibly notice.

"It's safe to go to the stable now," I said, "because Maggie isn't there."

"Just be careful."

"Don't worry, Daisy likes me."

"Well, that could be a problem."

Getting a couple of buckets of water was easy, and I passed them carefully down the ladder to Cynthia, and together we carried them through the compartment, the corridor, and the tunnel into the cave. And without much trouble, Cynthia's formula for mixing plaster worked, and she was able to cover the hollow cavity and smear enough of the paste onto the walls that, by the time she was done, our excavation efforts were barely visible.

Both of us were hot and sweaty, so we cooled off in the shed before heading back to the cottage. Once again, Cynthia moved the padlock to the front of the door, knowing all too well that the intruder would be back. As we walked across the lawn, the sun burst through the clouds, illuminating our path, filtering through the trees, and mottling the grass with shadows. Cynthia took my hand and started skipping. I could barely keep up, but somehow I did. And when we were about ten yards from the garden, Cynthia pulled away and sprinted toward the cottage. I could have done the same, but I didn't. I lagged behind and enjoyed watching her act like a kid. But as I got closer to the cottage, I dreaded my next encounter with Sandra and Josette, who were no doubt lurking around, plotting how to make my life more miserable.

In the distance I saw Maggie waving from the garden. She was pacing around the shrine that Josette and Sandra had built, stewing about everything she hated about it. Not only had they disobeyed her, but they had erected it in a place that was offensive, overtaking the garden and intruding on the pristine views of the grounds from the veranda.

While Cynthia and I were away, they had added to it and constructed an altar, using an old wooden shipping crate that they had found in the basement. With Sandra's help, Josette had lined the crate with aluminum foil and then positioned her sacred objects inside—laminated photographs of her venerated ancestors, a brass crucifix, two incense burners, three plastic snakes, and a resin-coated skull.

Maggie said, "I should have confronted them while they were

working. But I never thought they would go this far. And now I don't want to antagonize Josette further, because her injuries are so severe."

I swallowed hard and told her what Josette had said about the healing power rising from the garden.

Maggie rolled her eyes, "Andy, her right hand is essentially paralyzed. She has no movement in her fingers, and it now appears that the nerve damage is permanent."

I was stunned. I wanted to say something but couldn't find the right words.

Maggie tried to reassure me. "Everyone knows it was a terrible accident and you did the best you could to stop the bleeding."

Maggie sighed, "I talked again to my father, and he spoke to an attorney in Lenox who agreed to represent you at your deposition." Then she handed me a piece of paper that was folded up in her purse, on which she had printed the attorney's contact information with the text that her father had emailed to her, paraphrasing Section 12V of the Good Samaritan statute for the state of Massachusetts.

I read it aloud: "'Any person who, in good faith, attempts to render care and assistance to a person who is in need of care, and does so without compensation for the care from or on behalf of the person cared for, shall not be liable for acts or omissions, other than gross negligence or willful or wanton misconduct, resulting from the attempt to render such care and assistance.'"

Maggie said, "I hope this attorney can help you. But I have to tell you. I've been advised not to talk to you any further about it, especially since I might be called as a witness."

I understood all too well. I was on my own. I thanked her for the contact information for the attorney and trudged into the cottage. The reality of all the legal wrangling ahead of me sank in. My throat was parched. I needed something to drink, and, in the kitchen, Hannah was washing dishes. When she saw me, she smiled and said, "I've been praying for you."

As much as I appreciated her concern, I wasn't in the mood for talking, but she pleaded with me to tell her what was bothering me. So I sat down at the kitchen table, and she brought me a glass of ice water, offering to make a pot of tea. And I mumbled, "Okay."

While she filled the teapot with water, she told me about her day, reading Scripture and helping to clean up the mess the workers had left behind. There were muddy footprints on the Persian rug in the entry foyer and grungy leaves in the living room, blown through the shattered window by the storm.

Hannah prepared a tray with almond cookies and the blue Sorrentino tea set that she took down from a cupboard above the kitchen counter.

I knew that Hannah was hoping I'd open up to her, but part of me had already shut down. I couldn't handle it. I had nothing to say.

Hannah took my right hand in hers, acknowledging that she was breaking our rules of social distancing, saying that she felt compelled to do so because she could see I was suffering. I pulled back, but she tightened her grasp.

I took a deep breath, and she lifted her Bible from her purse and read to me Luke 10:25–37, the parable of the Good Samaritan: "'And, behold, a certain lawyer stood up, and tempted him, saying, Master, what shall I do to inherit eternal life? He said unto him, What is written in the law? how readest thou? And he answering said, Thou shalt love the Lord thy God with all thy heart, and with all thy soul, and with all thy strength, and with all thy mind; and thy neighbor as thyself. And he said unto him, Thou hast answered right: this do, and thou shalt live. But he, willing to justify himself, said unto Jesus, And who is my neighbor? And Jesus answering said, A certain man went down from Jerusalem to Jericho, and fell among thieves, which stripped him of his raiment, and wounded him, and departed, leaving him half dead. And by chance there came down a certain priest that way: and when he saw him, he passed by on the other side. And likewise a Levite, when he was at the place, came and looked on him, and passed by on the other side. But a certain Samaritan, as he journeyed, came where he was: and when he saw him, he had compassion on him, and went to him, and bound up his wounds, pouring in oil and wine, and set him on his own beast, and brought him to an inn, and took care of him. And on the morrow when he departed, he took out two pence, and gave them to the host, and said unto him, Take care of him; and whatsoever thou spendest more, when I come again, I will repay thee. Which now of these three, thinkest thou, was neighbor unto him that fell among the thieves? And he said, He that shewed mercy on him. Then said Jesus unto him, Go, and do thou likewise.'"

I sipped my tea slowly, and a quiet settled around us. As the daylight in the kitchen waned, I felt Hannah's love for me, and the love that I was beginning to feel for her. But at the same time, I wondered if either of us could ever truly fulfill the other's needs.

It was time for our group meeting, and no one knew where Eleanor and Barb were. Sandra and Josette were still upstairs napping.

Eleanor had said something about going back to the dairy farm, and Barb wanted to go with her. Maggie was impatient. She had changed into riding clothes and boots, but it seemed unlikely that she would have time to go the stable after our meeting.

When Josette and Sandra stepped into the kitchen, Hannah and I stopped talking. Sandra acted proud of herself. In her mind, she was in control, but she seemed less confrontational and exuded a strange self-confidence.

I could tell that Josette was hurting. Her face was pale, and she struggled to position her bandaged hand in her sling. Cynthia asked her how she was doing, and she grimaced as she and Sandra sat down on two stools on the opposite side of the kitchen from Hannah and me.

Maggie was ready to start the meeting but was disappointed that

Eleanor and Barb were late. She shifted her weight from foot to foot, and, after about ten minutes, she said, "If they don't show up soon, I'm going to postpone the meeting until later." She had a notepad under her arm and held a laser pen that she flipped on and off, drawing attention to herself in a way that made me uneasy.

Finally, Eleanor and Barb appeared and apologized for their tardiness, telling us that the old dairy farmer had died from the virus, which he had contracted in the hospital. And when they had gone to the farm to offer their condolences, his family members kept asking them questions about when and where his milk had been delivered in town. One of his sons, who worked as a tax lawyer in Pittsfield, said he thought the beneficiaries of his milk should make contributions to help cover the old man's burial expenses, even though there wasn't going to be a funeral.

Maggie was fidgety and asked Eleanor, as politely as possible, to save her story for later, and Eleanor shut up, a little bothered by Maggie's formality.

Maggie began, stumbling with her words in a way that seemed out of character. "I want to thank all you for your participation in our . . . well, this somewhat unique attempt to shelter in place together. Sadly, it didn't exactly work out as we all had hoped." Then she turned on her laser pen and pointed to areas of the kitchen that were still a mess, reminding us that we needed to do what was necessary, as we all had agreed, to leave the cottage in better condition than we found it.

Richard raised his hand, and Maggie reluctantly asked him to speak. Richard said, "Max and I are willing, in addition to assisting with cleanup, to make a cash contribution."

Cynthia, Hannah, and Eleanor all chimed in that they could also make a donation. And I stuttered, "I don't have much of a savings account, but I am certainly able to work."

Sandra said that she could help fund some of the repairs but that

Josette, because of the severity of her injury, shouldn't be expected to do so.

Barb was embarrassed and offered to do whatever, from scrubbing floors to raking leaves.

Maggie was pleased and said that she would post a list on the refrigerator, that each of us could sign up for times when we were available.

Sandra announced, "More subpoenas for depositions will be forthcoming for those who witnessed Josette's accident."

No one responded except for Cynthia, who maintained, "Sandra and Josette's legal maneuvering should no longer be discussed among ourselves. Not only is Sandra trying to poison our relationships with one another, but her vitriol is a form of harassment."

Sandra stood up abruptly, clamping her hands on her hips, and, just as she was about to let loose, Josette grabbed her forearm and said, "I'm sorry to have caused so much acrimony. But to be honest, I have to come to terms with what appears to be a permanent disability. And the liability for my medical and rehabilitation expenses has to be established. I don't have any health insurance."

I apologized to Josette for the damage I might have done and reminded her in as kind a voice as I could muster that it was just an accident, that I panicked and had to do what I could to help her.

Josette gritted her teeth and stomped out of the kitchen, with Sandra a few steps behind. Hannah asked for a moment of silence to pray for Josette, and for me, and we all bowed our heads. When we were done, Maggie said she wanted to continue our storytelling sessions on a nightly basis, stressing the need for us to not completely break apart as a group.

After all, Hannah added, "*The Decameron* involved ten days of storytelling, but it was spread over two weeks. One day per week was dedicated to chores, and, on the holy days, they didn't do any work at all."

Maggie nodded, "Okay, then, our next storytelling session will be the day after tomorrow. We need a day to work and a day to rest." All agreed. And as everyone split apart, Maggie oohed, "Look, at that full moon! It's breathtaking, Andy. You want to go with me for a horseback ride?"

"Yeah, sure."

Cynthia and Hannah acted surprised when I accepted Maggie's invitation, but then Cynthia said, "Sounds great. It will be good for you, Andy, doing something other than dwelling on your legal dilemma."

On our way to the stable, Maggie asked, "What are you and Cynthia really doing in the shed?" I didn't want to lie to her, so I told her the truth. "It's better that I don't talk about it. Cynthia made me promise that I wouldn't." And Maggie grimaced. I could tell she knew all too well that we were up to something more than just another Rube Goldberg invention, and any attempts by me to convince her otherwise weren't going to work. And the more I squirmed around in the generalities of my answers, the harder she pressed for details. But I resisted, and, finally, after I pleaded, "I need you to stop. It's too much for me to handle," she backed off.

Dusk streaked its last bursts of orange and red, and darkness descended as the moon rose above the horizon. Daisy and Harry neighed loudly when Maggie slid open the stable door. They were hungry. Maggie placed her hand on Harry's forehead, petted down over his nose, and encouraged me to do the same with Daisy. Then she pulled a baggie filled with sliced apples out of her purse and handed it to me to feed both horses while she filled two buckets with oats. And once Daisy and Harry were done eating, she asked me to help saddle them up for our ride.

The night air was brisk, and the terrain had an eerie iridescent glow. The rocks on the trail shimmered, drawing us deep into the woods. Daisy kept pace with Maggie and Harry without my having to do much at all. I was in awe. I felt like I was on a surreal journey into a landscape where everything around me was melting into a mélange of silky textures draping the moss-covered gorge in front of us.

Maggie slowed Harry to a stop and dismounted. And as Daisy eased up, she took the reins from my hands and tied them around the trunk of a sturdy white pine, then helped me to the ground. The moonlight streamed through the trees above the Ice Glen Ravine onto the maidenhair ferns blanketing the forest floor.

I reached for Maggie's hand, and she moved closer to me, but she only touched my fingertips with hers. My body yearned for her, but she was reticent, telling me without words that she didn't really trust me.

I squatted and picked up a handful of pine needles, dropping them one by one onto the ground. I looked up and said, "Maggie, I really am grateful for all you've done. And I don't really know how to tell you, but what I feel for you is deep. But somehow it touches part of me that hurts."

"I know you have problems."

"That's an understatement."

"How long were you and your girlfriend together before she died?"

"Not very long. I met my girlfriend kind of by accident."

"What was her name?"

I didn't want to tell her.

"Something wrong?"

My eyes were burning, and, as I wiped away the tears, which I hoped Maggie couldn't see, I blurted out, "Jessica."

"Why is it so hard for you to say her name?"

I couldn't answer. I asked Maggie if we should head back to the cottage. She shrugged *no*. "If anything," she said, "I wish we could spend the night on this site overlooking the ravine."

I cleared my throat. And Maggie whispered, "I understand, Andy. I do. But it's time to get on with your life."

"I guess."

I wrapped my arm around the trunk of the white pine where Daisy was tied off and joked, "How about a ménage à trois?"

But Maggie didn't think it was funny. "Don't you ever think *that* will happen again."

I told her that it was all new to me, too. She scoffed at my use of the word *it* and said in a blustery voice that it was a weak moment, when the three of us caved in to feelings that were no doubt driven more by loneliness than affection.

It was clear that my allegiance to Cynthia was a problem for Maggie and that nothing I did was going to make a difference to her, unless I revealed what we had found in the shed.

I untied Daisy's reins from the tree trunk and struggled to get back in the saddle. Maggie mounted Harry and took off without me. Daisy charged ahead, and by the time we got to the stable, Maggie was waiting for me with a sour look on her face.

"Maggie, I know you're under tremendous pressure, weighted down by the damage to the cottage and everything you can't tell me about your father and the property owner."

Maggie turned and marched out in front of me, and I lagged a little behind. As we neared the cottage, the smell of incense wafted through the air. We heard Josette chanting sounds and words that were barely audible. Candles were flickering in the darkness.

Day 11

THE HAMMERING OUTSIDE MY WINDOW WAS giving me a headache. I tossed and turned in my bed. I hadn't slept well. For most of the night, I dreamed I was standing in the middle of the street, with a group of people surrounding me and throwing balled-up sheets of paper at me that piled up at my feet faster than I could pick them up. And when I got up to pee, they stopped, but, once I returned to bed, I drifted back to that same street and all the people were gone. I swept up all the wadded-up sheets of paper and unfolded them one by one, only to discover that on each page there was a single word or phrase that I needed to arrange in the right sequence in order to form sentences that, when pieced together, turned out to be my deposition about Josette's accident.

I was a wreck.

Cynthia knocked on my door. "Andy, are you okay?"

I stumbled out of bed, and, when I was about to open the door, I realized that I was naked.

Cynthia knocked louder, startling me awake. I grabbed a robe, and when Cynthia entered my room, she seemed relieved. "I could hear you groaning in the hallway. It was that loud."

"I was having a nightmare."

We sat down on opposite sides of my bed. It was 11 a.m., and Cynthia told me that everyone else was doing chores. "I've already cleaned Sandra's, Josette's, Richard's, Max's, and Maggie's bathrooms. And in the process of doing so," she said in a mischievous voice, "I gathered samples of hair, toenail clippings, and even a couple of crumpled-up Band-Aids that I plan to send for DNA analysis to see how the results might line up with the traces of blood and bone fragments."

I was sleepy, but what she was saying was still registering with me.

Richard was in the hallway yelling that we all needed to get downstairs and out of the cottage.

There was a fire in the kitchen, and Eleanor called 911. Apparently, there was a gas leak in one of the pilot lights of the stove, and, when Barb was heating some oatmeal, the burner burst into flames. Luckily, Barb got out of the way in time.

The fire spread quickly from the stove to a dish towel, and, when Eleanor saw what was happening, she scooped it up with a pair of tongs and rushed it to the sink, but she bumped into the window valance and knocked the curtain rod out of its socket, and the curtains tumbled over and ignited in seconds.

Maggie doused the flames with a bucket of water and, thankfully, the damage was minimal. But smoke billowed through the kitchen.

Maggie was flailing her arms and shouting, "How could you be so stupid?"

Richard and Max were stunned, as were Eleanor, Barb, Hannah, Cynthia, and I. Everything had happened so quickly. We weren't exactly sure what to do.

No one knew where Sandra and Josette had gone.

Sirens were blaring outside. A policeman and three firemen charged through the front door.

The policeman looked at me suspiciously, and I turned away.

On the front lawn, another policeman and the fire marshal were talking with Maggie and taking notes for their report on the fire. But as I walked by, the policeman introduced himself as the lieutenant who had written the letter that Sandra had delivered to me with the subpoena and then asked when I wanted to come to his office in Stockbridge to make a formal statement about what happened on the day Josette was injured.

I told him that I was trying to contact an attorney to represent me but hadn't reached him yet. The policeman handed me his card with instructions for me to schedule an appointment as soon as possible.

Cynthia was concerned, and I assured her that everything was under control. But I needed to make a telephone call and told her that maybe once we finished our chores we could get back together later in the day. She strained a little smile, and I hurried off to my room where I could have more privacy.

The attorney, Charles Wilkins, answered after the third ring and said, "I've been expecting your call." And after about ten minutes of trying to explain what happened, he asked, "Can you come to my office today? You'll need to sign an engagement letter, and then we'll have a little sit-down to discuss a viable plan of action and the payment terms."

We made a two o'clock appointment, which gave me time to do my share of work around the cottage. I walked downstairs into the kitchen. Maggie had opened the windows and was placing a box fan on the counter.

She complained, "No one's listening to me. Instead of becoming more careful, it seems like everyone is more careless."

I asked her if I could help, and she pointed to the stove top and counters that were dusted with ash and soot. Then she handed me a few rags and a sanitizing all-purpose spray.

I felt myself welling up inside but didn't want Maggie to notice.

"What's wrong, Andy?"

"Everything."

In the distance, I could hear Hannah humming a hymn that I remembered from Sunday school when I was a kid.

In a strange way, Hannah reminded me of a little girl I knew when I was small. Maggie and Cynthia were like high school girls I was interested in but never got to know because I wasn't cool and didn't fit in with that crowd.

Maggie saw that I was preoccupied and asked, "So, what are you thinking about?"

"Right now? My appointment with the lawyer you told me about."

"Well, that's good. I'm sure he'll know what to do."

I could tell she still wanted to talk about the shed, but I avoided bringing it up until Cynthia showed up. Instead I offered to take out the trash and recycling. When Cynthia walked into the room, Maggie seized the moment to ask her straight out what she was excavating.

Cynthia was taken aback by Maggie's bluntness, especially by her use of the word *excavating*. Maggie glared at her, then at me. But Cynthia wasn't fazed and said, "Okay, I'll tell you. I'm focusing on the layers of soil compression to better understand the history of the site, which, I believe, predates the construction of the cottage and maybe has something to do with early Italian immigrants to Massachusetts and perhaps even Boccaccio himself, or his children."

Maggie looked at Cynthia as if she were nuts. I was just as weirded out as Maggie was. I had never heard Cynthia talk like that. She was always so scientific, and her reasoning was usually easy to follow. But connecting the layers of soil compression to Boccaccio was so out there that it didn't make much sense to me. That said, Cynthia's strategy worked, and Maggie stopped asking questions about the shed.

Cynthia and I wiped down the kitchen counters and cabinet doors, while Maggie struggled to remove the burn marks from the stainless sink, worrying that it was permanently stained.

Max came into the kitchen and said, "Cynthia, my dear, I overheard you talking about Italian immigrants, and I think that's so interesting, especially because I've been doing some family research about my Italian ancestors."

Cynthia replied, "All of a sudden, I'm *my dear*?"

"I want to know more."

"I don't know very much. I'm just in the beginning stages of my research."

Max laughed. "Well, I want you to know that I sent off a DNA sample to Ancestry.com, and I'm waiting for the results. Just thinking about the fact that we're actually staying in a replica of an Italian villa turned me on from the get-go."

I had to leave for my appointment. It was later than I thought, and I wasn't sure where I was going. But Lenox was small enough that finding the attorney's office on Pine Knoll Road seemed easy.

The office was located in a white colonial-style house, where, presumably, the attorney also lived with his family. But when I rang the doorbell and was buzzed in, I saw that it was subdivided into different office suites. The attorney was standing in the hallway with a powdery blue surgical mask on his face and latex gloves on his hands and said, "Welcome, welcome. Please call me Chuck. No formalities here."

I followed him into his two-room office. In the front, his secretary, Greta, greeted me with a nod, and Chuck shook my hand with a hearty laugh, his bushy salt-and-pepper hair bobbing above his Ralph Lauren denim shirt, creased khaki pants, and burgundy loafers.

The wood plank floor squeaked as we entered his office, and he gently closed the door. The walls were lined with oak bookshelves on which legal tomes were interspersed with Currier and Ives prints of steamships.

He grabbed a yellow pad off his desk and suggested that we sit catty-corner to each other, "friendly-like." I lowered myself slowly into one of his tufted leather chairs and stretched my back, and he joked, "Comfort, but not too much, means the world to me. Spring comes slow to Western Massachusetts, though winter often roars through and a leaves a pile of dirty snow, sometimes until May."

I squirmed uncomfortably in my seat.

"Well, well," Chuck said. "If I were in your situation, I'd be nervous, too. But I do hope I can set your mind at ease. I like to think that I can talk to anybody, a trait that makes me especially well-qualified for presenting my case to juries, young and old, Black and white and, these days, a spattering of Mexicans, Mohicans, and Chinese, among others. Ordinary folks, just like you."

I told Chuck everything I remembered about Josette's accident, and he began quizzing me about the witnesses who could testify on my behalf. I talked about the pros and cons of Maggie, Cynthia, Hannah, Eleanor, Richard, and Max. They all seemed supportive, but I had no idea about what each of them might actually say, except for Cynthia and Hannah, who I felt for certain would speak in my defense.

Chuck listened intently, and, when I was done, he said matter-of-factly, "Each of the potential witnesses needs to be deposed. And for me to get started, I can agree to an initial cap on my work of $25,000, an estimated fifty hours at $500 per hour. If I work more than fifty hours on the depositions, you wouldn't have to pay for the excess hours, except if the amount of my time exceeded sixty hours, then the time I work beyond sixty hours will be billed at $500 per hour up to a secondary cap of $50,000. However, if we were not able to settle the case out of court, then I would have to charge you $500 per hour up to a cap of $25,000 for the preparation for the jury trial, and then if the preparation were to exceed twenty-five hours, you would get the next five hours of my time free of charge. And unless we agree otherwise, I won't bill for any work on the depositions or trial preparation in excess of one hundred hours. And if I work less than the cap or secondary cap, if applicable, you will only have to pay for the time I actually worked."

My head was reeling. I didn't have $25,000, let alone $50,000 in case Josette's case against me went to court. But Chuck wasn't finished: "To represent you at your deposition to the police and for any subsequent work related to criminal charges that might be filed, I'll have to bill you at the rate of $650 per hour. Criminal proceedings are potentially far more complicated and costly than civil cases."

I was speechless. Chuck grinned, "Rest assured, everything I've told you up to this point was gratis, free of charge, given that you had been referred to me by an old friend."

I explained to Chuck that I only worked odd jobs and that, with the pandemic, I had filed for unemployment benefits as an independent contractor. He backtracked and said that, before moving forward with depositions, he would be willing to do a preliminary investigation of the insurance policies that were in place. "Surely," he said, "the homeowner's policy of the cottage must have some kind of liability coverage for injuries sustained on the property, and this vacant-building liability policy would cover any allegations of negligence leveled against the property owner or his assigns. Of course, if you were found to be criminally at fault, you could become liable for Josette's medical costs, time missed from work, and pain and suffering. So, to be properly prepared, you might want to explore getting a loan from your bank in Texas. Interest rates have never been lower, and in the worst-case scenario, I can recommend you to an attorney friend of mine in Houston who could, if necessary, help you to file for bankruptcy.

"Essentially," Chuck said, "the good news is no one died." In the end, he promised I'd emerge stronger on the other side, explaining that, barring any criminal charges, I might be judgment-proof, meaning that any judgment against me in a civil suit was essentially a waste of time, particularly if I had few tangible assets.

Chuck escorted me to the door, apologizing that he didn't mean to rush me off, but he had another appointment. But before I left, I turned toward him and said that I was ready to sign an engagement letter with him to represent me when I went to the police station in Stockbridge to give my statement about what happened. He stopped short and asked Greta to prepare the documents for me to sign, smiling that these days he had plenty of time.

Greta warmed up, and while she printed the paperwork, she checked Chuck's calendar and said it was wide open and that I should give her a ring after I confirmed a date and time with the Stockbridge police. Before the scheduled meeting, she advised, I should spend at least an hour with Chuck to discuss a plan of action.

By the time I left Chuck's office, the straps on my mask were hurting my ears. I couldn't wait to get outside. I was suffocating, gasping for air. And even though the streets of Lenox were empty, the world around me was closing in. Everyone had finished work for the day and had gone back into quarantine for the night. But then again, some people had probably never ventured out of their houses at all. The number of virus cases in Massachusetts was growing fast. In my car, I pulled off my mask and lowered the windows, turning on the air-conditioning full blast. The air was stale, and I needed to get back to the shed as quickly as possible.

I sped off, and an old woman sweeping the sidewalk in front of a house on Pine Knoll Road shook her broomstick at me to slow down. I did. There was a police car parked at the intersection ahead of me, and the officer inside glared at me as I turned north onto Highway 7.

The maple and hemlock trees were budding out, and the afternoon brightened the road, illuminating the squiggly ribbons of oil slick on the pavement leading me home.

The circular driveway in front of the cottage was crowded with utility vans. NRG Home Power technicians were stringing electrical wires to replace the ones that had been damaged in the storm, and painters were repositioning their ladders.

Maggie raked up leaves and debris while Hannah dragged a broken tree limb to a pile where Max was stacking broken branches. I started walking toward them but then took a quick detour and hurried across the lawn toward the shed.

The door was ajar, and I called out to Cynthia, but there was no answer. Her satchel was placed awkwardly near the ladder into the underground compartment as if, at the last minute, she had decided not to take it with her.

I grabbed the spade and lowered myself into the compartment as slowly and quietly as I could. I didn't want to startle Cynthia, but I worried that if there was an intruder, I had a better chance of defending myself and Cynthia if the unwanted person didn't know I was there. I heard talking in the distance, but I couldn't understand what was being said. And neither of the voices sounded like Cynthia's.

Once I was in the compartment, I was reluctant to enter the corridor that led to the tunnel. The voices were moving toward me, and I lay down on the ground and slid under the bed frame so that I wouldn't be visible. No one was expecting me, but I wondered if they had heard me shouting for Cynthia.

There were two men, whose voices were muffled as their feet scuffed along the ground.

Apparently, they didn't hear me, because they didn't hesitate or look around. After they left, I entered the corridor, still very cautious, fearing that someone might still be inside and that Cynthia might have been injured.

Nothing in the corridor appeared out of place. As I inched my way into the tunnel, I didn't hear or see anyone. I was relieved, but I didn't understand why Cynthia's satchel had been left near the ladder.

I rushed back through the corridor and up the ladder, took a deep breath, and called Cynthia on my cell phone. I tried not to sound as panicked as I felt. She said she couldn't wait to see me. I didn't want to go into much detail about how and why I'd gone to the shed but told her that we had a lot to talk about. When I got to the cottage everyone was buzzing around. Cynthia was in the living room cleaning up the mess the window glaziers had left behind. Maggie was with her, and they were talking about everything that needed to be done.

Both Maggie and Cynthia were eager to know about my meeting with the attorney, and I said as little as possible, though I did mention that I was going to meet with a detective from the Stockbridge Police Department to make a formal statement about Josette's accident.

Maggie raised her eyebrows and glanced at Cynthia, who said, "We were all served while you were away with subpoenas for depositions, and Josette's attorney is coming to the cottage tomorrow with a stenographer and a person qualified to administer oaths." I apologized for causing so much trouble, and Cynthia chastised me, "You're too self-deprecating. Stop it!"

Maggie backed away, telling us that she had to tend to some personal business upstairs, but it was clear that she didn't want to get in the middle of any tiff I might have with Cynthia.

Once Maggie left, Cynthia raised her hands and wiggled her fingers as if to say she was glad that Maggie was gone. I forced a little grin, and she laughed that it had been a very long day and that there were still a few hours of daylight to go.

We exited the living room, and, as we moved toward the veranda, Max appeared and asked, "Can I come with you to the shed?" I could tell Cynthia didn't like the idea, and she brushed him off: "To be honest, Max, we need a little privacy, you know, for our hanky-panky." I couldn't believe she had used the word *hanky-panky*, but it worked. And he joked, "Richard and I prefer the bedroom."

I was embarrassed. Cynthia and I had barely gotten it on. If anything, we were kind of stuck in the teasing and foreplay stage of our relationship. Both of us acted as if we desired more, but day-to-day life at the cottage and our ongoing fears about the pandemic were obstacles that seemed, at this point, insurmountable.

As we walked quickly to the shed, I spilled my guts to Cynthia, ranting that I could barely afford a lawyer to represent me during my statement and deposition, let alone at a jury trial, if it ever went that far. Cynthia was reluctant to ask too many questions about my personal financial dilemma because she could tell that, for me, talking about how I was pretty much broke made me self-conscious.

Cynthia changed the subject to the intruders I had stumbled upon in the shed. I replayed for her what I did, every step of the way, but she wasn't satisfied. She kept quizzing me until we entered the shed and immediately noticed that her satchel was splayed open and that a few of her tools were missing—her micrometer, a tape measure, and a pair of needle-nose pliers.

Cynthia stood up and moved the padlock to the interior doorjamb so that we could control the site while we were there. She donned her miner's helmet and descended with satchel in hand into the underground compartment as fast as she could.

When I lowered myself into the compartment, everything looked different. Whoever the intruders were, they had returned after I left. "Apparently," Cynthia said, "they knew you were there but didn't want to confront you, meaning that they likely live nearby and had probably been to the shed before we ever moved into the cottage."

Cynthia and I proceeded slowly through the corridor toward the tunnel, and, when we got to the lever in the wall, Cynthia activated the gear system. She had jammed a small, pointed rock between two of the teeth in the gears to keep them from moving.

We were relieved to see that the cave was untouched. Cynthia's patch-up on the wall had not been disturbed. I was ready to turn back, but Cynthia wanted to explore the cave more closely, thinking that there might be another hollowed-out section in the wall or perhaps some other apparatus that might open into yet another chamber.

Cynthia was serious. She got down on her hands and knees and methodically brushed her gloved hands on the ground, asking me to do the same, starting from the opposite side of the cave and inching toward the firepit in the center, where we had found the *corno* and *mano fico*. When we were about three feet apart, Cynthia motioned for me to hold still, saying that she heard some activity above where we were working.

We eased out of the cave back into the tunnel and waited, listening for any indication that whoever was there was going to break through the door of the shed. But after ten or fifteen minutes, we decided that it was safe to get back to our excavation. I was exhausted, and our inactivity had only made it worse. The downtime weighed heavy, and the anticipation of giving a statement to the police gnawed at me.

Cynthia said, "I know what you're thinking about," and I nodded that I was okay. Once we got back to work, I was able to yank myself out of the funk that was taking hold of me. Cynthia crawled up next to me and head-butted me in my back, and I slipped forward. Then she lowered her mask from her nose and mouth and kissed the back of my neck. Her lips tingled on my skin, and, by the time I turned in her direction, she had already fitted her mask back over her face.

She was playing a silly game of hide-and-seek, and I loved it. I pulled a mask strap off an ear and told her that, to be fair, I needed to kiss the back of her neck, and she giggled. She leaned over, and I nestled up to her. My lips and tongue touched her skin ever so softly, and she oohed that she felt like a lollipop. We both laughed.

Cynthia straightened up and showed me something in the corner that she had felt with her hand, but it was only beginning to make sense. There were some sharp edges jutting up from the ground that she realized were manmade structural elements in the cave. Someone had either chiseled the rock or maybe even created the cave with a jackhammer or some other industrial tool.

I was, once again, amazed. But I was sinking. I was hungry.

Cynthia offered me a granola bar that she had in her fanny pack, assuring me it wasn't one that Sandra had made.

Cynthia said, "It's time to go back to the cottage. Maggie left a note on the refrigerator about us all convening for another storytelling session around 8:00 p.m."

As we packed up, I asked, "So, when do you want to tell people about the bejeweled hand?" She replied, "I haven't quite figured it out. I'm worried that if it becomes public too soon, the owner of the property will no doubt make his claim, and/or Maggie's father will get involved and try to broker some kind of deal, when it's likely the skeleton or skeletons were stolen in the first place, which was the reason the intruders were poking around."

Cynthia had sent the blood sample and bone fragments via FedEx to a DNA lab in Boston that guaranteed twenty-four-hour service and hoped that the results would establish connections that at this juncture were unknown, speculating that, if we could identify the proprietary owner, there might actually be a significant reward.

I promised to keep our secret for as long as I could, though the pressure to reveal what we were doing was growing with each passing day, and we probably didn't have much time left at the cottage. And once we left, there wasn't much we could do. Cynthia wasn't convinced. Finding out the truth was of paramount importance, because the truth could wield a power that we would never have otherwise.

The walk to the cottage was peaceful. The sky was overcast and the fog rolling in from the east hovered over the grass. Cynthia was swinging her arms back and forth, as she often did, and I was beaming. But then she started whistling an eerie tune, and my mood plummeted. My head was throbbing. And in my mind's eye, waves were crashing into a seawall in front of us. Cynthia was wearing foul-weather gear, and I was ill-prepared, with a skimpy bathing suit and a thin T-shirt that was already soaked.

Cynthia saw me stumbling and took my hand to steady me. I

snapped out of it, whatever it was that had taken possession of me. I wondered if Josette and Sandra had cursed me in one of their rituals, but I was afraid to talk about it. It was too creepy, and I didn't want Cynthia to think I was sick. But the closer I got to the veranda, the more I began to worry that I might be coming down with something.

I had chills, and my body ached. Cynthia was concerned but said that, given my dry mouth and dizziness, it was probably dehydration. She led me into the kitchen and handed me a bottle of coconut water before guiding me upstairs to bed. I was really ready to rest, but Cynthia was uneasy about my sleeping, saying she needed to revive me first. She sat on the edge of my mattress and propped up my pillows so I could sit comfortably and not slip down.

Sandra and Josette sauntered past my open door, peering inside but not saying anything to me, though Cynthia did overhear bits and pieces of their conversation. Josette was complaining that she had been so overlooked by all the pseudo kings and queens that no one had given her an opportunity to tell her story. It seemed to her that they were treating her like some kind of quack because she believed in Voodoo, and this attitude seemed racist and homophobic.

But Sandra said, straight-faced, that Maggie had in fact posted a note on the refrigerator that the next story was to be told by Josette. Josette was surprised because she hadn't seen her name, and Sandra scoffed that it was in the fine print.

I asked Cynthia to please close my bedroom door, which she did. After I drank two glasses of coconut water, Cynthia wiped my brow with a silk hanky from her fanny pack and said I could doze off if I needed to. But she wasn't going anywhere, just in case I passed out from dehydration. I glared at her, but she insisted she wasn't playing around. I was at risk.

Cynthia's assessment definitely made sleep difficult, but maybe that's what she wanted. I did zone out, though, long enough to feel more rested and less woozy.

Cynthia brought me a tray of food, leftovers from a dinner that Richard and Max had whipped up with Hannah, Eleanor, and Barb. There were two pieces of roast chicken that Hannah had made, a green bean casserole that Richard and Eleanor had thrown together with canned mushroom soup, and a pasta primavera that Max said was an old family recipe. Barb had baked a loaf of what she called *hippie bread*, a dense mix of flax seeds, rye, and stoneground wheat flour. And at the last minute, even Josette and Sandra chipped in and made fresh tomato and pickled tofu caprese salad.

I chowed down with Cynthia at my side joking, "You eat like a truck driver, or maybe a wolf that doesn't know any better." She had already eaten with the group and said, "Everyone acted more civilized than I ever expected, given all of the acrimony of the last few days."

I thanked Cynthia, and she admitted, "I'm falling for you, Andy, in ways that are surprising me." But then she backpedaled and said, "Don't get your hopes up, because I've been in this place before."

"It's okay. I get it. After all, I'm pretty much an emotional basket case, alternately grieving and, to be honest, lusting for what I probably can't have."

Cynthia giggled, "We might actually be perfect for each other—that is, if we have the patience to keep it going, flirting and petting and who knows what else, over the next couple of months or years."

I smiled and we went downstairs to the storytelling session that Maggie had convened on the veranda. Maggie said, "I think it's only appropriate that we sit in a semicircle gazing out at the Voodoo shrine."

Josette looked shocked by Maggie's sudden acceptance of the shrine, but there was something about the way her eyes darted back and forth that made me feel she didn't really believe her.

Sandra draped a red cape over Josette's shoulders, and, when she began her story, she bowed her head and whispered a prayer that she said was both invocation and supplication.

"Please understand," Josette began, closing her eyes, "in the story

I am about to tell, I am channeling a voice that isn't mine. What you are about to hear passes through me like a stream, without beginning or end.

"Love can exert a mysterious power over all of us. Love can move us to do what we might never have foreseen possible, even if it involves consorting with an enemy or with someone who is already dead."

Josette reached into her sling with her left hand and removed a cloth figurine that she cradled in her palm as she closed her eyes. "Now, you are looking at me in ways that I cannot see, but only feel. Without sight, your stares are not visible to me. You are subject to my power, whether or not you accept what I have to say. First and foremost, I must tell you that Voodoo dolls, per se, do not exist, and the figurine you are looking at is significantly different. It has been blessed and will transform as I speak. My figurine can aid in the process of healing and provide protection from forces out of our control, but those who claim to be Voodoo dolls cannot. They are false prophets. So, how can we know the difference?

"The Voodoo dolls sold in tourist shops are a sham. They are the products of pop culture that play on people's fears and ignorance. They deceive, while pretending to enlighten. These Voodoo dolls were introduced in pulp fiction and Hollywood movies, and as much as we want to believe in them, they have no restorative value. Instead, they embrace evil and work to diminish the power of the one and only God that is greater than all of us.

"In your mind's eye, remember the cloth figurine that I showed you. With your eyes closed, hers appear red, and in the darkness, they have become more radiant. Next to her is another doll, one that will disappear if you open your eyes. She is made of cashew nutshells. She was exported in the 1950s to the United States from Haiti to satisfy the insatiable American need for exotica, but she has never aged. She was and is the embodiment of everything we yearn for but have never been found.

"In 1959, public health officials even issued a warning that these so-called Voodoo dolls were dangerous because cashew nutshells were poisonous. But in the end, the power of true Voodoo triumphed, against all odds. Embrace the Holy Spirit within you. Do not be afraid of what you do not understand.

"Please, keep your eyes closed. Trust me. Join me on a journey you will never forget. Take a deep breath. Again. Release the tension. Relax. But do not become complacent.

"Watch! The two dolls are fighting. The innocent girl with red button eyes stands toe-to-toe with the doll made from cashew nutshells, who wields a dagger. The innocent girl seems powerless, but somehow, she dodges the attack of the other doll and her strength grows. The landscape changes. The earth beneath their feet softens. They sink into the soil, gasping for breath. Who will survive? The girl with the weapon or the girl without one?

"Time passes.

"With every thrust and parry, the cashew nutshell doll weakens, and in the end, loses her ability to fight, because she has no endurance. She is obsessed with the moment, and that moment never comes, because it does not exist. It is illusory.

"Almighty God has intervened, lifting us out of the firestorms of hell, proving that all things are related, good and bad. The righteous always prevail. There is no coincidence. Belief heals.

"Evil will be vanquished. Now! Open your eyes, and see, as you have never seen before. The cashew nutshell girl is gone, but the eyes of the innocent girl have turned from red to blue. The sky opens before us and we are free."

Josette passed her cloth figurine around the room, and in fact, the eyes had turned blue as she told her story. But Maggie wasn't convinced, and said, "I think they were blue in the first place. You tricked us, telling us they were red, when they were not."

Tears welled up in Josette's eyes, eyes and she prayed, "Heal me, dear God, heal me! My spirit comes to you on bended knee. Heal my suffering, my pain. Grant me the power to overcome my weakness and rise up in your glory."

And Sandra said *Amen*.

Max and Richard clapped softly. Hannah squirmed in her seat. I glanced at Cynthia, who appeared as confused as I was. Maggie stoked up the firepit. Barb stretched her neck backward as if doing one of Eleanor's chair yoga exercises. Eleanor smiled.

Hannah looked at Josette and whispered, "'Be subject therefore unto God; resist the devil, and he will flee from you.' James 4:7."

Josette lifted her cloth figurine in front of her face as if shielding herself from Hannah. And Sandra said, "'Bless them which persecute you: bless, and curse not.' Romans 12:14."

The burning embers in the firepit crackled, and no one said a word. We all sat in silence, and, as the flames died down and the veranda darkened, we got up one by one and left.

Cynthia and I went upstairs to my bedroom, where we sat in chairs opposite each other pondering whether Josette, Sandra, and Hannah could ever reach a truce. I was skeptical. All three of them were so set in their ways. "Dogma is their armor," Cynthia said disparagingly, but then shifted her attention to me, sliding her chair closer and playfully twiddling her fingers into mine.

I asked what she meant when she said that I shouldn't get my hopes up because she'd been in this place before. She leaned back and told me about her engagement to someone she had met at a conference in Washington, D.C., about six years before: "He was a grants officer at the National Science Foundation, and, after a few months, I realized he was more interested in me than my research. That, of course, is not to say that he wasn't going to recommend me for funding. I was a graduate student, and he had a PhD from Stanford in microbiology. Well, the short of it is, we played around, kind of like what you and I have been doing, nothing too serious. It was just fun.

Every time we seemed to be on the verge of consummating our relationship something got in the way, though we worked hard to see each other. He'd come to Boston every other weekend, and I went to D.C. when I could. But because I was writing my dissertation, the demands on my time were greater. And over time, I had to accept the fact that he had become a bureaucrat, a boring one at that. Then our relationship ended abruptly. He met someone else at another conference, and that was it. Now, Andy, intellectually, I know you're nothing like him. It's simply that the more I think about another long-distance relationship, the more I'm turned off."

I swallowed hard and said, "I understand. The reality is, there are so many parts of our lives that couldn't be more different. I do odd jobs for a living, and you have a career. But as long as we're living in the cottage, it doesn't seem to matter. We need to make the most of what we have while we still can."

Cynthia perked up, laughing, "If we leave masks on, we can probably do anything we want, except kissing." I stood up with my hands on my hips, exaggerating my every move, and she knocked me over onto my bed. And we picked up where we had left off in the cave, except this time we took off our clothes.

Day 12

THE COMMOTION IN THE HALLWAY JARRED me awake. Sandra and Josette were looking at each other with disdain in their eyes. Hannah was crying, and Eleanor and Barb were trying to comfort her.

My cell phone was ringing. It was Cynthia, jabbering that she had tossed and turned all night and had gone to the shed just after dawn.

I told her that I was in a big hurry. I had overslept, and my appointment with Chuck was at one, followed by the police detective at two, and it was already eleven. But Cynthia pleaded with me to join her for breakfast, "I really need to talk to you, Andy. And I even brought some goodies I scavenged from the kitchen—a couple of apples, cheddar, yogurt, and a thermos of coffee." Reluctantly, I agreed.

I stripped off my underwear and headed to the shower, and the intensity of the hot water steamed me into a strange euphoria. I closed my eyes, savoring my memories of Cynthia's breasts heaving on my chest, her thighs enveloping mine. My skin tingled, and my breathing evened out.

My towel was warm on the rack outside the shower, and, as I dried off, I wondered what it would be like living with Cynthia in Boston. Would she ever want me to meet her parents, or her scientist friends?

I dressed quickly and decided that making notes for my meeting with the police was a waste of time. I knew what happened. I was only going to tell the truth. And I bolted out of the cottage with an urgency I hadn't felt in a long time.

The air was frigid, and there was an icy slick of dew on the grass. As I neared the shed, I saw Cynthia sitting outside on a folding chair, and next to her was another one, waiting for me. She had built a small firepit on the gravel and was rubbing her palms together.

I sat down next to her, and she pressed her lips lightly together, as if she didn't know what to say or how to begin. She stumbled around with her words and said, "I don't want you to get too attached," but then corrected herself. "I loved every second of being together with you, but when I went back to my bedroom in the middle of the night, I felt guilty, like I had done something I shouldn't have done."

My heart sank. I had finally been able to let go, to free myself from my mourning long enough to immerse myself in someone else, someone who at that moment seemed to meet my every need. But listening to Cynthia, the grief returned. I looked away, and the wind gusted in my face.

Cynthia said, "I need some time to sort out what I'm feeling, but that doesn't mean that I want to stop seeing you."

"That's okay. I'm willing to do whatever. I need time, too."

Cynthia poured me a cup of coffee, and I lowered my mask. And we ate the yogurt, apples, and cheddar slices that she lifted out of her satchel. Cynthia had a dreamy gaze and said, "I'm so grateful that you're so understanding. I really am."

"Back at you. I feel the same way . . . even though . . . I'm still hoping for more."

Cynthia stirred the embers in the firepit and covered it with gravel, and I carried the chairs into the shed and stacked them in the corner. Cynthia could tell that the intruders had been back. The latch on the trapdoor leading to the underground compartment was broken, and a couple of the rungs of the ladder had apparently been kicked loose.

Before descending into the compartment, Cynthia got down on her hands and knees, running her fingers over the ground to see if the intruders had planted some kind of trip wire or booby trap. When she didn't find anything, she lowered herself into the compartment, steadying herself as best she could. But as she stepped onto the last rung, it gave way, and she tumbled to the ground.

I shouted, "Are you all right?" and she mumbled, "I think so, but I kind of hurt my shoulder."

I navigated my way down and carefully helped her to prop herself up. She stretched her arms and said, "I don't think anything's broken. Only bruised." Fortunately, she was wearing her miner's helmet, which helped break her fall.

Cynthia got up slowly, and we found the rungs that had been removed and tossed to the side. We nailed them back into place, then did our best to reinforce the bottom rung, which had given way. "Clearly," Cynthia said, "the intruders messed with it and were hell-bent to sabotage our efforts."

Cynthia was determined to go deeper into the corridor and tunnel, but I was able to convince her that we had to come back later. She needed to ice down her shoulder, and I had to leave for my meeting with my attorney.

Cynthia was listless on our way back to the cottage. Everyone was getting on her nerves, and the last thing she wanted to talk about was how she had injured her shoulder in the shed. Maggie was too nosy; Hannah, too doting; Richard and Max, too busy in their own little world; Sandra and Josette, too angry; and Eleanor and Barb, too difficult to pin down in relation to everyone else.

I managed to help Cynthia to her room without the others noticing us. Apparently, Maggie had called some of kind of meeting and everyone was outside in front of the cottage assessing the state of the repairs and what else needed to be done.

I filled a couple of gallon-sized plastic bags with ice cubes and made a makeshift ice pack that I brought to Cynthia, who reluctantly got into bed. And while she said she appreciated what I was doing, she kept pushing me away, wincing in pain. I cushioned the ice pack against a couple of pillows and helped her to reposition herself. Her shoulder was swelling, and I pleaded with her to let me drop her off at the hospital emergency room to get X-rays while I was meeting with my attorney and the police. But she refused.

I left Cynthia's bedroom in a huff and charged through the front door of the cottage without looking back, ignoring everyone who had gathered outside. Maggie asked where I was going, and I said I had an important appointment with my attorney, Chuck.

Josette looked down, and Sandra scowled at me. Richard whispered something to Max, and Eleanor and Barb said they'd also been in touch with attorneys who'd been recommended to them.

Hannah offered to do some of my chores while I was gone. She knew I was supposed to clean out the broom closet, and I thanked her for her thoughtfulness but said I'd take care of it later.

I jerked open the door to my car and slammed it loudly. I was disgusted, not with Hannah, but with myself. I was hurting, and Cynthia's indecisiveness about me only made things worse.

Driving to Stockbridge, I tuned in to a classical station on the radio, and the delicate sounds of Segovia's *Spanish Dances* on guitar helped my head to clear. I was early and found a parking place on Main Street more easily than expected. The streets were empty. The town was shut down. Everyone was sheltering in place; even Theresa's Stockbridge Café was closed. And while I waited for Chuck, I read the historical marker identifying the café as the site of a place called The Back Room that was immortalized in Arlo Guthrie's 1967 hit song, "Alice's Restaurant."

I remembered finding that record in a stack of LPs my grandmother had put out in the trash after my grandfather died, when I was about ten years old. That was the day she told me that they were both hippies and that if she had to listen to that song once more, she might die of a heart attack, too. But she cheerfully brought it into her house and let me listen to it on her beat-up turntable, and, as scratchy as it was, I thought the song was funny.

Chuck seemed easygoing enough, but his homespun manner made me skeptical. He reminded me of good ole boys in Texas, except that he had a Yankee accent instead of a Southern drawl. He was both disarming and alarming. And as he described to me his philosophy on giving statements to the police, I started shivering inside. "Usually, Andy, statements are made as soon as possible, meaning if you get in a car wreck, you call the police, and each of the parties involved gives his or her side of the story so that the officer can write a report. But in your case, the circumstances of the storm and the nature of the injury dictated otherwise. That said, in most cases, people who give statements to a police officer during an investigation do so based on some general beliefs and assumptions: 1) Giving a statement makes it clear that you have nothing to hide. 2) If you tell the police what happened, they might be more understanding and not arrest you or go easier on you. 3) If you admit to the police that you did something wrong, the prosecutor and court will go easier on you. 4) Officers are more suspicious if you do not give a statement."

I looked at Chuck apprehensively. None of what he was saying seemed to apply to me. I was only trying to help someone who had injured herself when a pane of glass came crashing down on her. But Chuck pointed out, "You became part of the problem because you responded to it, which, unfortunately, makes it into a bigger problem than it already was.

"Andy, when we sit down with that detective, you must understand that prosecutors, juries, and judges—not police officers—decide cases. Police officers are trained to investigate crimes and wrongdoing by collecting facts and evidence. In America today, the police have virtually no discretion to make decisions regarding whether or not you will be charged for a criminal act, or if you will be found liable in a civil case. Prosecuting attorneys have the final say on all charging decisions, and, if the facts support a reasonable chance of conviction of a crime, a prosecuting attorney will almost certainly file charges. Moreover, they also weigh cases for plea or trial *based on the facts* they have gathered to prove their case. The role of the police is to collect evidence, write reports, and support the prosecuting attorney in criminal prosecutions. Any promise a police officer makes to you is, at best, only a good intention and may be just another method to induce you to provide a statement, facts, or evidence. If the investigating detective is annoyed with you, stay calm. Annoyance is just another form of pressure to get you to give a statement they know you do not have to give. If the detective is going to arrest you, nothing you say or do can change that. But if you lock yourself into a statement you do not believe to be completely true, you are in big trouble."

I struggled to get comfortable on the wood slat bench on which we were sitting, but the more I twisted around, the more fidgety I became. Chuck paused and urged me to take a deep breath. While he could tell that I was having a hard time listening, he said his intent was only to prepare me for what I was up against.

"If the detective sees that you are restless, he will press harder, knowing full well that statements are subject to bias, memory, and conflicting facts. But once a policeman takes your statement and swears in court that this is exactly what he heard, if you change your story, you will be accused of lying because officers don't lie. Officers do not make mistakes, and officers are not biased, especially in a courtroom in Western Massachusetts. These three tenets, for better and mostly for worse, are intrinsic to the criminal justice system, whether they are true or not. Trying to explain away misstatement is a lot more problematic than giving no statement at all."

I leaned forward and asked Chuck if I should try to postpone or cancel my appointment with the detective. He grimaced. "Certainly not. I'll be at your side. But you must introduce me before the proceedings begin as your legal counsel. And if at any point it appears that you are being led off course, or being inordinately pressured, I will intervene on your behalf."

Chuck pulled his shoulders back and said, "Let's go for a little walk. Take in the sights. It's a glorious day."

Before entering the police station, I looked back onto the street and, for a reason unknown to me, one of Eleanor's chair yoga exercises popped into my head. I was standing, but I figured it didn't make any difference. I inhaled slowly and raised my arms, pressing my palms overhead, and then exhaled, floating my arms back to my sides, releasing some of the tension in my shoulders and neck. I did it again and again, and Chuck asked if I was okay. "I'm as ready as I am ever going to be," I said with a sigh.

When we walked through the door, the detective was waiting for us at the information desk, file folder in hand. He greeted Chuck with a nod and me with a gesture that beckoned me forward to a windowless office with an empty desk and three chairs.

We sat down, and he offered me a cup of coffee or a soda or water. I was thirsty, and, just as I was about to say yes, a uniformed officer joined us and said he'd fetch drinks for everyone. The detective sensed my nervousness and assured me that while his goal was for me to make a formal statement, he didn't want to pressure me. He wanted to keep it friendly, get to know me better, learn more about me and what happened.

The first question he asked was whether our cohabitation at the cottage constituted a commune. He said he was older than I might think, that, when he was a rookie cop back in the day, hippies like

Arlo Guthrie were everywhere. And while the Western Massachusetts version of a commune wasn't anything like Woodstock, kids shared houses, smoked pot together, dropped acid, and probably had group sex. But, of course, he didn't think any of us at the cottage were doing anything like that, given the reality of the virus.

Chuck laughed and explained, "Everyone living at the cottage met through an internet chat room. Everyone was asymptomatic, and Maggie, the young woman whom you met on the day of the accident, made arrangements for everyone to move in for a couple of weeks, with, of course, the permission of her father, who's friends with the owner of the property."

The detective scratched his head and thanked Chuck, then turned to me.

I told him that on the day of the accident, I lost track of time. "I had been in the den with Hannah when everyone panicked. It was all hands on deck, and we all worked to protect the cottage from damage. The rain was pelting against the windows. Water was rushing under the door. And when we saw that two of the living room windows had cracked, we struggled to board them up with plywood. Then one came crashing down on Josette, and a piece of glass gashed her hand. Blood was gushing out of her palm, and no one could find a bandage or other first aid supplies. I saw a sewing kit, or maybe someone gave it to me, and I stitched the wound together, hoping to stop, or lessen, the bleeding until Josette could get to the emergency room."

The detective wasn't satisfied. "I need more details, something that I can match up with the statement Sandra and some of the others had made."

I couldn't believe that no one told me they had already spoken to the detective. Chuck asked if they had made their statements in the presence of legal counsel. The detective replied sternly, "They didn't choose to do so. They only wanted to help establish the truth of what happened."

Chuck objected to the detective's tone and reminded him that I had come to the police station voluntarily. Except, the detective interjected, that it was his understanding that I had been served a subpoena in a pending civil suit that had been filed against me to cover the cost of medical bills and damages.

Chuck scowled, but instead of confronting the detective further, he was proactive and said that I was not sufficiently prepared to make a written statement at this time. The detective knitted his brow, and Chuck escorted me out of the office.

Chuck said, "I was simply telling the truth. You weren't prepared, and the detective knew that. If and when the detective is able to gather enough evidence to charge you with a criminal offense, he will do so, and anything you say to him is only going to be used against you."

As we parted ways, Chuck reminded me that he would try to keep my billing to a minimum.

I wished Chuck had talked to me longer, but then again, it was only going to add to the expense. I wasn't sure what to do next, other than return to the cottage and not talk about what happened. The drive back to the cottage was lonely, and the darkening landscape was ominous. There was another storm headed toward Stockbridge, and I was driving into it. Possible tornadoes. Hail and sleet. The road conditions were harrowing, with patches of black ice, thunder, lightning, and cloudbursts that pelted my car with a wintery mix that jammed up my windshield wipers and made visibility almost nil. By the time I reached the cottage, I was wiped out.

As I rushed to the front door, my feet slid out from under me, and I crashed onto the flagstone path. I was dripping wet.

I trudged into the mudroom and plopped down on a folding chair Maggie placed near the door for me. She watched me yank off my sneakers and socks and asked how everything had gone in Stockbridge, but I was too worn out to say much. She acted as if she had already heard that my meeting with the detective was a bust. I told her that I liked my attorney, and she nodded. Her father had called about an hour earlier, and he was worried that the owner of the property was going to kick us all out.

"I'm sorry," she said. "Andy, it wasn't your fault. The storm was an act of God. And the injury to Josette's hand was a terrible accident with unforeseen consequences that are becoming increasingly problematic. Don't worry. Everything's going to be okay. But to tell you the truth, what bothers me the most is that you and Cynthia are keeping a secret from me about what you have found in the shed."

Before I could respond, she said matter-of-factly, "The owner has known for decades about religious relics that were buried on the grounds of the cottage. And he needs to know their whereabouts before selling the property."

I was shocked. Maggie knew more than I thought. Her father must have told her. But I didn't understand why he hadn't done so sooner.

Maggie glared at me and said, "I've spoken with Cynthia." But she didn't tell me what they talked about.

I looked at Maggie and asked her as politely as I could if we could all get together later. I needed some time to decompress. Maggie reluctantly agreed.

I walked barefoot through the kitchen, and, when I got upstairs, I knocked on Cynthia's door, but she didn't answer. I turned toward my bedroom, and Cynthia came out into the hallway, motioning for me to join her. She said her shoulder was better and that the ice pack that I made for her had really helped to take down the swelling.

I was a mess. I wanted to take a nap, but she insisted that we needed to talk. She followed me into my room and sat in a chair across from me. "You look awful, Andy, and, if you don't change your clothes fast, you're likely to catch pneumonia."

After a hot shower I emerged, wrapped in my terry cloth robe, and sat down on the edge of the bed.

Cynthia said, "I'm sorry that I acted the way I did. I was hurting emotionally, physically, both."

I appreciated her apology but wondered if she still felt guilty about making love with me. But before I could ask, she started telling me about her conversation with Maggie, and I told her that Maggie had also talked to me. Cynthia was amused. Maggie was just fishing around. Obviously, she'd heard some kind of gossip that Cynthia and I weren't party to.

Cynthia had emailed a query about bejeweled skeletons to an archaeologist friend at the Smithsonian, who wrote back that some had been pillaged from little villages in Germany after World War II. "And in the 1950s," Cynthia said excitedly, "some were smuggled piecemeal to antique dealers in the U.S. and were ultimately reassembled to be sold on the black market. In some cases, the jewels were removed from the bones, and the skeletal remains were incinerated." However, there was an archaeologist, her friend said, teaching at a tiny liberal arts college in New Hampshire, who had discovered the journal of a Venetian seaman in the Biblioteca Nazionale Centrale di Roma that spoke about an excursion into the Berkshires where stolen skeletons from Germany were buried. A copy of the journal was translated by an antiquarian in Stockbridge and distributed in a limited edition by real estate agents seeking to boost the mystique of selected historic properties scattered through the countryside that they were trying to sell. However, two years ago, the *Journal of the Venetian Seaman* was discredited by a researcher at Princeton, though the tales of the bejeweled skeletons were still being circulated and, to varying degrees, believed.

"So, the short of it is that, as I had suspected, and as Maggie has finally admitted, the property owner was aware of the possible existence of the skeleton or skeletons long before we ever arrived. And ever since we began frequenting the shed, Maggie has been reporting back to her father, who, in turn, was keeping the owner in the loop."

I pressed Cynthia for more information, and she said calmly, "I contacted the Archdiocese of Berlin about the terms through which the skeletal remains could be repatriated once my research was completed. And one of the archbishops stated that a reward of more than €500,000 had been offered by a church donor who had grown up in a village where the bejeweled skeletal relics of a patron saint had been desecrated and removed during World War I, not World War II. Of course, what Maggie and her father never anticipated was that first and foremost, I am only interested in the repatriation of the relics to the church where they were stolen. I have no financially driven motives, and, I assume, neither do you."

"Well, yes . . . except, to be honest," I said, looking down, "for me, the possibility of a reward does make the excavation project more intriguing, given how broke I am and the likelihood of a civil judgment against me in Josette's lawsuit."

Cynthia replied, "We'll see how it all plays out. But the bottom line is that Maggie, her father, and the property owner never anticipated that there would be an intruder onto the site or perhaps different intruders all pursuing the same booty. But, clearly, none of them has as yet discovered the skeletal remains."

Cynthia's DNA tests were due back soon. I didn't fully understand exactly what she wanted to establish, other than the relationship between the trace of blood on the tile and the skeleton, and possible connections to Sandra, Josette, Richard, Max, or Maggie. But then Cynthia said, "There are other correlations that I hope to make once I know more."

She started rattling off details that were hard for me to follow that had to do with the Italian and German documents she had been reading and had sent, or was sending, off for translation.

Cynthia was losing me, and it was unclear to me what she had most recently said to Maggie, who seemed more relentless in her efforts to determine the whereabouts of the sacred relics she knew existed on the property. Cynthia said, "I just need a little more time.

The pieces in the puzzle are coming together. Once the DNA results come, I'll know what to do next."

I was disappointed that Cynthia hadn't said anything about this flurry of emails earlier. And she was defensive. "Andy, I was going to tell you in due time. But there's so much more to do and know. I didn't want to give you false hope about any reward for finding the relics. And I still don't."

I grimaced, realizing I was overreacting. I was stressed out, and she could tell that my meetings with the attorney and the detective hadn't gone well.

Cynthia opened her arms, and we hugged, and neither of us wanted to let go. We fell backward onto my bed, and Cynthia giggled that she wasn't ready for more hanky-panky but that taking a nap together would be great.

Cynthia got up first, and, while I was sleeping, she prepared a dinner tray of her favorite comfort food—homemade macaroni and cheese with a green salad, two glasses of ice water, and a bottle of red wine. I asked her how she knew that I used to live on macaroni and cheese when I was in college, because I couldn't afford much more than the rent.

Cynthia laughed, and we chowed down, sipping wine until we both were a little tipsy. When we went downstairs, everyone was waiting for us in the den. We took our seats quickly, and Maggie announced that it was time to begin the storytelling.

Eleanor stretched her arms out to each side of her body, then brought one arm under the other in front of her at shoulder height. While bending her arms at the elbows, she twisted around so that her palms met. She held her breath, then unwound herself and repeated the same yoga position with her opposite arm on top.

Barb tried to keep up with her and said, "I'm starting to like that yoga exercise. Yes!"

Eleanor was pleased.

Maggie stomped the floor and pleaded for everyone to focus their attention on the story we were about to hear. "Yoga," she said, "is okay, but chattering is not."

Richard grinned, and Max quieted down.

Hannah relaxed, and I leaned back in my chair and crossed my feet in front of me.

Maggie smiled, "Andy, we have been waiting for days to hear your story. After all, you were the one who first brought *The Decameron* to our attention. So I think it's high time for us to know what you've prepared."

I squirmed in my seat and reluctantly stood up. "Okay, then. It's nothing profound. But I will say, I've been carrying around my notes in my back pocket for days. So I guess I'm ready."

I swallowed hard and began slowly. "My story takes place in Certaldo, a town in Tuscany in the Metropolitan City of Florence, where Boccaccio lived.

"Located in the middle of Valdelsa, with a population of about sixteen thousand, Certaldo is about thirty-five kilometers southwest of the Florence Duomo. In the heart of Certaldo is the Augustinian Convent and the home of the Church of Santi Jacopo e Filippo, which houses the Boccaccio funerary monument, built after his death in 1375, and the body of Blessed Giulia, beatified on the 18th day of May 1819.

"My story, however, focuses less on the Blessed Giulia but more on an episode in the long history of the church and convent when an impoverished friar came to Certaldo from a small fishing village because he had been told by an itinerant monk about the benefits of preaching there to local residents and tourists, who, upon hearing his fiery sermons, would lavish him with praise and money.

"The friar took the name of Aglio, 'garlic' in English, in honor of its integral role in Italian cuisine, where it was used often to add flavor and depth, but never to overpower the other ingredients. Friar

Aglio saw himself as vital to the life of the community he served, an enhancement to their faith without being dogmatic. But over time, he realized that fiery sermons were not always sufficient and, in some instances, were actually detrimental to the message he strove to deliver.

"Supplicants to the holy baptismal font in the Church of Santi Jacopo e Filippo flocked to see its relics, including the skeletal remains of saints or fragments of sacred objects, which many believed were endowed with healing powers and were known and, perhaps, influential to Boccaccio during the years that he lived in Certaldo.

"As people learned of the riches of Friar Aglio, legends grew about other friars from Sienna, Rome, and as far away as Positano, who made their way to Certaldo seeking the grace of God and the good fortunes that grace engendered. One such man who came to Certaldo had taken the name of Cipolla, 'onion' in English, in homage to the popular friar immortalized in the Tenth Story, told by Dioneo on Day Six of *The Decameron.*

"But unlike Boccaccio's Cipolla, this friar's hair was not red but instead was a purplish gray that he claimed was completely natural, when in fact a hairstylist in Certaldo, when interviewed by a reporter for a large urban newspaper in the United States, swore on her Bible that she had created this unique dye especially for him. Hair color aside, Cipolla was fiercely competitive with Aglio and often challenged him in ways that excited tourists but were scorned by local residents, who invoked the blessings of Giulia, the beatified saint who had turned away from fame and earthly glory.

"Ultimately, the objections of local residents were to no avail, and the heated exchanges between Cipolla and Aglio, in which each of them demonstrated his adeptness at rejecting sin and avarice with Bible verses of praise to the glory of God to elicit the awe of those in attendance.

"Aglio and Cipolla attracted huge crowds day after day, but it wasn't until Cipolla devised a plan to discredit Aglio that the interactions between them became more seriously adversarial. Each carried a small black box that he opened at the conclusion of a sermon to show a relic from the church. Frequently these relics, while purportedly authentic, were facsimile reproductions and not valuable at all. But the manner through which they were revealed and presented and passed around to the supplicants always increased the size of the monetary donations made to the coffers of the friars, who promised to use the funds they collected for the preservation of the artifacts in their possession.

"One day, Cipolla made an arrangement with a cohort to pretend to be a supplicant in pursuit of Aglio's blessing. When Aglio turned away, Cipolla opened his black box and stole its relic, a crucifix that he claimed had been found in the hand of Saint Giulia herself on the day that she died. In its place, Cipolla inserted a piece of volcanic rock that he had found in a creek bed on the outskirts of Certaldo. And when Aglio completed his sermon, he opened his black box with his usual fanfare. Closing his eyes, he said that he could feel the presence of God in the crucifix he was about to show, but when he reached inside and pulled out the piece of black volcanic rock, he was horrified. Within minutes, though, his expression brightened. He proclaimed that the transformation of the crucifix to volcanic rock was a miracle, demonstrating the power of God to imbue the ordinary with the extraordinary, quoting Exodus 17:5–6: 'And Jehovah said unto Moses, Pass on before the people, and take with thee of the elders of Israel; and thy rod, wherewith thou smotest the river, take in thy hand, and go. Behold, I will stand before thee there upon the rock in Horeb; and thou shalt smite the rock, and there shall come water out of it, that the people may drink.'

"Those in attendance were so completely wowed by the transformation of Aglio's relic that everyone turned away from Cipolla. The donations for the preservation of what he called the sacred volcanic rock exceeded all that had ever been contributed. And with the fortune he earned on that day, Aglio was able to retire at an early age and was known to have devoted himself to the study of the everlasting legacy of Blessed Saint Giulia for the rest of his days.

"And to this day, garlic is seen as having a significance far greater than onion in dishes prepared by certain chefs in private villas who pride themselves on creating a cuisine that Boccaccio would have no doubt enjoyed and that distinguishes Certaldo from its neighboring towns in Tuscany. The end."

I stuffed my notes into the front pocket of my jeans and sat down.

Maggie was beaming.

Hannah was ecstatic. "What a wonderful mix of the ludicrous, the spiritual, and the sublime! I was particularly impressed by the use of Scripture to emphasize the importance of faith."

Richard groaned, but Max and even Josette were enthused. Sandra was nonplussed, and Barb and Eleanor were indifferent.

Cynthia whispered to me, "I was so moved by your story in such an unexpected way. I especially loved how you alluded to our project in the shed but didn't overstate its relevance."

Hannah opened her Bible in her lap, nestled it in her hands, and began reading Exodus 4:1–9, in which Moses says to God, "But, behold, they will not believe me, nor hearken unto my voice: for they will say, The Lord hath not appeared unto thee. And the Lord said unto him, what is that in thy hand? And he said, A rod. And he said, Cast it on the ground. And he cast it on the ground, and it became a serpent; and Moses fled before it. And Jehovah said unto Moses, put forth thy hand, and take it by the tail. And he put forth his hand, and caught it, and it became a rod in his hand: That they may believe that Jehovah, the God of their fathers, the God of Abraham, the God of Isaac, and the God of Jacob, hath appeared unto thee. And Jehovah said furthermore unto him, Put now thine hand into thy bosom. And he put his hand into his bosom; and when he took it out, behold, his hand was leprous, as white as snow.

And he said, Put thy hand into thy bosom again. And he put his hand into his bosom again; and plucked it out of his bosom, and behold, it was turned again as his other flesh. And it shall come to pass, if they will not believe thee, neither hearken to the voice of the first sign, that they will believe the voice of the latter sign. And it shall come to pass, if they will not believe also these two signs, neither hearken unto thy voice, that thou shalt take of the water of the river and pour it upon the dry land: and the water which thou takest out of the river shall become blood upon the dry land."

Josette perked up, "Amen. Amen!"

Sandra joined in. "Amen. I've been praying for Josette's hand to heal and for the dexterity of her fingers to be restored—to be transformed by an act of God."

I sank deeper into my chair. It seemed like there was a new strategy afoot to make me feel miserable.

Cynthia sensed my discomfort and tried to console me with her eyes, which met mine with a compassion that seemed to embrace me, while the others in the den were chattering away.

And to make everything worse, Maggie asked me to talk to our group about my meeting with the detective.

I was flummoxed and refused to speak.

Sandra glared at me.

Cynthia implored Maggie to leave me alone, and Maggie said adamantly, "I've reached my breaking point. The sneakiness is driving me crazy. It's time for everyone to come clean."

Cynthia brushed her hand toward me. I straightened up and said proudly, "On the advice of my legal counsel I haven't made a statement to the police, and I don't intend to. I've done nothing wrong. There was no criminal intent."

Josette gasped.

Sandra got in my face and shouted, "But at the time, you said she got what she deserved!"

I was flabbergasted. I had no memory of ever saying those words.

Hannah jumped up and quickly came to my defense. "Remember, Sandra, you were the one who spread out the blanket on the floor. And you were right there at Josette's side while Eleanor helped to prop her up with pillows she had taken from the veranda."

Max added, "Yes, yes! I couldn't help with Josette because I was too busy trying to secure the other piece of plywood to the window."

Richard leaned forward, "I was so panicked that when I saw the pool of blood at Josette's feet I almost passed out."

"Look, we were all desperate to do anything we could to help Josette. And from my point of view," Eleanor maintained, "Andy's quick thinking was incredible and so completely on-task that I'm certain he kept Josette from bleeding to death."

But Sandra pushed back, "C'mon. Let's get back to reality. Andy is and was a homophobe whose rage couldn't be contained. He pushed everyone aside and insisted that he knew exactly what he was doing."

Josette was shivering. "That's right. Andy wanted to punish me. He intended to cause me harm, to teach me a lesson that I was inferior to him."

Cynthia was furious and lashed out at Sandra and Josette. "That's insane. Your accusations are vicious and paranoid. You're hell-bent on destroying Andy's life for reasons I can't understand."

Maggie admitted, "I was the one who found the sewing kit and handed it to Andy, not thinking that he was actually going to use it. But when I saw that needle in his hand and watched as he squeezed the gash in Josette's hand together, there was no way stop him."

Eleanor remembered, "All I know is that I heard someone screaming but wasn't sure who it was."

Sandra clamored, "It was me! I tried to stop him."

Max said, "It was definitely Sandra's voice. But the cacophony was deafening. It was chaos."

Sandra blathered on, "Now, Andy, it's your turn to be punished.

Big time! Why can't you just man up and plead guilty and ask for the mercy of the court?"

"I haven't even been charged!"

Sandra was seething and threw her arms in the air. Josette was shaking.

Maggie shouted, "I am so pissed off that if everyone doesn't shut up, I'm going to call the police."

Richard echoed the word *police*. And Sandra quieted down.

Maggie changed her tone and muttered, "What happened on that terrible day will become an ugly and protracted court battle."

"I certainly hope it doesn't go that far," Cynthia said.

Maggie continued, "Quite frankly, I don't want to have anything to do with it."

"In the meantime, I have to learn how to live with a dead right hand," Josette groaned.

No one had anything more to say except Maggie, who looked around the den with a severity that made it very clear that everyone had to stay right where they were. And when Sandra complained that Josette needed some rest, Maggie wasn't especially sympathetic but nonetheless asked Josette if she needed a blanket or pillow. Josette turned away without answering, and Maggie continued and announced that our stay at the cottage was coming to a close. "You're welcome to find other accommodations in Stockbridge, if departing Massachusetts isn't possible on such short notice. In fact, there's an inn in town that's completely vacant, and the owner told my father that he's willing to make rooms available at thirty dollars a night for up to a week."

Maggie was going to stay at the cottage to coordinate the final repairs, which might take another month. In addition to packing up our belongings, Sandra and Josette would have to remove their shrine and altar, and Cynthia and I would have to clean up the shed.

Cynthia was defensive and said, "You know the shed is in better condition now than when I found it."

Maggie corrected her, “You didn't *find* the shed. It was already there, and while it may have appeared to be a mess, the owner kept it that way for a reason.”

Cynthia was fuming. But Maggie wasn't letting up, “I know what you and Andy are doing. And your actions, or perhaps inaction, have increased the level of vandalism.”

Hannah leaned forward and said, “For a while I've had a feeling that there was something strange going on in the shed.”

Eleanor laughed, “I wasn't particularly concerned because I just assumed the shed was where Cynthia and Andy went to make out and do whatever else consenting adults do when they're alone.”

Josette said, “Sandra and I built the altar and shrine to express our devotion to higher powers greater than us and to also ward off evil spirits, which I immediately sensed when I arrived at the cottage.”

“If there are evil spirits, they stayed away from me because I eat lots of garlic,” Richard said, interlocking his fingers in front of him and cracking his knuckles.

Josette recoiled, and Sandra scoffed that Richard's corny joke was insulting.

Cynthia said, “I can't believe this. We all sound like a bunch of old biddies, and we aren't even thirty years old.”

Maggie stared at Cynthia and me and accused us of doing everything we could to avoid answering her questions about what we had actually found in the shed.

Maggie said, “As I've told you before, I knew of the existence of documents that seemed to contain details about the significance of the shed, but I don't read German or Italian.”

Max squirmed in his seat, as if he knew something that he didn't intend to share. I turned my attention to him and asked if he could tell us more about his Italian ancestry. Maggie objected, saying that, once again, I was introducing a tangent that was only going to take us further off course.

None of what Cynthia and Max were saying made any sense to Maggie, until Cynthia reminded her that she had already told her about her research into the layers of dirt in the shed to determine whether it predated the construction of the cottage. Maggie was dismayed. Everything Cynthia was talking about seemed so off-topic. But then Cynthia added, "I'm waiting for the results of the test samples I sent out, and more conclusive evidence will no doubt be forthcoming."

Maggie wasn't satisfied. She needed to know exactly what we'd found. And Cynthia pushed back, "If artifacts of significant value are discovered on the grounds of the cottage, they would, of course, belong to the owner of the property, unless they were stolen and the rightful owner could be identified."

Maggie demanded that Cynthia turn over the documents she had taken from the file drawers in the compartment beneath the shed. Cynthia fired back, "I'd be glad to give them to you, but I mailed them to a colleague working at the Smithsonian Institution who's preparing a fully translated and annotated transcript."

Maggie was angry. "You had no right remove those documents, and doing so was tantamount to theft."

Cynthia told her, "As a scientist, I had an ethical responsibility to act because I suspected malfeasance, and I'm preparing a complete dossier that details my field notes and findings, which I intend to provide to the property owner, who is apparently unaware that the family member who had bequeathed the cottage and its grounds had signed a contract with the Smithsonian Institution that granted its archaeologists and their assigns the right to excavate the site."

Maggie was stunned and left the den without responding.

Josette and Sandra got up, and Sandra snarled at me that she was looking forward to Josette's day in court. But when I asked Josette for the name of her attorney so that I could pass it along to mine, Sandra said, "We're still finalizing the details. Just give us your attorney's contact information, and I'm sure Josette's legal counsel will be in touch with him soon."

I reached into my pocket and handed Josette Chuck's card. Barb and Eleanor trickled out of the den, and Hannah stopped in front of me and said, "Andy, I will pray for you. I will." Richard added, "Well, I hope it works, because he's going to need all the help he can get." Cynthia and I sat together, not sure what we should say to each other. There was so much Cynthia hadn't told me, but when she took my hand in hers, it didn't seem to matter. I was confident Cynthia knew what she was doing, and when she said, "I want to spend the night with you," I was thrilled.

Day 13

WAKING UP WITH CYNTHIA SPOONED BEHIND me, her arm curled over my chest, I felt everything that had been weighing me down lighten up. In the warmth of my bed, the pandemic was, for the moment, more of a memory than a presence. But as the sun edged the curtains and seeped into the room, my thoughts darkened with the reality of what was yet to come.

I had scheduled another appointment with Chuck. Cynthia wanted to join me, but I didn't really want her to come. I was worried that if she got involved, it could ruin everything that was just beginning to fall into place in our relationship. But for Cynthia, it was a trust issue. If I didn't let her come to the meeting with me, she thought she wouldn't be able to ever trust me again. I understood her intellectually and emotionally, but I still felt vulnerable. It was hard enough talking to Chuck, and I knew that having Cynthia with me was only going to make it more difficult. But I gave in, and Cynthia was grateful. She did everything she could to help me get ready and even brought a breakfast tray up to my room with a glass of orange juice, coffee, toast, marmalade, and a thick slice of Vermont cheddar.

I murmured, "You're spoiling me."

She giggled, "I hope not."

Once we were in the car, Cynthia told me that when she was in the kitchen, she'd overheard Josette, Sandra, and Maggie talking.

Josette was complaining that her hand was more swollen. Maggie was urging her to go back to the emergency room, but Josette balked, saying that she couldn't bear it.

Hearing about Josette made me gasp. Cynthia tried to be consoling, "We can only hope for the best."

I nodded, changing the subject to Chuck, who had asked me to meet him at the bench across the street from Alice's Restaurant in Stockbridge. I was nervous. But Cynthia laughed, "How bizarre."

"I'm not joking."

"I don't want to make you feel bad. Quite the opposite. It's just such a pandemic place to meet. Outside. In the cold."

The closer we got to town, the more anxious Cynthia became. Every few minutes, she checked her phone to see if her friend at the Smithsonian had reviewed the documents. Cynthia couldn't sit still, clasping her hands together then pulling them apart. And when we were a couple of blocks from Alice's Restaurant, she got an email from her friend at the Smithsonian, informing her that there was some evidence that the bejeweled skeleton had been stolen from a small church in a German village, referenced in the documents that she had translated. However, she needed to see photographs of the crest on the ring on the index finger of the skeletal hand to confirm its identity.

Cynthia said she could go back to the shed by herself. But I told her no way. We were in this together. I could talk with Chuck later. Josette's civil suit wasn't going to court anytime soon. But when I called Chuck, he insisted that we meet. He'd been contacted by the attorney representing Josette, who informed him that they were seeking $2.5 million for pain and suffering, in addition to any medical expenses not covered by insurance.

When I told Cynthia I didn't have any insurance she was shocked, "I just don't get it. You could be forced into bankruptcy and/or debt for the rest of your life. I'm worried about you, Andy."

"But Chuck says I'm essentially judgment-proof because I have so few assets."

Cynthia replied, "Knowing that doesn't make me feel any better."

When we finally got to the bench across from Alice's Restaurant, Chuck was cranky. He wasn't happy that I'd brought Cynthia along, particularly since we weren't married, and reminded me that if Cynthia decided to blab about what we discussed, there was nothing I could do to stop her. I assured him that Cynthia was completely trustworthy. Chuck raised his eyebrows as if to say he didn't really believe me, but, instead of confronting me further, he tried to be proactive, laughing that I'd already bought an hour of his time and he hadn't done anything yet. Cynthia and I sat down, and Chuck rattled off a summary of recent trial court cases that he thought were comparable to mine.

"In *Murphy v. Smith Realty Corp.*, a jury verdict in the sum $2,200,000 for pain and suffering, reduced by the trial judge to $1,050,000 for a thirty-five-year-old factory worker whose nerve, tendon, and muscle damage left him with a permanent clawing deformity and a useless hand.

"In *Simpson v. City of Boston*, a thirty-one-year-old schoolteacher was injured when a heavy metal door was slammed on her hand. A Suffolk County jury returned a pain and suffering verdict in the sum of $1,200,000 which was upheld on appeal. Ms. Simpson's hand sustained nerve injuries that caused her to suffer from reflex sympathy dystrophy—a condition that often leaves her with unremitting extremity pain, burning sensations, extreme hypersensitivity, and loss of use. Ms. Simpson's case was so bad that her hand was clawed, she could not tolerate the slightest touch to her fingers, and she could not use her hand at all."

Cynthia said she'd heard enough and excused herself. Chuck looked at her as if he were glad that she was leaving. Cynthia apologized but explained she had other urgent things to do. Chuck said he would speak to Josette's attorney on my behalf and contact Maggie for more information about the property owner. And I said, "I'll call you later, after I take care of a few things with Cynthia."

Chuck scowled, "If you don't make the effort to nip Josette's lawsuit in the bud, it's going to grow into a nasty vine and strangle you."

Both of the plaintiffs in the cases Chuck described sounded too much like Josette. I felt terrible. I was speechless. Cynthia asked Chuck if he thought I was also going to face criminal charges, and he shook his head that it was highly unlikely. Proving intent in the aftermath of an accident of this kind was tough. But then Cynthia said, "Sandra and Josette are accusing you of being a homophobe. According to them, Andy, you knew full well the harm you were going to inflict when you started stitching up Josette's hand."

I gulped. "What? That's the first I've heard of that."

Cynthia seemed about to cry.

Chuck was concerned. "If what Cynthia is saying is in fact true, you could be charged with assault and battery or, in the worst-case scenario, a hate crime."

"Assault and battery? A hate crime? That's ridiculous."

Chuck was suspicious. "Is there anything you haven't told me that I need to know? Are you a homophobe?"

"No way."

"Right now, it's your word against theirs. But what are the others in your group going to say about you? I'm glad you didn't give a statement to the police. Remember, if you're not more careful, you could become your own worst enemy."

Chuck ambled away, exuding a strange confidence that made me uneasy. Cynthia could tell how upset I was but didn't say anything as we walked back to my car.

"I need to know more about what Josette and Sandra said to you."

"It was mostly Sandra. Josette didn't say much, but, then again, she didn't object to what Sandra was saying. I guess we have to remember Sandra told the scarecrow story because she identified with its plight. She's been hurt, maybe even scorned because she's a lesbian."

"Not by me."

"I know."

"Well, that's not what Sandra seems to think. Yesterday, she shouted that she remembers me telling Josette she got what she deserved."

"That's awful. Have you told Chuck?"

"Why should I? I never said that."

"But if Sandra says that in court, someone might actually believe her."

Driving back to the cottage, Cynthia was irritable. "There's something about Chuck that I don't like. He doesn't seem completely forthright. It bothers me that he's a friend of Maggie's father, who, for all we know, might be in cahoots with the property owner.

"I just sense that Chuck knows more than he lets on. Maggie might have told her father or him or even the property owner that we've been digging around the shed. Chuck says he's only trying to help you with your legal problems, but he might also be working to leverage you into telling him more about our excavation project."

I mumbled, "Rest assured. I haven't talked about the shed and I'm not planning to."

"Andy, what you don't seem to understand is that Chuck might be waiting for the right moment to pounce on you. Threatening you. If you don't do what he wants, he's going to do what he can to hurt you."

Cynthia saw that I was terrified and eased up. "You're in a very tough spot. But I want to help you if I can. One of my old college roommates is an attorney in Boston, and she might be able to represent you or at least recommend someone who can, no strings attached."

"But I signed an engagement letter, and Chuck is already doing stuff on my behalf."

"Andy, you have the right to terminate Chuck whenever you want."

I was about to tell Cynthia that I could handle Chuck on my own, but the more I thought about it, the more I realized that I couldn't.

"Right now, Andy, you don't have to rush to terminate Chuck, but instead let him make some preliminary inquiries on your behalf. And then, when he plays the quid pro quo card, shut him down. By then, I'll have had enough time to talk to my friend, who will no doubt be willing to help you explore other options."

When I turned onto Ice Glen Road, we heard a crow cawing in the distance. The air was damp and raw. Some kind of storm front had blown in, and everything around felt different. Fog billowed across the landscape, and, by the time we got to the shed, an eeriness had settled in.

The interior of the shed had been ransacked, and the ladder to the underground compartment had been demolished. Cynthia picked up her miner's helmet. It had been thrown into a corner, and the headlamp was smashed. We used the flashlights on our cell phones to peer into the underground compartment but couldn't really see much.

Cynthia wished she had a rope to lower herself down, but she couldn't find the one she had used just a few days before.

"I know there's one in the stable. I've seen it. I'll go get it."

"Just hurry. We don't have much time. I need to collect what evidence I can. The shed is now a crime scene."

The stable had a strange vibe. Daisy and Harry weren't there and apparently had been moved to another location. I didn't see a rope, but then I remembered I'd seen one coiled up in the hayloft, and, as I climbed up the wooden stairs, my memories of being with Maggie weighed heavy on my heart. Horseback riding with her had been great, and rolling around with her in the loft had transported me to a place I had all but forgotten. That seemed so far away, when it had only been about a week ago.

I grabbed the rope and hurried back to Cynthia, who took it from my hands and tied one end off on one of the timbers that supported the ceiling of the shed, pulling hard on it to be sure it was sturdy enough. Then she picked up a sledgehammer that she found while I was in the stable and said, "This must have been what they used to destroy the ladder to the underground compartment."

Cynthia was more determined than ever and told me to please do as she directed. We knew that at any moment the intruders might return. To get the photo of the rings on the skeletal hand, we had to dig into the wall with extreme care. And then we had to camouflage the site so that no one could find it before we could get the proper authorities to mount a thorough, and scientifically grounded, archaeological excavation.

Holding tightly to the rope, Cynthia lowered herself, sledgehammer in hand, into the underground compartment, and I followed close behind. We proceeded slowly into the corridor and the cave. Debris was strewn everywhere. Cynthia photographed the footprints on the path and concluded quickly from their irregularity that whoever it was had apparently panicked.

Cynthia pulled the lever to open the cave, and the stones barely moved. The lever had been damaged. So I squeezed my hands into the opening between the stones and managed to jar them apart but then pulled back. Cynthia picked up the sledgehammer and pounded on the lever, and the pulley system released. I pulled harder on the stones, and they inched apart wide enough for Cynthia to slither through into the cave.

I passed Cynthia my cell phone, and the light illuminated the wall enough for her to penetrate the plaster and photograph the family crests on the rings of the skeleton. But to seal up the wall, she needed water. I scurried back into the compartment and somehow was able to pull myself back up the rope into the shed, where I found a half-empty water jug in the trash can. I tossed the jug down to Cynthia, who rushed back through the corridor into the cave to patch the wall.

Outside, I heard people talking as they moved toward the shed. I shouted to Cynthia, "Maggie's headed this way! And she's with two men I don't recognize."

I paced back and forth until Cynthia called out to me, and I steadied the rope as she climbed out of the underground compartment. She was out of breath, and perspiration was dripping down her cheeks. "I did it, Andy, as best I could. The stones wouldn't return to their original position, and I figured out a way to stuff debris into the gap. Then I pounded on the lever with the sledgehammer until I was able to disable it by dislodging one of its bolts."

Maggie pushed open the door to the shed and acted surprised to see us, even though it was clear that she was proud of herself for catching us in the act of doing exactly what she had asked us not to do. She introduced the two men with her as friends of the property owner who had been assessing the damage and any needed repairs to the cottage, but who were also interested in checking out how the shed had been vandalized as a separate claim.

The two men surveyed the interior of the shed, and one of them said, "This is going to take more time than we have right now. We'll need to schedule a time to come back."

Cynthia wiped her brow with her scarf, and Maggie said, "It looks like your day has been as exhausting as mine. But no time to waste. I need you to tell me more about exactly what you know about the underground compartment."

Cynthia hesitated but then said, "It appears that someone had been living there, but I'm not sure when and for how long." Maggie mocked Cynthia's response and said, "More than likely, the shed and its compartment were the home of a groundskeeper many years ago, or perhaps the secret nesting place of the gardener described in Richard's appropriation of Boccaccio's story of Masetto."

Cynthia wasn't fazed by Maggie's sarcasm and said, "The documents I found in the file cabinet near the desk never mentioned a groundskeeper."

Maggie asked in a stern voice, "So what did you do with these documents?"

"I've already told you: after reviewing them, I sent them to the Smithsonian Institution to get them translated."

Maggie was irked, "So when do you intend to return them?"

"As soon as possible. Look, I've already taken care of it. Everything I sent off will be back before I leave town."

Maggie looked livid but held back saying anything more until the two men were gone. Then she confronted us again. "The property owner has hired a team of archaeologists to excavate the site, beginning sometime soon, and, if both of you don't cooperate, I've talked to the police about filing criminal charges against you for trespassing and theft."

Cynthia was defensive and said, "Good. There's no point in talking further about the documents or the site until we know more."

Maggie stomped away but was met by Max, Richard, Barb, Eleanor, and Hannah, who were all rushing in her direction. Maggie threw up her arms, as if she were too exasperated to speak, and Hannah shouted, "Sandra had to bring Josette back to the emergency room! Josette had a fever, and Sandra was afraid that her hand was infected, but also worried that it could be the early symptoms of the virus."

Maggie looked at her in disbelief.

My phone started beeping. I had a text from Chuck telling me that I needed to meet him in Stockbridge ASAP. I tried to get Cynthia's attention, but she was focused on Hannah, who asked if we could all bow our heads and pray for Josette. I turned away, "I'm sorry, but I gotta go. It's . . . uh . . . urgent."

When Cynthia looked up, she could tell something was wrong and chased after me. By the time she caught up with me, I was opening the door to my car. She shouted for me to wait. I apologized. I had to go back to Stockbridge to see Chuck, and I didn't know how long I would be gone.

Cynthia's face was backlit in the afternoon sun, and, as I moved closer to her, her eyes emerged from her silhouette. She was welling up, and I hurried toward her. She opened her arms, and we embraced. Cynthia lowered her mask, and I did the same, and our lips came together as never before.

I lost track of where we were and where I needed to be. But then the reality of everything that was pressing on us roared back. Cynthia pulled away and said she'd let me go into town by myself, on the condition that I called her as often as needed—before, during, or after I met with Chuck. She was still waiting for a return call from her friend in Boston.

Driving to Stockbridge, I felt my eyelids sag, but, as I neared the center of town, my adrenaline started to kick in. I saw Chuck on the sidewalk. He was pacing around in front of Alice's Restaurant. He was more impatient than the last time I had seen him. He looked at me with an intensity that straightened me up. He told me bluntly, "The police are indeed filing criminal charges against you. A warrant has been issued for your arrest, and I think it's best if you simply turn yourself in. If we go to the police station immediately, you might actually be arraigned before the end of the business day."

I was dumbstruck.

"While you're being booked," Chuck said, "I'm going to file a motion that the case be dismissed because the charges clearly have a very shaky foundation. In the worst-case scenario, I'm going to ask that you be released on your own recognizance, which essentially means that no bail money would be paid to the court and no bond would be posted. You could be released after promising, in writing, to appear in court for all upcoming proceedings."

Everything was happening too quickly. I could barely make sense of what he was telling me. I told him I had to make a phone call.

Cynthia picked up on the first ring. But my voice was so jittery she could hardly understand what I was saying. She kept telling me to take a deep breath and speak in complete sentences. But I couldn't.

Cynthia was shocked, "You're going to be arrested and arraigned for a crime you didn't commit? I'll be there as soon as I can. I'm leaving now!"

Chuck escorted me to his car, saying that if I took mine, it might be impounded and that if I were jailed, I'd have to pay towing charges and fines to get it back.

Sitting in Chuck's Jaguar was weird. Here I was, driving in a luxury car to the police station to be arrested for assault and battery and a hate crime. I repeated the words *assault and battery and a hate crime* to myself. When I got out of the car, I squatted on the sidewalk and puked.

Chuck helped me to my feet, and, once I was inside, two policemen made a formal arrest, reading me my Miranda rights before escorting me through the booking process. First they did a health check, taking my temperature and inquiring whether I had any virus symptoms or contact with anyone who was sick. Then they pushed me along as expediently as possible, recording my name, contact information, the nature of the alleged crime and other vital information. Then they confiscated my wallet, cell phone, and other personal belongings, took my fingerprints, and positioned me for a mug shot.

I noticed the detective who had interviewed me, and he saw me, but he didn't look up from his desk as I walked by. I couldn't believe it. As the arresting officers pulled my arms behind my back and handcuffed my wrists, Chuck chided them that that wasn't necessary. But one of them said in a gruff voice that they were just following protocol, and they led me from the booking area to a holding cell. While I was being booked, Chuck said he'd call Cynthia.

As much as I wished Cynthia was there, I knew it was best that she wasn't. There was nothing that she could do to help me. The holding cell was cold. I wrapped myself in my coat and stretched out on the steel bench bolted to the side wall. Somehow, I managed to doze off. When it was time for my arraignment, a policeman poked me in my side with his nightstick and told me to stand up. He cuffed my hands in front of me and led me through a long corridor to the courtroom.

Chuck was seated at a table about eight feet across the aisle from the Stockbridge prosecutor. The officer unlocked my handcuffs, and I sat down. I was perspiring and wiped my forehead with my sleeve.

The judge entered, we all stood up, and the judge called the arraignment to order. The prosecutor read the charges. Chuck entered my not-guilty plea and asserted that I should be released immediately on my own recognizance. The prosecutor objected on the grounds that I was an out-of-state resident who was likely a flight risk. Chuck argued that I had never been convicted of any crime, other than a speeding ticket three years ago. The judge, a woman who appeared to be in her midfifties, glared at me and then stated that she would release me after I promised, in writing, to appear in court for all upcoming proceedings. After the arraignment, the judge said that she would entertain a motion to dismiss, and Chuck asked, "When can you schedule a hearing, Your Honor?"

"I happen to have an opening for a hearing tomorrow morning at ten, and I will hear your motion then."

As we were leaving the courtroom, I felt relieved, but Chuck said he had a couple of other things he wanted to discuss with me before Cynthia arrived. I asked if he'd called her, and he nodded. Then he said, "I've spoken to the owner of the cottage, and, if you provide the proprietary information he requested through Maggie, he's willing to do what he can to help you get out of the mess you're in."

"But I didn't do anything wrong."

"Look, Andy, you're in trouble."

"I don't get it. What proprietary information?"

Chuck shrugged, "He didn't provide any details, other than to say that if you don't tell Maggie what she wants to know, no telling what might happen to you."

I looked at Chuck in disbelief and he left, grumbling, "Talk it over with your girlfriend, and text me your response by nine tonight."

I waited outside the courthouse for Cynthia, and when I got into her car, I was stunned to see that she looked so disheveled. Her hair was a mess, and her jeans were grimy. I asked her what had happened, and she said that she didn't really want to tell me but ultimately gave in.

"After you left, Maggie forced me to go back into the shed with her to explain step-by-step what I had been doing. I resisted, but she wouldn't relent. Out of frustration, Maggie pushed me, and I tripped, falling face first into the dirt. When Maggie tried to help me up, I pulled away and ran off."

Cynthia was fuming. As she calmed down, she asked me to give her a rundown of everything that had transpired. By the time I got to Chuck's request for the proprietary information, Cynthia was disgusted. "He's trying to blackmail you, Andy."

While Cynthia had been driving into Stockbridge, her friend had called back and given her the name of another attorney, whom Cynthia had quickly contacted on my behalf. Recognizing the gravity of my situation, the attorney was en route from Springfield, about an hour east of Stockbridge.

I didn't know how I was going to get rid of Chuck. But Cynthia was firm. "You simply have to tell him that you've lost confidence in his ability to represent you. If he asks you to explain yourself, you need to throw in his face the same verbiage he's already thrown at you."

Cynthia helped me to compose a text to Chuck, terminating his services immediately. Within minutes, Chuck called me. Cynthia instructed me not to answer, and I didn't. We were both nervous. He called again, and still I didn't answer. Every minute that passed was excruciating.

Cynthia dropped me off where my car was parked, and we drove back to the cottage separately. When we arrived, Eleanor, Barb, and Hannah were all so glad to see me that I could barely get a word in edgewise. None of them asked where I had been, because they already knew. Instead they yapped about the dinner they were planning, the last supper before we all departed the cottage. But then Maggie appeared and said, "I just got a call from Sandra. More surgery might be needed on Josette's hand. Her doctor was reluctant to reopen the wound, but it's necessary because the infection is spreading."

Hannah was dismayed that Sandra hadn't called her, especially since she had left her a few messages. "Sandra's a wreck," Maggie explained, "and it's almost impossible to get a straight answer from her about what's really going on."

I mumbled, "That's terrible."

Maggie looked at me with sad eyes and said, "It is terrible. But there's not much we can do about it. Not now. You ought to get some rest while you can."

After about an hour, the attorney from Springfield showed up. Cynthia led him quickly into the den, where he introduced himself to me. His name was George Wilson, and he had more than thirty years of experience as a prosecutor, defense attorney, and litigator. I laid out the criminal and civil cases against me as best I could, and he agreed to represent me. After I signed an engagement letter, George systematically reconstructed a timeline from the day of Josette's accident to my booking and arraignment. In the process of my describing every bit of minutia I remembered, he identified several procedural errors that, at first, I didn't understand.

By the time George finished, it was past midnight, and he joked that we'd better get some rest, because tomorrow was already upon us.

Cynthia didn't want to leave me alone and asked, "Do you mind if we spend the night together? In my room or yours?"

I was overjoyed. "Wherever. I'm ready."

Cynthia led me to her room. I pulled off my shoes and stripped down to my underwear, and Cynthia undressed and put on a flannel nightgown. Then she wrapped her arms around my waist and pulled me gently into her bed.

Day 14

AROUND 8:00 A.M., GEORGE CALLED TO TELL me that I needed to meet him at the courthouse no later than 9:30. I was exhausted, and my head was still fuzzy. But when George cleared his throat, I snapped awake and put him on speakerphone so Cynthia could hear what he had to say.

"I know this is tearing you up inside, but, please, keep it to yourself. When you stand before the judge, you must appear calm, responsible, and, most of all, respectful."

When I hung up, Cynthia asked, "Do you want me to drive you into town?"

"No, no."

"Are you sure don't want me to come with you?"

I patted my chest lightly with the palm of my hand. "Don't worry. I'll be okay."

Cynthia leaned forward and bussed my cheek with a tender kiss and said, "You better hurry!"

By the time I got to my car, my heart was beating hard. The sun was splintering through the clouds into the newly planted fields, glistening with sparks of light. I rolled down my window, and the cold, fresh air whooshed in, opening my eyes wide to the road ahead.

At the courthouse, George was waiting for me and said, "When the case is called, come up with me to the bench and pay strict attention and try, as best you can, to not ask any questions or make any comments. Here's a pad and pen. If you have anything you want me to consider, write it on a piece of paper and hand it to me."

The judge entered the courtroom exactly at ten o'clock, and the court was called to order. The clerk called our case and the judge said, "Mr. Wilson, I will hear your motion now."

George submitted his motion for dismissal in writing, and the judge looked at it quickly and said, "I'll hear you now."

George explained the facts of the case and argued that there was insufficient evidence to proceed and that the case should be dismissed.

The prosecutor, an assistant district attorney for Berkshire County, argued that there may not be sufficient evidence at this time but that the investigation was ongoing.

In response, the judge expressed her opinion that the case, at this point, was weak and that there was minimal evidence to take before a jury. But she denied the motion to dismiss without prejudice and said the defendant might bring this motion again after discovery was complete.

As I left the courtroom, George explained. "Andy, you need to understand that hate crimes, sometimes called bias-motivated crimes, are crimes committed against the victim because of the victim's actual or perceived race, national origin, ethnicity, religion, or sexual orientation. In your case, to secure a conviction for a hate crime, the prosecutor must convince the judge or jury that you committed the underlying criminal act, assault with a sewing needle, and did so with the requisite intent. Not every crime committed against a person who is gay is a hate crime. In order to convict you of a hate crime, the prosecutor must prove beyond a reasonable doubt that you committed the crime *because of* the victim's sexual orientation. Proving that you acted with hate crime intent will be challenging unless you admit, to police or others, that the crime was motivated by bias.

"But evidence of bias is difficult to establish. I don't want to BS you, Andy, but you need to tell me candidly: do you or have you ever harbored any bias against lesbian women?"

I said "No!" and George said, "I didn't think so," and then he stated in a more serious tone, "In my opinion, the charges are spurious and driven by other factors, a kind of quid pro quo, or blackmail, to get you to provide information that you are withholding from Maggie, her father, and the property owner.

"From my point of view, I believe you were a Good Samaritan to help Josette and should be protected and held immune by the Good Samaritan laws in Massachusetts. Moreover, Andy, you acted in a responsible and ingenuous manner. Taking the risk to stitch up Josette's hand was not a crime or a civil offense. It was courageous. But proving it is not going to be easy."

I didn't know how to respond, and George said, "I know it's a lot to think about. But we'll get through it. We will."

Driving back to the cottage, I was on autopilot. It was as if I had blinders on and was oblivious to everything around me. I was lost in my thoughts, trying to replay everything that George and the judge had said to me.

As I pulled into the circular driveway in front of the cottage, I saw a police car parked near the front door. The two officers who had arrested me marched toward me, one with his arms dangling at his sides and the other with a search warrant that he handed to me, explaining that it was only for my bedroom.

I fumbled in my pocket for my cell phone and called George, who advised me to stay calm and cooperate. I had nothing to hide.

I stepped back and the officer who had served me the warrant said that I shouldn't leave the grounds until they had finished. He demanded to search my car, and I reluctantly gave him the keys.

Richard burst out the front door, startled and irritated that the police were already inside. Max gawked at me, and I looked away, not wanting to make eye contact with him.

Cynthia turned toward me and said, "I'm not particularly concerned that the police are searching your bedroom. I kind of expected them to, and, if anything, I'm surprised they didn't show up sooner. Yes, the police are a nuisance, but I'm not going to let them get in the way."

Cynthia was excited and gushed, "I can't wait another minute to tell you my news. My friend has mailed via FedEx a report documenting the provenance of the bejeweled skeleton and a copy of the contract signed by the family member who had bequeathed the cottage to the current property owner, granting the Smithsonian Institution, its archaeologists, and their assigns the right to excavate the site. FedEx is due to deliver these documents today."

I called George, and he was pleased to hear what Cynthia's research had revealed but urged me to remind her to not present this evidence to Maggie until he was able to review it.

"Cynthia is going to do what she has to do," I said. George was irked but didn't seem to want to argue about it. Just before I hung up, I told him about the contract that had been signed with the Smithsonian concerning the excavation. George asked me to repeat myself. So I explained to him what Cynthia had told me, and it dawned on him that he needed to read the probated will for the cottage, which contained an inspection report that no doubt documented its condition prior to our arrival.

For me, the contract with the Smithsonian and the probated will were a disconnect, but for George, it was an *a-ha* moment. George apologized for ending the call so abruptly. He needed to get to the courthouse to do his research.

Within minutes, one of the policemen appeared holding a handful of brochures from the Steadfast Truth Ministries in Springfield, Massachusetts, that he said they found on the back seat of my car. As he shoved them in my direction, I pulled back, and he asked me sarcastically, "So, could you talk a little about your interest in the antigay international campaign that's been launched in Western

Massachusetts?" I took a deep breath. I didn't want to sound agitated. "I picked up those brochures on the counter of a convenience store and have barely even looked at them."

Some of the police officers reentered the cottage and found my computer, which I had left in the den. As they were getting into their car, I said, "Hey, that's my computer." One of the policemen answered, "We're taking it anyway," and they drove off.

Hannah, Barb, Eleanor, Richard, and Maggie trickled onto the veranda, with Max trailing behind. Richard was asking questions about the menu for our last supper. Barb wanted beef Stroganoff, but Eleanor's wish was for local seafood, having read that the striped bass and rainbow trout in the Berkshires were great. Richard insisted on lobster because it was the way our stay at the cottage began. Cynthia chimed in that there were still a couple of bottles of white Burgundy in the pantry, but Max stepped forward and countered that if he didn't prepare his grandmother's lasagna with a beef, pork, and veal ragù, he was going to feel that he had done everyone a disservice. Richard balked, saying that Max made no sense, though he couldn't wait to sample the bottles of Il Poggione Brunello di Montalcino Riserva Vigna Paganelli that Max had been saving for a special occasion.

For dessert, Hannah wanted to make rhubarb custard with streusel topping, using a recipe the Ox Yoke Inn in Amana had made famous, but she didn't know where she was going to find any rhubarb. Maggie looked dour but joked, "Rhubarb grows like a weed in the Berkshires."

I glanced at Hannah and said, "If you promise to make your custard, I'll go hunting in the forest for rhubarb."

"You're not likely to find any rhubarb in the woods," Maggie laughed. "Mostly, wild rhubarb grows on the edges of grassy meadows and along roadsides and marshlands."

Cynthia poked me in the side with her index finger.

I turned to her, "C'mon, you can come with me. We haven't explored the banks of the Housatonic River."

"I'd love to, Andy, but I need a little break. I thought my gas tank was on full, but it's really on empty."

Hannah complained that Maggie, Cynthia, and I were ruining everything she had prayed about for our last night together. "I hoped God was going to bring us back together, at least, for one last meal." Cynthia and I jumped in, assuring her that we'd be there.

Eleanor reminded us that someone had to make a vegan option for Sandra.

Hannah nodded, "Sounds wonderful. But remember, Sandra is still at the hospital, and Josette's not doing well."

"I don't know what I'm going to do," Barb said, "I had to let a couple of my needy friends stay in my apartment in Brooklyn, and I can't kick them out. I can't afford to pay the thirty dollars a night to stay at the motel in Stockbridge that Maggie said was willing to cut us a deal. And even if I could, the offer was only good for a week, and I still have to figure out where I'm going to sleep for another week before I can move back into my place in Brooklyn."

Maggie tried to be sympathetic, but her voice had a sharp edge as she declaimed, "Well, the cottage is still a mess, and it's not my idea of fun to have to stick around and babysit the repair crews and cleaning ladies."

Barb glared at Maggie, "I wish I'd never come."

Maggie shot back, "You're such an ingrate."

Hannah pleaded with them to stop bickering and offered to loan Barb the money to tide her over for a couple of weeks.

Barb cringed. "Thanks, Hannah, but I don't take loans. I suppose, if I have to, I can probably move in with my parents. But they live in a three-room assisted living apartment in Yonkers, about an hour and half by train and bus from New York City, which means to get to work, my commute back and forth will be three or four hours."

Maggie moaned, and Barb strutted away.

Cynthia went upstairs, and Eleanor called out to me. We hadn't talked in a couple of days, and she wanted to catch up. I wasn't much in the mood for talking, but she acted so concerned that I couldn't brush her off.

"You know, Andy, I'm not sure if I ever told you how much it meant to me when you went with me to see the dairy farmer."

"That's okay. I enjoyed it. Hey, it made me feel like I was actually able to do something that mattered at a time when the world is falling apart."

"Would you like a cup of tea?"

"Sure." And I went with her into the kitchen. She filled the kettle with water and talked about how she'd been keeping up with some of the nonprofits she advised but was totally frustrated by the lack of funding and the ignorance of the general public. "Domestic violence and child abuse are spiking. And the incidence of the virus in low-income neighborhoods is off the charts. Racism is rampant. And while people act like they understand the fundamental problems, little is being accomplished."

The kettle was steaming, and, as Eleanor brewed the tea, she apologized for ranting on. "I'm sorry for unloading on you, but I have a feeling you might be the only one here who gets what I'm all about."

I picked up the cup Eleanor placed on the counter for me, and we sat at the kitchen table across from each other.

I appreciated having the time to listen. But when the conversation turned to me, I didn't really know what to say about my situation. It wasn't hard for Eleanor to sense my uneasiness, and she took up the slack. She told me that in her statement to the police, she had attempted to exonerate me. For her, not only had I done nothing wrong, I was a hero. But in that moment, I was so self-conscious I could barely speak. I was grateful but overcome with a strange sense of regret that I hadn't done enough.

Eleanor was confused. I stumbled around with my words, and, biting my lower lip, I mentioned the antigay brochures from the

Steadfast Truth Ministries in Springfield that the police had found in my car. Eleanor was shocked. "I can't believe they're actually yours."

"They aren't. But they were in my car. To be completely honest, I'd never seen anything like them before. I just wanted to read them to see what we're all up against. I'm not antigay. I'm a strong advocate for equal rights of all kinds."

I swallowed hard, and the words stuck in my throat.

Eleanor's face softened, encouraging me to continue.

"I'm too embarrassed to tell Cynthia about the brochures. I'm afraid that, if I tell her, it will make me sound more guilty than innocent."

Eleanor sipped her tea slowly, and I gazed at her face, awed by her curly red hair, hoping in a strange and silly way to somehow find answers to my problems in the freckles spattered on her cheeks and forehead. And while I had never been physically attracted to her, there was something about her, as she sat across from me in the light streaming through the kitchen window above the sink, that imbued her with a very special beauty.

Eleanor was kind, and I could tell that she was measuring her words before she spoke them, like she was assessing the ingredients of a recipe that had been given to her but that she intuitively knew needed to be adapted to satisfy her taste. It seemed as if she recognized the complexities of my moral and ethical predicament and didn't want to say the wrong thing.

"I admire your honesty, Andy. But I have to tell you, in all the years I've worked in the public sector, I've never met anyone exactly like you."

"I mean . . . I appreciate what you're saying. But I think you might be exaggerating."

She giggled, "But in all seriousness, you're special."

"These days, I'm not so sure about that."

"Hate crimes are usually straightforward to the extent that those who commit them are usually bad people and the level of racism or sexism or homophobia is self-evident. Reading brochures from an antigay church is not a crime. Acting on the hatred they advocate is, but there's no evidence that you've done anything wrong."

"Except," I said woefully, "from Sandra's perspective, when I stitched up Josette's hand and punctured the nerve, I intentionally assaulted her."

I worried that I was talking in circles, saying the same thing over and over again. But Eleanor assured me I wasn't. We placed our teacups in the dishwasher and walked into the garden. Eleanor was a few steps ahead of me and turned toward me with open arms and gave me a hug. The afternoon light shimmered on the grass, energizing me. I asked her if she'd join me on my hike along the banks of the Housatonic River. "I told Hannah I'd try to find her some rhubarb." Eleanor's eyes widened in surprise, and she said, "I thought that's what you wanted to do with Cynthia."

Eleanor and I ambled past the shed and saw Maggie in the stable, saddling up Harry. I waved to her, hoping that she'd gotten over her tantrum. But she acted as if she didn't see us.

I wanted to tell Eleanor about what Cynthia and I had discovered in the shed, but I decided not to; she'd find out soon enough, more than likely at our last supper. And Cynthia and I hadn't really compared notes on when and where was best to reveal what we knew.

My cell phone rang. It was George. I told him I couldn't really talk, and he said it was urgent. He'd found what he was looking for in the will and asked if he could meet with me in a couple of hours.

George was going so fast, I could barely keep up with him, and he finally said he'd phone me back after he'd spoken to the property owner.

We turned back onto Ice Glen Road and made our way into Stockbridge, walking on the shoulder of Highway 7. The traffic was light, and while it didn't have the dramatic landscape views of the Ice

Glen Trail, I thought we might have a good chance of finding rhubarb along the way. And we did, in a clump of tall weeds about ten feet off the roadway. It was still very early in the season, and the plants were small, the stalks thin. I broke off a couple of leaves and tasted a small piece.

A tart, lemony flavor tingled on my tongue, and I handed a leaf to Eleanor, who said, "I've never tasted raw rhubarb." I smiled, "It's perfect."

I pulled off more leaves and broke up a few of the bigger stalks, and Eleanor stuffed them into a plastic bag she had in her purse. We continued on our trek to the Mary Flynn Trailhead at the end of Park Street, across a stone bridge. And as we neared the Housatonic River, we saw a blue heron at the water's edge. We stepped forward, careful not to scare it, but, once we were about eight feet away, it spread its wings and soared off.

The Housatonic River meandered into the horizon, the landscape layered with cumulus clouds and long shadows that stretched across the hazy Berkshire Hills. The trail was flat and led us through leafy underbrush and a grove of young hardwood trees to a short loop at the end and then back to where we started.

Eleanor said, "I can tell you want to get back to the cottage."

"Sort of . . ."

"Hannah's waiting for her rhubarb."

I sighed, "It's not that. It's everything else that's weighing me down."

On our way back to the cottage, Eleanor got a call from Hannah, who said she'd heard from Barb that Josette was being discharged sooner than expected. The infection in her hand had not spread into her arm, as they had thought, or to any other parts of her body.

Hannah said Barb had gone to the hospital, but they wouldn't let her visit with Josette. She sat in the waiting room for more than two hours before she was given any updates, and when she finally got to see Josette, a nurse's aide was helping her from a wheelchair into Sandra's car.

I was happy to hear Josette's infection was under control, but I told Eleanor that I felt trapped. The case against me was gaining momentum.

Eleanor struggled to find words that weren't loaded with false expectations. I didn't have much more to say, and we walked the rest of the way in silence.

As we turned into the circular driveway in front of the cottage, the last of the policemen were leaving. The detective in the front passenger seat lowered his window and waved to me, shouting out to me that we'd be talking again very soon.

Inside, Barb was sitting alone in the living room, her head cradled between her hands, her elbows propped on her knees. Eleanor walked slowly past her into the kitchen, but I stopped.

Barb looked up at me with sad eyes and complained, "I have a terrible headache. My sinuses are throbbing, but I took a decongestant, so I'll feel better soon."

I sat down next to her, "I'm down in the dumps, too. Part of me is glad that our stay at the cottage is drawing to a close, but, to be honest, I'm terrified about what might happen to me once I leave. It might be smarter if I plead insanity and get committed to a mental hospital."

Barb laughed, "I should probably do the same thing. Maybe after a couple of weeks of observation and testing, they'll let me out and I can move back into my apartment in Brooklyn.

But on a more serious note, I've been wanting to tell you, Andy, I'm willing to testify on your behalf if the criminal or civil case ever goes to trial."

Then she leaned forward and whispered, "There's been a new development, something you need to be aware of. When I was in the waiting room of the hospital, I overheard Sandra and the nurse's aide chatting away. At that point, Sandra hadn't seen me, and she was blabbering on about what you'd done. But the nurse's aide didn't agree with her. When Sandra insisted that your stitching up Josette had punctured the nerve in her hand, the nurse's aide said that, after the surgeon opened the wound earlier in the day, he discovered a shard of glass that the emergency room physician had apparently missed on the day of the accident. Your stitching was superficial, indicated by the tiny holes that the needle made. It was the shard of glass that tore the nerve and caused what was likely permanent damage. Well, needless to say, Sandra was pissed off. But when she saw me sitting there, she shut up."

I was shocked. "Did you get the name of the nurse's aide?"

"I am so sorry. I didn't think of that. But certainly, it should be in the surgeon's report."

I didn't know how to respond and excused myself to call George.

When I told him what had happened, George assured me that he would subpoena all of the medical records related to Josette's injury. But he needed to caution me that he might be able only to establish a timeline, which he said might yield some evidence that Josette's treatment was hurried and inadequate. He was skeptical, though, because surgeons often left out details of the procedures that they undertook to protect themselves from a malpractice suit.

I ended the call, dejected but not completely discouraged. What Barb had told me was potentially very helpful. I was certain Sandra was going to lie, but I couldn't figure out exactly why she had it in for me. But then I began to replay my interactions with her. I didn't like Sandra, but not because she was a lesbian. She had a chip on her shoulder, and no matter what I did, I couldn't get through to her.

Sandra and Josette were in the foyer.

Sandra was leering at me, and I looked away. She started telling Barb about a mushroom and truffle casserole she wanted to make for dinner. I heard Josette whimpering, and my heart sank. I needed to reach out to her. In a raspy voice, I asked her how she was doing. And she turned toward me and with sad eyes said, "Poorly."

Sandra stepped between us and barked, "Take a good look! Josette will never be able to use her hand again. She might one day be able to hold a pencil, but she'll never be able to write with it."

I could hear George telling me not to talk to them, but I had to. I couldn't hold back. And I said, "Can we . . . uh . . . pray together at the Voodoo altar?"

Sandra glowered at me, but Josette stared deep into my eyes and said, "As a matter of fact, Sandra and I are on our way to the shrine now. You're welcome to join us."

Sandra objected, "Please. No!"

But Josette overruled her, murmuring something about *maybe he's learned his lesson.*

At the Voodoo altar, Josette handed me a small butane fire starter. "Please, light the incense burners on the perimeter of the shrine and help Sandra reposition the candles in the altar."

Josette slipped her left hand awkwardly into her sling, her eyes welling up with tears, as she removed the cloth Voodoo figurine she had placed on her bandaged right hand and prayed, "Gracious God, I open my heart to you. I ask you now to touch me with the power through which you created me. Fill me with the healing power of your spirit."

Sandra bowed her head and said *Amen,* and I did the same.

Josette raised her left arm and moved her feet counterclockwise around the shrine. Sandra clapped her hands in a counter rhythm as Josette chanted "Run Old Jeremiah," a ring shout that she said she had learned from her great-grandmother.

> By myself, by myself, by myself, by myself. You know I've got to go.
> You got to run.

I've got to run.
By myself, by myself, by myself.
I got a letter, I got a letter,
Ol' brownskin
Tell you what she say,
Leavin' tomorrow,
Tell you goodbye
O my Lordy, O my Lordy, O my Lordy, O my Lordy
Well, well, well. Well, well, well
O my Lord, O my Lord
Well, well, well
I've got a rock.
You got a rock.
Rock is death.
O my Lordy.
O my Lord.
Well, well, well.
Run here, Jeremiah. Run here, Jeremiah.
I must go.
On my way.

Josette shrieked and Sandra's clapping trailed off. And Josette prayed, "Restore me, Lord. Restore me."

I gazed at Josette, in awe of the intensity of her chanting. The incense and the flickering candles were overwhelming. I was dizzy and knelt down, lowering my face between my knees to steady myself.

Josette was shivering, and Sandra led her back into the cottage.

I sat and watched the candles extinguish themselves, feeling that I had finally connected with Josette in the most unexpected way. But I wasn't sure if it was because of the Voodoo, or just some amalgam of African and Christian beliefs that Josette had adapted to meet her needs.

As I turned toward the cottage, I saw Sandra walking toward me with cardboard boxes in each of her hands, telling me with a coldness that made me shudder that it was time to dismantle the altar and shrine, before Maggie and Hannah destroyed it. I offered to help, and she sneered, "Josette asked that you not touch anything. She said that the spirits, the Loas, are swirling about, that they had welcomed you, but, in the end, we know we can't fully trust you until you confess your guilt and beg for forgiveness."

I looked at Sandra, and, struggling to contain my anger, I spoke as calmly as I could. "I don't believe you. If Josette had something to tell me, she'd say it herself."

Sandra dropped the boxes and charged at me, knocking me back onto the ground with her hands, screaming, "Stay away! From Josette. From me!"

I sat up, planted my feet in the garden soil, the dirt oozing into my sneakers, slowly stood up, emboldened by my resistance to Sandra's fury, and shouted, "Barb told me what the nurse's aide said to you about Josette's injury on the day she was discharged from the hospital. I know!"

Sandra was aghast and yelled, "Stop! Are you threatening me? Get away from me!"

I stepped back.

Cynthia burst out of the veranda door into the garden.

Sandra quieted down and began to systematically pack up Josette's shrine.

Cynthia asked if I was okay, and I nodded yes. There was no point in saying anything more yet.

My head hurt. The back of my neck was damp with what I thought was perspiration but then realized was blood. When I fell backward, I must have hit my scalp on one of the paving stones Sandra and Josette had used to build their shrine. When Cynthia saw that I was bleeding, she rushed into the house to get a first aid kit.

Cynthia blotted the back of my head with a gauze pad soaked in peroxide, and, after a few minutes, the bleeding stopped. Pulling back my hair, Cynthia said, "Luckily, it's only a scrape."

Sandra ignored her and finished packing the boxes she had brought with her.

I was still reeling but didn't say anything more. I needed to shower, and Cynthia followed me back into the cottage.

Hannah and Eleanor were in the kitchen, dicing up the rhubarb stalks for the custard. Hannah said they had heard the commotion outside but hadn't wanted to interfere. I smiled and said everything was under control, thanks to Cynthia.

Eleanor looked skeptical but pointed to the announcement she had posted on the refrigerator about our last supper and storytelling session to begin at eight thirty, saying that she hoped everyone would be there, even Sandra and Josette. The dinner was going to be more of a potluck than a feast, with each of us taking turns in the kitchen. There was a sign-up sheet on the counter, and most of the time slots were already filled in.

My cell phone rang. It was George. He needed to see me sooner than he thought, in Stockbridge, at his office. There were documents to review, and possibly sign. I told him I had to shower first and change clothes. George quickly changed his tone, reiterating that he could help me, if I'd let him do his job.

Cynthia led me upstairs and said that she wanted to accompany me into town, even if it meant waiting in the car while I met with George. I was glad that she was willing to make the effort but worried that, once she found out about the antigay brochures, she was going to explode.

I was sweating, though I didn't feel especially hot. My body was buzzing. And my hands quivered as I turned on the shower. The water running through my hair cooled me down and soothed the scrape on the back of my head. I dried off and dressed as fast as I could. In the hallway, Cynthia was talking with Max, who was pressing her for information on the DNA samples she had collected. She was alarmed that he seemed to know as much as he did but said coolly that she would discuss her findings after dinner, as part of the storytelling session.

I hurried past them toward my car, but Cynthia caught up with me and said she was going to drive. She could drop me at George's office and pick me up when I was done. I reluctantly gave in but didn't want to talk. I was too stressed out. And she said, "Okay, Andy. I'm fine with whatever you need to do to keep yourself together."

I leaned back and closed my eyes, and by the time we reached George's office I was sound asleep. Cynthia tooted the horn, and I snapped awake. And at the last minute, I decided to ask her to join me for my meeting, telling her that I welcomed her support. Cynthia said she needed to stop at FedEx to print out and make copies of her report and the documents that her friend at the Smithsonian had sent her.

George's office was more spacious than I'd expected. There were a waiting room and four desks, all of which were empty. George offered me a cup of Nespresso and passed me a plate with chocolate mints, each individually wrapped and sealed. As the light waned outside, George flipped on his desk lamp and said that he had completed the discovery phase of his investigation. He handed me a copy of the timeline of Josette's treatment, from her arrival at the emergency room to her discharge, and summarized his findings, stating that it was clear the attending physician had delegated the triage of her wound to a nurse practitioner, who took the necessary steps to have the patient admitted and scheduled the surgery.

Hearing all these details was exhausting. George had already covered much of this terrain, but, when I interrupted him, he rambled on. He finally got to the property owner, who referred him to his attorney, a managing partner of the firm where Maggie's father worked. "This attorney," George said, "argued that the window shattering was simply an act of God, when in fact it wasn't. The inspection done when the property was appraised as part of the probate process, which I reviewed, clearly indicated that the windows in the living room had been flagged—not only that they were in poor condition, but that they were unlikely to withstand foul weather, and you and your friends were not informed of that fact."

I couldn't believe it. "Does that mean I'm free of any liability?"

"Unfortunately, Josette can still sue you. If you are liable is a question for a jury. That said, I don't understand why the owner is not making a claim to his insurance company. Once he did, the insurance company would control the defense of this claim and the payouts. And all you would then have to do is make your own claim to the insurance company to defend and indemnify yourself."

"I'm confused."

"It's possible, I suppose, that when the owner inherited the cottage and its grounds, he thought that he only needed coverage for property damage, not for personal injury protection. But then again, his reluctance to make a claim might have something to do with the so-called proprietary information Chuck was seeking from you, which at this point is not my main concern.

"The bigger issue right now is the criminal case against you—the assault and battery and hate crime charges, which look as if they might gain momentum, especially after the police raided the cottage, confiscated your computer, and discovered the antigay literature in your car."

The blood drained from my face, and I explained how I had stupidly picked up the brochures at a convenience store and neglected to throw them in the trash. The police found them on the back seat of my car.

"But," George continued, "culling through your computer, the investigating detective found a history of you searching antigay sites during your stay at the cottage."

"I was looking at the website of the Steadfast Truth Ministries in Springfield, which had published the brochures, and that site linked to others."

George leaned toward me and said, "I believe you, Andy, but I'm not sure if a judge and jury will."

I covered my face with my hands.

George tapped my shin with the toe of his shoe and said, "You're overreacting. There are a lot of steps between there and here, and from here to the courtroom. Right now, I need to review the warrant that was issued to search your bedroom in the cottage, because it sounds to me that the police may have obtained the evidence illegally, especially if the warrant only granted them the right to search your bedroom and they went ahead and searched your car and snatched your computer out of the den."

George escorted me to the door, telling me that he was on his way to court to get a copy of the search warrant or warrants that were issued, and warned me to not talk about any of this with anyone.

Cynthia waved to George from the driver's seat of my car, and he waved back. On the floorboard was a bag with a couple of mason jars filled with homemade pickles and relishes Cynthia had bought at the corner market for our dinner. And next to the bag was a stack of red file folders, each filled with the documents Cynthia had assembled.

I started to go through the documents, but Cynthia asked me to stop. She wanted to know everything that I had discussed with George. And I told her that he had advised me against talking any further about it. Cynthia looked surprised. I didn't know what to say. But after a couple of miles, I loosened up and said, "I trust you, but right now, it's crucial that what I tell you stays between us." Cynthia grimaced, and I explained, "I might be off the hook for the civil suit Josette filed against me, but I'm facing other challenges in the criminal case that are difficult to talk about."

"Andy, I had hoped that we'd grown closer, but listening to you now, I'm starting to feel that you're pushing me away."

So I told her everything, and when I got to the antigay brochures, I started sobbing, "I know I've messed up my life."

And she raised her eyebrows, as if she was about to say that I was *so stupid* but didn't.

When we got back to the cottage, Maggie, Hannah, and Barb were gathered in the den. Max had just put his lasagna in the oven. And Sandra was showing Eleanor and Josette how to prepare a vegan mushroom casserole.

Cynthia and I rushed upstairs to change clothes.

When we went downstairs, Cynthia grasped my hand in hers.

Richard said, "You two do make a cute couple, but not as cute as me and Max."

Barb, Eleanor, and Hannah acted happy for us, but Sandra and Josette were fighting in the kitchen. Sandra was shouting that she had done so much for Josette that if she had to do one more thing, the weight of it all was going to crush her. Josette yelled back, "If you tell me one more lie, I'm never going to talk to you again!"

None of us knew exactly what they were arguing about. But it seemed as if it had something to do with me and with Josette's injury. We looked at each other with anticipation, wondering what consequences our last supper and storytelling session might bring. Hannah glanced at me and said softly, "'The wicked plotteth against the just, and gnasheth upon him with his teeth. The Lord shall laugh at him: for he seeth that his day is coming.' Psalm 37:12–13."

Richard groaned *please* and passed us glasses of wine. Hannah beamed, "I try to be in the world, but not of it." Maggie placed a charcuterie board on the counter with more toothpicks than I'd ever seen in one place, and we took turns helping ourselves to the goodies. Cynthia said that she had a story, and Eleanor chimed in that she had one, too, as did Max, who muttered, "It's going to be a long night."

"To be fair," Hannah said, "the storytellers should draw straws to determine the order of presentation."

Maggie had her doubts and joked, "As reigning monarch, it's up to me. That said, I will exercise my last duties of supervision and guidance as queen before abdicating my throne."

Richard said, "For the purposes of mixing it up, I've written out place cards so that we can sit next to and across from people we don't usually talk to."

The setup seemed ridiculous, and when I saw that I was between Josette and Barb and across from Richard and Hannah, I was uneasy. At the other end of the sprawling table were Maggie, Cynthia, Eleanor, Sandra, and Max.

Richard had arranged the salad plates on two serving carts, and Max said, "We need to be patient while the lasagna cools because if I cut it too soon the perfect squares will fall apart."

Hannah clasped her hands together and said, "On this night of our last supper, I pray Psalm 136: 'O give thanks unto the Lord; for he is good: for his mercy endureth for ever. O give thanks unto the God of gods: for his mercy endureth for ever. O give thanks to the Lord of lords: for his mercy endureth for ever.'"

Hannah paused, and then continued, "Bless us, O Lord, and these Thy gifts, which we are about to receive from Thy bounty. In Jesus's precious name, Amen."

Maggie raised her wine glass and toasted, *Salute!*

Everyone cheered, except for Eleanor, who said, "For me, God is not a *He*. And while I respect Hannah's Christian beliefs, the patriarchy of the Bible bothers me. I'm sorry if I'm out of line. I've been patient, but, since this our last night together, I have to speak my piece to set the record straight."

The room went silent. Hannah said, "I adhere to the principle of complementarianism, that men and women are equal in personhood, meaning that they were created for different roles: In Ephesians 5:21,

Paul writes that we must submit ourselves 'one to another in the fear of God.'"

Eleanor asked to see the Bible that Hannah always carried in her purse and quickly thumbed through the pages to read aloud more from Ephesians 5:22–23, "'Wives, submit yourselves unto your own husbands, as unto the Lord. For the husband is the head of the wife, even as Christ is the head of the church: and he is the saviour of the body.'"

Eleanor looked up and said, "This is unacceptable."

Hannah countered. "In Galatians 3:28, Paul proclaims, 'There is neither Jew nor Greek, there is neither bond nor free, there is neither male nor female: for ye are all one in Christ Jesus.'

"Thereby, Paul espouses, my friends, an egalitarian view. Men and women are equal in role capabilities as well. And from this perspective there are no gender restrictions on what roles men and women can fulfill in the church, at home, and in society. Jesus and the New Testament abolished gender-specific roles as well as roles related to race and class."

Barb chuckled, "Wouldn't that be great?"

Max cleared his throat. Richard said that he'd heard enough.

Eleanor wasn't done, and Maggie pleaded with her and Hannah to let it go and simply agree to disagree.

Josette began chanting in a deep and resonant voice the last lines of her Voodoo prayer that she had recited a few day earlier: "Heal my suffering, my pain. Grant me the power to overcome my weakness and rise up in your glory."

Josette bowed her head, and we all did the same. And Cynthia whispered *Amen.*

One by one, we took our seats around the table. Once we started eating, the mood in the room changed. I could tell Hannah and Eleanor were holding back, but the less they said the more they seemed, for the time being, to accept a truce.

I was glad to be next to Richard. We hadn't really talked much.

He wanted to hear about Texas, and I was curious about his ancestor Henry Wilcox Evans, but once we got past the pleasantries of answering each other's questions as briefly as we could, we delved deeper and finally got around to talking about our grief.

"Since my partner, Jack, died," Richard said, "there hasn't been a day that I haven't thought about him. Loving Max doesn't change that. He has his own grief triggers that hit him hard, and I have mine. The thing that triggers me is usually something unexpected, a quip someone says in an offhand way, or a bit of trivia, or even the weather at a particular time of day. While the specifics usually blur together, the sinking feeling that descends on me is sometimes overpowering and difficult to shake off."

I understood exactly what he was saying. "It's like when I walked past someone on the street the day after my girlfriend died and got a whiff of perfume that reminded me of her, or a giggle I overheard, or the color of the fingernails of a woman in front of me in line at the grocery store."

Richard nodded, "When something pops into my head about Jack, I lose track of where I am, and I have to start all over again.

"Sometimes I become temporarily paralyzed by a memory and start to spiral down, not knowing how long the feeling will last. And if a thought pops in in the middle of the night, I toss and turn until I get up in the morning, and then I'm exhausted all day."

Josette chimed in, "When my uncle died from the virus, I was devastated."

I turned toward her as she continued, "My uncle meant the world to me: literally, spiritually, and emotionally. He was the center of my life. He belonged to a social and pleasure club and was a Mardi Gras Indian who took me to practices, parades, and marches year-round when I was a kid. He didn't have any children, and I was more of a daughter to him than I was to my own parents. He was the one who introduced me to Voodoo."

Interested, Richard asked, "So, did you have to go through some kind of initiation ceremony?"

Josette sighed, "Richard, I think you need to slow down on your drinking."

"I'm only sipping."

Josette shook her head, and continued, "Voodoo for my uncle was a way of life, a way of rebelling against the racist society in which he was forced to live and work. He drove a garbage truck in New Orleans and prided himself on helping the people in need that he met along his route. In fact, my uncle probably caught the virus from a guy he was trying to help who had been released early from the county jail.

"I never really knew if my uncle was trained in Voodoo. He said it just came to him naturally, and he did whatever the spirit moved him to do, whether it was reading from the Bible or shouting a Mardi Gras Indian chant or practicing what he believed to be a Haitian or West African ritual. He was a leader and activist in his community."

Josette sounded so sincere, and, once again, I sensed the same connection I'd felt with her during the ceremony at her shrine.

The stories were about to start. Maggie inched over to the cupboard and handed Hannah dessert bowls, and she scooped out the custard, sprinkled her crunchy streusel on top, and passed each of us a serving.

I was the first to taste Hannah's custard and smacked my lips. "Oooh . . . the flavors of fresh rhubarb, the spices . . . the silky texture."

Hannah was beaming.

Eleanor raised her hand and asked if she could go first. Maggie objected, saying she had decided that Hannah was right; each of the storytellers should draw straws to determine the order. But Eleanor balked, saying, "I volunteered," and Cynthia said, "I want to go last."

Exasperated, Maggie caved in, and Eleanor tapped her dessert spoon on her wine glass, and everyone focused their attention on her.

Eleanor began by saying, "My story is based on one told by Neifile on the third day in *The Decameron*, and, while the characters might bear some resemblance to those created by Boccaccio, mine are totally made up, more of an absurd riff than an accurate read of the sheet music.

"Neifile was only eighteen years old and was an inexperienced young woman whose face, Boccaccio wrote, 'was like the rose that blooms at dawn in early summer, whilst her eyes, which had lowered slightly, glittered and shone like a morning star.' In other words, her appearance was quite the opposite of mine. And when Neifile was elected queen, she blushed, but I certainly did not. Instead, my friends, I raise my fist in solidarity with the oppressed women of the world, one of which is the subject of my tale tonight, one who rises up and triumphs in the most unexpected ways.

"Corrine was the daughter of a physician in Washington, D.C., who curried the favor of high-ranking political officials. His diagnoses, though often unorthodox, were remarkably spot-on. He was quick to recognize the early symptoms of heart attack, stroke, and various neurological disorders when they might in fact be years away from causing life-threatening harm.

"As a girl, Corrine loved to accompany her father on his house calls to some of the most prodigious homes in the District, and, by the time she had graduated high school and gone on to college and then medical school, she had learned the tricks of his trade.

"Surprisingly, his most notable patient was not an elected official but another physician, one who had ceased practicing medicine and had been appointed chief of an influential government agency with the capacity to punish his foes and reward his loyalists with funds and prestige. And this particular physician had a son, named Walter, who, though slight in build, had a divine complexion and facial features that were both soft and hard. Walter was not a typical male, and, much to his surprise, and sometimes chagrin, girls in his classes at school found him to be irresistible. Among them was Corrine, who fell in love with him when she was introduced to him as a child.

"But Walter never showed much interest in Corrine. He was being groomed as an entrepreneur, and Corrine as a physician, and, while their paths sometimes crossed, they lived worlds apart until they were brought together one unexpected day in the emergency room of a local hospital after their fathers were critically injured in the same car wreck, driving from D.C. to Baltimore in the middle of a blizzard.

"Ironically, by the time of the accident, their fathers were no longer friendly and were embroiled in a legal and ethical battle related to the FDA approval of a drug that many believed was a cure to a rare form of cancer. How this cancer metastasized as rapidly as it did was a mystery, and both cocktails, as they were called, that each of their fathers advocated as a remedy and likely cure derived from a protein that had heretofore not been identified in the human body. It was believed that one of the fathers had plagiarized the research of the other, but, in the end, the hard drives containing their research and data relevant to the manufacture of the respective cocktails were destroyed in their head-on collision.

"Sadly, Corrine's father died from internal bleeding within days of the accident. And while Walter's father survived, he spent the rest of his life mentally incapacitated, requiring the constant attention of the nurses who were hired to care for him. It was rumored that, after his discharge from the hospital and nearly a month of rehab, Walter's father accused his wife of being a sorceress. He was convinced she had tried to poison him when he was at his most infirm.

"Walter loved his mother, but he also resented her for reasons that seemed to have more to do with his father's disdain than with anything she had ever done to him. What happened to Walter's mother remains unknown, though, by some accounts, she was banished, or possibly murdered, but there were reports that she had fled the contempt of his father and moved to an undisclosed location, where she changed her name.

"Walter, by then, was a business mogul, and Corrine was a practicing physician, highly regarded among some of her colleagues but not particularly successful, because she was often associated with her father's scurrilous activities. Like him, she was generally known as a quack, or even worse, a *drug whore,* willing to prescribe anything if the price was right. Nevertheless, Walter's father pleaded with Corrine to become his personal physician. Corrine resisted but was ultimately blackmailed into doing so. Logic aside, the financial benefits for Corrine were potentially huge, but, instead of accepting his monetary rewards, Corrine agreed to attend to Walter's father personal care on the condition that he persuade Walter to marry her.

"Why Corrine was so obsessed with Walter was and is difficult to comprehend. But by all accounts, her passion for Walter seemed more driven by what he represented in her mind than by the man he actually was.

"At every turn, Walter rebuffed Corrine's advances.

"The years passed. Walter was a jet-setter who traveled the globe in pursuit of romantic liaisons that were fodder for gossip in the social circles to which he belonged. On more than one occasion, Walter was known to have lured women into his lair only to humiliate them by taunting them with his masculinity and rejecting them for their inadequacies, sexual and otherwise.

"Corrine was not discouraged. She continued to provide care to Walter's father for his various ailments, real and imagined. And after he passed away, Corrine and Walter met up again.

"At the funeral, Corrine professed her love to Walter, who pretended not to hear her, because on his arm was a young woman. He introduced her as a high-dollar fashion model, but, in fact, she was not. Corrine sensed that Walter was miserable deep inside and was trapped by the superficialities of the life he had constructed for himself.

"That afternoon, while Walter was having drinks with some of his father's cronies, Corrine confronted the 'fashion model' and insisted that she stop seeing Walter immediately, promising her an unspecified sum of money.

"That night, when Walter staggered back to his hotel room, drunk, he saw a woman facedown on the bed who, from the back, looked like the fashion model, but was, in fact, Corrine. Walter lay down next to her, and, in the darkness, Corrine whispered that she would make love with him only if he wore a sleep mask. She had elaborate fantasies of him fondling her body as if he were blind. Their relationship was consummated, hot, sweaty, and kinky, without his ever knowing that he was being deceived.

"When they were both spent, Walter drifted off to sleep. When he awoke hours later, Corrine was gone.

"Walter tried every means possible to contact the fashion model, but she never responded to his queries, per her agreement with Corrine. As the weeks passed, Corrine discovered that she was pregnant. But she vowed to herself to give birth alone. In her mind, if she were ever to marry Walter, he needed to come to terms with his indiscretions over the years.

"Corrine's pregnancy was difficult. She moved to Stamford, Connecticut, where a friend took care of her. During her first appointment with her obstetrician, a sonogram revealed that she was carrying twins, a boy and a girl. The months leading up to the births were hot and long. And once the babies were born, she decided to seek out Walter, who lived by himself in the Adams Morgan area of D.C., desperate but ultimately unsuccessful in his drive to find the love he craved. Sex for Walter had become boring and unfulfilling. He started therapy, took antidepressants, and even underwent electroconvulsive treatments, but nothing seemed to work.

"Corrine called Walter and told him that she had tricked him and that he was the father of twins. But he didn't believe her, and she told him that she had paid the fashion model to abandon him. After months of resisting and finally consenting to DNA testing, Walter's paternity was confirmed. He broke down, sobbing that his life was ruined. But instead of ridiculing him, Corrine told him, in as sincere a voice as she could muster, that he had one more chance to redeem himself.

"Corrine traveled back to D.C. with the twins in tow, and, upon seeing them, Walter fell to his knees and begged her for forgiveness, but it was not until he admitted, in tears, that he had broken the chains of his past that Corrine accepted his apology.

"A few days later, Corrine and Walter were married in a private ceremony. When they exchanged their vows, they pledged their commitment to one another and to their twins.

"Walter proclaimed that he had learned the true meaning of love. And Corrine's lifelong dream was realized.

"Sadly, however, a month after their wedding, Walter was blindsided by a speeding car that swerved onto the curb, slamming him into the street, where his head was impaled by a piece of steel rebar jutting from a section of concrete pavement in need of repair. Eyewitnesses recalled Walter's bloodcurdling screams and the excruciating anguish that flashed across his face as he died. Corrine, of course, was devastated. After a forensic autopsy revealed that Walter had suffered not only from blunt force trauma but from congenital neurological abnormalities, Corrine established, with money she inherited from Walter, a foundation dedicated to the research and treatment of brain injuries and abnormalities. But once the assets of the foundation were made public, Walter's mother came out from hiding and sued Corrine for what she was entitled to by virtue of her prenuptial agreement with Walter's father. After two years of court proceedings, she was awarded a huge settlement, but instead of keeping it for herself, she donated it all to the foundation that Corrine had created, stating in a press release that in the end women were more powerful than men."

Eleanor sat down. Richard was chuckling, "I'm so glad Eleanor chose a fairy tale that was utter nonsense but was nonetheless enjoyable in the convoluted way we delight in what appears to be divine retribution, coupled with an unexpectedly happy conclusion."

Hannah was offended by Richard's sarcasm. "Corrine's behavior raises difficult moral questions. But what bothers me the most is that she never prayed to God for guidance, or forgiveness for herself."

"Well," Max snickered, "she was a sinful woman."

"Be that as it may," Hannah countered, "Walter was a sinful man."

Hannah whispered, "'Take heed to yourselves: If thy brother trespass against thee, rebuke him; and if he repents, forgive him.' Luke 17:3."

Sandra scratched the back of her neck and tried to change the subject. "Putting the God talk aside, I . . ."

Hannah was incensed. "Never!"

Everyone stopped talking. We all looked at each other, not sure what to say or do.

Sandra apologized. "I appreciate what you're saying, Hannah. Believe me. But I feel there's a bigger issue I'd like to bring up, and it relates more directly to Eleanor's story and not so much to the subtext which you have elaborated on."

"Please," Hannah said. "'How much better is it to get wisdom than gold! And to get understanding is rather to be chosen than silver!' Proverbs 16:16."

"All right, then," Sandra continued, "I'll cut straight to the chase. I think Eleanor effectively echoed Boccaccio's misogynist sentiments. Clearly, Walter was the embodiment of a man who reviled women and whose final act of misogyny was getting himself killed after Corrine had forgiven him. But ultimately, what frustrated me was that Corrine did not exact revenge. After all, she could have cut off his balls when she had the chance."

Maggie disagreed, "Corrine was a feminist who refused to accept the traditional role of being subservient to men and having no say in a male-dominated society. But she wasn't going to stoop to violence. Corrine was strong and determined, with a clear vision of how to be as aggressive as Walter."

Barb laughed, "That's right! Corrine was everything but submissive. She was in control."

Hannah questioned the appropriateness of Eleanor's story on our last night together in the cottage. "Why? Just why?"

Eleanor said, "I told this story because I had to. I wanted all of you to think about what's wrong, and what's right. Yes, I played the game, knowing full well the rules weren't fair. But, in the spirit of *The Decameron,* Corrine triumphs through her capacity to not only deceive Walter, but to actualize her deep-seated sexual fantasies and her earnest desire to bear children."

I defended Eleanor. "For me, this absurd story was perfect for the occasion and provided us the opportunity to put *The Decameron* in a contemporary context that is at once stupid and smart. Corrine was as courageous and outspoken as Gillette of Narbonne, upon whom she was based. And to cap it all off, let's not forget, Walter's mother was vindicated."

"That's right," Max said. "She was a victim, too. Misogyny and patriarchy, they go hand in hand."

Maggie was disgusted and said, "The only way I'm going to listen to the other stories is if everyone stops drinking."

Richard balked: "This is the last supper, after all."

Sandra insisted, "It's time to sober up."

Richard lifted his glass to his lips, savoring every sip, "Delicious. Truly delicious." Then he placed his glass on the table. Max picked it up with his and took both to the kitchen.

Sandra and Hannah helped Josette to her feet and led her to the living room sofa. Richard, Max, Maggie, Barb, and Eleanor followed along.

Once we were all seated, Cynthia offered espresso and tea. I wheeled one of the serving carts into the kitchen to get cups and saucers.

Maggie was fidgety, squirming in her chair, not talking to anybody. The moment there was a lull in the small talk, she asked, "Max, are you ready to tell your story?"

Max recoiled, "I've changed my mind. I prefer to go after Cynthia."

I straightened up as Max quibbled with Maggie, insinuating that Cynthia was going to shed light on the subject of his story and said, "I worry that I might be upstaged or contradicted." Maggie was impatient and demanded that Max proceed.

Max was nervous. He cleared his throat and reluctantly began. "I know some of you, particularly Cynthia, Andy, and Maggie, and maybe Hannah, are familiar with my efforts over the last several years to home in on my Italian ancestry. Part of the appeal of coming to the cottage was always its Italian roots, being a replica of a Tuscan villa from the Renaissance. Little did I know that I was to meet here a man named Richard, who has become so dear to my heart, and that I'd also meet all of you. Despite our differences and difficulties, I will always cherish my memories of our time together.

"Just last week, I received a report from Ancestry.com that documents a 98 percent DNA match with my paternal ancestor Loretto Abianato, who was a governing official in the commune of Barberino Val d'Elsa, located above its namesake Tuscan valley. Now, the DNA to which mine was compared was found in the beard hairs of Loretto's death mask, which had been excavated from a site in close proximity to the original fortifications that still ring the town.

"In the medieval communes of Tuscany, allegiances of mutual defense (both physical defense and defense of traditional freedoms) were sworn among the citizens of a town or city, where leadership positions, such as archbishop, abbot, mayor, and others with civic responsibilities were elected in keeping with public and canon law.

"By all accounts, Loretto was admired and respected by the citizens of his commune. He had married young but well. His wife, Maria Gaetana Agnesi Pinotti, and her family were held in high regard. And around 1790, Loretto and Maria's only son, Luigi, was born. Growing up, Luigi was tutored by priests in Barberino Val d'Elsa, and, as a young man, he worked at the Orto Botanico di Firenze, also known as the Giardino dei Semplici, the *Garden of Simples*, a botanical garden today maintained by the University of Florence. The garden was opened on December 1, 1545, by Cosimo I de' Medici, Grand Duke of Tuscany, and was first laid out by the landscape gardener Niccolò Pericoli to a botanical system and plantings selected by Luca Ghini, with Pier Antonio Micheli as its director, to whom Luigi apprenticed himself. The garden's primary purpose was to propagate medicinal plants. However, when the Società Botanica formed in 1753, the garden shifted its focus to experimental agriculture and its design was ultimately modified to suit its new mission.

"Luigi showed great promise and was at some point introduced to Lewis De Patry (or Patri), who migrated to Western Massachusetts and married a Massachusetts woman named Rebecca around 1814 and continued to live in the area into the 1820s. The only documentation of Luigi's associations with Lewis De Patry appears in a fragment of a diary page mailed with a few botanical samples from an unknown source to my great-grandmother, in which Luigi wrote that he had found 'the hills of Tuscany in Western Massachusetts,' and that he had brought with him a wooden box filled with rare and precious gems that he intended to sell to generate the funds necessary for him to build a homestead. But the diary page ended there. No one knew what had happened to Luigi or his treasure.

"Years later, before my great-grandmother died, she was contacted by a one hundred-year-old man named Hans Wohler, who claimed that he had been Luigi's lover and partner. In a typed letter to my great-grandmother, Hans wrote that Luigi, suffering from a rare lung disease, had asked him to reach out to her on his death bed, but he had lost her address. Hans did, however, confirm that it was Luigi who had mailed to her the diary page and botanical samples but was afraid to send more information. He and Hans were forced, because of the nature of their relationship, to live in isolation, away from the world but nonetheless in it. Luigi worked in a hardware store by day, and by night he tried to sell his precious gems on the black market, but no one would buy them, because it was believed they were fakes. In desperation, Luigi buried them on a parcel of land that he intended to buy before he died, just a few miles away from what today is known as Ice Glen Ravine.

"The old man hoped that my great-grandmother would help to recover the treasure, which he believed rightfully belonged to him, because he was Luigi's designated heir. And when my great-grandmother asked for proof of their relationship to one another, he sent a Bible in which both their names were inscribed. Pasted on the inside cover of the Bible was Luigi's handwritten last will and testament, in which he described meeting Hans in a small village in German-speaking Switzerland and then traveling with him on the *SS Edenhurst* from Hamburg to Boston. Hans was a deckhand, and Luigi worked in the boiler room. En route to the United States, there was a fire on board. Hans's face was badly disfigured, as were the faces of a dozen or more deckhands. Luigi did what he could to save Hans, and, thanks to his diligent care, Hans and a few of the others survived. However, weeks passed before Hans and the others were able to speak, and only then could Luigi be sure which of the maimed men was in fact Hans. When they finally landed in Boston, Hans was admitted to a hospital for burn victims, and Luigi got a job in a confectionary in the Italian North End. Within months, they traveled together to Springfield, Massachusetts, and eventually settled in a small house Hans called 'the shed,' in an unspecified location on the outskirts of Stockbridge. Why Luigi left out any mention of Hans in his diary entry remains a mystery, though it was likely because he could not admit to his family that he was gay.

"The circumstances of Luigi's life and untimely death have haunted me since I first learned about him as a teenager, at the time when I first became aware that I was not the same as most of the other boys in my school. I was a troubled kid who grappled with who I was deep inside, thinking that something was wrong with me. My school guidance counselor urged my parents to send me to a summer reeducation camp, which they did. I was mentally and emotionally tortured for two months. When I came home, I was psychologically scarred and avoided my parents at all cost. Finally, when I finished high school and went to college, with a scholarship to Dartmouth, I was liberated. Then, after graduating magna cum laude, I found a job back in Seattle and did my best to reconnect with my mother after my father died of a heart attack. My mother was always more accepting of me, and we grew close. But then, just days after we had dinner together at her favorite seafood restaurant, my mother contracted the virus. A week later, she was hospitalized and intubated. I was tested and found to be asymptomatic. Four days after that, she died.

"Please forgive me if I've been too personal. I realize I shouldn't be talking so much about myself. I went down this rabbit hole and barely found my way out. What I really want to say is that I have a nagging sense that what Cynthia and Andy have been doing in the shed might be relevant not only to my quest to learn more about Luigi, but to the final disposition of the treasure he brought with him to the New World."

Max sat down, and, in a self-deprecating voice, apologized again for not telling a very good story. Then he looked at Cynthia, imploring her to share what she knew about the buried treasure.

But before Cynthia could speak, Maggie announced that the excavation of the shed was to begin tomorrow, after we had all vacated the property. She doubted that Luigi and Hans had ever lived on the grounds, but, then again, the cottage was not built until 1915.

Cynthia rolled her eyes and started to talk: "It is important that we all understand that the region around Stockbridge, which had been settled by English missionaries in 1734, was not only hospitable to Christianized Mohicans but also to Italian immigrants in the early nineteenth century. Census records, as Max indicated, list Lewis De Patry as perhaps the first Italian to live in Western Massachusetts in the 1820s, around the time that Lenzoni Medici acquired and began to repair the remnants of Boccaccio's house in Certaldo, Italy. Now, the connections here are tenuous at best. But if one considers that little is known about the three children that Boccaccio reportedly had out of wedlock, the possibility, unlikely as it may sound, that a descendent of Boccaccio found safe passage to America is not so far-fetched."

Richard and Max oohed.

Josette and Sandra yawned.

Maggie sighed.

Barb and Eleanor said *Wow* almost in unison.

Hannah was stunned.

I was entranced.

"Initially," Cynthia said, "I went to the shed because I needed a private space away from the cottage to collect my thoughts, to meditate, to get away. It wasn't that I didn't like being with all of you in the cottage, but I am, by nature, a loner. In the process of tidying up, I discovered a trapdoor covered with dust and leaves under the table in the center of the shed. I got a broom and rake from the mudroom of the cottage and swept up what I could. But when I cleared the surface of the trapdoor and pried it open, I could see the top rung of a ladder that was buried in dirt. And just as I was about to start shoveling, I realized that the dirt was layered, and each layer had different degrees of compression, meaning that the dirt had been accumulating over a long period of time. So with my micrometer, I began to chart measurements of the different layers and attempted to determine whether or not the site on which the shed was built actually predated the construction of the cottage.

"Once Andy and I had excavated the dirt from the ladder, we climbed down and found an underground compartment. And in this compartment were an old desk, a bed frame, and file cabinets that contained handwritten documents in German and Italian that revealed details about the history of the shed and its contents."

Maggie interrupted and barked, "But Cynthia, you violated the ground rules that we had agreed upon. Anything you discovered was proprietary information that belongs to the property owner."

Cynthia ignored her and said, "Of course, I understand your concerns. However, when I contacted my colleague at the Smithsonian Institution about the underground compartment, she informed me that there was a contract, signed by the family member who had bequeathed the cottage to the current property owner, granting the Smithsonian Institution and its archaeologists and their assigns the right to excavate the site."

Cynthia lifted the top file folder from her stack, removed a copy of the contract she called *Exhibit A,* and handed it to Maggie. "As you can see, I have prepared a complete dossier that details my research for all of you to see."

Maggie scowled.

"Technically," Cynthia asserted, "the archaeologists, or whoever was coming to excavate the site, needed to contact the Smithsonian for written authorization to proceed." And then she produced the authorization she had been granted and an agreement she had signed with the Smithsonian concerning the ultimate disposition of her findings.

I was surprised. Cynthia had never mentioned any of this to me.

Maggie sneered, "I need to call my father, and he'll contact the property owner."

Cynthia replied, "I suspect the property owner is already very much aware of this contract. Sadly, Maggie, you have been duped and not appropriately informed."

Maggie was defensive and said, "I've never even met the property owner. And what he did or did not know was not my business."

Cynthia was proactive: "Look, I have so much more to tell that I really don't want to get bogged down arguing with you."

Maggie crossed her arms.

Cynthia raised her eyebrows, and I blurted out, "Maggie, I even found a *mano fico,* which fits the description of the one you told us about on our first day here. You know, the one you said was discovered by a gardener in the 1920s."

"You found what?" Maggie asked in disbelief, and I reached into the pocket of my jeans and placed it in the palm of my hand to show her. Everyone craned their necks to see it.

"Maybe," Cynthia added, "the compartment in the shed was the gardener's hiding place and possibly was where he actually lived. After all, there's a bed frame, desk, and file cabinet."

"Without a sink or a toilet!" Maggie exclaimed.

"Be that as it may," Cynthia continued. "There's more. On one of the walls, we uncovered what looked like a mechanical lever-and-pulley system. And I figured out how to operate it to wedge open the stones in the back wall of the underground compartment, uncovering a corridor that was tiled in mosaic patterns that had much in common with those I had once seen in Fez, Morocco, and seemed to have some correlation with mystical beliefs. But after thorough examination and consultation with the Smithsonian, there was no definitive proof. And if anything, the patterning was more decorative than ethnographic."

Cynthia then showed Exhibit B, translations of the documents; Exhibit C, a preliminary report on the lever-and-pulley system; and Exhibit D, an analysis of the mosaic tiles.

Max asked, "Cynthia could you please spare us the technical details?" And Cynthia maintained, "It's important that everyone here witness everything I have to say, but I will try to simplify my explanation wherever possible."

Eleanor said, "I'm mesmerized," and pleaded, "Max, let Cynthia tell us what she knows. No one cut you off."

I interjected, "There was evidence in the corridor that an intruder had not only been there, but had apparently slipped and scraped themselves, leaving a trace of blood on the tiles that Cynthia spotted."

Cynthia perked up and said, "I don't know how I could have forgotten to mention this very important detail."

Maggie scoffed, "It sounds like you're just making everything up as you go along."

Cynthia snapped back, "I have a small request. Could each of you roll up your sleeves and show your hands and forearms so that I can inspect them for cuts and bruises that might have been the source of the trace of blood?"

Josette moaned, "But I only have one good hand."

Cynthia apologized. "At first, to be honest, I thought the blood could have seeped out from Josette's bandage, but I learned soon enough that was highly unlikely."

Cynthia ambled around the room, glancing quickly at everyone's hands and forearms, but when she came to Max, he resisted, baying, "I'm not a little kid, and, quite honestly, Cynthia, your *inspection* is out of bounds."

"Only if you have something to hide."

Richard reached over to Max, trying to cajole him into acquiescing. But Max recoiled and pushed away Richard, who fell backward but was caught by Sandra, who sprang from her chair and helped him to steady himself.

Max showed the cut on the side of his index finger, stuttering to

Richard that he was so sorry. "I never thought exploring the shed was such a big deal, and, moreover, I had cause to do so. Certainly, to the extent that Cynthia and Andy were digging around."

Maggie was fuming. "Don't you understand? This is private property!"

Max stared at Cynthia, and he and Richard quietly took their seats.

Cynthia thanked us for our cooperation and said, "Next, I'd like to discuss the DNA evidence in greater detail. But at this point, I want to describe the passageway with hanging stalactites of different sizes that led from the corridor into an interior cave."

"I'm having a hard time believing you," Richard said, "because it all sounds too much like an Indiana Jones movie," and everyone laughed. But Cynthia and I sat straight-faced. This was real and not to be diminished by Richard's or anyone else's bad jokes.

Maggie was exasperated.

Barb asked, "So, Andy, what was your role in the excavation?" and I simply said, "I was Cynthia's assistant." Eleanor giggled, and Josette mumbled, "You were certainly more than that."

I looked at Josette, and her eyes widened, "This is the first time in days that I actually feel no pain." And Richard said, "Thank God, the hydrocodone is finally working."

Hannah closed her eyes and raised her hands, as if praying quietly to herself.

Cynthia leaned forward and said softly, "Well, what happened next exceeded all expectations. The walls of the cave were natural, not man-made, but, in one area, the stone was discolored, and, as I ran my hand across the surface, I realized there was a thin layer of plaster covering a hollowed cavity in the wall. And when I pressed against it, it cracked, crumbling into my hands and revealing a skeletal hand with jeweled rings on its fingers."

Max jumped up. Everyone else oohed and ahhed, except for

Maggie, who insisted once again that Cynthia cease and desist. But she didn't.

"I knew that we had discovered the buried treasure," Cynthia said, "but I was extremely careful to not intrude upon the site. I collected bone fragments for DNA analysis and photographed the rings so that my colleague could analyze them."

Max was excited, pronouncing that Luigi had been found.

Cynthia said, "The skeleton is not your ancestor, and I can prove it. When I cleaned the bathrooms in the cottage, I gathered strands of hair, toenail clippings, and even a couple of crumpled-up Band-Aids that I sent for DNA analysis to see how the results might line up with the traces of blood and bone fragments."

"The DNA results in Exhibit E," Cynthia maintained, "were not conclusive but were nonetheless highly suggestive. There was a 99 percent match between the trace of blood on the tiles and the hair removed from Max's sink, meaning that Max was in fact the intruder, but there was only a 60 to 65 percent match with the skeletal remains."

Max raised his eyebrows as if to say, "So what?" But then he broke down crying. "I needed this. I've been trying so hard. It's not just about me. It's about the world today. Everyone's suffering. The virus has affected all of our lives. We're all wounded, whether or not we want to admit it. And somehow, just thinking I was finally connecting with my ancestor, someone I never knew, gave me hope. I know all this sounds screwy."

Richard moved closer to Max, grasping his hand and stroking his thigh.

Hannah was in tears.

Everyone was silent. But then Cynthia spoke up. "There were, however, two distinguishing features that my colleague at the Smithsonian identified: one skeletal ring displayed heraldic elements, most notably two lions, from a small village in Bavaria, Germany, about thirty kilometers west of Munich.

"My colleague emailed church officials in Bavaria, who confirmed that during World War I, the abbey that housed the bejeweled skeleton had been pillaged, presumably by German soldiers. But there was anecdotal evidence among local residents that three soldiers in the American Expeditionary Force, who had been dispatched to Bavaria to recover the remains of a mortally wounded colonel, stumbled on a bombed-out church near Fürstenfeldbruck, removed the skeleton of an early Christian saint from its display case, and shipped it back to the United States in a sealed casket.

"But regardless of its exact point of origin, the skeleton is clearly stolen property. Interestingly, further analysis of the DNA in the bone fragments confirms the presence of medieval *Y. pestis* genomes, which scientists believed caused the Black Plague, but that also resemble strains of *Y. pestis* that still exist today. And while there is probably no correlation between *Y. pestis* and the virus, the fact remains that they both spread rapidly worldwide by coughing and sputum without intervening action by fleas, mosquitoes, or other insects."

We were all mystified by what Cynthia had to say, even though she kind of lost me when she started ranting on about the Black Plague. Cynthia grinned, "I know my colleague and I jumped off the deep end, but that's what some scientists like to do when not doing serious research."

"Ultimately," Cynthia concluded, "while the science of our discovery is still open to speculation, my colleague did identify the crest on another ring on the middle finger of the skeleton's hand. And that crest, my dear friends, belongs to the family of Boccaccio."

We all looked at her in disbelief, and Cynthia admitted, "The presence of this ring is completely circumstantial. And the relationship to Boccaccio cannot be definitive without further DNA testing, meaning that the skeleton of Boccaccio, or his children, would have to be exhumed. However, if the skeleton found under the shed is in fact the remains of one of Boccaccio's illegitimate children, who was mistakenly identified as an early Christian saint that had been transported from the catacombs in Rome, or perhaps Tuscany, to Bavaria, the chances might be greater. Except, while the bones might establish a familial connection to Boccaccio, the gemstones were undoubtedly imbedded by nuns after the remains were brought to Germany, and thus, legally belong to the Church. But in any event, the terrible irony of finding a skeleton who died from the Black Plague in the age of the virus is even more bizarre."

Richard looked bewildered. Max frowned. Hannah, Barb, and Eleanor seemed frustrated by the improbable logic of Cynthia's meandering hypotheses. Sandra and Josette zoned out.

Maggie flushed red, "I doubt the contract with the Smithsonian will hold up in court, and, even if it did, the patrimony of the bejeweled skeleton would be challenged."

"While Maggie might be correct," Cynthia said, "the Smithsonian has filed a petition for an injunction against the property owner for undertaking any further excavation of the shed without a court ruling on the patrimony of the artifacts found."

Maggie was stunned but collected herself quickly. "Well, I guess that means it's time to adjourn."

Josette raised her hand. Her voice was shaky, but, once she started talking, she gained confidence. "I'm not sure how to say this. But I have to come clean. I've been anguishing about the hate crime charges I filed against Andy, and, after one sleepless night after another, I've decided to withdraw my complaint."

Sandra glared at her. "You can't do that! Technically, the decision to prosecute belongs to the prosecutor, who, in this instance, is the district attorney for Berkshire County."

Josette turned toward Sandra and scowled, "I'm sick and tired of being ordered around by you!"

"Josette, dear Josette," Sandra said defensively, "I've only been acting in your best interest. When I saw Andy reading those antigay brochures from Steadfast Truth Ministries in Springfield, Massachusetts, I was certain that he had it in for you, that he was going to teach you a lesson you'd never forget."

Josette shouted, "Stop!"

Sandra pulled her cell phone out of her purse and flashed it in front of me, ranting that the district attorney had texted her earlier in the day, when she began to suspect that Josette might pull out, that there was sufficient evidence to bring the case to trial, even without a complaining witness.

I jumped out of my chair and yelled at Sandra, "The police did not have probable cause to search my computer or my car. They only had a search warrant for my bedroom, and they found nothing, and when they asked to search my car and computer, I never really gave them my consent. The police coerced me!"

Sandra shouted, "Stand down, Andy! You're threatening me, and everybody in the room is a witness."

I inched away, and Cynthia said, "I have your back."

Sandra snarled, "Even if you can weasel your way out of the criminal case, Josette is going to win the civil case, and you're going to be in debt to her for the rest of your life."

I shook my head *no way.* "First of all, I'm essentially judgment-proof—and, if by some weird rule of law I lose in court, I can go bankrupt and owe nothing. But most important, it isn't my fault."

Sandra snorted, "You're in denial!"

Once again, I shook my head. "It's the property owner's problem. The causal chain of liability began with the gross negligence of the property owner, who failed to inform us of the dangers inherent in the instability of the windows, and this instability was the primary reason that the glass panes shattered and Josette was critically wounded."

Maggie was angry. "A jury will decide who was liable and what percentage of that liability is yours."

Barb interrupted Maggie and stated matter-of-factly, "I don't think so. I was in the waiting room the day Josette was discharged from the hospital, and I heard what the nurse's aide told Sandra. It wasn't Andy stitching up Josette's hand that punctured the nerve in her hand, it was a shard of glass."

Josette took a deep breath and bellowed at Sandra. "I knew you were lying to me! I knew it!"

Sandra was shaking, "I was only trying to protect you."

Josette was wailing, "I don't believe you!"

"Oh, Josette . . . please. I love you."

"I don't ever want to speak to you again!"

Sandra stormed out of the room.

Hannah tried to console Josette, "'Take therefore no thought for the morrow: for the morrow shall take thought for the things of itself . . .' Matthew 6:34."

Max and Richard stood up and were ready to leave the room. Eleanor and Hannah looked into each other's eyes, as if they had finally agreed it was okay to disagree.

Maggie closed her eyes and stretched her head and neck backward.

I was trembling. Cynthia reached for my hand.

Freezing rain pelted against the window glass, and the midnight landscape iced over.

PARTNERS

FIRST EDITION MEMBERSHIP
Anonymous (9)
Donna Wilhelm

TRANSLATOR'S CIRCLE
Ben & Sharon Fountain
Meriwether Evans

PRINTER'S PRESS MEMBERSHIP
Allred Capital Management
Robert Appel
Charles Dee Mitchell
Cullen Schaar
David Tomlinson & Kathryn Berry
Jeff Leuschel
Judy Pollock
Loretta Siciliano
Lori Feathers
Mary Ann Thompson-Frenk & Joshua Frenk
Matthew Rittmayer
Nick Storch
Pixel and Texel
Social Venture Partners Dallas
Stephen Bullock

AUTHOR'S LEAGUE
Christie Tull
Farley Houston
Jacob Seifring
Lissa Dunlay
Stephen Bullock
Steven Kornajcik
Thomas DiPiero

PUBLISHER'S LEAGUE
Adam Rekerdres
Christie Tull
Justin Childress
Kay Cattarulla
KMGMT
Olga Kislova

EDITOR'S LEAGUE
Amrit Dhir
Brandon Kennedy
Dallas Sonnier
Garth Hallberg
Greg McConeghy
Linda Nell Evans
Mary Moore Grimaldi
Mike Kaminsky
Patricia Storace
Ryan Todd
Steven Harding
Suejean Kim
Symphonic Source
Wendy Belcher

READER'S LEAGUE
Caitlin Baker
Caroline Casey
Carolyn Mulligan
Chilton Thomson
Cody Cosmic & Jeremy Hays
Jeff Waxman
Joseph Milazzo
Kayla Finstein
Kelly Britson
Kelly & Corby Baxter
Marian Schwartz & Reid Minot
Marlo D. Cruz Pagan
Maryam Baig
Peggy Carr
Susan Ernst

ADDITIONAL DONORS
Alan Shockley
Amanda & Bjorn Beer
Andrew Yorke
Anonymous (10)
Anthony Messenger
Ashley Milne Shadoin
Bob & Katherine Penn
Brandon Childress
Charley Mitcherson
Charley Rejsek
Cheryl Thompson
Chloe Pak
Cone Johnson
CS Maynard
Daniel J. Hale
Daniela Hurezanu
Dori Boone-Costantino
Ed Nawotka
Elizabeth Gillette
Erin Kubatzky
Ester & Matt Harrison
Grace Kenney
Hillary Richards
JJ Italiano
Jeremy Hughes
John Darnielle
Julie Janicke Muhsmann
Kelly Falconer
Laura Thomson
Lea Courington
Leigh Ann Pike
Lowell Frye
Maaza Mengiste

ADDITIONAL DONORS, CONT'D

Mark Haber
Mary Cline
Maynard Thomson
Michael Reklis
Mike Soto
Mokhtar Ramadan
Nikki & Dennis Gibson
Patrick Kukucka
Patrick Kutcher
Rev. Elizabeth & Neil Moseley
Richard Meyer
Scott & Katy Nimmons
Sherry Perry
Sydneyann Binion
Stephen Harding
Stephen Williamson
Susan Carp
Susan Ernst
Theater Jones
Tim Perttula
Tony Thomson

SUBSCRIBERS

Ned Russin
Michael Binkley
Michael Schneiderman
Aviya Kushner
Kenneth McClain
Eugenie Cha
Stephen Fuller
Joseph Rebella
Brian Matthew Kim
Anthony Brown
Michael Lighty
Erin Kubatzky
Shelby Vincent
Margaret Terwey
Ben Fountain
Caroline West
Ryan Todd
Gina Rios
Caitlin Jans
Ian Robinson
Elena Rush
Courtney Sheedy
Elif Ağanoğlu
Laura Gee
Valerie Boyd
Brian Bell

AVAILABLE NOW FROM DEEP VELLUM

MICHÈLE AUDIN · *One Hundred Twenty-One Days* · translated by Christiana Hills · FRANCE

BAE SUAH · *Recitation* · translated by Deborah Smith · SOUTH KOREA

MARIO BELLATIN · *Mrs. Murakami's Garden* · translated by Heather Cleary · MEXICO

EDUARDO BERTI · *The Imagined Land* · translated by Charlotte Coombe · ARGENTINA

CARMEN BOULLOSA · *Texas: The Great Theft* · *Before* · *Heavens on Earth*
translated by Samantha Schnee · Peter Bush · Shelby Vincent · MEXICO

MAGDA CARNECI · *FEM* · translated by Sean Cotter · ROMANIA

LEILA S. CHUDORI · *Home* · translated by John H. McGlynn · INDONESIA

MATHILDE CLARK · *Lone Star* · translated by Martin Aitken · DENMARK

SARAH CLEAVE, ed. · *Banthology: Stories from Banned Nations* ·
IRAN, IRAQ, LIBYA, SOMALIA, SUDAN, SYRIA & YEMEN

LOGEN CURE · *Welcome to Midland: Poems* · USA

ANANDA DEVI · *Eve Out of Her Ruins* · translated by Jeffrey Zuckerman · MAURITIUS

PETER DIMOCK · *Daybook from Sheep Meadow* · USA

CLAUDIA ULLOA DONOSO · *Little Bird*, translated by Lily Meyer · PERU/NORWAY

ROSS FARRAR · *Ross Sings Cheree & the Animated Dark: Poems* · USA

ALISA GANIEVA · *Bride and Groom* · *The Mountain and the Wall*
translated by Carol Apollonio · RUSSIA

FERNANDA GARCIA LAU · *Out of the Cage* · translated by Will Vanderhyden · ARGENTINA

ANNE GARRÉTA · *Sphinx* · *Not One Day* · *In/concrete* · translated by Emma Ramadan · FRANCE

JÓN GNARR · *The Indian* · *The Pirate* · *The Outlaw* · translated by Lytton Smith · ICELAND

GOETHE · *The Golden Goblet: Selected Poems* · *Faust, Part One*
translated by Zsuzsanna Ozsváth and Frederick Turner · GERMANY

NOEMI JAFFE · *What are the Blind Men Dreaming?* · translated by Julia Sanches & Ellen Elias-Bursac · BRAZIL

CLAUDIA SALAZAR JIMÉNEZ · *Blood of the Dawn* · translated by Elizabeth Bryer · PERU

PERGENTINO JOSÉ · *Red Ants* · MEXICO

TAISIA KITAISKAIA · *The Nightgown & Other Poems* · USA

JUNG YOUNG MOON · *Seven Samurai Swept Away in a River* · *Vaseline Buddha*
translated by Yewon Jung · SOUTH KOREA

KIM YIDEUM · *Blood Sisters* · translated by Ji yoon Lee · SOUTH KOREA

JOSEFINE KLOUGART · *Of Darkness* · translated by Martin Aitken · DENMARK

YANICK LAHENS · *Moonbath* · translated by Emily Gogolak · HAITI

FOUAD LAROUI · *The Curious Case of Dassoukine's Trousers* · translated by Emma Ramadan · MOROCCO

MARIA GABRIELA LLANSOL · *The Geography of Rebels Trilogy: The Book of Communities; The Remaining Life; In the House of July & August*
translated by Audrey Young · PORTUGAL

PABLO MARTÍN SÁNCHEZ · *The Anarchist Who Shared My Name* · translated by Jeff Diteman · SPAIN

DOROTA MASŁOWSKA · *Honey, I Killed the Cats* · translated by Benjamin Paloff · POLAND

BRICE MATTHIEUSSENT· *Revenge of the Translator* · translated by Emma Ramadan · FRANCE

LINA MERUANE · *Seeing Red* · translated by Megan McDowell · CHILE

VALÉRIE MRÉJEN · *Black Forest* · translated by Katie Shireen Assef · FRANCE

FISTON MWANZA MUJILA · *Tram 83* · translated by Roland Glasser · DEMOCRATIC REPUBLIC OF CONGO

GORAN PETROVIĆ · *At the Lucky Hand, aka The Sixty-Nine Drawers* · translated by Peter Agnone · SERBIA

ILJA LEONARD PFEIJFFER · *La Superba* · translated by Michele Hutchison · NETHERLANDS

RICARDO PIGLIA · *Target in the Night* · translated by Sergio Waisman · ARGENTINA

SERGIO PITOL · *The Art of Flight* · *The Journey* · *The Magician of Vienna* · *Mephisto's Waltz: Selected Short Stories*
translated by George Henson · MEXICO

JULIE POOLE · *Bright Specimen: Poems from the Texas Herbarium* · USA

EDUARDO RABASA · *A Zero-Sum Game* · translated by Christina MacSweeney · MEXICO

ZAHIA RAHMANI · *"Muslim": A Novel* · translated by Matthew Reeck · FRANCE/ALGERIA

JUAN RULFO · *The Golden Cockerel & Other Writings* · translated by Douglas J. Weatherford · MEXICO

ETHAN RUTHERFORD · *Farthest South & Other Stories* · USA

TATIANA RYCKMAN · *Ancestry of Objects* · USA

OLEG SENTSOV · *Life Went On Anyway* · translated by Uilleam Blacker · UKRAINE

MIKHAIL SHISHKIN · *Calligraphy Lesson: The Collected Stories*
translated by Marian Schwartz, Leo Shtutin, Mariya Bashkatova, Sylvia Maizell · RUSSIA

ÓFEIGUR SIGURÐSSON · *Öræfi: The Wasteland* · translated by Lytton Smith · ICELAND

DANIEL SIMON, ED. · *Dispatches from the Republic of Letters* · USA

MUSTAFA STITOU · *Two Half Faces* · translated by David Colmer · NETHERLANDS

MÄRTA TIKKANEN · *The Love Story of the Century* · translated by Stina Katchadourian · SWEDEN

SERHIY ZHADAN · *Voroshilovgrad* · translated by Reilly Costigan-Humes & Isaac Wheeler · UKRAINE

FORTHCOMING FROM DEEP VELLUM

SHANE ANDERSON · *After the Oracle* · USA

MARIO BELLATIN · *Beauty Salon* · translated by David Shook · MEXICO

MIRCEA CĂRTĂRESCU · *Solenoid*
translated by Sean Cotter · ROMANIA

LEYLÂ ERBIL · *A Strange Woman*
translated by Nermin Menemencioğlu & Amy Marie Spangler· TURKEY

RADNA FABIAS · *Habitus* · translated by David Colmer · CURAÇAO/NETHERLANDS

SARA GOUDARZI · *The Almond in the Apricot* · USA

GYULA JENEI · *Always Different* · translated by Diana Senechal · HUNGARY

UZMA ASLAM KHAN • *The Miraculous True History of Nomi Ali* • PAKISTAN

SONG LIN · *The Gleaner Song: Selected Poems* · translated by Dong Li · CHINA

TEDI LÓPEZ MILLS · *The Book of Explanations* · translated by Robin Myers · MEXICO

JUNG YOUNG MOON · *Arriving in a Thick Fog*
translated by Mah Eunji and Jeffrey Karvonen · SOUTH KOREA

FISTON MWANZA MUJILA · *The Villain's Dance,* translated by Roland Glasser · *The River in the Belly: Selected Poems,* translated by Bret Maney · DEMOCRATIC REPUBLIC OF CONGO

LUDMILLA PETRUSHEVSKAYA · *Kidnapped: A Crime Story,* translated by Marian Schwartz · *The New Adventures of Helen: Magical Tales,* translated by Jane Bugaeva · RUSSIA

SERGIO PITOL · *The Love Parade* · translated by G. B. Henson · MEXICO

MANON STEFAN ROS · *The Blue Book of Nebo* · WALES

JIM SCHUTZE · *The Accommodation* · USA

SOPHIA TERAZAWA · *Winter Phoenix: Testimonies in Verse* · POLAND

BOB TRAMMELL · *Jack Ruby & the Origins of the Avant-Garde in Dallas & Other Stories* · USA

BENJAMIN VILLEGAS · *ELPASO: A Punk Story* · translated by Jay Noden · MEXICO